ROGUE WARRIOR®

Curse of the Infidel

ALSO BY RICHARD MARCINKO

FICTION

Violence of Action

With John Weisman

Red Cell

Green Team

Task Force Blue

Designation Gold

Seal Force Alpha

Option Delta

Echo Platoon

Detachment Bravo

With Jim DeFelice

Rogue Warrior®: Vengeance

Rogue Warrior®: Holy Terror

Rogue Warrior®: Dictator's Ransom

Rogue Warrior®: Seize the Day

Rogue Warrior®: Domino Theory

Rogue Warrior®: Blood Lies

NONFICTION

The Real Team

Rogue Warrior (with John Weisman)

Leadership Secrets of the Rogue Warrior:
A Commando's Guide to Success

The Rogue Warrior's Strategy for Success

ROGUE WARRIOR®

Curse of the Infidel

RICHARD MARCINKO
AND
JIM DEFELICE

A Tom Doherty Associates Book
New York

ROGUE WARRIOR®: CURSE OF THE INFIDEL

Copyright © 2013 by Richard Marcinko and Jim DeFelice

All rights reserved.

A Forge Book
Published by Tom Doherty Associates, LLC
175 Fifth Avenue
New York, NY 10010

www.tor-forge.com

Forge® is a registered trademark of Tom Doherty Associates, LLC.

Library of Congress Cataloging-in-Publication Data

Marcinko, Richard.
    Rogue warrior : curse of the infidel / Richard Marcinko and Jim
    DeFelice.—First Edition.
        p.   cm.
    "A Tom Doherty Associates Book."
    ISBN 978-0-7653-3294-3 (hardcover)
    ISBN 978-1-4299-6547-7 (e-book)
    1. Rogue Warrior (Fictitious character)—Fiction.   2. Special
forces (Military science)—Fiction.   3. Terrorism—Prevention—
Fiction.   I. DeFelice, Jim, 1956–   II. Title.   III. Title: Curse of
the infidel.
    PS3563.A6362R63 2014
    813'.54—dc23
                                                                2013025794

Forge books may be purchased for educational, business, or promotional use. For information on bulk purchases, please contact Macmillan Corporate and Premium Sales Department at 1-800-221-7945, extension 5442, or write specialmarkets@macmillan.com.

First Edition: January 2014

Printed in the United States of America

0 9 8 7 6 5 4 3 2 1

Dedicated to Tyrone Woods and Glen Doherty, SEAL warriors to their last breath while serving as contractors in the Benghazi, Libya, debacle. To their very last breaths, they lived up to the SEAL code. The damage they inflicted on the attacking hordes was the essence of courage.

NAVY SEAL CODE:
1. Loyalty to Country, Team, and Teammate,
2. Serve with Honor and Integrity on and off the Battlefield,
3. Ready to lead, ready to follow, never quit,
4. Take responsibility for your actions and the actions of your teammates,
5. Excel as warriors through discipline and innovation,
6. Train for war, fight to win, defeat our nation's enemies, and . . .
7. Earn your Trident every day.

PART ONE
CURSE OF THE INFIDEL

The value of tradition to the social body is immense. The veneration for practices, or for authority, consecrated by long acceptance, has a reserve of strength which cannot be obtained by any novel device.

—Rear Admiral Alfred Thayer Mahan,
"The Military Rule of Obedience,"
National Review, March 1902

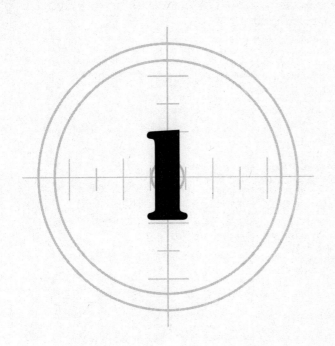

[1]

Y ou are an infidel and will confess to slandering the name of the most holy and
sacred Prophet, sacred be His name!"

As the voice screamed, a stick snapped across my back. The stick, long
and thin, was made of plastic. It hadn't hurt much the first time it touched
my skin. But that was over an hour and a hundred flails ago. Now every swat
felt like I was being smacked by a baseball bat.

A bat spiked with 20-penny nails.

"You will confess!" shouted my tormentor. "You will fall on your knees
before the one true God, blessed be His holy name."

"Screw yourself," I said between my gritted teeth.

Thwack.

"Ugh."

"Confess! Or we will beat salvation into you!"

I was seeing a part of Saudi Arabia that the Tourist Board doesn't adver-
tise. You can call it the belly of the beast; to my mind, it's a much lower part
of the anatomy.

"Do you confess?"

"No!"

Thwack. Thwack.

Under intense international pressure a few years back, the Saudi government reformed its prison system. The new rules give certain guidelines for
"corrective measures"—that is, beating the crap out of a prisoner. The "cor-
rector" must hold a book under his arm while administering lashes. The idea
was to keep the torturer from raising the cane too high over his head.

I can attest that the letter of the law was observed in this case. I even
know the title of the book, which was an illustrated comic collection entitled
Brave Men in Saudi History. The book, four pages long (two of them were
blank), was duct-taped to his underarm.

Thwack. Thaaaaa-WACK!

Somewhere around whack number sixty-eight, I had begun fantasizing
about what I would do to the bastard with the stick. My thoughts were very
creative, and in no case would the stick have been recognizable as a stick
when I was done.

By now, though, I was beyond any sort of fantasy. I was, as the football
play-by-play analysts put it, grinding it out. I just hoped the end of the game
wasn't going to be signaled by a gun.

The Apaches, among other Native American tribes, have an especially useful mechanism for dealing with intense pain. I adopted it now, focusing my concentration on a point just outside my body. As the beatings continued, my mind stepped away and observed the scene.

This got me through another thirty or forty lashes. Finally the pain overwhelmed my body and I blacked out. Oblivion was a welcome reprieve, but it didn't last long. I came to only a few minutes later, as I was being dragged along a dank and dark cement corridor.

I have no idea why the corridor was dank—the prison I was in was located at the edge of the Saudi desert, which has to be one of the driest places on earth. But dank it was. Moss, crud, and slime water blended into a horrendously smelling mélange between the inlaid stones of the floor. I tried not to breathe.

I'm far from a connoisseur, but I think I can say with some authority that Saudi jails are among the worst in the world. It doesn't even take that much to get into them. The surest way is by opposing the government or insulting the royal family, but you can get there with much lesser offenses if you know what you're doing. Drink a beer in your yard or drive a car with a woman who's not your wife—supposed outrages to Islam—and you will land there in a flash, even if you're a foreigner. Even random victims of crime who had the audacity to file police reports have found themselves guests of the state.

They were lying, you see. Because the Kingdom is PERFECT, and thus there is no crime, and anyone who says different is a slanderer who deserves to lose his tongue.

Being a traditionalist, I had chosen an oldie but a goldie to ensure my incarceration: I had insulted the Prophet and the Kingdom by proselytizing a vermin religion.

Said religion being Coptic Hinduism, which I had invented solely for the purpose of running afoul of the authorities.

Not that Coptic Hinduism preaches violence or anything remotely touching on the state or other religions. It borrows freely from all pantheons and pathways, seeking peaceful coexistence with all. We're not much on sacraments, and the heavy burden of conversion is best left to those of other beliefs. In fact, the most definite (and important) thing you can say about it, at least in the context of Saudi Arabia, is that it is not Islam, and therefore fit for repression.

The two guards dragging me to my cell were kindly fellows, and they tried cheering me up along the way by shouting various slogans in Arabic.

"You're a blessed fellow!"

"You're going to be very popular in jail!"

"Now you will have a real chance to pray."

My Arabic is mostly of use in brothels and street fights, so maybe my translation is a little soft. I will say that the others in my cell, all twelve of them, welcomed me with open arms and hard feet as I was hurled into the tiny space.

Walled by solid concrete on three sides, the room was roughly eight by six feet and smelled of sweat and human excrement. I curled myself into a corner at the back, hoping to be left alone.

Unfortunately, one of my fellow inmates had deputized himself as the Welcome Wagon. As he bent over me, a shiv appeared in his hand and he took a swipe at my face.

Coptic Hinduism has very strong precepts against having your face cut up and eyeballs gouged out. It has been heavily influenced by what many readers will recall as the Rogue Warrior's First Commandment:

Do unto others before they do unto you.

I decided that this was a good time to do some preaching. My opening text was a fist to the nether regions of my new congregant. This was followed by a fist to the throat.

The convict was impressed. He had never before encountered the spiritual depth of Coptic Hinduism.

Still, he was firm in his own primitive convictions, and pressed forward in his attempt to make a blood sacrifice to his gods. While I wanted nothing to do with such primitive religious practices, my retreat was cut off by the thick and immovable wall behind me.

He cut a halo across my forehead. I decided to return the favor by encouraging him to kneel and reflect on the holy light of the universe. Given that he was clearly devout, all he needed was a little push.

Or shove.

I sent him sprawling against the nearby wall. The others were looking on anxiously, perhaps hoping for their chance at conversion as well. So I leapt up, grabbed the little knife that had fallen from my convert's hand, and baptized him in the name of the Rogue, the Warrior, and the decidedly Unfriendly Ghost.

Duly impressed, the others backed away.

Exhausted by my spiritual experience, I dragged myself to the corner of the cell.

You may very well be wondering what I was doing in Saudi Arabia in the first place.

The truth was I was here to find another American, Garrett Taylor. Garrett was the son of a friend of mine; he'd gotten into a bit of trouble in the Kingdom Oil Built a few days before. I'd heard that he was currently a guest at this esteemed Saudi institution. I had therefore posed rather ostentatiously as a preacher in hopes of meeting him.

Be careful what you wish for.

Not long after the blood stopped flowing from the neck of my new convert, a series of loud shouts announced the approach of the guards. We were ordered to clear the cell. I got up, hiding my shiv in the waistband of my pants. My knees were creaking and my spine felt as if it had been removed from my body and rearranged in a random pattern. Being last made me a target for the guards, who proceeded to give me a series of gentle love taps as a reward.

I thought they were coming to investigate the ruckus, but they made no move to do so beyond kicking over the limp body of my follower. I kept my head low and eyes peeled as I stumbled down the hall. When we came to the end of the corridor, we took a turn right and made our way up a set of concrete steps. Two guards behind me very kindly assisted my progress with a few kicks; otherwise I was left alone.

We were led to the courtyard behind the building. Stumbling, I took my place at the end of a line of prisoners who were kneeling in the direction of Mecca. I'm not very big on praying, especially to Allah; a guard watching the line helped me into position with a punch between my shoulder blades; I put my head down and caught my breath as a loudspeaker began barking the call to prayers.

A few phrases into the proceeding, I recovered enough to raise my head slightly and look around for Garrett. There were maybe a hundred inmates in our little corner of paradise; none looked even remotely like the man I'd come to rescue.

Prayers over, the inmates were allowed to walk for a few minutes before being led to dinner. I mingled silently. The courtyard was about twenty by fifty feet—spacious for a Saudi jail—and bounded by a high chain-link fence topped by barbed wire. There was another fence a short distance away, with another courtyard on the other side of that.

I circled around, mumbling to myself in a combination of random street Arabic and the occasional French and English. Anyone who heard me would think I was deranged—all in all, not a bad assumption, actually.

He didn't seem to be in our courtyard. I sidled next to the fence and slid down to my haunches.

"Garrett?" I asked, raising my voice loud enough to be heard in the neighboring yard. None of the men close to the fence looked anything like him.

"Garrett?"

Some of my cellmates had gathered nearby and started talking loudly. I couldn't make out what they were saying, but the glances they threw me convinced me I better pay some attention to them. I was just about to when someone pressed against the fence behind me.

"You? What are you doing here?" said a voice in perfectly enunciated English.

I turned and looked through the fence. A young man who looked remarkably like my old shipmate was staring through the chain links. His face was battered—eyes bloodshot, cheeks checkered with cuts, his left temple the color of an eggplant at harvesttime.

"Garrett Taylor?" I whispered, though I was sure I had found my man.

"Marcinko?" He shifted a bit, trying to get a better view. "Demo Dick? Here? Why?"

"I came to get you out."

"Oh yeah?"

He sounded a little more skeptical than I would have liked. Admittedly, his location in the other building presented a problem, but that was only temporary.

"You could sound a little more enthusiastic," I said.

"Well, we'll see how enthusiastic you are after you get the crap knocked out of you."

"That's already happened," I told him.

"I meant from them," he said, pointing.

I turned back around. Three of my cellmates were stalking across the small courtyard in my direction. They didn't look like they were in the mood for prayers.

But before I get pummeled, let's go back to the beginning of this twisted tale. Like Paul on the Road to Damascus, my route to enlightenment in the Saudi prison was anything but direct.

It started in Germany, a few days before, when I went to a bank to make a withdrawal . . .

(II)

Actually, I had an experience many of us do when we go to a bank—I was shafted.

In my case, though, this wasn't a figure of speech. I was literally in an air shaft, *die Luftshact*, of a large international bank. The narrow, brick-lined vertical tunnel smelled of rotting garbage and at least one dead cat. It was also extremely dark. But it happened to be the easiest way into the computers used by the American International Bank, a modest institution of some $875 billion in deposits, with branches all over the world.

I'd been hired by the bank to investigate some suspicious transactions. The person who hired me, however, soon acted suspiciously himself. Which aroused further suspicions.

My thoughts shaded toward embezzlement. And here's the beautiful thing about that: federal law provides for a 15 to 30 percent "finder's fee"— also known as a Whistleblower's Tax—for exposing fraud. Slap some zeroes around and that's serious money, more than enough to endure all manner of discomfort, including the growls emanating from the stomach of my assistant, Paul "Shotgun" Fox, who was crawling up the shaft behind me.

"God, I'm hungry," griped Shotgun.

"When have you ever not been hungry?" I said. "Let's go. We have two more stories, then we'll be at the computer center."

In order to reach the air shaft, we had rappelled down a much larger one in the center of the building, crawled through a four-foot-square ventilation hole, and then begun climbing upward through the cramped rectangular space. The odd construction was the result of a long series of renovations to the building, performed over several decades. Pipes and several large bundles of wires ran up all four sides of the shaft. We had to avoid the temptation to use them as handholds—if they were broken, the penetration would be easily detected.

Feel free to insert the prophylactic joke of your choice.

I maneuvered myself diagonally, placing my hands between two boa constrictor–sized runs of wire, and pulled up against the bricks. A thick wedge of slime blocked my next handhold; I shifted around and found another.

When I pulled up I knocked my head against the top of the shaft.

Which shouldn't have happened for another two floors.

I glanced up, playing the small LED light around the ceiling. It was concrete, and fairly new.

I mentally recalculated, hoping I'd made a mistake and lost track of the floors. But I hadn't. The computer center was on the eighth floor of the building, and we were on the seventh.

"What's up?" asked Shotgun, coming up behind me.

"We're a floor short. I'm going to kill Shunt."

Shunt—Paul Guido Falcone—had stolen the building's architectural plans by hacking into the Berlin code enforcement office's computer system, where all the building plans were conveniently stored online. Apparently they hadn't been updated.

You could blame Murphy—the author of the ubiquitous law that states anything that can go wrong will go wrong, but only at the worst possible time. I preferred to blame my wop genius.

"Can we get through it?" asked Shotgun.

I pounded my knuckles against it, listening to see if it was hollow.

"Anyone home?" asked Shotgun.

Instead of dignifying that with a response, I reached into the pouch at my waist and took out the little Dremel tool I had there. I had to balance myself with one hand and use the drill with the other, which not only made my leverage weak but meant I was drilling on an angle as well. It was slow going.

I figured that if I could cut a small hole, I'd use the miniature crowbar I had in my ruck to hammer out the rest of the concrete. But the barrier was too thick; the Dremel's drill bit didn't go all the way through.

Worse, it snapped off about halfway around the hole. I put in a backup and completed the circle, but the plug wouldn't come out. Running the drill across the diameter of the circle, I snapped the new bit; that left me as the only functional item in the tool kit.

It was time to go to Plan B.

"This isn't going to work. We'll have to back out," I told Shotgun. "I'll tell Mongoose. Wait for me on the roof."

"Already heard," radioed Mongoose, aka Thomas Yamya. The team radios were set to always transmit. "Things are quiet out here."

Mongoose was in the rental up the block, listening to us on the radio circuit and monitoring the video cameras we'd planted around the building. The cameras—or "cams"—beamed their signals via satellite to a Red Cell Internet site. Mongoose accessed the site via a tablet computer in the car. The devices gave him a full view around the perimeter of the building, in effect doing the work of a small army of lookouts.

(The computer looks like an iPad, but has a number of improvements, including a faster processor and a proprietary operating system. I got it from a friend and Team Six plank owner, Frank Phillips, who first used it in one of his operations with Golden Seal Enterprises, a Class A training and special operations company. Shunt made a few customizations.)

Plan B called for us to enter via a bathroom on the floor where the data center was located. Getting into the room was easy—a fire escape ran right by the window. But according to the schematics Shunt had stolen, the hallway between the restroom and the computer center was protected by a motion detector. I'd have to defeat it before we could proceed.

Motion detectors generally fall into one of two categories: those that work by infrared—heat sensors—and those that work by ultrasound—a little like radar. The techniques for each group are very different, as you can imagine: you can't freeze a detector that's sending out sound impulses, and you can't hum your way close to an IR unit.

The mechanical plans indicated where the sensors were located. They also stated that the whole building system was wired together. We had been inside the building two days before, and confirmed that the detectors used on the floor *downstairs* were all thermal. It was therefore reasonable to expect that the one on the computer floor was thermal as well.

But the appearance of the ceiling where there shouldn't have been one meant I couldn't take anything for granted.

Shotgun was waiting on the roof, eating a bag of potato chips—or "crisps" as they were called in Europe.

"Hungry?" he asked as I emerged from the shaft. "They're onion and garlic."

"I can smell them. No thanks."

"You're missing a treat," he said, rising to join me as I made my way to the fire escape.

"Sure you don't want me to come down with you?" Shotgun asked.

"No, I need you out here to create a diversion if we need it," I told him. "Just like we rehearsed. There's no place to hide inside."

"You got it." He reached into his tactical vest and took out a candy bar as I started downward.

The restroom window was locked by a flimsy turn screw. This was easily pried to the side; I was past it in less than a minute. The red emergency exit sign at the window, indicating the fire escape, was all the light I needed to see as I squeezed inside, checked to make sure the stalls were empty, and then went to the hallway door.

Now the fun began. The door was almost certainly within "sight" of the sensor; if I opened the door there and attempted to reach it from the opening, it would have registered the fact that the temperature of the air in front of it had changed.

I needed to defeat the sensor without exposing my warm body to it. This would mean I'd have to climb the wall behind the door, open it ever so slightly, and maneuver a small piece of glass over the sensor unit. The glass would be held in place by the metal arm I used to get it there, thanks to a spring-loaded piece at the back. We'd remove it on the way out.

Yes, I have done this before.[1]

While detection units are generally aimed so that they can't pick up something close by at the ceiling, you can't necessarily take this for granted. So the first thing I had to do was get the glass and arm at room temperature.

My laser thermometer found a ten-degree difference. That might not actually be enough to trigger the motion detector.

Then again, did I really want to take the chance?

I went to the sink and ran the cold water over the glass and rods for a few minutes, until my laser thermometer declared the apparatus a perfect 18.23° Celsius, or 65° Fahrenheit—the bank kept the data center floor relatively cool.

Then I took two of the waste cans from next to the sink and taped them together with the help of some duct tape. This gave me a small platform behind the door.

With everything in place, I climbed up, dug my fingernails into the edge of the wood, and eased the door open. Slipping in a small wedge of toilet paper from one of the stalls to keep it ajar, I examined the sensor with the help of a pair of low-tech but powerful opera glasses.

I spotted the telltale plastic shield of the IR detector immediately. The arm pointed downward, covering the area where anyone exiting the stairs would walk. The detection angle was definitely aimed at the stairs, but would sweep around in an angle behind, making it harder to approach from where I was.

Harder, though not impossible.

But wait. There was something else on the wall to the right.

An ultrasonic device. This was smaller, and looked a little like an electric razor with a circular head. The red light in the hall—another exit sign—glinted off the metal mesh at the detection dish.

---

[1] The glass is specially treated and cut to block light waves that are larger than a certain wavelength. By placing it over the entire detector, it ensures that there are no hot spots on the sides that can be seen. The latter is why using a huge pane of glass to walk across a room won't work, as a quality sensor will note the temperature emanating from your body at the edges.

I thought the Germans believe in documenting everything they do. Why wasn't the ultrasound system in the plans?

Sloppy, sloppy.

In theory, ultrasonic devices don't have to be completely defeated—by wearing padded clothing and moving very s-l-o-w-l-y, you can fool the device into thinking that its waves are returning normally. (The devices look for a Doppler shift in the waves, but the shift has to be relatively large or they'd always be going off.)

That's the theory. The reality is, most people, burglars especially, don't wear padded clothing. Nor do they have the patience to walk very slowly across a room—so slowly that it might take a half hour to go thirty feet, which is generally the distance the devices are reliable at.

I had patience, but neither the time nor the clothes. So instead I took out a small radio scanner and turned it on. The scanner "listened" for a few seconds, then declared that it had found the wavelength of the sound waves the device was using.

Pushing a button at the side of the little device, I set it to the detector's frequency, then climbed down and slipped it near the crack in the door. By squawking in the same frequency as the detector, the device masked any other returning waves.

That taken care of, I went back to work on the infrared detector. It was only a few feet away from me; I could practically slap it with my hand. But the closeness worked against me, putting it at an odd angle. I had the damnedest time getting the glass in place over the curved sensor. This took a good five minutes.

Fortunately, the suction cups to hold it in place went on smoothly. I got down and packed my gear.

"How's it looking, Dick?" asked Mongoose from outside.

"Just about ready to go down the hall," I told him. I hadn't bothered to put a video feed in the building.

"You have another ten minutes before the security guys are due," he warned.

"That's all?" I checked my watch. He was right.

"Sorry."

We'd cased the building for nearly a week. Security was provided by an external company that made the rounds of several buildings each night. They were also tied into the security system, which besides the detectors up here included an array of video cameras on the first floor and outside the building. (We'd had to bypass one at the rear of the building to get on the roof.)

The checks generally occurred between five and ten minutes after the hour. The one thing we couldn't be sure of was what the guards would do when they arrived. Most often, they went into the downstairs floor, took a quick look around, and then left. Occasionally, they simply looked through one of the large plate-glass windows at the front and decided that was enough. But about once a night they conducted a top-to-bottom run-through of the building.

By my calculations, ten minutes would be plenty of time for me to get down to the end of the hall, past the lock, and into the data center. But doing what I needed to get done in the computer center was another story.

Shunt had fashioned a small chip containing a Trojan horse program that would allow us into the system. The chip was attached to a small doo-hickey that I had to place in a specific board in a forest of similar boards in a room full of machines that all basically looked the same to me. I had practiced doing it for two days. My best time—twelve minutes.

"I better wait," I told Mongoose. "Give me a heads up when they're at the building."

"Roger that," he answered.

"What's the status?" asked Shotgun.

"I'm in the restroom. I have the detection devices defeated. If it looks like they're coming up I'll have to pull them out."

"Need help?" Shotgun's words were garbled by whatever he was eating.

"Negative. Hold your position. What the hell are you eating?"

"Devil Dogs."

"They sell those in Germany?"

"Ship all over the world," said Shotgun.

"Don't get crumbs on any of the equipment."

"Roger that."

I decided to do a little reconnoitering while I was waiting. I eased out of the doorway tentatively. When nothing sounded, I slipped all the way into the hall and walked down the short corridor to the door where the data center was.

There was a fingerprint lock, which was about what I expected.

Impossible to defeat, right?

Actually, easier than using a bump key. I dug into my magic bag of tricks at my belt and took out a small bottle of forensic dust, the CSI-friendly material technicians use to lift fingerprints. I dusted the reader, but it had been wiped clean after its last use.

Not a problem. I went back to the restroom and the large plate anyone wishing to enter pushed to get in. I had three different hands to choose from. Choosing the largest, I took a few snaps with my iPhone.

"Here we go," warned Mongoose. "Security car is coming up."

He gave me a play-by-play as the car parked in front of the building.

"Guards are getting out of the car," said Mongoose. "Checking the front door."

"I can see the car," said Shotgun from the roof. "They going in?"

"No," said Mongoose a few seconds later. "They're coming back."

Sure the guards were leaving, I went back to the fingerprint reader and held my phone over it.

Nothing happened. The LED light on the side of the reader blinked red. *Fail.*

I tried two more times, but without any luck.

The process had never failed before. I thought maybe there was some sort of heat sensor on the touchplate instead of just a simple scanner, so edged the side of my hand over it and tried again.

Nada.

Either the reader wasn't working, or I had taken the wrong print. Obviously someone other than data center employees used the restroom upstairs.

Like the janitor.

I glanced around for another source of prints. The best candidate was the door to the stairs, but I suspected I would have the same problem there.

There was a closet on the left side of the hall, almost directly opposite the door to the data center. The knob looked like it might be a better bet; the only problem was that the fingerprint, if there was one, would be on the side and difficult to photograph.

What about in the closet?

Eureka. It was filled with shelves of stationery. About three-quarters of a bottle of fingerprint dust later, I had three fresh index prints that the app claimed were all different from the others.

The first one worked. I opened the door gingerly, scanning to make sure there wasn't another unmapped detector nearby.

I'd just completed my scan without seeing anything when Mongoose came on the radio circuit.

"Something's up, Dick," he warned. "Two guys just walked down the street and stopped in front of the bank."

"What are they doing?"

"Looking in the front window," said Mongoose a few seconds later. "They're dressed in black."

"They looking for the ATM?" asked Shotgun.

"If so, they're blind."

I told Mongoose to keep me informed, and went to work. The red light over the door here was dim and the room large, so I turned on the miner's lamp. The LEDs revealed a forest of large mainframe computers and peripheral equipment.

We'd had to guestimate the room's arrangement, and my little light now revealed that our guesses were more than a little off. Working with layouts from other data centers, we'd assumed that the machines would be pushed back near the walls, with a large open area at the center. But here the large units formed a corridor immediately inside the room, and to get to the operator area, you had to walk between them. This actually made my job easier, though; there would be a lot more area to work in when I removed the access panel from the machine.

Assuming I could find the right one.

The bank used an IBM System Z, a rather impressive computer system. The machine cases themselves are high couture—for silicon. The large black boxes with the occasional slash of blue were joined together by bundles of wires that ran along the floor and some of the sides of the units, a bit like ivy without the leaves.

It took me several minutes to find the right box. I narrowed it down to three based on the outside covers, then used a small plug-in device to see which one had the right addresses in the system.

I'm parroting what Shunt told me—I have only the vaguest idea of the technical details of what I was doing. From my perspective, I was plugging what looked like a fancy thumb drive into a diagnostic panel on the bottom of the machine. If the LED light lit, I had the right machine. It took all three tries—when I got to the last one, I had to cross my fingers: there was no backup plan if the device didn't work.

Unit located, I opened the front of the case and looked for the support processor unit, which looked like a stamped card with two little boxes for plugs. I put a jump wire and card into the left opening. Then I counted off cards until I found the bulk power hub. This contained a long row of connectors, which looked very similar to the network connectors you might use on your own home computer. I slipped Shunt's doohickey into the third hole, connected it to the jumper, then pushed a little switch at the very end of the doohickey.

Then I stood back and waited.

According to Shunt, the device would open a path for him within two computer cycles or some other odd measurement of time that only he knows. He would call Mongoose once he was in. At that point I could dismantle everything and go grab a beer.

But instead of Mongoose, I heard Shotgun blaring in my ear.

"Hey, Dick—those guys are breaking into the bank. Shit!"

The next second, the bank alarm began to sound.

We had reached the most marvelous stage of any operation—the condition known to aficionados as SNAFU. As in *Situation Normal: All Fucked Up.*

Somewhere on the other side of the Atlantic, Shunt and his assistant were hunched over a pair of computers, attempting to connect with the mainframe I was kneeling in front of. According to our plan, he would get into the system—his little doohickeys made the computer think he was a diagnostic routine—and once there, call and tell me I could shut everything down.

Apparently, his coding wasn't as perfect as he thought.

"Shotgun, pack up," I said over the radio.

"I'm ready to go."

"Dick, I don't like the looks of this," warned Mongoose. "You better get out of there."

"In a minute. You hear from Shunt?"

"Negative. I hear police cars."

"Stand by."

I pulled out my sat phone and quick-dialed Shunt. It probably only took a second or two to connect, but it certainly felt like forever.

"I'm working on it," said Shunt, answering.

"I have two idiot bank robbers downstairs, and cops on the way," I told him. "Make it work *now*."

He answered with a string of curses, echoing my unvoiced thoughts. Then he was quiet. "Try the backup address switcher," he said finally. "Then go back and move the dip switch forward."

"What the hell are you talking about, Shunt?"

He walked me through the changes, which involved putting the doohickey into a new slot on the same card, then moving a small switch on the board. One of those changes—or maybe the swearing—did *something*—lights began flickering madly inside the machine.

"Dick, the police are out front," warned Mongoose.

"I'm waiting on Shunt," I told him. "What about the robbers?"

"Still in the building somewhere."

I have to confess that part of me wanted to go downstairs and teach those knuckleheads a lesson. But sneaking downstairs and gift wrapping them for the police would expose me to the surveillance cameras at the base of the stairwell and on the main floor. I consoled myself with the hope that they might venture upstairs, whereupon I would greet them warmly.

"Shunt, what's going on?" I demanded.

"I need sixty more seconds."

"Bad guys are running out the front door," cut in Shotgun over the radio. "They're armed."

Good, I thought to myself, *that will keep the police busy for a few minutes.*

A second later, the floor came up from beneath me, and what sounded like a freight train drove over my head.

The boys downstairs had blown the place up.

(III)

Having witnessed more explosions than I care to recall, the pop and crackle of a mere grenade going off behind a distant wall no longer excites me.

This blast was on a different order entirely. Seven on a ten scale: it blew a hole in the floor a few feet away from me. Flames shot up through the hole in an impressive display of color and heat.

I observed the flash from my back.

"Shunt!" I yelled as I struggled up from the floor. My voice must have been loud enough for him to hear all the way back in New York.

"We got it," he answered. "Go, go, go!"

I reached into the computer. Flames had spread out from the hole. The ceiling seemed to be on fire. Something flared to the right of me.

Black smoke began pouring from a computing unit behind me. Something yellow poked out of the black grill of the one next to it.

I grabbed the doohickey and turned toward the door—which was not only on the other side of the hole, but blocked off by one of the computer units, which had fallen just beyond the hole.

Without thinking, I grabbed the computer unit I'd just been working on and climbed to the top, then scrambled over the large cases and moved toward the door. The air was thick with smoke and acrid fumes. My eyes felt as if they had been soaked in pepper spray, and my throat could have sanded down an oak tree.

The explosion had blown the door inward, where it rested on one of the fallen computer units. I was able to slide down headfirst, landing in the hall in a tumble.

I'm not sure what the temperature was, but it was certainly hot enough not to have to worry about the infrared motion detectors. I threw myself to the floor, then crawled toward the restroom.

The air near the floor was a bit clearer, and the damage out here wasn't nearly as bad as in the data center. Still, I seemed to be moving in slow motion. Mongoose yelled in my ear, but it was impossible to make out with the symphony of alarms set off by the explosion. Besides those in the bank and the buildings on either side, it seemed like every car alarm in the city was sounding.

I was about six feet from the men's room and escape when a dark shadow burst into the hall ahead. It moved so fast that my first thought was that it was a cloud of smoke.

The next thing I thought was that it was a fireman. But firemen, even in Berlin, don't dress head to toe in black.

I'm guessing we stared at each other for a full second before either of us moved.

I ducked toward the restroom. He did, too—and kicked me in the face. I hadn't seen it coming, and took practically the full force of his size 20E boot to the front of my skull.

I'm guessing at the size. The impact certainly seemed to warrant it.

I rolled back, then tried to grab him as he rushed past me toward the data center. The hook of my hand was just enough to throw him off-balance and he crashed down against the doorjamb and rolled onto the floor.

Twenty years before, I would have jumped to my feet and stomped his face a few times for good measure. But I'm older now, and either lazier or smarter, depending on your perspective: I took the easy way out, grabbing for my pistol.

My shot caught him in the back of the head. As he fell down, I realized he was wearing a breather.

I grabbed it, then took a quick look at him. Between the smoke and the confusion, I doubt I could ever identify him in a lineup, but I did note one thing—he was definitely a Caucasian.

"Dick?" said Shotgun over the radio. "What's going on?"

"OK. I'm OK," I managed. "I'm coming."

I held the mask of the breather—it looked like a gas mask—then crawled into the restroom and over to the window. Shotgun pulled me out, and we made our way down to the back alley. I took a half step, then fell off-balance.

"We gotta move, boss," yelled Shotgun. He spun around and hoisted me over his back as if I were a seabag filled with unwashed clothes. Then he hustled out to the street, where Mongoose had moved the car. Shotgun threw me into the back as the car sped off.

My head had cleared but my jaw and the side of my skull ached. I reached up gingerly to see if my ear was still there. It certainly was—at about three times its normal size, it wasn't hard to find. My lungs made a wheezing sound that would have made an organ-grinder proud.

I slumped back, content to let Mongoose drive—which gives you some idea of how battered I felt. The streetlights blurred. I finally got my strength back to the point where I could lean forward and pull the ruck off my back. As I did, Mongoose took a hard turn and nearly sent me into the dashboard. I dropped the backpack and grabbed for my seat belt.

"Careful with your driving," I told him. "Aren't you going a little fast?"

"Tell that to the idiots on my bumper."

I turned around. The idiots on his bumper had their bubblegum lights going full blast.

Fortunately for us, the police officers behind us were driving in one of the force's relatively new Prius Toyotas. I'm sure they were getting fantastic gas mileage, but the 3.6 liter six-cylinder in the CC had them beat by a hundred horsepower. Veering through traffic, Mongoose managed to build up a decent lead, zigzagging his way around the Tiergarten into a tangle of *Strasses* and *Sackgasses*.

I don't know how familiar you are with Berlin, but undoubtedly you know the streets better than Mongoose. We had rehearsed three different exit routes to get us out to Bundesautobahn 2, the major highway running west from the city, and another two apiece to Tegel and Schönefeld, the airports north and south of the city, respectively. But in his haste to duck the policemen, Mongoose had lost his way. The navigation unit in the car—programmed for Schönefeld—was no help. It kept telling him to turn right, then became frustrated as he missed the turn, announcing in a loud, English-accented voice that it was "recalculating."

We had lost the policemen, but we were lost as well. Even I was confused—we had zigged and zagged so much that I had a hard time making out exactly where we were. The roar of a jet nearby revealed we were near Tegel airport.

"Should we go to the airport?" asked Mongoose.

"Negative," I told him. While we had a set of reservations for a plane—a backup getaway plan—I figured we'd be easy prey there.

"There's a paper map in the glove compartment," I told Shotgun. "Get it and let's figure out where the hell we are."

"I got it," said Shotgun. He took it and managed to direct Mongoose onto Stadring, one of the major roads that cuts south through the residential areas of the city. But we had hardly gone a half mile when a pair of flashing blue lights cut across the highway from the other direction. They slammed on their brakes, blocking our path. Mongoose took evasive action, cutting hard to the right, which took us across a lane of traffic, and out over the shoulder of the road.

Into thin air.

We hung there for a moment or two, the Volkswagen apparently trying to remember if its engineers had stowed wings somewhere in its trunk. But they hadn't.

"Brace for impact," yelled Shotgun, who obviously had been watching too many reruns of *Star Trek: The Next Generation* on our off days.

We slammed down a second or two later, airbags exploding on all sides. Though rough, our landing was much better cushioned than I had any right to expect.

Which made me suspicious.

"Water!" yelled Mongoose.

"Let it sink," I told the boys. "Swim to the south. The cops will be on the north."

There was no time to argue—the car's hood sunk low, and water surged over our chests.

In case you're keeping track, this would be the FUBAR stage of the operation—*Fucked Up Beyond All Recognition.*

The Volkswagen was a great car. It was a miserable boat. It filled with water quicker than a kid's bucket at the seashore.

I took one last glimpse of my position in the car as the water filled and pulled it downward. The idea is simple: while you can see (if you can see), you spot an orientation point. Then once you're in the darkness and under the water, you make for that spot.

In this case, it was the door handle, right next to me. I held my breath as the water rose, undid the seat belt, then pulled at the handle. Had I tried opening the door before we sank, the outside pressure would have made it extremely difficult. But now there was just as much water inside the car as outside, and the door opened relatively freely.

I pushed out, kicking my legs free. I couldn't see where I was—the water was extremely murky, and it was night besides. Propelling myself topside, I took a quick gulp of air, then ducked back down, doing an improvised side-stroke toward the opposite bank.

Mongoose is a former SEAL, and reached shore well ahead of either of us. Shotgun took a little longer, reaching the rocks just about when I did.

The police car was directly across the channel, blue lights spinning in a panicked arc across the water's surface. I pointed to our left, and we made our way, still in the water, along the shadows for nearly a hundred yards, until we reached a small construction barge. We clawed our way to the other side of the barge, then clambered up behind a large construction crane that was being used to add new bulkhead sections to the shoreline.

"Think they're coming for us?" Shotgun asked.

"Not yet. Soon." I looked around. There was a construction trailer on land, behind a four-foot fence. "Maybe there are clothes in there. Let's find out."

There were clothes, workmen's overalls to be exact, though none of them came even close to fitting Shotgun. I'm sure he was a rather comical sight to the cabdriver who picked us up a few minutes later. The man never uttered a word, however—this was Berlin, and he was used to seeing very strange sights.

Then again, the frown on Mongoose's face couldn't have encouraged much interaction, let alone comments.

I had the cabbie drop us off about a quarter mile from the hotel where we had rented a pair of safe rooms the day before. We made our way to the building quickly, entering through a back door. Two showers and fifteen minutes later, we readjourned at a nearby *biergarten* for first aid and a debrief.

[IV]

Let's start by stating the obvious:

The bank building had been blown up by people who knew, more or less, what they were doing.

The computer center was a target. Robbery was, at most, a secondary goal.

And German beer is very good.

The televisions at both ends of the bar were tuned to a German news station, and by the time we had finished our first round of drinks, they were showing live footage of the fire at the building. Apparently a neo-Nazi group had phoned in to take credit for the attack, supposedly because it allowed foreigners to work there.

Even in translation, that sounded to me like a rather pathetic attempt to divert attention from what had really happened.

"Gotta be related to our project," said Mongoose as he waved to the bartender for refills. "Too much of a coincidence."

I didn't give my opinion. I wanted to hear from Shunt before making up my mind.

Though I, too, am not a big believer in coincidences.

Shotgun fell into a conversation with a nearby *fräulein*, trying to convince her to teach him some German. Mongoose, something of a connoisseur of explosions, began analyzing the way the building had been blown up. He deduced that it had been designed to look like the target was the safe, which was several stories below the computer center. It would look like they just used too much explosive—a common problem. Strong evidence to the contrary would be destroyed by the resulting fire.

"I'd be willing to bet they used accelerants, but by the time this is done, it'll be hard to know for sure." He gestured to the screen. "They must have had stuff preplanted, because they didn't go in with enough explosives for this."

"Hmmm." I sipped my beer.

"Inside job," he added.

My sat phone rang. I thought it was Shunt, but the number belonged to Dan Barrett, who handles a lot of my business in the States and acts as exec officer when I'm away.

"Veep just called to tell you about a problem the bank is having in Berlin," said Danny.

"You don't say."

"Some sort of explosion in a building. Wanted to make sure you knew about it. He called from his cell phone—he's on his way to his office. You can reach him there."

Veep was Jason Redlands, one of about two hundred vice presidents of the American International Bank, though possibly one of the few with actual responsibilities: he was in charge of computer security.

He was the man who had hired Red Cell International—though not to look for embezzlement. He was also the reason we had come to Germany.

"I'll call him," I told Danny.

"He thinks you're in Texas."

"I'll speak with a twang."

I had been in Texas a week earlier, appearing as emcee of a mixed martial arts show there. It was a good show, raising money for disabled veterans, one of my favorite pastimes. Mongoose had been with me, hoping to take part in one of the early-round matches—but that's another story.

After ordering another beer, I took myself to a corner of the bar and gave Veep a call. His secretary wasn't there, but he picked up on the second ring.

"Commander Marcinko, thank you for calling," said Veep. Though his office was in New York, he was a Midwesterner, and retained his native politeness.

"Danny tells me there's been some sort of excitement?"

"That's not the word I would use," he said gravely. "Our bank in Germany has just been attacked, we think by terrorists."

"In Germany?"

"Our European servers are there. The computer operations," he added, as if I didn't know what servers were. "Our whole system is down. It will be hours before we can go to backups."

"That's terrible."

"I'd like to get your input on this," he said. "The terror group."

"Of course."

"They say neo-Nazis."

"Uh-huh."

"We'll extend the terms of the existing contract, if that's OK."

It was, of course, completely OK. Veep didn't want me to actually solve the case, let alone apprehend the bombers. All he needed, he claimed, was someone who understood the world of counterterrorism.

"Interface with Interpol, that sort of thing," he said. "Of course, if there are things we can do to prevent a recurrence—"

"I'm sure there are. I'll be in touch."

———

Shunt called a few minutes later, by which time I'd gone from beer to Bombay Sapphire—the doctor's elixir does wonders for aches and pains.

"We got nothing useful," were the first words out of his mouth. "We weren't in long enough to pull down all of the accounts, let alone start analyzing them. I'm afraid what we have isn't going to give us much information."

I made the mistake of asking Shunt why it had taken so long for them to get the virus working in the first place. This was a strategic mistake on my part: Shunt began explaining that what I had inserted was a Trojan horse, not a virus, and that it was considerably more complicated than Zeus,[2] whatever that was. I let him babble while the waitress brought me another drink, then asked him to tell me in actual English what the situation with the bank was.

"They've shut down their overseas accounts. If those computers are physically destroyed, they'll go to a backup system. It should be a mirror—"

"Which means what?"

"Exact duplicate. Once I know where the backup operation is, I can figure out how to penetrate it. I know a little more about their system now," he added. "And Junior gave me a couple of ideas—we might be able to get inside without having to get the machine itself."

"And we won't be detected?"

"Matt suggested a way we could make it look like we were Russian mobsters. I kind of like that."

So did I. Junior and Matt, by the way, are the same person: Matthew Loring, my prodigal son.

Actually he wasn't the prodigal; I was. I didn't know I had a son until he showed up on the doorstep, fully grown and ready to rumble. We've been making up for lost time; he joined Red Cell International as a tech guy and has been working his way over to the field. It seems like he joined us just the other day, yet he continually surprises me with his grasp of *reality*.

He's also a bit of a rogue in his own right, but we'll get to that by and by.

"I talked to Veep a little while ago," I told Shunt. "He wants me to consult with the police."

"Wow—you think maybe he's not stealing the money?"

"I remain agnostic."

Veep had hired us two weeks before "at the behest of"—read, "under heavy pressure from"—the bank's board of directors because of some

---

[2] "Zeus" is a famous, or infamous, piece of malicious programming that steals information from online transactions. Trojan horses are programs that may look benign or be presented within another program, but are actually designed to do something bad. They don't generally spread to other machines like viruses do.

European transactions that seemed suspicious. He had told the board that the transactions appeared to have been made to charity organizations that were known fronts for al Qaeda and other radical Muslims.

Veep seemed to feel that shutting down the accounts would end the matter. But apparently one of the board members was actually awake when Veep gave his presentation, and started asking questions. To get him off his back, Veep promised an outside investigation.

My name came up in the discussion. Someone must have been reading one of my books.

Hiring an American to investigate a problem that originated in Europe—questionable, even if yours truly does have an international rep. After all, the word "international" is part of my company name, Red Cell International.

Encouraging me to wrap up the investigation quickly, then barely cooperating with the work?

I smelled a well-perfumed rat. And my suspicions were strengthened when Junior discovered that the accounts had been erased from the American side of the operation.

Should what seemed like a carefully orchestrated attack on the bank remove the scent of an inside job?

Not yet.

"Can you break into the Berlin police systems and find out what's going on?" I asked Shunt.

"*Can I?* You have to ask?"

"I was being polite."

"Wow, Dick. That's a change for you. Are you jet-lagged or something?"

"Get your ass in gear. I expect a report in two hours."

"I'll have it in one."

You have to know when to pat 'em on the back, and when to kick 'em in the arse.

Forty minutes later, Shunt was on the line, and sounding like he had been drinking even more cherry cola than usual.

"Year ago," he sputtered. "Ethiopia—government office—bombing used a combination of explosives and fire bombs—took out computers—interior ministry—files—terror orgs."

"English is your first language, isn't it?" I asked.

That stopped him short.

"Uh, yeah. That and Perl. Well, maybe HLASM assembler.[3] Why do you ask?"

---

[3] Perl and HLASM are programming languages. Or soft drinks; I'm not sure which.

"Maybe you could try using it? English, I mean."

By breaking into the police system, Shunt had managed to get pictures and details of the remains of one of the devices. He had then run a simple search in the databases we maintain cataloguing terror incidents around the world.

He came up with an 85 percent match with attacks in Somalia and Kenya two years before by a group whose Arabic name translated into English as Allah's Rule on Earth.

Shunt went on to say that the group responsible had at least a tangential relationship to al Qaeda—it had received some money from a charity that had been used as a front by bin Laden in the late 1990s, and two men associated with the group were at a guerilla camp in Pakistan sponsored by al Qaeda around 2008.

An al Qaeda camp in Pakistan?

Goodness. Who would have thought?

"Maybe it wasn't embezzlement at all," said Shunt. "Maybe it is a legit group, trying to cover their tracks."

It wouldn't be the first time I was wrong—not even that day.

The contemplation of my fallibility, as well as the conversation, were cut short by another incoming call. I glanced at the ID, thinking it might be Veep. I immediately recognized the name, though: Flushing Taylor.

I would venture to say that not too many people in the world have the first name of Flushing. It just so happens that I know one of them: Chief Petty Officer (Ret.) Flushing J. Taylor, former SEAL Team Six and Red Cell member, personal security maven, and sometime drinking companion to yours truly.

"I have a little problem, Commander," he said. "I don't know where else to turn."

Flushing's son is Garrett, and you've already met him—we've almost come back full circle to where we started.

Garrett had just been arrested in Saudi Arabia for drug trafficking. Flushing said Garrett had gone to Saudi Arabia on a vacation, and while in the capital of Riyadh come across a man selling hookahs, those fancy water pipes used to smoke flavored tobacco. They're common enough in Riyadh, where you can find dozens of small cafés dedicated to their use.

You can also find dozens of policemen anxious to make arrests, which are magically "forgotten" once the proper fine is paid—to the policeman, of course. When it turned out that the dealer had included a substance other than tobacco as a deal-sweetener, they pounced.

"It musta been a setup," said Flushing. "The cops asked him for a bribe—not in so many words—but he had only a hundred bucks. It didn't cut it.

Now to get him out, it's going to cost a small fortune. I'm desperate. I can't let him stay in jail."

"Absolutely not."

"Someone at the State Department told me to hire a fixer," he said. "But that's a rip-off, too. What should I do?"

"Don't do anything until I talk to some people."

"Thanks, Dick. I knew I could count on you."

Garrett's arrest and our bank job should have stayed two different story lines, and probably would have, had I not called a not-to-be-named source in the Saudi royal family, who owed me a personal favor for reasons that cannot (yet) be given. He took my call, listened to the situation, then promised an aide would get back to me.

By now it was pretty late—or very early—in Berlin. It was an hour later in Saudi Arabia. You can judge how much of a favor he owed me not by the fact that he took my call, but that the aide called back within a half hour.

"Your friend is in a very bad situation," said the aide, whose accent was somewhere between Oxford and Cambridge. "He is involved with a drug-smuggling ring that we believe funds a terror group."

"He is?"

"I am sorry to tell you. Yes, there is evidence."

"What group?"

He used the Arabic name, a tongue twister that sounded like *PeterPiper-PickedaPintofPickledPotheadPenisHeads.*

Then he translated it for me.

"The Arabic means Allah's Rule on Earth. They are not so famous yet, but have acted in Somalia and Kenya. Very dangerous, indeed."

We have now reached the educational part of our program. I believe the following will be of use to members of the general public, informing them of the "business side" of international terrorism. But if you're anxious to get back to my little tea party in the Saudi jail yard, or just can't wait to see me squealing like a baby pig-boy, you have my encouragement to skip ahead.

Allah's Rule on Earth typifies the multi-faceted terror organizations that present the greatest challenges in the twenty-first century. It was small, highly secretive, and, most importantly, self-sustaining. It had associates in Africa, Asia, the Middle East, and Europe, which gave it the ability to strike in any of those areas.

Allah's Rule was led by two different figures—one a Pakistani expatriate thought to live in Egypt named Haji Khan Noor Muhammad Kalhoro, usually known as Noor Muhammad; the other Sameer Haddad, a Yemen cleric who at last report was holed up somewhere in the southern portion of the country.

Sameer had once been associated with al Qaeda in the Arabian Peninsula—today one of the most powerful terror groups in the world—but split with them over some perceived slight. Both men had various "intersections" with al Qaeda over the years, though neither seems to have actually met Osama bin Goatherder before his timely demise at the hands of SEAL Team Six.

Noor and Haddad had different abilities, and while their roles occasionally overlapped, in general Haddad recruited members and set goals for the group; Noor trained and did tactical planning. The two men were rarely together, but communicated through emissaries and the occasional cell phone and e-mail link. They were smart enough not only to vary their routines but to constantly get rid of anything that might help lead investigators to their doors. A cell phone might be used only once or twice; a sympathetic mosque might host a week's worth of sermons and classes, then never be visited again.

Terror operations are relatively cheap. Still, like all organizations, they need some money to run. An operation like Allah's Rule, with connections over a wide area of the earth and ambitions to match, needed more than many. So where did they get their funds?

Drug smuggling. Having all those connections makes it much easier to get things from one side of the world to another. And the most lucrative things to move are drugs. Not just for Allah's Rule, but for many terror groups with serious ambitions.[4]

In the case of our friends, poppies grown in the mountainous regions of Afghanistan and Pakistan were processed into heroin in Pakistan, then transported by ship to locations around the world. The routes were rotated, presumably to lessen the chances of detection, but the final destination was generally Europe.

We were able to turn up a number of Egyptian contacts among suspected Allah's Rule "associates," and the presumption was that the drugs went from Egypt to Turkey or Greece, and from there to the rest of Europe. Getting the drugs to Egypt was a bit tricky—not because of police activity, but because other groups had already monopolized the ports. Therefore the network used overland routes—including one from Saudi Arabia.

On the surface, driving drugs overland through Saudi Arabia was dangerous—the Kingdom has rather draconian penalties for drug trafficking. But these penalties only apply to the person caught. And even that's not much of a risk if you have the right connections.

Money from the operation flowed in several different directions. A good portion went to buying and moving the drugs. What was left over went to a small number of members as stipends, and to schools and mosques sympathetic to the cause. Only a very small portion went to actual operations.

In fact, compared to the damage done, the amount was, and is, shockingly small.

Except for 9/11 and some of the attacks on India that received state backing, the bombing in the Madrid subway system in March of 2004 was one of the most successful operations of all time. Four separate trains were attacked with a total of thirteen improvised explosive devices (IEDs). Three of the bombs failed to go off and were later exploded by bomb disposal experts, but the ones that did ignite killed 191 people; another 1,800 were injured. Estimates of the cost to Spain begin at 17.62 million euros and go way up.

How much did that attack cost the perpetrators?

Between ten and fifteen thousand dollars, using the exchange rate prevalent at the time. Or about $78.53 per life.[5]

---

[4] Taking drugs is forbidden under Islam. Because of that, there are varying opinions on whether devout Muslims are allowed to traffic in them, even to fund jihad. Osama bin Laden wrote a very long letter to one of his minions saying they were not. Obviously, not everyone agreed with the old goat.

[5] In case you're interested, no direct link to al Qaeda has ever been proven. Most experts believe that bin Laden's network inspired the Madrid bombers, but didn't guide them.

A few more numbers before we return to the mayhem: a kilo of heroin will fetch about one thousand dollars for a farmer in Afghanistan. That's just about twice the annual per capita income. When that kilo reaches Europe, it's worth in the range of one hundred thousand.

Mecca and Medina, holy cities of Islam, are altogether different. It's not simply that they are ancient Muslim cities. Both cities regularly handle crowds that put the Super Bowl to shame. Of course, if you're not Muslim, don't try making a reservation; they don't want you. In fact, they'll arrest you if you try to get in.

Riyadh, the capital, is open to all religions—as long you don't practice them. Like most of Saudi Arabia, worshiping any God other than Allah will get you a quick trip to jail.

Riyadh looks like a very modern city, nothing like you might expect if you're focused on camels and dust storms. Though it is by reputation more puritan than John Smith, you can find a fair amount of vice if you know where to look. Of course, with no house numbers, and street names written only in Arabic, looking is not as easy as you'd think. Even if you know where you're going, driving can be a hassle. Perfectly paved roads seem to be against the law, and the authorities have an annoying habit of throwing up checkpoints to harass citizens and foreigners at irregular intervals. The biggest landmark in the city is a giant zipper latch (Kingdom Centre); I'm still trying to figure out what that says about the place.

Mongoose, Shotgun, and I flew in through Dubai, and after running the gamut of louts and touts at the airport, found an "official" taxi to take us out of the city to the home of Prince X, a (distant) member of the royal family whom I won't name in hopes of staying somewhat in his good graces.[6]

Like most members of the extended—and in his case, extremely extended—royal family, Prince X is very wealthy.

How wealthy?

I met him on an indoor ski slope in his backyard.

Housed inside what looked like a huge spaghetti box held at an angle by toilet paper rolls, the slope was some 230 meters long, with enough width for a separate mogul section toward the bottom. The facilities at top and bottom rivaled anything you'd find in an Aspen condo, though I suspect the waitresses that work in the States wear a few more clothes than the attendants my friend had working that day.

Prince X was entertaining a few foreigners when I arrived, including a junior member of the American diplomatic corps, who was a charter member

---

[6] Yet another member of the Saudi family who owed me a favor.

of the "terrorism is no longer a threat" crowd. It's marvelous what they're doing with the developmentally disabled these days.

Prince X and I spoke between salmon egg canapés. He provided a few contacts in the prison administration that he thought would come in handy, along with the name of the engineering firm that had constructed the jail where Garrett was being held. I didn't tell him exactly who I was there to get, but given the paucity of foreigners in Saudi jails, it surely wasn't hard to guess.

"Before you do anything rash," Prince X told me, "first allow me to tell my lawyer, and he will arrange release immediately. For you, justice moves swiftly."

This naturally sounds like the matter would be taken care of quickly, but in fact, not even an immediate order from the prince himself would have gotten the young man out of the prison in less than a month. Going through his lawyer would mean using the courts, which might result in an "immediate" order to get the kid released in the next twelve to eighteen months.

Admittedly far better than the usual grinding wheels of justice, but not exactly fitting the definition of what I would call swift.

And so I returned to Riyadh, dabbed some gray in my beard and hair, and began spreading the word of Coptic Hinduism. My original plan was to set up shop at As-Sufaat, aka Deira Square, aka Chop-Chop Square, the picturesque plot of concrete and stone where convicts have their heads chopped off. But there didn't seem to be any police officers in sight when we drove past, and even fewer people to preach to. So instead I headed to Batha, one of the immigrant areas of the city, populated by so many Pakistanis that they call it Little Karachi.

I found a little patch of grass across from the Pia theater and set up poster and bullhorn. The poster featured the religion's (naked) patron saints ascending to heaven to join other (naked) saints. This immediately attracted the attention of the dozen or so men already in the triangle. Within moments, the nearby traffic had stopped.

I'm sure they were more interested in my preaching than the photos, but who's to say?

It took the police about ten minutes to arrive, and all of ninety seconds to arrest me. If I'd have known I would last that long, I would have passed a hat—I'm sure I could have gotten a few hundred riyals from the crowd.

Those were happy times.

A little more than twenty-four hours later, I had my back pressed against the chain-link fence in the Saudi prison as three men with grimaces and hard fists walked toward me. They didn't look like they wanted my autograph.

The best advice I have ever heard about fighting against overwhelming odds came from a wise old sea daddy whose name escapes me at the moment:

Run!

Unfortunately, that option was not open. So the first order of business was to even the odds with a preemptive strike against the most vulnerable goon, a stocky and swarthy Arab whose nose looked as if it had been sliced off and relocated a half inch to the right of its original position.

I tried to do the same thing for his head. Grabbing his shirt with my left hand, I pulled him forward as my right hand swung with the shiv across his neck. Then I pushed him backward with my knee, dumping him in a heap on the ground.

The knife was too small to go all the way through his neck. In fact, it barely looked as if he was scratched when he first fell. But then blood began spurting out like the Disney fountain at Epcot, a perfect quartet of jet streams.

The other two lugs didn't seem to notice. The nearest lunged with both fists flailing. I ducked, then jerked up quickly, aiming my knife at his belly. But he was faster than he looked. He ducked and I missed his stomach, flying forward.

The other managed to trip me, and as I hit the ground I lost the shiv. Until now, the rest of the crowd had been feigning disinterest, an admirable survival technique in a confined space like a jail yard. But the knife was too much to resist; a naked female would have gotten less attention. Everyone in the yard dove for the shiv, swarming over myself and my assailants. Unable to spot the blade in the scrum, I crawled for daylight, propelling myself through the squirming crowd on my knees and elbows.

Somehow I made it to the side of the building, where a pair of jail guards were waiting out the fight. Seeing me as easy pickings, they grabbed hold of my legs and dragged me without ceremony into the building, through a hall, and up a pair of steps to a luxurious lounge complete with a sauna and bargirls, very soft pillows, and a masseuse whose fingers should be numbered among the ten wonders of the world.

At least, that's how my fevered brain remembers it. The reality may have been slightly grittier. In any event, I soon fell into an undisturbed slumber, and didn't wake until the next morning, when we were summoned for prayers by the blare of the prison loudspeaker.

My eyes opened into the dim blue light of predawn filtering through the window above my head. There were only two other inmates in my cell; even though it was about half the size of the one where I'd initially been locked up, the lack of nearby bodies made it feel like a hotel.

"Come, come," whispered one of my companions, nudging me gently. He was Pakistani, and spoke in English. "Do not be caught in the cell. It would be worth many lashes to dally. Come."

I followed along to the yard, did the prayer thing, then wandered around in search of Garrett. He was standing near the fence about where I'd seen him the day before, away from the other prisoners. It was still relatively dark, but I noticed that he had some bruises to his eyes and the side of his face that hadn't been there before.

"You again," he muttered as I walked over to him.

"Me."

"You shouldn't hang around me. It's bad luck for both of us."

"I'm going to get you out," I told him.

He snorted contemptuously.

"Tomorrow at ten," I said. "Where will you be?"

"At night?"

"In the morning."

"Studying the Koran." He didn't sound particularly enthusiastic. Maybe they hadn't given him a good verse to memorize.

"Where will you be?"

"In the library."

"I'll come for you."

"Right." I've heard assurances that Iran doesn't want to build nukes voiced with more conviction.

"Make sure you're there," I told him. "No matter what else happens. You understand?"

He made a face. I pointed to his eye. "You want more of these?"

"Fuck off."

"Make sure you're in the library. Ten o'clock. Sharp."

He looked at me like I had the plague, and moved away.

———

My conversion to Islam began twenty minutes later. It was an extremely moving event.

Dragged into the interview suite, I was happy to see that my usual spot on the floor had been spruced up with some fresh applications of bleach. They hadn't gotten all of it—a myriad of dull brown splatters covered the spot where I was tossed, face-first—but it's the thought that counts.

I wallowed in the dust for a moment. Then, lo, a holy voice began speaking to me, and I was filled with the spirit of the most holy and glorious Messenger, the one, true Voice of the one true and glorious Allah.

Suddenly I understood the sacred writ. Nay, more than understood. I began propounding it, albeit in every foreign tongue known to man, and several that weren't. As I cited chapter and verse of the Holy Koran, even the most skeptical of my observers was moved to the deepest emotions: they kicked, they punched, they screamed, they pummeled. Through it all I continued my litany of praise for the Prophet, for the Book, for the one and only force of life, the being I am not worthy to contemplate, let alone mention.

For thirty solid minutes I spoke in tongues, imparting blessings upon all in earshot. By the end of the session, not only had my interlocutors and their aides joined me in prayer, but three other guards and two supervisors were now proclaiming the verity of my Truth, a special aspect of which revealed the very Holiness of the Saud family not just as defenders of the faith, but as veritable UNIVERSAL ETERNAL HOLY MEN SENT DIRECTLY FROM THE MESSENGER HIMSELF!!!! (Editor—yes, we need those caps!!!!)

It was, clearly, the most tremendous and spiritually uplifting conversion to Islam ever, certainly in this prison. And that, naturally, required an e-mail message to headquarters that very morning.

A message intercepted by Shunt, who had hacked his way into the pitifully primitive system used by the jailers.

The response from Riyadh was immediate—a high-level team of clerics would arrive the next day.

I'm not sure if it was the shower or the meal, which included something similar to meat, that tipped me off that salvation was on the way. Maybe it was the fact that the afternoon beating wasn't nearly as severe as the earlier ones, or that the waterboarding was at best halfhearted. I should note that Saudi law does allow certain prisoners to be released if they memorize a passage from the Koran and truly convert, revert, and pervert, and the administration was undoubtedly used to dealing with phony prophets.

My conversion was anything but phony. I propounded on the Divine Plan for the Kingdom, which naturally included exalted places for the conduits of my message—the torturers who had corrected my grammar and helped with the difficult questions of where to place the accents.

Whatever. I slept better that night than I had in months, aware that salvation was at hand.

I woke to the fervent baritone of the jail guard as he sang his praise of the early dawn, muttering in Arabic that the curs of Allah better get their butts up before they were flailed with the stick of heavenly persuasion.

I greeted him at the door of my cell most reverently, head bowed.

"You," he muttered. "I have heard of you."

I lowered my head even farther. "I am not worthy of your attention," I muttered in poorly accented Arabic.

How poor was my accent? To the uninitiated, the words might have sounded like "You are the bastard son of a goat-fucked mother." But surely I can't be blamed for my poor diction.

He rapped on the cell with his stick. I bowed my head lower.

"True believers fear the almighty and powerful," I told him. "And screw your mother, too."

This clearly placated him, as evidenced by the fact that he only poked me twice in the face with his stick before moving on.

I sang his glorious praises, thanking him for his gift of compassion.

My two cellmates were understandably cautious, and gave me a wide berth as I shuffled out to the hallway. I found new inspiration in the hall, realizing that the entire staff was worthy of a place in paradise, and all should get bonuses of five thousand dollars (American) come the Sabbath. My proselytizing reached a fevered pitch as I walked trembling out to the yard. I was moved by the spirit—and the prods of the guards behind me.

Word of my conversion had spread through the jail. Practically everyone was watching as I took my spot for the morning prayers. I'm sure they were expecting me to lead them with some profound revelation. But conviction is best understated. I went deep within myself, barely moving my lips in prayer.

My words wouldn't have been heard even if I were shouting, for as I began uttering them, a helicopter thundered overhead. The Russian-made Mi-8 was in so-so condition, offered for sale at the bargain price of only $550,000: an incredible deal, though at that price one had to expect some sort of mechanical deficiencies. Which no doubt explains the engine problems and the near crash landing in the second courtyard of the building, a feat that took considerable skill.

Have you met Trace Dahlgren, vice president of Red Cell International and part-time helicopter pilot?

I know what you're thinking: Dick is going to scoop Garrett up and run to the helo in a blaze of gunfire. Trace will gun the engines and they will sail off into the sunrise, just like in that movie . . .

The Saudi guards thought something similar. They rushed to the helicopter en masse, discovering Trace and the very frightened salesman trying to put out a small fire under the instrument panel. There were shouts and complaints and drawn guns.

The salesman fainted, leaving Trace to stare down the Saudi officials on her own. She did this in a yellow sleeveless shirt about two sizes too small and a pair of jeans that defined the term "painted on." She proceeded to get out of the helicopter, demonstrating with a series of complicated hand gestures where she thought the problem had actually originated.

Garrett, meanwhile, was at the edge of the crowd near the fence. I wouldn't say he was leering, exactly, but he certainly had the expression of a man who admired manual dexterity.

Suddenly he was also overcome by heat exhaustion—that or the sharp pop to the neck I administered.

I've carried heavier men—Shotgun comes to mind—but Garrett weighed enough to provoke a mental review of the signs of hernia as I toddled from the courtyard into the building in search of medical assistance. The guards had moved out into the yard for a better view. I descended the stairs to the lower level, carrying my load ever lower as I walked past the "interview cells" to the steps on the far side. Both Garrett and my butt were practically dragging the floor as I climbed up to the small yard where the garbage was collected in a series of small Dumpsters and largish bins.

The smell was absolutely delightful. It got even better as I approached the half-filled rolloff.

Mechanical problems cured and salesman revived, the helicopter took off from the rear of the yard, much to the regret of the population. Meanwhile, I clamped my teeth shut and went to work. Not five minutes later, a garbage truck rolled up. Two hulking attendants hopped off the back, pushed the Dumpster over, and had the lift empty it into the rear.

Someone shouted as the truck started to pull away.

"Two prisoners are missing!" he yelled. "Stop the garbage truck!"

It was a trick nearly as old as Sharia law. Alarms began sounding and guards began running. In the back, the helicopter began hovering unsteadily over the compound.

Meanwhile, two members of the night shift began making their way out the front door of the building, heading for the approaching bus with the other employees at the main gate. One of them tripped after exiting the building and struck his head on the sidewalk. His friend kindly helped him up and walked with him toward the stop.

That was us: the garbage bins were just a ruse, and a convenient place to dump the bodies of the two men whose clothes I stole. It was a perfectly executed getaway, out the front door.

Or it would have been, had Murphy not been driving the damn bus.

[IV]

The bus had pulled away from the curb and started down the narrow lane to the exit when it stalled. It was right in the middle of the road, blocking all traffic to the main building. When the driver couldn't get it restarted, we were ordered off.

Garrett was still out of it. I put my arm under his shoulder and eased him down the aisle, half walking him, half pushing him toward the exit. The driver eyed us suspiciously, but I managed to get him down the stairs without being stopped or asked about my sexual preferences. Nearby, the guards had hauled the two would-be escapees from the back of the garbage truck. Though clearly unconscious, they were being questioned ferociously.

I shuffled toward the back of the crowd, hoping not to be examined too closely. I had my beard, and in the shadows could probably pass semi-plausibly for a sunburnt nomad. But Garrett looked about as white as white could be, and no amount of fussing with the collar of his long prison uniform shirt could hide that. We stood out from the other patients, and I knew we were eventually going to be found out. So rather than waiting for that to happen, I pushed my still comatose comrade upright and walked with him in the direction of the garbage truck.

We were about halfway there when someone began to shout, but I didn't start running until I heard the gunshot.

Bullets exploded in the dirt nearby, fired by one of the guards back near the garbage bins. I threw my legs into overdrive, pulling Garrett with me to the cab. Yanking open the door, I pushed him inside, then I jumped up after him and put the truck in gear.

The truck promptly stalled. Murphy obviously hadn't done well in auto school.

As calmly as I could, I reached and turned the key.

Rrrrrrr—ping—ping-ping—rrrrrrr.

The pings were the bullets hitting the top of the cab. The *rrrrrrr* was the truck's starter, grinding the crankshaft over and over but failing to catch. Finally the engine coughed and caught, sounding like a pig with bronchitis. I managed to give the engine just enough gas to keep from stalling, and with a series of bucks and jerks, we began moving ahead.

The bus was blocking our path. There wasn't enough room to get around it, and I didn't have enough momentum to ram it and push it aside. So instead I threw the truck into reverse.

The crowd behind us scattered. Loose garbage flew from the rear as we jumped up the curb, drove across the sidewalk, and slammed into the low fence separating the garbage area from the rest of the driveway. I imagine all the guards were firing now, but I couldn't hear them. I was too busy cranking the wheel and shoving the tranny into drive, angling for the narrow space between the buildings on the left.

The truck's engine stuttered when I tried mashing the gas. I lifted my foot from the pedal just enough to keep the engine running without flooding; right about the time my stomach started looking for a new home at the back of my throat, we began moving forward.

We stuttered and bucked, but we were moving. A low fence stood between us and a wide, open field. The main road out was on the other side of the field.

As I picked up speed, something pounded on the side of the truck. It was one of the truck drivers, trying to recapture his vehicle. Fortunately, he didn't have a weapon. I swung my forearm at his face; he ducked, then reappeared at the window. He leaned in and bit my arm.

Either he didn't see the fence or didn't care. We hit it hard enough to sheer it in half; as it broke, the shattered links grabbed his clothes and pulled him away.

Clear, I turned hard right. I had a straight, unobstructed run to the main road. Except for the man with the M16 standing in my way.

"Duck," I yelled to Garrett, who was already slumped in the seat.

He croaked a response, the first peep I'd heard from him since the yard.

"Duck!" I yelled again.

I pushed my head down beneath the steering wheel as bullets raked the windshield. At some point soon thereafter, we crashed through the main gate. I'm not sure what happened to the guy with the rifle; either we ran him over or he jumped out of the way.

Steam was pouring from the front of the vehicle when I raised my head again. I didn't have to look at the gauges to know we weren't going to get very far.

"Garrett, we're going to bail," I yelled as the cabin began fogging.

He didn't answer. Fearing the worst, I glanced to the right and saw he was fending off a Saudi who was clinging to the window.

Garrett's dad was tough sea salt and a better-than-average brawler, which is pretty much what you would expect as a SEAL. He calmed down considerably at Six—mandatory behavior if you want to stay on the Team. But like father like son: the way Garrett pounded the Saudi with his right fist while holding his hair with his left hand made me nostalgic for his dad and bar fights gone by.

A loud boom and the sound of eight pistons shattering brought me back to the present. The truck immediately began to slow.

I threw it into neutral.

"Out!" I yelled as we coasted toward a halt. "Come on!"

Garrett let go of the guard, then grabbed at the door handle. As he flew out of the truck, I hopped out from my side and began running.

The Saudis were about two hundred yards behind us, rallying their forces from the prison. They had a pair of Humvees, with a .50 cal mounted in a turret on the top. The up-armored Hummer started spitting bullets. I grabbed Garrett and pulled him alongside, trying to keep the garbage truck between us as cover.

We'd only taken a few steps when something threw me forward into the grit. Sand swirled over me. For a moment I thought it was a Saudi sandstorm— one of the massive storms they call a *shamal* in Iraq.

Then I realized it was manmade.

The thick cloud of dust rolled over the Hummers. The dust blinded the driver and the gunner; they not only stopped firing but turned the vehicle to the side to escape the brunt of the dirt-laden tornado.

The next thing I knew, I was being grabbed by the back of my shirt and carried through the twister of dirt. Garrett was nearby, yelling that he was going to tear whoever was carrying him into a thousand tiny pieces.

There was a roar above us, and suddenly we were thrust out of the storm and into the hold of a helicopter.

"Better grab on to something!" yelled Mongoose as the Mi-8's motors roared overhead. "Trace is driving and she seems to be in a very bad mood."

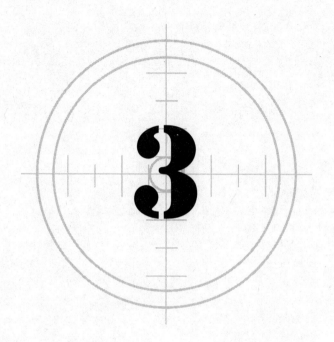

Trace took the helicopter east to Abu Dhabi, flying low over the desert to avoid Saudi border radar and the two aircraft that had been scrambled to intercept her. I was in the back of the chopper, so I have no idea how close the F-15s ever got to us; for all I know the fancy acrobatics she pulled and the wild zigzagging were simply an effort to show off.

The movements were extreme; they sent Mongoose and Garrett to a pair of large buckets at the rear.

I didn't feel all that well myself, but fortunately there was little in my stomach to remove. Shotgun had only one comment the entire flight:

"These jalapeño potato chips need more jalapeño."

There were some complications with the officials at the airport. While Trace and Shotgun stayed behind to straighten those out, Mongoose, Garrett, and I cabbed to a hotel in the city.

Abu Dhabi is the capital of the Arab Emirates, a very modern and surprisingly multicultural city. It has skyscrapers. It has race cars. It has alcohol—at least in hotel bars and restaurants designated for tourists. We went to one of the latter, located on the top floor of the Emirate Emerald, a la-di-da luxury high-rise hotel located right on the water.

Before making my way to the bar, I hit the head and the shower. The first splatter of water against the welts on my back stung, but gradually the pain melted away. Feeling better, I toweled off and got dressed, then went to partake of the magical healing powers of Dr. Bombay.

Mongoose and Garrett had taken a table near the windows. Garrett had been more or less comatose in the helicopter when he wasn't throwing up, and he didn't seem much better now. He stared at the far wall with unfocused eyes, his cheeks so bruised and puffed they looked like rotten potatoes. A beer and a shooter were sitting in front of him. Neither one had been touched.

"Damn," he muttered as I settled in. "Damn."

There seemed to be thoughts in his mind somewhere, but they were having trouble getting to his mouth.

I sat patiently, expecting . . . oh, I don't know, maybe a thank-you for rescuing him from that hellhole. Maybe a promise to name his first kid after me.

Instead, I got this:

"You fucking asshole."

I get that a lot, but generally not from people I've risked my life to rescue.

"You screwed everything up," continued Garrett. "You screwed it all up. I can't believe you screwed it all up."

He unleashed a stream of curses so severe even Mongoose appeared embarrassed. He grabbed our glasses, got up, and went for some refills.

Garrett was still spewing when Mongoose returned. I may have gotten out of my chair by that point, because Goose looked concerned. "Maybe you two should take it out to the street," he suggested.

The street was some eighty stories down. It was tempting.

"Let's go out to the terrace," I suggested, pointing to the doors on the side of the room. I could always toss him down to the street if I changed my mind.

Garrett hopped up with more energy than I'd thought he possessed. In the short walk across the room, he became rejuvenated, shedding the ill effects of the prison as if they were dandruff flakes on the shoulders of his jacket. Mongoose furled his brow—a frightening look that reminds me of a war pig—then trailed after him. I grabbed my gin and one of the beers.

I was barely through the door when Garrett launched into a fresh tirade. I'd heard enough and snapped back.

"I ruined your life? Is that what you're saying?" I demanded indignantly. "Your life would have ended at the point of a sharp axe when they chopped off your head after declaring you guilty in a few months."

"You don't know crap." Garrett's eyes flashed. I had a sudden flashback to my navy days with his dad, when he and I faced off against a dozen marines.

I love the marines. Except when I'm fighting them in a bar. And especially when I'm outnumbered six to one.

But Flushing Taylor's temper was a legendary force multiplier. He lit into those marines like an A-10A Warthog ripping through a squad of tanks. None of them were standing when he got done.

Now, the infamous family temper was about to explode on me. Mongoose took a step between us, ready to grab Garrett if he took a swing.

"Who sent you?" Garrett demanded. "Who pulled the plug?"

"What plug? No one sent me. I talked to your dad."

"My dad?"

"Look, I don't know what you're doing with your life, and I don't want to know. If you want to associate with the scum of the earth, that's your business. Your father was a plank owner of mine, and that brings certain obligations. That's why I'm here. If you have a beef, take it up with your father."

"My father."

"You're on your own. If I were you, though, I wouldn't go back to Saudi Arabia."

"You're an idiot, you know that?" Garrett began to laugh. "You went through all this trouble because my father was worried about me?"

"What's so funny about that?"

"How much did he pay you?"

"Not a cent."

"This—all this—you did out of the kindness of your heart?"

"I did it because your dad is an old friend," I told him. I was also hoping to get information about Allah's Rule on Earth from him, but under the circumstances I decided this wasn't a good time to talk about it. And frankly, I had the feeling I wasn't going to be getting much of anything in the way of cooperation.

"This was none of my father's business," said Garrett, shaking his head. "I work for the agency, you idiot. The CIA. You just blew six months' worth of work."

[II]

Oh yeah, I felt foolish.

Here I was, thinking I was living a Father's Day greeting card, and it turned out I'd actually stumbled into a Christians in Action Playtime Adventure.

Contrary to popular belief and my occasional roguish jibes, the CIA is not entirely clueless when it comes to tracking terrorists and their use of drug smuggling to fund operations. In this case, they were ahead of me, just not far enough to avoid tripping me up.

Concerned that Allah's Rule was making inroads into Europe, the Christians in Action had tried for months to get information about its hierarchy and drug smuggling operations. At some point they decided that the best way to flesh out the hierarchy was to insert someone inside it.

They'd placed an Arab inside the network, but the cell-like nature of the organization prevented them from finding anything out about the European side. So they set Garrett up as a possible mule, getting him arrested in Saudi Arabia, where they hoped he would come in contact with Allah's Rule operatives.

"How'd that work?" I asked him.

"It was working," he insisted, folding his arms.

"So it wasn't working at all. You're lucky you're not dead. What bright bulb at the agency thought of that? None of my friends, I hope."

It was purely a rhetorical question. Garrett turned red, and stomped back inside the hotel.

"You think we screwed up an operation?" asked Mongoose.

"No. We saved him from being killed," I told Mongoose. "He was pretty beat up the first day I found him, and he got worse. By the time he would have found anyone to make the connection for him, he'd have been cut up into little anchovy pieces. If you're not a Believer in that prison, you're not coming out alive. It was a stupid idea. Probably not his."

"He's probably not going to see it that way."

"I don't blame him."

Garrett had left for his room. Mongoose and I shared a few more drinks, a couple of stories about his misadventures between deployments as a SEAL, then turned in.

Four or five hours later, I was woken from the middle of a dream by the ring of my satellite phone. I reached for it groggily, and found myself talking to Karen Fairchild.

"Honey, are you awake?" she asked. "Admiral Jones just called."

"Damn." I figured he'd get around to calling at some point. Admiral Jones heads the CIA. We have what you might call a beneficial but bendable relationship: it benefits him, while I get bent, spindled, and generally masticated en route to a payday. "I hope you told him you didn't know where I was."

"I couldn't lie. Besides, he already knew where you were. He wants to talk to you."

"Tell him I'll meet him for lunch."

"He's on the other line. I can connect you."

"I wish you wouldn't."

The phone clicked, and the gravel-laden voice that sunk a thousand careers came on the line.

"What the hell are you doing out there, Dick? What the hell are you doing?"

"Sleeping. Isn't it past three there? Shouldn't you be on a golf course? Or have you taken up bowling?"

"One of my people is downstairs in the lobby of your hotel," barked the admiral. "I expect you to talk to him, pronto. Or I'll approve his request to send two men up to roust you."

"Aye, aye, Admiral."

"Don't 'aye, aye' me, Dick. I understand you screwed up something my people have been working on for over a year."

"I saved one of your junior officers' lives," I said, sitting up in bed. "You ought to be a little less reckless with them."

"I'm sure Clayton Magoo wasn't reckless. Get down there and talk to him, or all those contracts that are keeping Red Cell International one step away from bankruptcy are going to vaporize in the morning."

The name sounded vaguely familiar, though I couldn't quite place it, and was sorely tempted to go back to sleep. But being a conscientious sort of person, I decided to get up and see what this Magoo fellow wanted.

For the record: Red Cell International is not now, and has not ever been, one step from bankruptcy. Two or three, maybe.

Two large goons fresh from the Farm (the CIA's training facility) came out from the shadows as I pressed the elevator button in the hallway a few minutes later. They flashed agency IDs, but acted more like Mafiosi. Obviously they'd seen a few too many *Sopranos* reruns.

"Boss wants to see you," said Tweedledumb. He looked all of nineteen. He tried to neutralize his baby face by frowning as much as possible.

"Downstairs," added Tweedledumber. He actually did look mean, or at least ugly, but the effect was ruined by a squeaky voice that a rubber duck would envy.

Both kids were about six-three or six-four, and probably weighed around two hundred pounds.

Big, but not nearly big enough to intimidate Shotgun, who stepped out of the shadows behind them.

"Should I clock 'em, Dick?"

Dumb and Dumber would have jumped through the ceiling if Shotgun hadn't clamped his hands on their shoulders. No mobster has a grip quite as pulverizing as his.

"Leave them be," I told him. "They look kind of heavy, and I don't feel like carrying them downstairs. I've done enough lifting for one day."

Fresh off the elevator, I was met by a skinny man in a brown polyester suit, who squinted at me through a pair of the thickest glasses you have ever seen.

Magoo. The last name could easily have been a mocking nickname, though apparently it wasn't. Then again, except for the glasses, he didn't look much like the cartoon character[7] either—he stood about six feet tall, with a thick carpet of black hair cut almost razor tight to his scalp. The vague hint of a scar ran down from his hair to his right eyebrow, following the square corner of his head. He was probably in his mid-thirties, though he had the sort of face that seemed a good deal older.

"You're in a shitload of trouble, Dick," he said. He pushed his face forward when he talked to me, a little like a chicken poking at a fence in hopes an onlooker will give it some food.

Chickens, remember, are not exactly the smartest animals in the barnyard.

"I don't believe we've met," I told him.

He poked his head up and down. Career CIA men get a certain smell about them that you don't find on a scratch-off page in a magazine. It's called ARROGANCE. All capital letters.

"We'll discuss this upstairs," he said.

"The bar's still open?"

"In my room."

"Let's go up to the bar and have a nightcap instead. It'll put me in a better mood."

---

[7] My editor suggests some of you may never have heard of Mr. Magoo, the nearsighted cartoon character who first appeared in 1949, and has been a perennial kids' favorite ever since. I think he overestimates my audience.

"I heard you were a drinker," he said smugly, waving his hand to signal agreement.

Well, at least he had done some homework.

Magoo and his two henchmen secured us a table toward the far end of what was now an empty room. Dumber pulled out a device that checked for bugs. Shotgun went over to the bar, hovering near the pretzel bowls and watching protectively from a distance as I got myself a beer.

"The admiral says hello," I told Magoo, sitting down across from him at the table.

He blinked from behind his glasses. "This doesn't concern him. I'm in charge of this operation."

"Which operation?"

"Don't get cute with me. I know Garrett told you everything."

"What Garrett told me was enough to get you fired for gross incompetence," I said.

"We all take risks."

"The only risk he was taking was on the size of the coffin they were measuring for," I said. "Putting a white guy in that jail was foolish."

"You seem to have made it out OK."

"Just barely." I sipped my beer. "I'm sorry if I interfered with your operation. Next time you might try giving his dad a heads up."

"The infamous SEAL network." Magoo made it sound like a disease. "A brother SEAL is in trouble, and you rush to his aid?"

"I didn't realize helping a friend was a bad thing."

"Well, you owe me one now. A big one."

"They only have eight-ounce glasses here," I said. "You might want to wait until tomorrow when we can find a real bar."

Needless to say, Magoo wasn't talking about a drink. He wanted me to help him continue his "investigation"—his word—into the network smuggling the drugs. And I was to start by telling him everything I knew.

I suppose I could have laughed and gone back to bed. But there was still the matter of the bank, and I needed to find out what the connection or non-connection with the terror group was. Magoo didn't realize it, but he was offering to help me figure it out.

"I don't know all that much," I said. "Just what Garrett told me. What do you know?"

"There's a European connection, that I know."

"Are they just bringing drugs in, or are they trying to blow things up?"

He shook his head. We danced around a little bit more, neither one of us revealing what we were really thinking, aside from the obvious contempt.

Then finally Magoo got to the reason he'd come by.

"You owe me a favor," he said. "And I intend to collect."

He took off his glasses to wipe them. They'd fogged up with perspiration—obviously he was thinking hard. I ordered a refill and asked him to explain what he had in mind.

Note for the file: never make important business decisions after midnight in Abu Dhabi.

Two days later, rested, restocked, and rejuvenated, I came face-to-face with an old friend.

A Heckler & Koch MP5, to be exact. The submachine gun has been my weapon of choice for many years. It's light, deadly, and most important of all, dependable. If a dog is a man's best friend, a decent submachine gun is not far behind.

Unfortunately, this one wasn't mine. And it happened to be pointed at my nose.

"You are an enemy of the state," said the man holding the gun.

"Probably," I admitted.

"You are an infidel and a demon."

"Absolutely."

"You are worth more to me dead than alive."

"There I'd have to disagree."

"In Somalia, even here in Mogadishu, white men are worth their weight in gold," countered the man with the gun. He wore a gray suit, which somehow seemed loose-fitting despite his considerable girth and broad shoulders. The perfectly pressed cuffs of his pants edged over the tops of his gleaming blue vinyl Nike athletic shoes. A small line of sweat glistened at the edge of his mahogany-colored scalp, a dotted line where his hair had once been.

Hopefully, the sweat was a result of the heat, not nervousness. Nervousness in Somalia is very bad for your health, especially if you're on the wrong end of a gun barrel.

I held my arms out a little farther. The Somalis are world-renowned for their friendliness. In ancient times, it's said they often held feasts for visitors, generally about a half hour after they were killed. These days, they party a little less, but the same welcoming spirit prevails.

"No one will pay my ransom. You'll have to pay the cost of my burial."

"Well, that wouldn't do." The man lowered the submachine gun and grinned. "How are you, Mr. Dick?"

"Good, Taban," I managed before he extended his arms and pulled me into a bear hug that could have squeezed life out of a tree.

"So long since we have seen you."

Taban released me and stepped back. Then he glanced to his left, where a thin young man of about twenty was standing, holding an AK47. The young man seemed confused, or maybe disappointed that he wasn't going to get a chance to use the rifle.

"Let me introduce my nephew Abdi," continued Taban. "Abdi—put the gun down. This is my friend, Mr. Dick. We have done much business together. The Good American. Mr. Dick—the Rogue Warrior. Very famous in America. He has come to eat in our restaurant, no?"

Taban turned back to me.

"Sure," I told him. I had already eaten, but turning down an offer of hospitality in Mogadishu is more dangerous than stepping into a room filled with king cobras.

Abdi eyed me suspiciously. I couldn't blame him, really—paranoia is a survival skill in Mogadishu.

"Come, and have something to eat," said Taban, pulling me into the restaurant. "I have something very special for you—Mogadishu meatloaf. This is an old family recipe. Very good."

"Your family had meatloaf?"

"No, no, not my family. A family in Minnesota. I found it on the Internet."

I'd met Taban ali Mohammad nearly a decade before, when I did some "consulting" work for a shipping line, during the days when piracy was still a growth industry. My clients got their item back without having to make a payoff, which meant quite a big payday for me. Taban got a commission. We've had several opportunities to work together since then, though Somalia being Somalia, we haven't seen each other all that much.

Taban had worked for several of the revolving-door governments, and had ties to two different clans along the coast. More important was his connection to a Somali entrepreneur whose unpronounceable local name translates as something like Fat Tony. Fat Tony started in the pirate business as a grunt, then climbed the ladder to commander and CEO. As competition increased, he did what many businessmen do: he sold out his shares and retired from day-to-day operations.

Not that he was really retired. He still invested in different pirate groups, bankrolling expeditions and seeing to a number of other concerns, including smuggling and gun running. Rumor had it that he owned several khat "farms," a potentially lucrative arrangement given the popularity of the narcotic, which was not only the drug of choice for ministers of mayhem on the high seas, but more popular than coffee in much of northern Africa.

I knew of Fat Tony only by reputation, and needed Taban's introduction to make the connection. The connection was necessary, for I'd come to Somalia to buy things unavailable in Europe.

Magoo's plan had been extremely crude—he wanted me to make a connection in Somalia, where the drugs shipped en route to Europe, and he'd take it from there. I refined the plan once I realized Fat Tony was one of the connections used by the terrorist/smugglers.

I should say that, as far as I could tell, Fat Tony wasn't a member of either Allah's Rule or al Qaeda; he was Muslim in name only, if that. That was certainly not unusual—the terrorist hierarchy contained only true believers, and no true believer would have a direct connection to drugs. The network made use of many Fat Tonys in its day-to-day affairs.

I hadn't told Magoo about the connection between Allah's Rule and the bank. I'm sure there were things he didn't tell me as well.

As for Magoo himself, he wasn't too well-known among my network of CIA contacts. "A fast-mover," one friend I'd known since my SEAL days told me. "Shooting up the ranks like a rocket."

I'm not sure he meant it as a compliment.

"How long have you been in Mogadishu?" asked Taban, making small talk as dinner cooked.

"I just got here. They didn't want to give me a tourist visa."

"This is not surprising. Maybe they gave you a head exam first, no?"

"They probably thought about it."

Actually, I had obtained a tourist visa before flying into Mogadishu, but I knew from experience that it would be useless for anything other than getting on the plane, which flew from Dubai to Kenya, stopping here mainly for fuel. Once we landed, I joined the short queue of Turks waiting for a tourist visa in the terminal, which looked like a cross between a bus garage and a 1960s strip mall. The line moved at a snail's pace under the wary eye of soldiers from the African Union, who were there to provide the security that the government couldn't. They looked at me and rolled their eyes, sure that my tanned but still white face would never be seen again.

The Turks were "contract workers" for the government—aka, mercenaries who would man "peacekeeping posts" and shoot the daylights out of anything smaller than a tank that crossed into the government-controlled area of the city without permission. For them, tourist visas were a convenient fiction. For me, it was an inconvenient one, as the customs official at first refused to believe my story that I was expected, and tried to send me back to the plane.

Fortunately, the aircraft was already taxiing down the runway, and I eventually got my visa, for twice the normal bribe. That was a bargain, though—I paid five times what the Turks did for the room at my hotel.

All told, I spent about what you'd spend at McDonald's for a super-sized lunch. Isn't the Third World wonderful?

"Mr. Dick, here you are," said Taban, gesturing as Abdi came out of the kitchen with a covered plate. "Special meatloaf."

It looked about as appetizing as my shoe, and proved nearly as tough. Slices of mystery meat were aligned on the plate beneath a thin sauce.

I picked up my fork and carefully tried a bite. "Goat?" I asked.

"Dog," he said triumphantly. "With a touch of oxen and just a hair of rat."

"Rat hair, or hair of rat?"

"Both."

Calling it roadkill stew may be giving it a culinary upgrade; it seemed to have been baked au naturel by the sun. Compared to some of the things I've eaten in Africa, it wasn't half bad.

Taban talked about Somalia while I ate. He was as optimistic as ever— killings in the city were down to a manageable level, and the government zone had actually expanded in the past few weeks. Business at his restaurant had improved: he could count on half a dozen customers each week.

"Soon, soon, as big as New York City," he proclaimed.

His nephew frowned from the corner. The expression seemed permanent.

Taban's optimism faded when I told him why I had come.

"A very risky trip for you, Mr. Dick," he warned. "Fat Tony is very far from here, and if we drive, there will be many risks."

"You'll be well paid."

"I am not worried about me. For me, there is no risk. For you . . ." He shook his head.

"What's life without risk?" I asked. "Speaking of which, how 'bout a second helping of that roadkill stew?"

(IV)

Taban and his nephew Abdi met me at my hotel the next morning. Dressed in a light tan suit over a black T-shirt with a pair of Ray-Bans and a NY Yankees baseball cap, he looked vaguely like an American actor on holiday.

I, on the other hand, looked as African as I could manage with my white skin. I wore an oversized green khaki military uniform "borrowed" from some African Union soldiers for a few dollars, and a very loose head scarf that concealed much of my face. Even Taban was impressed.

"You look Russian, Mr. Dick," he said approvingly. "Very good. You are ready?"

"Very ready."

"Abdi, take our friend's bag."

"I have them," I said, picking up my battered overnight bag. Aside from a change of clothes and a few electronic items I might need, the bag was empty. The narrow ruck on my back had some more tactical gear, but it too was very light.

Abdi frowned, and walked toward the door.

"Is he ever in a good mood?" I asked Taban.

"But he is very happy today," said Taban. He didn't seem to be joking. "He is a very good boy, Mr. Dick. To me, like a son."

Taban led me through the lobby, past the two bellhops who accessorized their uniforms with bandoliers and assault rifles. A pair of Land Rovers and six men with rifles were waiting at the curb. Taban walked to the rear of the first and retrieved an assault rifle—the MP5 was too valuable to take on the road.

"Take, take," he said, sounding as if he were talking about hors d'oeuvres.

I took an AK47 for myself. (Paratrooper's model with the folding stock.) It was one of the lighter weapons in the back of the truck. Besides a pair of RPGs and a British mortar, there were two Belgian light machine guns and a Russian PKP "Pecheneg," a light machine gun used by the Spetsnaz special op troops. There were also two boxes of grenades, and dozens and dozens of spare magazines for the AKs. I helped myself to plenty of the latter, then took a seat in the front of the first Rover. Taban was driving; two of his men, Rooster and Goat, were in the backseat. Abdi was driving the others in the second vehicle.

Mogadishu sprawls like a cockleshell from a small downtown area near the port. The federal government controls only about a quarter[8] of the city proper, its pie-shaped wedge bordering the water in the south quadrant.

There aren't any skyscrapers, but if you happen to visit—something I don't recommend—you'll be surprised by the number of modern buildings. Somalia was an Italian colony and protectorate until 1960, and by African colonial standards at least, was relatively civilized.

At first, the difference between the government zone and the area to the north dominated by al-Shabaab was subtle. Teenagers with AKs patrolled the streets in front of rundown buildings—barely a difference there. Then I started noticing graffiti and walls with more holes than bricks. Then came the open pit fires and crowds of women standing and staring, as if they'd just received electroshock therapy and were waiting for the buzz to subside.

We were headed inland, but our destination was a village named Eyl, some five hundred miles north on the coastline. Eyl has gained some notoriety of late as the supposed capital of the pirate force terrorizing the waters off northeastern Africa. It's located near the bottom of Puntland, the spear-shaped northern region that includes much of the area used as a base by various pirates. Everyone—except the UN and Foggy Bottom[9]—pretty much considers Puntland a country separate from the rest of Somalia. It has its own lawless government, meaning that it's basically ruled by its own set of tribal leaders, warlords, and ne'er-do-wells.

The different categories are significant to actual Somalis. If you're an outsider, the chaos is pretty much seamless.

The region itself is your basic desert scrubland, with marginal ability to support agriculture. Drive up the highway from Mogadishu and you'll see vast rolling hills of gray rocks and tan grit pockmarked with clumps of stunted greenery.

We drove northwest out of the city, then angled up on a long, straight road that stayed some eighteen or twenty miles from the coast. Taban claimed this was for security, and there was some truth in that—the road along the sea is (slightly) more dangerous. But there was also less chance of running into a government (local, mostly) checkpoint. Given that Taban didn't like to pay tolls, the route had probably been chosen because it was cheaper as well.

Dust furled from the Land Rovers in a pair of vertical tornados as we drove. Once outside the city, Taban became talkative again. A few months before my visit, SEAL Team Six had made a rather dramatic rescue of two

---

[8] This was changing during my time there, with the government slowly taking over territory.

[9] Also known as the State Department.

American hostages in Gadaado—a village in Puntland not all that far from where we were going. Since then, said Taban, his services as a negotiator had been in more demand. He was a rare thing for Somalia, an honest person.

"Soon, this will all end," he told me solemnly and with more than a little sadness. "The insurance companies are taking a harder line. The pirates and kidnappers will learn that they will be punished rather than cheered, they will begin to find other work. There will be no more big paydays for them—or for me."

"Then what will you do?"

"I will have my restaurant," he said brightly. "Tourists will come, and I will be a very rich man."

Mogadishu, tourist destination? I'm sure it would rank right up there with Orlando and New York. But I didn't have it in my heart to step on his dream.

We got to Eyl about midafternoon, and drove through the dusty main road at a steady but slow clip—too fast and you were obviously scared, too slow and you were too good a target. Steel-roofed houses were scattered along the scrub almost like a child's toys left out overnight. Just beyond them were much larger houses with high walls around them to keep the animals in and the riffraff out. The center of town looked like a downtrodden mishmash of one-story buildings dating from the mid-twentieth century. There were maybe two dozen lean-to storefronts, open to the street, and a handful of simple but new brick-block buildings that dwarfed everything around them. Most of these, Taban explained, were restaurants, built for the hostages who were kept here.

"There must be quite a lot for them to have restaurants," I said.

"Two hundred here. But in all this city, there is still only one good place to eat."

Pairs of men in light brown khakis sporting AKs stood in front of several of the buildings, but otherwise the main drag looked like any other sleepy town in Africa. In many respects, Puntland was safer than Mogadishu—*if* you belonged here.

If not, you were soon either joining the guests at the restaurants, or a permanent addition to one of the farm fields that checkerboarded the nearby hills.

We stopped in front of a newer two-story building on a street just off the main drag. Taban put the car in park, but left the motor running as we got out.

Rooster and Goat clung to me as Taban led the way into the building; Abdi and the others spread out along the street. I was surprised to see that the front door was made of plate glass, but wasn't sure exactly how to interpret that—was it an eccentricity, or a sign that the place was becoming more stable? Then again, for all I knew, the glass had been boosted from one of the ships they'd hijacked recently.

The door opened on a hallway with a set of stairs on the right. The scent of fresh paint hung in the air, though the pale blue walls were covered with enough smudge marks and gouges to give Martha Stewart a heart attack. We went up the stairs to the strains of a British rock 'n' roll song from the early 1960s—"Ferry Cross the Mersey," by Gerry and the Pacemakers. How I recognized it is as much of a mystery as why it was playing here.

The music was coming from the large room on the right at the top of the steps. I looked inside; four very large African women were dancing in what looked like a class, doing a kind of free-form interpretation of the 1960s Twist. The walls were bare, except for a rail that ran along the sides.

"This way," said Taban, pointing to a door on the left side of the landing.

He knocked, and without waiting for an answer went inside. Rooster and Goat practically pushed me to follow.

A middle-aged man sat at a desk to the left of the door. He had an iPad in his hand and was playing Angry Birds when we walked in.

He practically jumped from his seat, jabbering and grabbing Taban in a bear hug. Taban reciprocated, and the two men carried on like a pair of old ladies comparing notes at a grandniece's wedding. I couldn't understand a word they were saying, since it was all in Somali. Finally, Taban shook his hand and led me back to the door.

"What was that about?" I asked as we began trudging down the steps.

"We have to go to the port," he explained. "We will meet the people you want there."

The "port" consisted of a beach with a dozen small skiffs scattered around the dunes, and another three or four in the rocks. Twenty years before, the people who lived here were all fishermen. They took small, hand-carved boats out into the ocean, where they heaved out nets that would have looked familiar to the Roman soldiers who first passed through in the years before Christ was born. There were still fishermen here, but now they were in the minority—piracy was the lifeblood of the village, and the families who mined the sea were considered old-fashioned.

A herd of six or seven camels scattered up across the dunes as we turned down the narrow road from the main city, which was roughly two miles away. The shanties that had dominated only two years before had been replaced by larger buildings. These weren't about to appear in *Architectural Digest* anytime soon; the stucco and block construction had as much charm as your average bomb shelter. Still, here it passed for great wealth, and was a pretty visible symbol of how piracy had turned the economy around.

So were the brand-new Jeep Cherokees parked in front of the squat, purple building on a rise overlooking the polluted creek.

"Whatever you do, praise the food," Taban whispered as he pulled the truck up the street to park. "Just don't eat any of it."

The stench that struck me as soon as I was through the door told me the food was almost surely anything but good. My stomach kicked at my chest as we walked past a tall screen decorated with a Chinese-print fabric of an African safari. The dining room beyond the screen reminded me of a high school cafeteria. Long tables covered by vinyl tablecloths flanked a center aisle that led back to a set of double doors to the kitchen.

Two men in checkered pants and cooking smocks stood over a counter, arguing vigorously over some fine point of food preparation. The one on the left had an eight-inch chef's knife, which he flicked against a chopping board to accent his points. The other had a cleaver, which he flailed around in the air, either chasing some unseen fly or demonstrating how he would install several new scars to the other man's scalp.

Taban continued past them to a set of steel steps in the right corner of the kitchen. I followed. The door at the top was open, and we walked into a room filled with personal computer stations. Only about half were occupied; I counted a dozen men hunched over the keyboards, pecking furiously.

"Fat Tony has been branching out," whispered Taban as we walked toward the back of the room. "They are now doing e-mail solicitation."

"My old friend, Taban," said Fat Tony, rising from an upholstered chair in front of a TV set. "And my very good friend, Mr. Dick. We have met in the flesh for the first time."

He clasped my hands as if I were a long-lost relative—one who'd recently won a very big lottery.

"Very pleased to meet you," I told him as he released me. I resisted the temptation to count my fingers.

"It is the pleasure mine, to meet a man of your caliber." Fat Tony's accent if not his grammar shaded toward Britain, where he had gone to school. "Have you seen my restaurant?"

"Yes."

"For our clients," he confided in a stage whisper. "They are not used to the local food. Taban gave me the idea."

Taban beamed proudly.

"Unfortunately, we didn't have sufficient notice of your visit," continued Fat Tony. "Or we would have prepared a great feast. We will still have a dinner, though—our best food on short notice."

"Please, don't go to any trouble," I said.

"Trouble? For a famous American? There is no trouble!"

"We have some business to discuss," said Taban.

"First, some refreshment," insisted Fat Tony. He started for the door.

"What's with all the computers?" I asked.

"Data processing. New area of business growth."

You know those scam e-mails that fill your in-box with news of a lottery you've never heard of? And the notes about a downtrodden widow who needs an American connection to liberate ten million dollars? They don't just come from Nigeria anymore.

Fat Tony took us downstairs to the restaurant and sat us in the middle of the room. A pair of skinny young men appeared within a few moments carrying pitchers of water and a few cans of soft drinks. I passed on the water—always wise in Africa—but took one of the soft drinks to be sociable. It tasted like a cross between coconut juice and very weak ginger ale; nothing that couldn't be improved by a little gin.

"So, Mr. Dick," said Fat Tony finally. "How can I help you?"

"I represent a group of investors who will have a ship sailing in the area very soon," I told him. "And they want to insure safe passage."

His eyes widened, and he asked for details. I gave him a cagey response, enough to make it clear that I was buying safe passage for a shipment of drugs without actually saying that.

"The ship will have a Russian flag and will sail past in about two weeks," I told him. "Payment will be made when it reaches its destination. In a foreign currency, and we will arrange for a delivery."

Foreign currency meant not in American dollars or euros, something that was a deal breaker in Puntland. Fat Tony insisted on American dollars, and a bank transfer. I hemmed a bit for show, then finally told him I would have to speak to my employers to see what I could do.

"I believe that it can be arranged," I conceded. We shook hands. This time I looked to make sure I had them all when he released my grip.

Fat Tony called over one of the skinny young men, and whispered something to him. The young man disappeared into the kitchen, reemerging in a few moments with a dusty bottle of Dewar's Scotch to cement the deal. The bottle had apparently come from a previous business arrangement.

I'm not a Scotch man, but having a toast was necessary to seal the deal. And so I dutifully accepted a glass.

"As a Muslim, I cannot share your drink," Fat Tony said with some sadness—right before the young man poured two fingers' worth of Scotch into his glass. He finished his before I even tasted mine.

We engaged in some light conversation. I noted that my clients had interests in many parts of the world, and were especially enthusiastic about shipping items from places like Afghanistan and Iran and Pakistan to places in Europe.

"What sort of shipments?" asked Taban. Beads of sweat began to sprout on his forehead; he obviously knew me well enough to realize the arrangement had just been an excuse to meet Fat Tony.

"Any sort of shipments," I said, looking at Fat Tony. "Anything that might be sold for a profit elsewhere."

Fat Tony smiled. Maybe the Scotch agreed with him.

"Sometimes there are the sort of shipments that you are speaking about," he said. "They are not easy to arrange."

"No," I agreed. "But that only adds to their value."

The rest of the conversation was pleasantly disjointed, with Fat Tony discoursing on local politics and the trials and tribulations of a businessman trying to make an honestly dishonest living. The international community had recently begun yet another initiative to bring legitimate government to Somalia, something that of course he opposed, though taken at face value his words gave every indication of the opposite. The Western media, he claimed, slandered many legitimate tribal leaders and businessmen by calling them warlords.

"Slander, slander, slander," he said, banging the table with his glass for more emphasis—and not so subtly indicating that the young waiter should refill his glass. "Nothing but slander."

"Join the club," I told him.

Having accomplished my mission, I wanted to get the hell out of Eyl as quickly as possible. So did Taban. But I couldn't afford to be impolite, which could jeopardize both my ultimate mission and my life, so I remained at the table, nodding and studying the Scotch, until finally Fat Tony's one-sided conversation ebbed.

"Thank you very much for your hospitality," I told him, rising. "Taban will be authorized to make the final arrangements. He can contact me, if there is a need."

"A very pleasure to do with you," said Fat Tony.

"I do not like your new employers," Taban told me when we were on the road. "Russians and mobsters. You must consider who you associate with."

It was interesting to hear a lecture on morality and ethics from a man who made his living by dealing with pirates and other criminals, but I let that pass. Taban was so sincere I could almost hear an angel whispering over his shoulder.

Actually, it was the whip of the wind as rifle shot blew through the windshield.

"We're under fire!" I yelled to Taban.

He didn't answer. He did have an excuse: it's hard to talk with a bullet hole where your mouth was. So much for the old adage, bite the bullet.

[V]

Taban's foot had been pressed firmly against the accelerator when he was shot. It remained there as his head flew back against the seat, propelling us at an increasing speed. I lurched over to the wheel, trying to keep us straight, but it was too late; we veered off the road, careening through the shallow ditch flanking it.

I yanked us back onto the road, only to have Newton's Third Law of Motion—*For every action there is an opposite but equal reaction*—meet Murphy's—*Anything that can go wrong will go wrong, at the worst possible moment.* The Land Rover careened across the pavement, swung over the apron and then back into the center of the road, only to hit a pothole that pitched it onto its side. We tumbled sideways and then skidded across the macadam on the driver's side of the Rover, flying off the shoulder and onto the flat desert. Sparks, bullets, and dirt flew everywhere.

Then we slipped down into the ditch at the right side, which happened to be deeper and sharper-angled here than anywhere else along the way. The SUV flipped over. Not once, not twice, but three times, coming to rest on the side where I'd been sitting.

Bullets began popping against the chassis. By the time I managed to break out the window with the butt-end of my gun, the two bodyguards, Rooster and Goat, had jumped out. They were hunched at the side of the SUV, firing at a row of bushes about two hundred yards away.

Whoever was in the bushes had a machine gun, a few assault rifles, and at least one high-powered rifle.

Our second vehicle was nowhere to be seen.

"Hold your fire," I told Rooster and Goat, motioning with my hands. "Conserve ammo. We're going to be here awhile."

My warning came too late—both guns clicked empty, loud and clear.

The ground directly behind us was flat; there was no cover for at least a hundred yards, so retreating that way was not going to work. More promising was a rock outcropping about thirty yards to our left. If we could get there we might be able to sweep around and flank our enemy from the rear.

Getting to the rocks without getting killed wasn't going to be easy. They were thirty yards away: a good seven or eight seconds for the swiftest of us, and that wasn't me. If the guy with the sniper rifle was even halfway decent, he'd have at least five shots. The machine gun would have plenty more.

Run, dive, tumble—maybe it would work. After all, Somalis were notorious for being bad shots. Maybe they'd already spent all their luck killing Taban.

Staying here was out of the question. The Rover was taking a pounding. Sooner or later something inside was going to blow up.

But if that was the case, why not make it sooner?

"We need some more ammo," I yelled, more or less talking to myself, since neither Rooster nor Goat spoke English. I waited until the gunfire from the bushes died down, then dropped my gun, grabbed the edge of the roof, and did a pull-up onto the side. I fell face-first through the window as a fresh wave of bullets flew into the bottom of the truck. I smacked my neck on the console as I fell, but it was a small price to pay in exchange for not having the rest of my body perforated.

I grabbed for just about anything I could—ammo boxes, magazines, grenade launcher, guns—and began tossing them out the window. I may not have been particularly accurate, but I was certainly fast, and if there was an Olympic event for weapons tossing I would have taken the gold. I hunted around for one of the boxes with the hand grenades, but could only find three loose ones. I shoved them in my pockets. With the truck now rocking to the beat of gunfire, I decided I'd pressed my luck as far as I could and did my best snake dive from the Land Rover onto the ground.[10]

Rooster and Goat had grabbed more mags for their AKs, but the rest of the gear lay on the ground. I picked up the rocket grenade launcher and got it ready to fire. Then I took out one of the hand grenades and held it up, a bit like a priest displaying the chalice at Midnight Mass.

"We'll run as soon as I yell 'go,'" I told the others, pantomiming what we would do. I threw in a few generic curses; obscenity is universal.

Goat nodded. Rooster looked perplexed.

"I'll count three," I added, gesturing with my fingers. "I'm going to drop it into the gas tank—"

Before I could get any farther, two of the men firing at us dashed out from behind the bushes and darted toward the road, trying to flank us from the side. Goat saw them, and immediately emptied his AK in their direction without hitting either. He threw the rifle down, grabbed another from nearby, and once again fired until he ran out of bullets—maybe a third of a minute or less on full auto.

---

[10] The copy editor is asking for a definition of a "snake dive." It's what you do when bullets are flying and you try to make your body as narrow and lithe as possible so you somehow slink between them. You'll find the full definition in *Webster's* between "Get the Hell out of There!" and "Kiss Your Ass Good-bye."

Every one of his bullets missed, but the men scurried back for cover.

I grabbed a grenade, pulled the pin, and leaned up to drop it into the gas tank of the Land Rover.

Or would have, had Murphy not flipped the SUV onto the side where the gas cap was.

Shit.

I spun around, not quite sure what I was going to do instead. As I turned, Rooster tried getting behind me to the other side of the truck and a better firing position. He hit my hand as he passed.

The grenade flew upward. Then down to the ground.

The pin was in my hand, the grenade was at my feet, and I was about as far up the proverbial creek without a paddle as you could go, ready to kiss my ass good-bye.

(VI)

I'm not exactly sure what I did, but I'm pretty sure it wasn't praying. Either I scooped, kicked, or levitated the grenade away, because the next thing I knew it was exploding some seventy or eighty yards from us.

The explosion threw dirt and dust everywhere. It wasn't exactly a shield, but it was better than nothing.

"Run!" I yelled to the others, taking a second grenade and lobbing it just over the truck, in the area of the gas tank. "Run!"

I scooped up the grenade launcher and an AK and took off, not bothering to see if they were following. I took three, maybe four steps, when something pushed me down hard.

The explosion had lit the gas tank, which responded with a very strong secondary *ka-boom*. Laden with ammo, the Land Rover caught fire spectacularly, shooting a cascade of flames skyward in a pyro display that would rival any you've seen at WrestleMania. Thick, pungent black smoke curled across the landscape, a veritable band of airy ink that blocked out the sun and hid everything behind it from view.

I struggled to my knees, coughing from the smoke. I felt myself lifted upward: Rooster and Goat were dragging me away.

We collapsed behind the rocks, exhausted. I could have slept for a good week straight, but there was no chance to rest.

The ground behind us dipped down gently, which would make it possible for one of us to crawl from behind the rocks to a point where he couldn't be seen. From there, he could move around the flank to the rear of the bushes, and make an attack.

I decided I'd do the flanking because it was the hardest part to explain. I mapped out the operation for them, trying to show that they had to provide cover fire and then be patient. When Goat gave a halfhearted nod, I decided that was as good as I was likely to get.

"Do it!" I shouted, pantomiming their firing. I grabbed the AK and grenade launcher, then dove on my belly. As soon as they started firing, I began crawling away from the rocks. Within seconds I realized it would take too long. I pushed up and sprinted like a track star coming out of the blocks.

Too bad I couldn't run like a track star. Bullets whizzed around me; after maybe a half-dozen strides I threw myself back to the ground.

Fortunately, I was now far enough down the gentle slope that I was no longer a target. I went a little farther, then made a sharp right and began inching toward their position.

I guessed that whoever had ambushed us would have a guard posted, and that I would see him first. What I didn't expect to see, though, were camels—a baker's dozen were milling placidly, chewing their cuds as I approached from the north.

At first, I ass-u-me-d that they were a wild herd; I was too far from the bad guys to connect the camels with them. But then a flash of light just beyond caught the corner of my eye.

I was a lot closer to our antagonists than I'd thought. Fourteen males of various ages from twelve to twenty-five were crouched in a ditch no more than five yards beyond the camels. I froze dead in my tracks—metaphorically speaking, though I realized I was damn close to making that figure of speech a reality.

All but one of the men turned and saw me near the herd as I took a step back. They may have been as surprised as I was, but there were a lot more of them than there were of me.

Instinctively, I pulled up the grenade launcher and fired. The RPG sailed right at the clump of men—and kept going, its rocket motor not even igniting until it was beyond them.

By that point, I'd dropped the launcher and raised my AK, sweeping right and spraying the ditch with 7.62 mm rounds. I swung left, dropped the mag, and threw in the next.

Two rounds spit out as my finger pressed on the trigger. Then the AK47, the remarkably simple, dope-proof gun that never ever jams, jammed.

Murphy is a son of a bitch, and forever at my side.

PART TWO
SIX, DRUGS & ROCK 'N' ROLL

In any problem where an opposing force exists, and cannot be regulated, one must foresee and provide for alternative courses. Adaptability is the law which governs survival in war as in life—war being but a concentrate form of the human struggle against environment.

—Captain Sir Basil Liddell Hart,
Strategy, 1954

1

I kept pressing my finger against the trigger, not quite believing the gun wouldn't fire. My brain screamed a succession of curses, but the rest of my body was incredibly calm. My central nervous system hadn't yet communicated just how completely screwed I was.

There were a half-dozen Somalis left alive in the ditch about twenty yards from me. They looked at me with something approaching awe.

As in *"Aw shit, we are so going to nail this son of a bitch and cut his skin into little triangles of flesh to serve to our enemies."*

I did the only thing I could do in that situation: I held the gun up as if it were a bayonet and leapt forward, screaming my best rendition of an Apache war cry.

The man at the center of the line threw down his weapon and bolted away. The others raised their weapons to fire.

Just then, something exploded right behind them. Bodies and dirt flew in every direction.

I fell, or was pushed down by the shock wave of the explosion. As heavy machine-gun fire raked the Somali line, I did my best impression of an earthworm.

The gunfire continued for what seemed like another half hour. Each time I thought it was going to let up the gunners seemed to double down. When the roar finally stopped for good, I raised my head and peeked through the still settling dust.

A pair of beat-up Nike sneakers walked toward me. Abdi had returned.

All of the Somalis who'd ambushed us were dead, their bodies close to pulverized. What the grenade hadn't blown to bits the machine gun bullets had perforated. The scene looked like the floor of Kino Der Toten in *Call of Duty Black Ops* after you've sprung a trap on the zombies. Bits and pieces of flesh were littered everywhere. The air smelled of blood, cordite, and burnt metal. Vultures were heading from as far away as Morocco to get in on the feast.

"My uncle," said Abdi as he helped me to my feet. "Where is he?"

I shook my head. His face clouded.

For a moment I thought he was going to try and shoot me. But he didn't. He lowered his gaze to the ground slowly, his machine gun drooping with it.

"Take me to him," he said softly.

We went back to the Rover, leaving two of the men who'd been with him to clean up the bodies as best they could.

Taban's body had been burnt badly in the fire, but had miraculously stayed intact. It was still belted into the seat. It wasn't a particularly pleasant sight, but Abdi took it stoically. Goat and Rooster joined us, then helped me fold a sheet around the body.

Tears fell from Abdi's eyes as we hoisted his dead uncle's remains to the roof of the other Land Rover. But that was his only expression of emotion.

"I hate this place," he said, pulling open the driver's side door. "I'll drive."

II

Four people in a Land Rover is comfortable. Try and squeeze in three more, though, and you understand why sardines never smile in a can.

Rooster wedged himself into the cargo compartment behind the seat. Goat tried fitting in the front, then gave up and climbed onto the roof, next to the body.

We rode like that for about an hour, until we stopped to put more gas into the truck from our jerry cans. At that point I traded spots with Goat. Riding there was much better than sitting between the two beefy bodyguards, neither of whom seemed at all familiar with the concept of soap.

We stopped again about two hours later. We'd lost most of the food in the other Rover; Abdi parceled out a box of dried fruit, taking none for himself. I didn't take a share either, but it was more because of what the stuff reminded me of than altruism.

Except for Abdi, none of the others spoke English, but the man who had driven Abdi's Rover on the way up knew enough Italian to engage in a halting conversation. According to him, the men who had ambushed us were probably just bandits, who saw the vehicles and figured they'd take their chances attacking. The Rovers alone would have been worth losing a few lives over.

"You don't think it was Fat Tony?" I asked.

The driver had a little trouble understanding. Maybe my Italian was rusty.

"Fat Tony—the man we met in the village?"

"Ah—no, no, no. Fat Tony is our host. He cannot shoot. The Prophet, blessed be his name, would be very unpleased."

Unpleased—the Italian word he used was *scontento*, which means "contented" until you throw the "s" in front of it. Unpleasing the Prophet isn't much of a disincentive in my experience, but then what do I know.

The road got better as we drove southward. Abdi, who hadn't been going slow to begin with, pressed harder and harder on the gas. Between the wind and jostling from the potholes, I could barely stay on the roof. Finally I lay down next to poor roasted Taban, hooking my arms through the rope we'd used to keep him in place. It wasn't my worst traveling experience—remember, I've been hauled through the air by a C-130—but it was up there.

Five miles outside of Mogadishu we came to a checkpoint. The sun had set by then, but fires in a trio of barrels in the road tipped us off as we approached. When we were still a mile away, something was tossed into one of the barrels that made the flames flare, illuminating the area. Sandbags had been piled on both sides of the road, with a pair of two-wheel wagons poised between them as a makeshift gate. The wagons didn't quite block the entire road, but it would be impossible to get past without ramming at least one of them, and besides the damage that would do, there were men with guns on both sides of the narrow highway. A particularly large gun pointed out from the emplacement on the left side. It was a Russian DShK machine gun. Better known to users and abusers alike as a Dushka—"sweetie" in Russian—it was the sort of weapon that wrote love letters in lead.

The roadblock had been set up by the militia of one of the local warlords. The soft ground on both sides of the road made it impractical to go around, and, besides, the men manning it would undoubtedly have followed. Abdi, probably tired and anxious to get home, decided it was easier to simply deal with it than chance backing up and finding another way.

I kept my head down but pulled up the rifle as the truck stopped.

"You're dead," hissed Abdi.

Stage direction? Or a threat?

I hoped the former. I held my breath—and my rifle beneath me—watching two men come up along the side of the road.

Abdi yelled something in Somali. The men answered. Abdi yelled back. None of the words sounded like they fit in a love song.

One of the men came over to the driver's side and pulled at Taban's body. Abdi jumped out and began yelling at them.

The man backed off. Abdi continued to yell, no doubt complimenting them on what excellent taste their wonderful mothers had had in lovers. In the middle of the tirade, he took a few bills from his pocket and threw them on the ground, then stomped back to the Rover and got in.

That, I thought, was the end of the transaction. But the bills he'd tossed failed to inspire the men back at the gate. The Dushka swiveled in our direction.

I'm not much on poetry, so I didn't wait to hear what it had to say. I raised my rifle and fired, dousing the machine gun's crew. Abdi, meanwhile, hit the gas.

Our left fender clipped the wagon on the left, spinning it aside. We hit the other full-on. Its wheels collapsed and sparks flew as we pushed it forward, metal screeching against the pavement. One of the guys in the back fired from the driver's side. I emptied the rest of my magazine, then hung on, not daring to let go of the rope long enough to trade out the box.

We drove a good three or four hundred feet with the trailer screeching and sparking beneath the front bumper. Abdi tried swerving left then right to get it free, but the damn thing was stubborn. Finally his maneuvers took us off the road. We bounced down a shallow embankment. The wagon broke apart, and pieces of metal flew up into the front of the truck. One shattered the windshield. Another grazed my shoulder, though so lightly I barely felt it.

Abdi jammed on the brakes. The Rover skidded into loose sand, and quickly wedged itself there as Abdi spun the wheels unsuccessfully, trying to get us out.

The others piled out of the Rover to investigate. I dropped down. My knees were a little wobbly from all the shakin' and bakin' we'd been doing.

Goat and one of the other bodyguards went to the front and started pushing the SUV. I joined them, but it wasn't until everyone got out and pushed that we were able to get back on the road. We were lucky the men at the checkpoint didn't decide to investigate; if they even bothered to fire in our direction, I never heard the bullets.

"Why did you shoot?" demanded Abdi as I started to climb back on the roof.

"To save your ass. The machine gunner was about to tattoo it."

He scowled at me. "Get inside," he said. "Having a white man on the roof isn't a good way to travel through Mogadishu."

Ordinarily I would have had them drop me off a few blocks from my actual hotel, but given the hour and how tired I was, I wasn't sure I'd be able to make it there on foot without becoming someone's meal ticket. And besides, they wouldn't have to go to too much trouble to figure out where I was. There weren't too many Americans in the city, nor were there many places to look.

I grabbed a second AK and stuffed my pants with mags before hopping out.

"Thanks," I told Abdi.

He didn't answer. Clearly he blamed me for his uncle's death, and just as clearly there was nothing I was going to do about it.

Upstairs, in my room, I checked in with Trace. It doesn't pay to let her worry too much about my general health—when in doubt, she's likely to show up at the door with a pot of chicken soup and half an army.

She picked up on the first ring, and greeted me with warm affection.

"About time, asshole," she said. "What sort of trouble are you in now?"

"I'm not in any trouble, aside from the fact that I'm in Mogadishu and talking to you," I told her.

I explained what had happened. With Taban dead, I was unlikely to make any connection with the drug dealers. The only question was when to leave. Though Mogadishu was such a beautiful place, parting would be sweet sorrow.

"You should get the hell out of Dodge right away," she told me. "While you can still do it without a medevac."

"I'll decide when I'm leaving in the morning," I told her. "I have to stay for Taban's funeral, at the very least. It should be tomorrow."

"Make sure it's not a double ceremony," snapped Trace before hanging up.

Both Magoo and Shunt had left several messages asking me to call. Magoo could wait until morning—if then. But there's nothing like technobabble to put me to sleep, so I fluffed up the pillows and gave Shunt a call.

"Would it surprise you to find out that black-market Viagra is being sold through the same network that's moving heroin into Germany?" Shunt asked when he picked up the phone.

It did, actually.

"Explain," I told him.

Over the past forty-eight hours, our resident geek had infiltrated half a dozen police forces, banks, and in one case a news organization, pulling together different bits of information to profile the drug dealers connected with Allah's Rule. Interestingly, he was no longer convinced that the bombing of the bank in Germany was their handiwork; the plastic explosives had come from a European source, different than what the terrorists, and other al Qaeda groups, typically used. But he had a much better picture of what was going on with the drug operation, and believed it included prescription drugs.

"It makes a lot of sense," said Shunt. "It's a growth industry—not only in Europe but here in the States."

He talked about it the way a stockbroker talked about the offering of a new stock. The drugs were originating somewhere in Asia—he hadn't tracked that down yet, though I'm sure Pakistan was on his suspect list. Fake Viagra, hydrocodone, a few other painkillers—potentially, the pharmaceuticals could bring more money than heroin and hashish. Even better from an Islamic nut job's point of view; because they were intended as medicine, there was no Koranic proscription on moving them.

"Connection to the bank?" I asked.

"Haven't found it yet."

"You get into the network?"

"Working on it."

"What about Veep?"

"Nothing. I'm going to have to come up with a way to track what he does online without him knowing he's being tracked. He's too sophisticated to be nailed with a simple keylogger."

"Why do you think that?"

"Well, he *is* the head of security."

In my experience, among the people most vulnerable to the simplest attacks are the so-called experts. They're so busy telling others what to do that they forget to do it themselves. Or maybe they just think that they're above it all because of their position.

At this point, of course, there was a definite possibility that Veep was entirely innocent. Maybe even a probability. But I didn't want to admit it, not yet anyway.

Shunt rattled on about his various plans, which had the desired effect: my eyes were soon gluing themselves shut.

"Update me tomorrow," I told him. "Right now I'm hitting the hay."

I drifted off to sleep.

My sat phone was ringing when I woke a few hours later. I groped for it groggily.

"What the F do you want?" I growled after punching the talk button. It doesn't pay to be too friendly when you're answering the phone—it only encourages people to bother you.

"Dick, this is Danny. Where are you?"

"In bed. Alone," I added.

"Sorry to hear that."

"Me, too."

"I just thought you'd want to know—French police and Interpol just made a big drug bust."

"Uh-huh."

"They raided a ship that had just come into Marseilles. Looks like it might have been the guys who were getting goods from Allah's Rule. I just got off the phone with Shunt—he's checking it out."

On the one hand, the bust would help—Allah's Rule would need new buyers, and I'd already made a connection. But if Fat Tony had set up the ambush the night before, the only thing I'd be in line to buy was a whole lot of lead.

I called Magoo. The call was routed to one of his underlings, who was about as helpful as the people on a computer help desk. I told him to have Magoo call me, then took a shower.

By then it was light. I went down to the desk and asked the man there to get me a ride, thinking I would go over and see Abdi and find out about the funeral. I'd retained a car and driver who'd worked for us before; he had no phone, and the only way to get him was to have the hotel clerk send a boy to fetch him.

While I was waiting, I took a peek out on the street. There were about a dozen people up, businessmen mostly, though I noticed two teenage boys sizing me up. The assault rifles slung over my shoulder convinced them I wasn't an easy mark, and they quickly found something else to look at.

"Hey, Mr. Dick!"

The shout, in English, came from up the street. It was Rooster.

"Abdi sent me," he said. "Funeral this morning."

"You speak English?"

"I have a little."

"Why didn't you say anything yesterday?" I asked.

He gave me an African smile. "Taban ali Mohammad tell workers always mind business. Keep mouth shut. Good business in Somalia. Always keep tongue quiet."

"Good business anywhere."

"Taban ali Mohammad great man," declared Rooster. "Funeral? You come?"

"Absolutely."

Rooster gave me a quizzical look.

"Yes, I come," I told him, spotting my car. "Here comes our ride."

The wake was being held in Taban's restaurant. All of the tables had been pushed to one side, except for the three placed at the center of the room that held his corpse. Taban's remains had been wrapped in a white *kafan*, three sheets that together formed a simple shroud.

The sheets made him appear much smaller than he had in life. Unlike in the West, the bodies are rarely if ever displayed at Muslim funerals; given what had happened to the corpse, that was a blessing.

There is a certain democracy in death. Whether we've been rich or poor, famous or infamous, achievers or couch potatoes, we all go into the afterlife as naïve souls without a clue of what we're going to do next.

There were several dozen mourners, all packed into the small front room. Six of Taban's female relatives sat, bent over, in a row of chairs in front of the body. His wife stood in front of them, facing Taban, her hand on the shrouded leg of the corpse. She stared at his head, silent, looking as if she were communicating with him somehow.

"I didn't think you would come," muttered Abdi, coming over through the crowd. He was dressed exactly as he had been when I last saw him: dusty Nikes, stained black pants. The shoes were a size too large; belatedly I realized that they must have been a pair Taban had worn before passing them down.

"I had a lot of respect for your uncle."

"Hmmmph."

An imam arrived, and within a few minutes everyone began praying in Arabic. I stood quietly, watching the mourners. Taban had supported most of the people in the room, either directly or indirectly, with jobs, handouts, and houses. Now that he was gone, more than one would find it tough going. Even in the government-controlled zone, there were few real jobs, and none could pay anything near what Taban offered.

I slipped outside as the prayers continued. A large crowd of people had come to pay their respects. They too were praying, eyes fixed in Taban's direction.

I was surprised to find Abdi on the sidewalk, standing alone, holding a homemade cigarette.

"A friend of Fat Tony's wants to meet you," he said. Abdi dropped the cigarette, and shuffled back a few feet to get some distance from the others. His fingers were trembling. He tightened them into a fist.

"You are involved with some very nasty people," he said. "Fat Tony is not someone to trust."

"Did he kill your uncle?"

He frowned. I wasn't sure whether he was having trouble finding the right words in English to use, or having trouble deciding what to say in general.

"They were thieves, trying to rob us and kidnap you," said Abdi. "You are the reason my uncle died."

I might have defended myself—Taban certainly knew the risks, and probably had been in such situations before. But I didn't say anything. Abdi changed the subject.

"My uncle was a very important person here," he told me. "Many people depended on him."

I nodded. He raised the cigarette to his lips and took a long pull. Tobacco is one of the things devout Muslims aren't supposed to indulge in.

"The arrangement you had with him," he said. "I will continue it."

"I don't know that that's possible."

His eyes flashed, and I saw some of the anger he'd displayed when we had first met. That was encouraging, actually.

"You don't trust me?" he said.

"It's not a matter of trust. You saw what happened to your uncle. I don't know that we can trust Fat Tony."

"He didn't kill my uncle. That I am sure of."

"Why did you keep driving past when his car was hit?" I asked.

"He always said to do that. He would have known I was coming back. He would have taken cover and waited. I loved my uncle," Abdi added. "I respected him. He was everything. For me and others. For them inside."

I didn't doubt that was true. What I wondered was whether Abdi was a coward.

But even granting the best possible interpretation of his actions—that he had driven on by design, then come back fully expecting to save his uncle—I doubted he would do the same for me.

"Your uncle was a great man," I told him. Then I turned toward the street, looking for my car and driver.

"Where are you going?" asked Abdi.

"Kenya, probably."

"You aren't going to meet with Fat Tony's man?"

"I don't trust him," I said. "And I'm not so sure about you, either."

He looked like I had slapped him. "You should come with us to the grave-yard," he muttered.

"I really have to get going."

He grabbed my arm as I turned away. I tensed, swung around, and barely stopped myself from clocking him.

"I want to help you the way my uncle would have," he told me. "I need the money."

"I don't think you can help me."

"Try me. What do you lose?"

My life, for one.

I told my driver to meet me at the cemetery, then joined the procession to the grave. The cemetery was several blocks away on a hillside overlooking the ocean. Squat hovels flanked it north and south. The gravestones were simple but lined up meticulously; if they had been more uniform in size and shape the effect would have rivaled the fields for fallen Allied soldiers in northern Europe. I found it difficult to look at them, not just because of Taban, but because of all the comrades I've had to bury over the years. Death is a constant companion in my business, and while I have been far, far luckier than most, still I've seen a legion of friends lowered into the ground. The fragility of life humbles you, lingering long after the adrenaline of battle dissipates. Each time I consider the fact that I may be next, I promise myself I'll live to at least one hundred, just so I can piss off many more no-load people.[11] Everyone needs to focus on a meaningful goal in life.

After some prayers, Abdi stepped over to the grave to speak. Rooster and Goat had come over to stand next to me, heads bowed. I didn't understand a word Abdi was saying—it was all in Somali—but it sounded appropriately somber.

Then the words changed suddenly to English.

"Mr. Dick knew our uncle well," said Abdi, looking in my direction. "He is a great man who will pay tribute to our uncle."

Everyone stared at me. Apparently Abdi had already said this in Somali and was now translating into English so I would understand.

Put on the spot, I cleared my throat and took a half step forward.

"Taban ali Mohammad was a great man," I said.

Abdi translated, which gave me a moment to think of what to say next. I didn't think it was appropriate to mention that he did business with pirates and kidnappers, though very possibly the people here would have viewed that a lot differently than most of us would.

---

[11] "No-load people"—The heavily redacted version of the *RW Dictionary* defines them as people loaded with "no's." The unredacted and not-safe-for-work version uses more colorful language.

"He provided for his very large family," I said, "and was a friend to many people."

There were a few murmurs from the crowd as Abdi translated.

"Taban had many ambitions, but what he loved most was his restaurant," I continued. "He had a very generous spirit. I think his restaurant was the best in Mogadishu."

One of the women started to wail. Within seconds, three-quarters of the crowd were crying aloud as well.[12]

Talk about having an effect on your audience.

I said something about him having gone to a better place, then stepped back. Abdi's voice cracked as he repeated it.

"Good speech, Mr. Dick," said Rooster. "Very good. Taban ali Mohammad was a great man."

Abdi picked up a fistful of dirt and dropped it over the body after it was lowered. He did this three times, then everyone else followed. I joined the procession, sandwiched between Rooster and Goat.

When everyone had dropped in their fistfuls of dirt, some of the family took up shovels and finished covering the grave. They stomped down the mound, then had one last prayer before the funeral was over.

Walking past the thin iron gates that marked the boundary of the cemetery, I realized my driver and his car were nowhere to be found. Rooster, trailing behind me, came up and asked where I was going.

"Back to the hotel," I told him. "If I can find my car."

"We can ride you," said Rooster. "To hotel, yes?"

"Yeah."

Rooster led the way to a small Toyota parked down the hill, two blocks away. The car looked about twenty years old. Once white, the paint had faded to a dusty gray, pockmarked with reddish brown splotches of rust. The quarter panels were fringed gray with epoxy filler, apparently in a forlorn effort to keep the corrosion from creeping completely up the sides.

Goat and one of the other men had followed us. I got in the front seat on the passenger side, tucking the rifle muzzle down between my legs. The seat was close to the dash; I tried adjusting it, but the rails were either rusted or jammed and it wouldn't budge.

A large wedge of wire had been stuffed into the ignition; this served as the key.

---

[12] Technically, wailing aloud is not considered proper at an Islamic funeral, but either the local custom permitted it or no one was worrying too much about proper form. As Taban's was the only funeral in Mogadishu I've ever attended, I'm not sure which of those is correct.

"Tricky," said Rooster. He pumped the gas, then played with the wire. It took him four or five tries before the engine turned over, then several more before it coughed to life.

"Coughed" being the technical term for stuttering and backfiring. Mourners had flooded the street, and Rooster made his way gingerly around them, riding the brakes. The street had once been paved with bricks, but there was only scattered evidence; mostly it was a collection of ruts and potholes. At the intersection we turned right, driving into a district of tightly but irregularly placed houses, none larger than a good-sized garden shed back home. The road was dirt, and an orangish haze rose from the wheels and crept in through the windows as we picked up speed. Rooster drove through a maze of shanties, heading us southward and down the hill until we came to a road flanked by high walls. This was a high-rent district, or what passed for it here, a kind of suburbia on the south end of the city.

I knew the hotel was to our right somewhere, but with the crazy patch roads I had no idea how to get there. Finally we came to an intersection. I saw a highway in the distance. Rooster turned toward it.

"I want my hotel, not the airport," I told him.

"I make the wrong turn, Mr. Dick," confessed Rooster.

"Just get us there," I growled.

"We are not going to hotel," said Goat behind me. He shoved a pistol into the side of my neck.

Rooster said something in Somali to Goat. I don't think it was "be gentle with Dick"—he jammed the snub-nose barrel forward and hard into my chin.

"Keep your hand away from rifle," said Rooster. "Better not to make a mess in the car."

[IV]

There is something about the feel of a snub-nosed revolver against your anatomy that gets your pulse racing. And when that happens, there's no sense lollygagging around.

"I think we're going a little slow for the highway," I said in a calm voice, extending my left foot under the dash to mash Rooster's on the gas pedal. The Toyota lurched, hesitated, bucked, then burst forward. Goat flew backward—but not before I managed to slap the gun out of his hand.

Unfortunately, the snub nose of the gun and bucking of the car threw my aim off, and I couldn't grab the pistol as it bounced into the back, beyond my reach.

Rooster had taken his left hand off the wheel to try and punch me. Rather than hitting back, I opted to help him steer—I jerked the wheel to the right, then hard to the left. He flew back against the seat, flailing at me. Unable to get his right foot off the accelerator, he tried stabbing the brake with his left. An elbow to his throat took his hands off the wheel. Before I could grab it, the car twisted around in a 360. Rooster's foot flew off the brake. The Toyota engine had finally found its sweet spot, revving steadily now as we spun. I grabbed the wheel and managed to get us moving straight— straight at a stone wall.

We rammed into the wall at about forty miles an hour. The airbags exploded, burning my face and pushing Rooster back in his seat.

Goat jackknifed over the back into the window, sliding between and over the two airbags. They may have slowed his momentum, since he didn't hit quite hard enough to do more than spiderweb the glass.

I grabbed at the door, got it open, then realized I still had my seat belt on. I unbuckled it and tumbled out of the car, pulling my AK with me.

Rooster looked at me over the prone body of his comrade. He had a dazed look on his face.

"Always wear your seat belt, Rooster," I told him.

Then I shot the son of a bitch through the head, and put a few holes into Goat's ribs. I've always admired a car with a bright red interior.

I fished the revolver from the back. It was a Colt, worn from decades of hard living but still serviceable. I was just pushing the cylinder back in place when a horn sounded. I looked up and saw a Land Rover rushing toward me.

I tucked the revolver in my pocket and lifted the AK. The Rover stopped and Abdi jumped from the passenger side, waving his arms. He was unarmed.

"Come! Come!" he yelled. "We must get away from here."

"Your two henchmen just tried to kidnap me."

"They don't work for me. They—" He looked at the Toyota. "You killed them? You have to get away from here quickly."

"They were working for you yesterday."

"No," he insisted. "They were just in the crew my uncle hired. They are not our people—my uncle didn't know them."

By now, people had come out of the nearby buildings. It was definitely time to leave, and not on foot. But it would be an understatement to say that I didn't trust Abdi.

"Up against the car," I told him.

"What?"

"Against the Rover, asshole." I helped him assume the position.

"Mr. Dick—"

He was unarmed—foolish in Mogadishu.

"You don't trust me," said Abdi.

"Damn straight."

Taban's MP5 was in a special holster in the front of the Land Rover. Still holding my gun on Abdi, I reached in and grabbed it. Then I told him to get in and drive.

"We go to the airport now," I said. "Straight to the airport."

I trotted around to the other side. He could have hit the gas and left me there—he wouldn't have gotten very far, but he could have tried. Still, I wasn't about to be lulled into trusting anyone in Somalia. From what I saw, I was just a target here—very possibly Magoo had set me up, knowing what would happen. The bust of the European side of the drug ring must've been planned for some time, and very likely Magoo was in on it. He'd "enlisted" me just to get rid of me.

Maybe that was too harsh, but it was what I was thinking. Time for a strategic retreat to rethink the situation.

"I want to make money," said Abdi as he wended his way toward the airport.

"We all want to make money, Abdi," I told him. "But that doesn't give us the right to kidnap people."

"I am not a pirate," he said. "I want to open a restaurant, like my uncle."

"That's fine."

"I want to open it in Brooklyn."

"Brooklyn is in New York."

"I have visited it. I went to school for two years in Pennsylvania. I want to get out of Mogadishu. America is a free country—that is where I want to go."

"Uh-huh."

"I will help you with Fat Tony. You will pay me, then with money I will leave. I know you are doing bad things," he added. "I will not judge."

"What bad things am I doing?"

"My uncle said—" Abdi suddenly lost his tongue.

"Go ahead."

"He said you helped people arrange ransoms. But when we went north, I knew something else was happening. You were talking about buying things. You would be open for this. Then, when Fat Tony sent his man, it was about purchases. Purchases are not ransom. So—it is smuggling."

"What if it is?"

Abdi shook his head. "It is none of my business."

"That's right."

"I will still help. For the money."

"If you're so hot on money, what's stopping you from holding me for ransom?"

Abdi's head pivoted. He seemed shocked; he might have been faking.

"That would be an offense against my uncle," he said, turning his eyes back to the road. Then he chuckled softly. "Don't want to end up like Rooster and Goat."

"Damn straight."

We had the airport in sight when my sat phone rang. It was Shunt.

Perfect timing. I needed him to hack his way into an airline ticketing computer and secure a seat out of this hellhole.

"You wouldn't believe what Veep's password is," he said as I clicked the phone on. Some people don't believe in long good-byes. Shunt doesn't believe in long hellos. Or any hellos. "Password1. P-a-s-s-w-o-r-d-1! The easiest password to guess. It was so simple I didn't even try it."

"I need you to arrange a plane ticket."

"He has an account in Djibouti. There are transfers between it and a bank in Pakistan. I tracked an e-mail down—he's using phony names, off-shore accounts—there's a lot there. There's definitely a connection between those accounts and Allah's Rule. One of the accounts that received money from al Qaeda also had two transactions with an account that got money from Veep. It's going to take me time to flesh this all out, but there's definitely a connection between Veep and the terrorists."

"Is he laundering money?"

"I can't tell yet. It's going to take me a few days to track through all the accounts and break the encryptions. But this is bigger than embezzlement."

Or simply hosting terror accounts, I thought.

"Another thing—he spent a lot of time on Google News this morning, running searches on drug busts," added Shunt. "Think there's a connection there?"

"Good work."

"So what's this about a plane ticket?"

"Never mind," I told him. "I'm sticking around for a while longer."

"Really? What's Somalia like these days?"

"Beautiful place. Everyone should spend their vacation here."

[V]

Roughly thirty-six hours later, I stood in the prow of a speedboat, zipping in toward the "port" of Eyl. Trace was at the wheel. Shotgun and Mongoose were sitting at the stern, Mongoose frowning at the smudge of light brown growing in front of us, and Shotgun munching on some sort of African snack he had brought with him from Kenya. Abdi was with us, unarmed, and looking more than a little seasick. The sun had set four hours before; there was only the barest sliver of a moon. Fat Tony was expecting us—the next afternoon.

I like being early for certain appointments.

To catch you up while we're in-bound for the beach:
- Magoo had called back. He claimed he'd had no advance warning of the raid on the European side of the drug deal. I didn't believe him.
- Magoo: "But that should help your op." You can figure out my response yourself.
- Veep had changed his passwords, and upped security on the bank system. Clearly, something we'd done had tipped him off. Shunt didn't think he could track the penetration back to us, but there was no way of knowing for certain.
- We were currently shut out of both Veep's computers and the bank accounts. Shunt was working on a solution that didn't require us to go on-premises.
- Before that had happened, Shunt had been able to get a nice read of *all* the bank's accounts, which was how he had found the connections he'd told me about. He'd also found something else interesting: the accounts that had started the entire investigation and gotten me involved did not exist on the backup set, which was now the bank's sole record of accounts.
- As suspected, the Allah's Rule network now needed new buyers. Fat Tony had thought of me. I sent his messenger back to Eyl with the promise of a meeting, then spent the following day and a half getting asses and assets in place.

Trace cut the engines. Snugging my waterproof ruck, I hopped out with the boys into knee-deep water. Trace would stay with the boat, its engines running—I wanted to be able to get the hell out if things didn't go quite the way we planned.

The water was cold. Abdi handed off his waterproof ruck, then hopped out, his teeth chattering.

"If I don't hear from you in an hour, I toast the town," said Trace, by way of saying good luck.

She was speaking literally—we had a mortar and several napalm and tungsten charges ready to go.

Shotgun and Mongoose were armed with FN Minimis with large plastic boxes of bullets under their bellies. I had my MP5 and the AK I'd gotten from Taban; when I hit the beach I took my PK from my ruck and holstered it on my leg. I secured the snub-nosed Colt I had retrieved from Goat to my other leg, and made sure my knives—*plural*—were in easy reach. I was carrying enough spare ammo to open a gun shop in Arizona.

I would have brought a cannon with me if I could.

I took point, with Abdi more or less at my side and Shotgun and Mongoose spread out behind me. The village was quiet, except for the hum of diesel-powered generators supplying electricity to the better-off houses and larger buildings at the center. A few lights flickered here and there, but the place was mostly dark.

The street in front of Fat Tony's building was deserted. I went to the door and tried it—it wasn't locked.

Honor among thieves? Or an open invitation to walk into a trap?

I slipped inside the door and attached a small video camera and a sending unit to the jamb. The camera itself was about the size of the one in your cell phone. The sending unit, which transmitted the video back to a receiving unit on the boat, was bigger, about the size of two decks of cards. Red Cell International has a variety of bugs, video and audio, purchased from various vendors. This one came from a Nevada company where I serve on the board of trustees.

I checked the volume on the team radio, then hailed Trace.

(On the radios: Think AN/PRC-148 Joint Tactical Radio System, then go about two sizes smaller. Most of the internal logic is supposedly the same, only it's been made on a smaller chipset. We don't have quite the range of options the military units made by Thales do—no provision for "future wide-band waveforms" as the brochure for the military unit brags—but the range is at least as good, and according to Shunt, the encryption beats the NSA standards the military uses.)

"Trace, you seeing this?" I asked.

"Yeah, it's a regular rerun of *Father Knows Best*."

"The Pad working OK?"

"IPad, Dick."

"Whatever."

"Yeah, it's working. It better, for the money."

Always keeping up with the times, our technical section—Shunt and Junior—had recently procured some "upgraded" iPads to use in place of the laptops we'd used to receive video and do other tasks. There were a variety of special "apps" on them, small programs that could automatically monitor video feeds and do a couple of other things. Personally, I think Junior wanted them just so he could watch Netflix when he was out on a mission.

"How is it out on the boat?" I asked Trace.

"Quiet here. Tell Shotgun he got crumbs all over the deck."

"I'll make him lick them up when he gets back."

"I'll lick anything you want," said Shotgun, listening in on the shared team circuit.

"The only thing your lips are going to taste are my shoe heels," snapped Trace.

It warms my heart to hear the kids show genuine affection for each other. Living proof that we are a *family*.

We set up video bugs on the other possible exits and the general area at the front of the building, then moved to the back where Fat Tony's living quarters were. We didn't have to be too quiet—the alley thumped to a mix of American heavy metal rock 'n' roll and lame African rap and hip-hop.

Mongoose's assessment, not mine. My knowledge of rap music is limited. Though Run DMC always gets my trigger finger bouncing.

A single outside door led directly to Fat Tony's apartment at the back of his building. He had a video camera positioned on the corner, which covered the approach; we suspected there would be a guard outside as well.

The video camera was not fancy. A floodlight was mounted above it, which limited its view to just under twenty feet from the corner; anything beyond that small circle of light would be in shadow.

Shotgun and I climbed atop the generator shed about six feet from the front of the building, and from there got to the roof. Most of the roofs in the village were covered with steel panels or rolled asphalt paper, the sort of cheap though waterproof covering you see on sheds and some houses in the States. This one, however, was covered with gravel that had been laid over pitch. Gravel and bits of tar stuck to my shoes and my hands as I pulled myself up over the side. Bob Vila would never have approved.

A satellite dish stood on a pedestal at the center of the roof, one set of cables running directly from the power generator, the other running downstairs with the signals. A large dish grabbed television signals—DirecTV without the subscription hassle. Next to it was a smaller dish, used for secure communications. We attached bugging collars to the cable—the collar looks like a fat hose that clamps over the wire—to pick up signals, then connected them to a sending unit. The devices are a little picky, even with the old-style cables Fat Tony used, and it took me a few minutes to get them set before the green LED on the box lit to tell me it was live. Meanwhile, Mongoose was getting restless down in the alley; music makes him antsy.

"You having trouble up there, boss?" he asked.

"We're just about ready," I said over the radio. "Be down in a second."

While I'd been fussing with the cables, Shotgun was posting another one of our video bugs to cover the back lot of the building. Then he took a rope from his backpack, tied off against the frame of the satellite base, and lowered himself down to have a peek.

"Bad news, Dick," said Shotgun, climbing back. "There's a grate on the outside of the window. I'm not going to be able to get in quickly if I need to."

I went down to take a look for myself. The steel grate was mounted over the window, held by a set of bolts. There were drapes inside, and the room was dark. I'd wanted Shotgun to be able to get in quickly if things went wrong, but to do that we'd have to remove the grate.

A minor inconvenience.

I dug into the pouch at my belt, took out a Crescent wrench, then went to work on the bolts. There were only four. The first three were easily loosened; the last one stuck, and all my elbow grease and curses failed to budge it.

Having come this far, I was loathe to give up. I went back into my pouch and took out the small battery-operated Dremel tool, attached a diamond bit, and went to work drilling out the bolt head. When I was done the head was no more than a stud.

"Dick, it looks like some people are coming down the street," warned Trace from the boat.

"Mongoose?"

"I heard. Abdi and I are ducking next to the generator."

I climbed back up to the roof and waited. Two men walked down the street and then the alley, passing within a foot or so of Mongoose and Abdi as they went to Fat Tony's apartment at the back. We couldn't hear what they said to the guard, but apparently they were expected.

"Were they armed?" I asked Trace.

"Didn't see any rifles."

"Mongoose?"

"Didn't get a good look. If they got a party going on, Dick, there's going to be a lot more people in there than we were counting on."

"Worried?"

"Fuck you."

That's the spirit.

I gave Shotgun the wrench so he could finish unscrewing the grate on his own, then went back to the other side of the roof. I climbed over the side and let myself drop down onto the shed. The fall couldn't have been more than eight feet; I've probably dropped that amount a thousand times over the past ten years without a problem. But this time both knees not only creaked but buckled, and I tumbled off the damn roof onto the ground in the middle of the alley.

It was embarrassing, but worse, my right knee hurt like a son of a bitch,[13] and my left knee was worse. I got up, a little shaky, and steadied myself against the pole supporting the shed roof as Mongoose looked on nervously.

"You OK?" he asked.

"Perfect."

I stowed my ruck and fanny pack behind the generator with Mongoose's, then checked my MP5 carefully, trying to give my knees a little time to recover.

"I'm ready," said Shotgun.

"You got your dick in your mouth or are you eating something?" snapped Mongoose.

"Twizzlers. Strawberry. What's the over-under on how many people are inside?"

"I say six," said Mongoose.

"Eight," said Shotgun, his mouth stuffed with licorice.

"A dozen," I said. "Three-quarters of them women."

I stiff-legged down the alley.

Shooting the guard would complicate business with Fat Tony, so I'd brought along a little gizmo called the Dazer Guardian. The Dazer, which is supposed to be available to military personnel within a year or so, is a modulating green laser that temporarily blinds whoever you shoot it at.

I'm sure you've read the stories about airline pilots being temporarily blinded by laser pointers "shot" from the ground. Developed by Laser Energetics, the Guardian is a laser pointer on steroids, with a much more effective light wave. The weapon is small; it looks and feels like a high-tech flashlight in your hand. As a nonlethal and silent device, it's perfect for situations where you want to get past someone without making a racket.

---

[13] Trace read the manuscript and asked, "Why is it always 'son'? Women deserve equal billing." I told her "bitch of a bitch" would just be piling on.

A blackjack at the back of the head works even better, and there's a lot to be said for a knife at the throat. But variety is the spice of life.

As we came around the corner, the guard spotted us and raised his gun, looking like he was going to shoot first and ask questions in the afterlife. I hit the trigger on the Guardian, and his whole world turned to dazzle. By the time he managed to get his hands in front of his face to block the light, Mongoose had sprung a kick to the side of his head. The guard crashed backward, bouncing off the door frame before rebounding into Mongoose's fist. We cuffed him with a zip tie and went inside, walking up a narrow set of steps.

Another guard met us at the top of the stairs, AK ready. I slapped the laser on again, blinding him. But my right knee gave out as I hustled up to take him down. I slipped and fell back against the wall of the stairway, dropping the light. The flashing green beam slipped from our antagonist's eyes, and the blind could now see.

I was a miracle worker, but definitely on the wrong side of Paradise.

[VI]

Something like a tornado or a freight train rushed by me. I thought it was Mongoose, running up to take a bullet for me. But it turned out to be Abdi, who bowled into the man, carrying him backward and landing in the chest of another guard who'd come in behind him. The three of them fell in a tumble. By the time Mongoose pulled them apart, both guards were out, knocked unconscious by either the fall or the shower of punches Abdi had thrown.

The landing opened into a foyer about ten feet square, dimly lit by a pair of flickering overhead lights. Fat Tony met us in the hall with a Beretta in his hand. By now the music had stopped, though my eardrums were still vibrating.

"Sorry for the commotion," I told him. "I forgot my invitation."

He squinted at me. A sweet, pungent odor drifted in from the interior rooms. I'm not a connoisseur, but the words "Moroccan hashish" crossed my mind.

"Mr. Dick," he said, looking at my submachine gun. "I expect you tomorrow."

"I was in the neighborhood, so I thought I would come early."

"You are . . . robbing me?"

"No."

He glanced at the two men on the floor behind me. I just smiled. Abdi began talking quickly in Somali, explaining that we had run into scheduling difficulties and decided to come north sooner than expected.

"I heard what happened to you when you left," said Fat Tony, sticking to English and addressing me, not Abdi. "I understand—you are nervous about me."

"I'm not nervous. I just don't trust you."

He frowned. "Taban ali Mohammad brought good business. His death pains me."

"Not nearly as much as it pained me."

Fat Tony brushed my comment away. "We are relaxing tonight. You come in and relax. In the morning we will have our meeting."

"If you want to talk business, we need to talk now. You have items for sale."

"It is not me," he said. "Persons I know. I personally have no interest."

"A commission, no?"

Fat Tony pretended not to understand. I glanced at Abdi, who translated.

"A small percent," admitted Fat Tony. "Well, then, let us speak inside."

Inside looked like the common room of a frat, assuming the frat was in the
position to host a dozen women in various stages of undress. Five of Fat
Tony's cronies slouched on a pair of couches that looked as if they had been
abandoned by the Italians some fifty years before, their gaudy colors now
worn and the stuffing showing in countless places. There were two large
hookahs on the floor, elaborate water pipes with multiple hoses and dishes
that could have held five pounds of tobacco. Everyone in the room had
glassy eyes.

The men barely noticed us. The women, on the other hand, were eager
to make the acquaintance of the exotic strangers.

"You can look, but don't touch," I told Mongoose.

"Don't worry. I ain't coming out of here with no disease."

Fat Tony ordered one of the women to make us some tea, then put his gun
down on a trunk that was being used as an end table. I decided to help him be
a good host—I picked up the gun, dropped the magazine to the floor, and
checked to make sure a round hadn't been chambered.

I did the same with my gun, putting the magazine in my pocket. Fat
Tony nodded, and pointed to the pipe.

"Not tonight," I told him. "Thanks, though. Tell me what arrangements
you wanted to make."

Friends had recently come into possession of a number of items that
could be sold in Europe at a very good price, he said. Would I be interested
in making an investment?

Perhaps. If the investment was a modest one.

We negotiated long enough for me to decide that Fat Tony really was a
principal in the network. This was somewhat important for Fat Tony's
health: if I had thought that he was part of the al Qaeda network, he would
have been uninsurable.

You may object that anyone who is working with the al Qaeda network
is, in essence, an ally of theirs, and any disease or other ill will that befalls
them is justly deserved. I seem to recall that is the "official" line of the suits at
Foggy Bottom (aka, the State Department) when addressing their peers
at highbrow cocktail parties.

Fat Tony would disagree—as far as he's concerned, his friends might
just as well be cardinals in the Catholic Church. His involvement was only
aimed at one thing, making money for himself.

The long and short of our discussion was that we arranged to have a meeting with representatives of the shippers the next morning. I set the time—six thirty, about twenty minutes after sunrise.

I said I would call to tell him where.

Six thirty was too early, he told me, and his friends would have to name the place; they were as wary of walking into an ambush as I was. Plus, he wasn't about to give me a phone number.

"I'll call this phone," I told him, retrieving one from my pocket. "Don't use it for anything else. Destroy it after I've called."

"You know it's not bugged?" he asked.

"Of course not. But the Americans have spies everywhere."

"Yes, this is true. You are working for Russians, yes?"

"I told you before, I can't say who my partners are. As far as anyone is concerned, I'm the person to deal with. I'll take care of the money. This—" I reached into my pocket and took out a stack of hundred-euro notes. "—is to show we're serious."

He eyed it suspiciously. "A down payment?"

"No. A tip for you. Or your partners."

Fat Tony took the bills and fanned them. They totaled ten thousand euros.

"Counterfeit?" he asked.

"I think they're real."

He smiled faintly. "I still do not think that my friends will be comfortable with you naming the place."

"That's my requirement. If they don't want to do business, fine," I told him. I glanced over at Mongoose, who looked like he was about ten seconds from forgetting his vow not to touch the women. "I'm leaving."

"Man, I never have any fun," groused Shotgun when we were all back on the boat. "All those women."

"I didn't touch them," said Mongoose.

"Yeah, but they touched you."

"Look at it this way, Shotgun," said Trace. "There was no food."

"I can't believe that. You'd think one of them would have gotten the munchies."

We floated offshore until roughly four A.M., then made our way to an inlet about thirty miles north of Fat Tony's village. An arm of rocks extended into a small bay, and the water was deep enough for us to pull the boat right up against them. Once more Trace stayed with the boat while we went ashore and scouted the area.

On the iPad's satellite map, the faint outline of a road was visible about two hundred yards from the shore. Between the gray predawn light and the hard-tack ground, we couldn't find it, and had to double-check our position against the GPS device to make sure we were in the right place. But the flat ground would give us a perfect view of our friend's approach, and with the nearest settlement a mile and a half away, it would be difficult to ambush us.

To make it even harder, we launched a small UAV for a bird's-eye view. The UAV was a new little toy, smaller and we hoped more dependable than the backpack UAVs we'd used on earlier operations. It was about the size of paperback book, and in many ways was similar to AeroVironment's Nano Hummingbird, developed for DARPA. The Hummingbird flies with flapping wings and looks very much like a small bird, especially in flight. Ours does, too. The skin is a rubbery plastic, and the body and wings are filled with hydrogen—the thing probably weighs less than a bird of the same size. But the real innovation is in its engine. Nearly silent, it's a small fuel cell that is supplemented by small solar panels on the upper wing that extend the flying time. Two video cameras on the underside provide real-time surveillance. The aircraft has a flight time of roughly two hours.

The little bird was made by a company—called Innovate Solutions and headed by one of my old sled dogs—that has been of great help to Red Cell International. Their best devices, like the UAV, involve nanotechnology straight out of sci-fi movies—but I digress.

Flying the aircraft isn't all that hard; there's a primitive autopilot that will fly in a circle or a figure eight, providing constant coverage of the area. Getting it into the air is the trick—the rear of the fuselage is a little heavy, and it takes a slippery wrist to get it up.

Mongoose got it on the first try. Draw your own conclusions.

Mongoose flew the plane through a quick routine of tests, then handed it over to the autopilot and adjusted the image on the video screen. Trace had her own video feed back in the boat.

"Looks good," she said, watching the screen.

I took out a cell phone and called Fat Tony.

"You have a half hour," I said. "The coordinates are coming in a text."

"But—"

I clicked off the phone, sent the text, and waited.

Twenty minutes later, a pair of camels appeared on the horizon to the south. Mongoose took over direct control of the aircraft, zipping it closer to the animals.

"Is that Fat Tony?" asked Trace.

I looked at the screen. Fat Tony was riding in the lead; a thin, short figure rode on the second camel. There were no bodyguards or other escorts.

Awful confident.

"That's him."

"I thought he wasn't one of the principals," said Trace.

"Maybe they nixed the meeting," said Mongoose.

"Or maybe the other guy is the deal maker. Can you get the aircraft around and get a good glimpse of the second rider's face? I want Trace to send it to Shunt and see if he's in a file somewhere."

"Working on it," grunted Mongoose.

Shotgun checked his machine gun, made sure his ammo was ready, and positioned a backup Twinkie.

I nudged Abdi and we started walking forward to meet them.

Fat Tony stopped when we were about ten feet away. The camel twisted its head slightly and parted its lips, as if to say, *Who the hell are you.*

"Looks like they have pistols under the camels' blankets," said Trace in my ear.

Fat Tony began talking in Somali. Abdi said only a few words in response.

"What's up?" I asked him.

"He says that if this is an ambush, my family will be wiped out. I told him it is not."

"This is Shire Jama," Fat Tony told me. "He is a representative of the people I told you about."

Shire Jama bent his head.

I went over and held up my hand. He didn't take it.

"Nice to meet you," I said.

You'd think that was fairly universal. He gave no sign that he understood.

Fat Tony began speaking. A quantity of drugs would be available for a shipment arriving in southern Europe within a few days. It was a modest amount, at least by international standards—fifty kilos of pure heroin and twenty kilos of black hashish.

A little explanation for those of you who are not connoisseurs of hashish. Hashish is classified by its color: black, as in this case, pretty much looks black; Moroccan is more a reddish brown, and Lebanese is lighter, usually green or red. (The names don't necessarily correlate with where they come from.) All are made from cannabis—aka, marijuana, mary jane, weed, smoke, etc.

I'll leave it to the experts to describe how the stuff is made by squeezing the hell out of the plants. Afghanistan—big surprise, right?—is a key source of the black variety of hashish, and since it's also the place of origin for a lot of heroin, it was reasonable to hypothesize that I was now being admitted to the terror pipeline the CIA was trying to plug. The skinny man was either a member of Allah's Rule, or, like Fat Tony, another cutout.

Then again, he could have been associated with another organization entirely. The information that linked Fat Tony with the Allah's Rule people could have been completely wrong—remember, some of it came from the CIA, and their track record is about as pure as yellow cake uranium.

But I did say "hypothesize" rather than "assume." I wasn't assuming anything, and Fat Tony wasn't giving out more information than he deemed absolutely necessary to close the deal. One hundred and twenty pounds (or so) of heroin is a good amount of high, but in the world of contemporary drug smuggling, it's not a major haul. The numbers Magoo had thrown around earlier for a single shipment were ten to twenty times that high.

I mentioned that I could handle more and would be very interested in doing so, but Fat Tony demurred.

"This is where we start," he said. "If you are not interested, then never mind."

"No, no. We are interested."

"We can add some other things, perhaps," he said, glancing at the other man. He mumbled something I couldn't hear; the man nodded. "Vicodin and Viagra, to start. Later something else."

"How many?"

"Two cases of each."

"They're good?"

"The best. I sell some myself."

"We will need an earnest payment in Djibouti by the end of the week."

"I'm not paying for anything until it arrives."

Fat Tony went back to speaking Somali with Abdi, this time because he was more comfortable with his native language when it came to numbers. A three-way conversation ensued on how much we would pay, when, and where. It was amicable—used car negotiations should be so smooth—and with minimal haggling he agreed to accept a down payment in Djibouti of only ten thousand dollars "earnest money," with additional money to be wired into two different accounts when the ship reached port and a final payment upon delivery.

I probably could have gotten a better price, but since I was dealing with Magoo's expense account, I didn't push all that hard. Making multiple payments was actually in our favor—it would give the agency more leads to follow as they tried tracing the money route.

And that was the deal. Fat Tony handed down a pair of clamshell mobile phones. A thick wad of masking tape encircled each; the number "1" was written on the tape of one, "2" on the other.

"The first cell phone will tell you where to go with the money in Djibouti," said Fat Tony. "Number One. It will only work there. You will need to be there very soon. Throw it away when you are done. Do not use it for another call. You will receive instructions on what to do with phone Number Two."

"Very good."

"We will do other business if this goes well," he said, pulling the reins of his camel. "Allah be with you."

〔 1 〕

If that all seems anticlimactic and blasé, you're right. In the space of five minutes, I'd just made a significant break in a case the CIA had been working on for a year—and didn't even know the full dimensions of. A quick walk through the desert, and I'd secured a million-dollar drug deal. All I had to do now was hand off the information to Magoo and let him take it from there.

Heh.

We recovered the UAV and headed back to the boat. By the time we got there, Shunt had managed to verify that Shire Jama's image and name matched that of a man identified by Interpol as a drug smuggler possibly associated with Allah's Rule and al Qaeda. I called Magoo, who was his usually cuddly self:

"I want those phones," he said, curtly. "Meet me in Djibouti."

Quick geography lesson for those of you who didn't have Sister Mary Elephant for your fifth-grade geography teacher:

Somalia is the weirdly bent seven on the eastern African coast directly below Saudi Arabia and Yemen. Djibouti is a set of false teeth that sits on the edge of the seven, to the east of Somalia, where the Gulf of Aden pinches into the Red Sea. Keep going north on the water and eventually you get to the Suez Canal.

And don't let Sister catch you drawing in your notebook rather than reading. The metal side of her ruler packs more wallop than brass knuckles. The sister has a bonfire of a track record when it comes to dealing with wayward scholars and other riffraff. She and my family go way back: she taught my father, George Leonard, and blessed my knuckles on countless occasions.

Our boat didn't carry enough fuel to make it to Djibouti, and Somalia being Somalia, finding a hospitable marina along the way was about as likely as finding a Buddhist in the Vatican. It was also a rental. I'd borrowed it from a company that did business with the African National Congress, and probably ran guns on the side; while I'm sure we could have kept it for a while, they were charging an outrageous day rate, and taking it to Djibouti would have dented Red Cell International's yearly dividend. So we motored back toward Mogadishu.

No sojourn in the waters off eastern Somalia is complete without a tête-à-tête with pirates, and so I wasn't surprised when Mongoose spotted a long fishing boat on a course toward our bow. It wasn't out for a leisurely sail, either—the prow was up, and there was a good wake behind it.

A prudent captain would have rung for full power and told the helm to steer us away. Then again, a prudent captain wouldn't have been in these waters to begin with.

"I see eight guys, all with AKs," said Mongoose, looking through his binoculars. "Looks like they're hungry."

"And we're the main course," said Shotgun, never one to miss a metaphor involving food. "Yum, yum."

"Well, let's give them something to chew on," I said. "Keep your weapons down until they're in range."

Trace eased off on our speed. As the boat grew closer, everyone was alone with their thoughts, contemplating the looming engagement.

I think I know my people well enough to summarize their thoughts:

MONGOOSE: Should I use the SAW or the grenade launcher for my first shot?

TRACE: I hope I get a little hand-to-hand action in. I haven't choked someone in weeks.

SHOTGUN: What is the proper pre-pirate snack, Yodels or licorice?

Abdi, sitting between Shotgun and Mongoose, looked anxious and a little seasick.

"You all right?" I asked.

"I could use a weapon, Mr. Dick."

"Just stay down," I told him. "We'll take care of it."

He frowned. I suppose you could argue that he had earned my trust in the hallways at Fat Tony's, but I wasn't convinced yet. And the last thing I was going to do was give him a gun so he could feel better. The United States tried that sort of thing in Iraq and Afghanistan; I think you're familiar with the results.

As they closed to two hundred yards, one of the pirates raised his rifle and fired a burst in our general direction. It could have been meant as a greeting to fellow sailors, the way different navies sometimes welcome visitors with a cannon salute. Or it could have been intended as a warning salvo.

We pretty much took it as an open invitation to fill the wooden vessel and its occupants with as much lead and high explosive as possible.

I kicked things off with a burst from my MP5, taking out the gunman.

A half second later, Mongoose fired the RPG into the boat, sending a spray of splinters and steam skyward. Shotgun emptied the magazine under his SAW on the forward section of the boat. He worked quickly, since his target was rapidly disintegrating. Mongoose fired another grenade—"overkill" is not a word in his vocabulary—and a second, larger cloud of steam appeared over the first one. I reloaded, but there was nothing left to shoot at but debris.

One or two men flailed in the water. We immediately commenced rescue operations . . .

Be serious. They were lucky we didn't run them over. Here's hoping they were strong swimmers. I'd simply *hate* to think they turned into shark shit on the bottom of the ocean.

Besides being an eating machine, Shotgun can strike up a conversation with just about anyone on the planet. Maybe because he's the size of a gorilla—you look at him and you know you *need* to keep him happy.

He started talking to Abdi about what sort of snack foods Somalia has. The concept of "snack food" is pretty much nonexistent in Somalia, though since he had been to America Abdi did understand the concept.

"Cheez Doodles!" yelled Shotgun. "Your restaurant should feature Cheez Doodles. You could build your whole menu around it."

"You eat so much," said Abdi. "How come you have no fat belly?"

"Intake matches expenditure."

Mongoose snorted.

"He's part of a deviant race," said Trace. "His parents were from Alpha Centauri."

"When I open my restaurant in Brooklyn, I will have these snacks," said Abdi. "Then you will come and be a customer."

Shotgun beamed. "I got plenty of ideas for a restaurant. You should have a snack-off, for one."

"What is that, a snack-off?"

"It's what Shotgun does in his room when the door is closed," snapped Mongoose.

"Don't pay any attention to him," said Shotgun. "He doesn't understand anything he can't blow up."

Shotgun filled Abdi with advice on what his restaurant should offer for the next thirty or forty minutes, until Mogadishu came into sight. By then, even Abdi had had his fill of Shotgun's "advice"—which, if followed, would have made his restaurant the only Somali restaurant in Brooklyn exclusively devoted to selling bagged junk food. We sailed in blissful silence the

rest of the way south. If there was a harbor patrol or coast guard craft anywhere, we missed it. The U.S. Navy had two ships off the coast near the
port, but we were so close to the shoreline they took no notice of us.

Finding a place to dock in Mogadishu was not a problem. Finding a
place to put your boat without having to worry about it getting stolen was
something else again. Even in the government-controlled area there were
few docks where you could safely tie up your vessel, and those were not only
crowded but expensive by Somali standards.

Fortunately, Somali standards are somewhat lower than those of the rest
of the world. Still, we had to pay one hundred bucks in cash to have the boat
watched, and that wasn't counting the ten dollars I slipped the two with the
machine guns patrolling the dock.

"Remember my face," I told them in English. "I'll be back for the boat in
an hour. If anything's touched, you'll be swimming with your ancestors."

I had Abdi repeat it in Somali.

"There's no chance they'll forget," he told me. "You've tipped them
more than they'll make in a month, even here."

My arrangement with Taban was the customary small percentage of the
overall deal, which I now owed a small down payment on. I was going to
throw in a per diem for Abdi, bringing his fee to several thousand dollars: a
fortune in Somalia, though hardly enough to get him to New York, let alone
open a restaurant there.

"I need you to open a bank account," I told Abdi as we walked from
the dock. "Once that's set up, I'll have your per diem wired in. Then when
the deal with Shire Jama is concluded, you'll get the rest."

Abdi was disappointed—he thought I was going to give him cash.
That would have made him a target for everyone in the city, as I tried to
explain.

"You set up the account with a business name, to lessen the possibility of
gossip," I told him. "You might even use your uncle's name. We wire it in, it
stays in the bank. No one can touch it."

I had to make the point several times. "You have a lot of people around
you who are very poor," I told him. "If they know you have a lot of cash,
they might try and steal it."

"My relatives would not steal from me. They didn't steal from my
uncle."

"You're not your uncle. They'll look at you as if you're a boy, and try and
take it."

Abdi was too dark-skinned to show much color in his face, but I could
tell the blood was rushing there and he was displeased.

"I'm not insulting you," I told him. "I'm just telling you the way it is. People are scumbags."

"No. You do not know the Somali people. I could walk the street anywhere with the money in my pocket. I would be safe."

"If Somalia is such a wonderful place, then why are you leaving?" I asked. I reached into my pocket.

"Here," I said, handing over a hundred-euro note. "Take it as an advance."

He stared at it as if it were the Hope Diamond. Meanwhile, I took a business card from my wallet. "Call this number when you've set up the account. We'll forward the rest of the per diem right away."

"I want to come with you," said Abdi.

"The hotel's not far. We'll be OK."

"No. To Djibouti. I can be very useful. There are many Somalis in the city—you will need a translator."

"They speak French there, *merci beaucoup*."

"Only government, not people. It would help to have a black man with you," added Abdi. "It means more places you can go."

"I'm not planning on going any place where that would be a problem," I told him. "I'm going for a meeting, and then very likely going home. Same with the rest of my team."

"But you said—plan for all contingencies."

"I was talking about wearing shoes on the boat."

"It is a general rule. I know this."

"Are you looking for extra pay?"

"Pay me if you use me. Nothing if you don't. You said yourself, be prepared. It is the SEAL way."

I hate it when people use my words against me.

"Look, I'm not coming back to Mogadishu," I told him. "I can't take you to the U.S., if that's what you're thinking."

"No, I don't think of that. I know I am on my own-some."

Own-some? Tell me he didn't pick up that English gem from Shotgun.

"You have a passport?" I asked.

"I do. What time should I be at hotel?"

"We'll pick you up at the restaurant," I said. "Be ready to leave a half hour before dawn."

"I will not sleep until then."

The next few hours were filled with phone calls and computer sessions, trying to gather more information on Shire Jama and Allah's Rule on Earth.

What we came up with can be summarized with one word: *bupkis.* This is a Yiddish expression meaning קאָזעבאָפקע.[14]

Shunt had temporarily run out of places to look for new information, and his various methods of drumming analysis—from standard data mining to something he calls context analysis—weren't feeding him any new ideas. The bank's new security measures had so far kept him out.

We were now pretty sure that the bank had hosted accounts for Allah's Rule. But without proof that they knew the accounts were connected to terrorists, there was no crime involved. On the contrary, the bank could point out that they had hired me to investigate the matter, and therefore done their civic and lawful duty.

As for the connection to Veep—the more I thought about it, the more tenuous it seemed. I relish biting the hand that feeds me, but I needed more to go on.

All of this meant that I put off updating Veep in New York. Telling him about the accounts we had found would shut them down; once that happened, we'd have an even harder time investigating.

Was Veep stealing money from the bank, or involved with the terrorists? Both? Or neither?

Both was best for me—it meant a much higher fee. I tried not to let that prejudice my thinking.

Even talking to Karen was frustrating.

"Your meeting in Mumbai has been pushed up. They need you there the day after tomorrow," she said. "And there's a reception tomorrow evening being held in your honor. They want to thank you for saving the Commonwealth Games."[15]

"That's an exaggeration."

"I told them that."

I can always count on Karen to keep my ego in check.

"Junior volunteered to go in your place," she added. "To the meeting, not the reception."

"I'd rather he went to the reception."

"He'll do fine at the meeting, Dick."

I trust Junior, but I wasn't ready to let him represent me at a business meeting, especially in India. And despite the reception, not everyone there was appreciative of how I had handled the terrorist plots at the Games.

"Can you get a plane from Djibouti?" I asked Karen.

---

[14] It has to do with goats.

[15] See *Domino Theory*, available at fine bookstores, online, and from the neighborhood pawnbroker at a substantial discount.

"It will cost you."

"I'll pay your fee any time."

"I meant that the airline connections are outrageously expensive. I'll figure it out. Junior will pick you up at the airport in Mumbai."

We spent the next ten minutes saying how much we missed each other. Since I'm not writing *Fifty Shades of Rogue Grey*, I'll spare you the gory details. Suffice to say I needed a cold shower when I hung up.

The team was suitably grumpy when we assembled at four the next morning and piled into the hired car. We drove over to Taban's restaurant, where, true to his word, Abdi was waiting when we arrived.

So was a crowd that looked like half of Mogadishu.

"Not good," said the driver, stopping halfway down the block.

"Put it in reverse. Fast," said Trace.

"Whoa, whoa," I said, grabbing the driver's hand as he reached for the shifter. "Let me see what's going on."

There was a general murmur of disapproval as I got out of the car. Then the others jumped out to cover my butt.

One or two people in the crowd had what looked like early-model M16s. The rest had AK47s. "Abdi, what's going on?" I said, walking past the outer ring.

"Sorry, Mr. Dick," he said. He had a small cloth bag with him. Three or four women trailed close behind. I recognized one as his uncle's wife.

"What's with all the people?"

"Family matter."

I gave him the hairy eyeball.

Abdi sighed, then pointed to a girl over by the doorway. "It is about Rose.[16] She is to get married, but she doesn't wish it."

I glanced over. A long, flowing scarf partly hid the young woman's face. Even in the bulky dress she was wearing, Rose looked like a scarecrow of a thing, little more than a stick figure, except for a suspiciously round belly.

"How old is she?" I would have guessed twelve.

"Fourteen," said Abdi. "In a few days."

"She's getting married?"

"It is the families' wish. Because . . . of circumstances . . ."

"Which are what?"

Rose had been raped by a cousin some months before. She'd kept it a secret from her family because of her shame—as in much of the Muslim

---

[16] Damned if I can pronounce her actual name, let alone spell it. A Rose is a Rose by any other name, anyway.

world, such events are considered the woman's fault. Worse, if it becomes known that the girl has been raped, it's impossible for her to marry. In Somalia, that's a death sentence, since a woman without a family is a) an easy target and b) unlikely to find a way to support herself.

Rape is not particularly rare here, and by common agreement such matters are handled by looking the other way—something that perversely is in the woman's interests. But the girl had become pregnant, and as I had seen, there was no way to hide it.

There was quite a bit of consternation, especially since the rapist was in the extended family. Eventually, the matter was brought to the local imam and a tribal council suggested that the matter be handled by marriage, proscriptions against cousins marrying notwithstanding.

Otherwise, the rapist would be turned over to the government for punishment, with the expected sentence to be five years in jail. That would probably equate to death, though I suppose the unpredictability of when and how it would come added a certain entertainment value for the prisoner.

"So why are all these people here?" I asked Abdi.

"They have spent the night trying to convince her to marry. And now they want me to order her."

"Order her?"

"Yes."

"And she doesn't want to?"

Duh.

Abdi didn't say that, but his expression made it clear that's what he was thinking. And he was right: why would *anyone* want to marry their rapist?

Even if it is sanctioned by the Koran.

"Why did they come to you?" I asked.

"Because my uncle is dead."

"The rapist was related?"

"No, no, no. But he would have helped settle the matter. With him gone, they look to me."

"What would he have done?"

Abdi sighed. "The solution would not be easy. I don't know what he would do, but Taban ali Mohammad always thought of something."

"We have to get going. If you're coming, come."

"I am." He turned and said something in Somali. The women wrung their hands together and begged him; Abdi repeated whatever it was he said, then turned and started for the car.

"What did you say?" I asked, falling in beside him.

"I told them I am going north. I said I will be back tomorrow."

"I don't know about tomorrow," I said.

"Yes, but please don't tell them." He turned quickly and said something in Somali to the crowd, which was still trailing. They pressed close to us, trying to touch him. It was like being with a rock star.

Things were so tight in the car that Abdi volunteered to run behind. Not only did he keep up, he barely seemed winded. I have a feeling he could have beaten us to the airport.

Getting our weapons aboard the aircraft would have entailed paperwork and a large bribe, and given that I could make adequate (and cheaper) arrangements if necessary in Djibouti, I decided not to bother. A five-minute phone call to Djibouti resulted in a promise that a set of pistols and ammo would be in the cars that met us at the airport. To keep our weapons in Somalia safe until they could be retrieved, I arranged to store them in a lockbox owned by a French company that had a contract with the African Congress security force. The French company was actually a front for the French military intelligence agency, Direction du renseignement militaire, similar to our DIA[17] with fancy accents and a hankering for wine instead of beer.

The arrangements had been made with the day shift; the sole person at the hangar when we arrived was a thirty-year-old Senegal native whose French was turgid and his English worse.

He was sleeping inside when we arrived. After picking the door lock, we went in and woke him by shaking his desk chair. He opened his eyes and saw us standing there with our guns; a puddle appeared beneath his chair.

"I need to use one of your lockboxes," I told him. The large metal boxes looked like slightly downsized shipping containers, which is basically what they were.

"Who you?" asked the guard.

"Dick Marcinko. I'm with Red Cell International."

"Who to sell?"

The word play might have been amusing had the airplane we were supposed to catch not been on final approach. I managed to straighten out the misunderstanding and we made the plane just as the ground crew was about to button up the cabin.

If you think flying on an American airline is a joy, try flying on African planes sometime. The plane we were on—a British-built Viscount four-engined turboprop—dated from the early 1950s. Some of my friends claim propeller-driven aircraft are romantic; I say they're loud. The seats were as comfortable as a concrete garden bench, and had half the flexibility. The cabin smelled like a donkey barn.

---

[17] DIA=Defense Intelligence Agency, also known as Daft, Insolent, and Angry

There was one similarity with Western airlines—it was full. We held our noses and our breath the whole flight.

We pause the narrative to bring you an unpaid public service announcement on behalf of the Djibouti chamber of commerce and tourist boards:

AMERICANS!

Djibouti is not like other places on the Horn of Africa or bordering on the Gulf of Aden. Djibouti is a peaceful place. Djibouti has kick-ass sand beaches, nice port facilities, and people who want your money, not your blood!

We speak French, but we really don't mean it!

Come! COME!

Djibouti is a small country on the coast, sandwiched between Eritrea, Ethiopia, and Somalia. With neighbors like that, most people would assume it's well down the staircase to Hell. But for various reasons—including those neighbors—it's an island of hospitality toward Westerners. Odds are against your vacationing there any time soon (unless you're French), but if you happen to have business there, you won't have to go around with armed guards.

It's estimated that somewhere around half of the country's population lives in or around the capital city, which is conveniently named Djibouti as well. The city is located right on the water about twelve miles from the Somali border; the location is strategic and convenient for ships transiting the Suez Canal to the north. It's also a good place to be a spy.

Did I mention there's also a decent large-sized U.S. military base next to the city airport, Camp Lemonnier? Its proximity to Somalia is not a coincidence, but you should forget about those Predators you see on the runway, and pay absolutely no attention to the U-2s at the far end of the field. Those are just weather observation aircraft.

We had two sets of reservations, one at the Sheraton and the other at Palace Kempinski, both highly rated hotels. Of course, we planned to stay at neither, since they were the first places anyone trying to check on us would look. Instead, we split up and took two separate taxis to a hotel about four blocks from the water called the Eastern Gate—a strange name given that it was on the west side of the city.

But the strangest thing was the man waiting in the lobby for us when we arrived: Garrett Taylor, erstwhile Christian in Action.

And his boss, Mr. Magoo, who looked about as happy to be in Djibouti as a SEAL at a church picnic, and twice as ornery.

The marines behind him were just window dressing. What I couldn't figure out was who the man in the gray suit was.

It soon became obvious.

"That's him," said Magoo, pointing at me.

Gray Suit stepped up, and pulled a small wallet from the pocket of his jacket. He flipped it open, revealing an FBI badge.

"Richard Marcinko," he said, in a voice that boomed through the lobby, "you are under arrest for illegal gun dealing in a foreign state. Take him, men."

(II)

The marines came forward quicker than you can say "bullshit." Ditto for Shotgun, Trace, and Mongoose, who had just entered behind me. We were about ten seconds from a whole lot of blood.

I put up my hands to calm everyone down.

"Relax," I said. "What's this about Magoo?"

I may have added a few other tender words of endearment when I addressed him, since Magoo's face flushed.

"You heard the man," he told me, sticking out his jaw even as he took a step back to make sure he was out of arm's reach. "You're an international gun smuggler. We have the evidence in Mogadishu. AK47s, grenade launchers, even an MP5 submachine."

"What the hell are you talking about?"

"Your instructions were to clear the arrangements with me beforehand," said Magoo. "You weren't to take the meeting yourself. Or is that part of your plan—you're going to make a little money on the side, right?"

Magoo had decided that, because I didn't give him a minute-by-minute rundown of what I was doing, I was conspiring to cheat the government— trying to skim some of the money I claimed was for the smuggling operation. He made some other accusations as well, accusing me of everything from breaking international gun laws to withholding information from him.

Granted, I had done both of those things. But I had my reasons. And skimming money off Uncle Sugar wasn't one of them.

I'm not convinced that Magoo thought that was really the case. More likely, he saw me as an impediment to his claiming the glory of nailing Allah's Rule and closing down its drug-smuggling operation. The French had gotten the glory for the earlier bust; he wanted no more competition.

Not that he was going to admit anything close to that, or even concede that I had done everything he'd asked and then some. Hell, I was about to hand him a connection twenty times more valuable than any he'd managed.

Our discussion attracted more than a few stares from the desk. I agreed to continue the discussion at Gray Suit's office, which happened to be on the military base back on the other side of the airport we'd just left. Gray Suit wasn't a particularly bad sort for an FBI (Fornication & Butt Implants) agent, even one of the overseas variety. He and I drove to the base with

Trace and a pair of marines. By the time we got there, he understood what Magoo was up to and was fishing for a date with Trace.

The car ride took some of Magoo's venom away, but he really didn't start to backpedal until I suggested we call the admiral to straighten things out.

"Maybe we can ignore the charges if you start cooperating," he said finally, glancing at Gray Suit.

Gray Suit looked at me and smirked.

"Listen, Marcinko, I want to impress on you that this is an *agency* operation," continued Magoo. "*Agency.* I want you to understand that we're the ones who are doing the job here. We're tracking down the terrorists. That's our job."

"I'm glad you understand that," I told him.

Magoo got a confused look on his face.

Garrett Taylor, who'd been standing at the side of the room the whole time, stepped forward and cleared his throat.

"I think Mr. Mar-Marcinko is right. I think he's absolutely, uh, just uh, on board here."

As these were the first words he'd said since Saudi Arabia, it was a bit of a shame that he stuttered. But Trace's death stare has that effect on people.

Magoo said something that might generously be interpreted as agreement. I convinced him that it would be foolish to do anything to make our contacts suspicious, like handing over the phones and changing the arrangements. He agreed, reluctantly, then assigned young Mr. Garrett as our "liaison."

And money holder. He handed over a small attaché case with ten thousand in euros, the down payment.

"I have other business, Dick," he said, as if I'd been the one wasting his time. "Don't make a move without clearing it first."

"Aye, aye, Cap'n." I sealed my promise with a one-finger salute.

Aside from having to babysit Garrett, the biggest practical effect of Magoo's intervention was the need to find a new hotel, since our cover had been blown. While Trace and I had been listening to Magoo's harangue, Shotgun and Mongoose had spent their time more productively, first by locating another nondescript hotel, and then by meeting the supplier who'd arranged some gear and additional weapons for us. The latter was not a particularly honest man, as it turned out; when he tried to double the agreed-upon price, Mongoose instead demonstrated how an MMA-style punch could break a rib. The supplier was so impressed he went back to the original price, and threw a few extra mags in gratis.

The hotel sat on the outskirts of the tourist area. The French-run place dated from the colonial days but now catered mostly to businesspeople from other parts of Africa; the desk clerk told us cheerfully that we were the first white people he'd seen in months.

We were just getting rooms when cell phone Number 1 began to buzz. I took out a voice recorder and held it close to the phone. Then I unwrapped the tape with great ceremony and unlocked the mobile so I could answer. "Yes?"

"Go to Banque La Monarch. De-posit ten thousand euros in a-count 1-0-9-7-7-6-5-5-5."

The instructions were made by a voice that sounded a lot like the auto-reader in the Kindle, assuming the Kindle had been dropped in a few swimming pools. The message repeated once—I grabbed a pen from Trace and jotted down the numbers—then cut off.

I checked my watch. If things went quickly at the bank, I could just make the flight to India.

As the name suggests, Banque La Monarch was a French-owned bank. Located not far from the central market, Banque La Monarch was small in international finance terms, but it had the ability to wire funds anywhere in the world, which was undoubtedly the only thing Shire Jama was interested in.

We had fifteen minutes. I sent Mongoose and Shotgun out ahead to take a look at the place and report back. I told Trace and Garrett to pose as a pair of tourists and shadow me and Abdi while we took our time walking over.

Garrett was very much up for the job.

"We could pose as a honeymooning couple," he said.

"I don't think we have to be on our honeymoon," said Trace. "Just a married couple."

Garrett was slightly younger than she was—if I say how many years, she might kill me. But aside from his affiliation with the Christians in Action, he didn't look like a bad catch. He'd already started to recover from the Saudi prison, and while still a bit underweight he had an athletic frame at six-three or so. He knew a couple of languages, spoke well, and seemed genuinely embarrassed by Magoo. Plus he came from good stock.

Garrett put his arm around Trace's waist. She removed it swiftly, though without violence—clearly a sign that she was attracted to him. I've seen her toss people through windows for less.

They left first. I gave them a three-minute head start, then Abdi and I left the building.

"What do you think I should do, Mr. Dick?" he asked.

"Just keep up with me," I told him. "Most likely you won't need to do anything."

"I meant with my cousin. Rose."

"Oh." I'd forgotten about the girl. "What would your uncle do?"

"I have thought about it the whole flight. He would have a solution, but I don't know what it would be. I don't think I can take her with me to America."

"Probably not."

"She should marry her cousin," he said. "That is the best solution for all."

I didn't say anything. It wasn't my job to be the kid's conscience.

Like a lot of the Third World, Djibouti City combines the modern with the colonial. The port area has machinery that would put American ports to shame, while for tourists there's a nice selection of fancy resort hotels along the beach. But the bulk of the city wears its poverty openly. Pick a street away from the port and downtown, and you're likely to find a narrow, dirt-packed thoroughfare littered with garbage and lined with rubble. It's as if the original buildings fell fifty or sixty years before, were pushed into a pile, and then forgotten. More often than not, their replacements are steel panels joined together slightly off-kilter.

Assuming you're in the high-rent district. Elsewhere, crates and discarded boxes are the popular building material.

Even though it was midmorning, the streets were mostly empty, everyone either off to work or doing their chores inside. Abdi had been here before, and took to playing tour guide as we walked toward the bank. The street opened into a wide field, and we passed what looked like a car junkyard. He assured me it wasn't a junkyard at all; the cars surely belonged to workers in the buildings just beyond.

"No one would abandon something worth that much here," he said. "And no one would steal it either."

"I'm surprised at that."

"Very honest place, Mr. Dick. Africa is like that."

"Somalia is not."

"Yes, it is. If you are one of us, it is very honest."

"But not if you're not."

"If you are not of the tribe, then you are not us. The rules are different."

"We don't think that way in America, Abdi. You should remember that."

"Yes, yes, I know. That is one thing I like. That and to make money."

We passed back onto a paved road, ignoring a pair of stray goats as we headed near the market, a square with various booths selling different items. Think Wal*Mart au naturel. If that image is too jarring, then conjure up a flea market and chill.

I was the only white man around. I got a few stares, but not as many as I thought I would. I stopped to sample some fruits, discreetly checking to see if I could find anyone watching us. I was sure that there would be surveillance, but if so I couldn't find it.

Abdi stepped in to negotiate the price. Unfortunately, I hadn't had time to get any of the local money—aside from the money to make the down payment for the drugs, all I had were the few euros I'd been carrying, and the worthless Somali script. I ended up giving the proprietor a one-euro note, about a 3,000 percent markup, according to Abdi.

"Now many people will want to do business with you. Watch."

"We're not going to hang around to let them."

I set a good pace over to the bank, a block and a half away. There was a guard inside the foyer, dressed in a brown uniform with what looked like a police cap from the 1950s practically covering his eyes. He had a wad of khat in his mouth, and chewed it with great purpose and deliberation as he watched us walk past and look around. Ordinarily, I would have chosen the cutest teller and explained my business. The tellers here were all men, though, so I went to the one in the middle.

"I need to make a large *dépôt bancaire*."

"*Il ne s'agit pas d'un problème, monsieur,*" he assured me in French. "Not a problem at all. What is the account?"

I told him. He hesitated for a moment, then pulled over a pen and asked me to repeat it. "How much euro?"

"Ten thousand." I glanced at Abdi and he popped open the briefcase on cue, setting it on the counter.

"Just a minute and I get the form," said the teller, practically hopping toward the office at the back.

Abdi and I were the only customers. There were two other clerks behind a high wooden counter topped with metal dividers. The interior offices could only be reached from the clerk's side of the counter.

The interior was plain, with a few wood panels beneath walls that were painted a dull beige. There were no paintings on the wall, and the incandescent arrays of lights that hung down would not have looked out of place in a water plant or maybe a large truck garage. The one fancy touch in the customer area was a skylight composed of large panels of clear glass that filled the ceiling three stories above. Two panels had faded designs on them, symbols I would guess of the bank, or maybe a previous owner of the building. Both were so faded it was impossible to tell what they signified.

The teller came back a few minutes later, a big smile on his face. He had me fill out a form for the deposit. The form asked for my name, and I gave it to him:

State of Virginia.

It even agreed with the license I showed him for identification.

He gave me a receipt, and wished me a *bon jour.*

I *bon jour*ed him back and took my leave, mentally calculating how long it would take me to get to the airport for my flight to India.

Just as we reached the door, a pair of women entered, dressed in black burkas. Abdi nearly fell over trying to get out of the women's way; I had to hook his arm in mine as I pushed through the door and went out on the street.

Trace and Garrett were strolling in our direction, looking very much like a married couple—there was a good five or six feet between them.

"What was that about inside?" I asked Abdi.

"The woman had a gun under her dress," he said. "I thought—"

He stopped speaking as an AK47 began barking inside the building, its metallic stutter nearly overwhelmed by the sound of shattering glass.

The bank was being robbed.

(III)

Is it me, or is there no safe bank to put your money in anymore?

While I was considering the horrible state of the international banking system, Trace was running past me in a blur, charging into the building.

"Stay out here," I barked at Abdi, following her inside. Garrett, barely comprehending what was going on, trailed me by a few steps.

One of the "women" had pulled a paratrooper model of an AK47 out from beneath her long tunics and was holding the staff at bay while "her" partner grabbed cash from behind the counter. The guard—I should probably use quote marks there as well—had thrown his weapon to the middle of the floor and was gazing at the robbers with stoned admiration. Clearly he went for dominating women.

As she entered the large lobby, Trace slid to one knee, pistol raised, voice steady.

"Drop the weapon!" she said.

It's debatable whether the robber understood English or not, and he's not around to say: he made the mistake of turning toward Trace with the gun still in his hands, and she put two bullets through his forehead.

The second thief ducked behind the counter, pulled out a pistol, and grabbed one of the clerks as a hostage. Then he began spouting something in Arabic. He was talking much too quickly for me to make heads or tails of what he was saying, but the general gist was clear enough—drop your weapons or the clerk gets it. To my surprise, Trace tossed down her gun, put up her hands, and moved sideways, giving the gunman and his hostage a clear path to the door.

Except for me. The gunman—as you undoubtedly know by now, two men had disguised themselves as women to make it easier to get inside with their weapons—yelled something at me and jabbed his weapon into the hostage's neck.

I wasn't particularly impressed, and held my ground. He shouted again, once more jabbing the automatic into the skinny clerk's neck.

"You speak English?" I asked.

He responded with an even louder tirade in what can only be called ferocious Arabic.

"You want me to drop my weapon?" I asked, gesturing.

He said something else. It might have been "yes," with a few gutter words thrown in.

"Why?" I asked. "Do you think I'll miss?"

I didn't. My bullet went right between his eyes and he fell back, his pistol clattering harmlessly to the ground. In his anger, the hostage taker had neglected the first rule of threatening hostages—don't put your head out where someone else can shoot it.

"Crap, you took your time," griped Trace as we cleared the room to make sure there were no confederates hiding nearby. She was holding a second pistol, which she had pulled from some nether region of her body. "I thought I was going to have to wing him myself on the way out."

Place clear, we exited to accolades of the local police force, who immediately whisked us to city hall where we were awarded the key to the city and feted with a day named in our honor . . .

Actually, we didn't stick around for the honors, or the police.

Taking positions outside the building as our backups, Shotgun and Mongoose noticed a car lurking nearby. When the car sped to the front of the building, obviously waiting for the bank robbers, they closed in. The driver stepped on the gas and jerked the wheel. As he pulled away, Mongoose somehow found himself on the hood of the car. Face-to-windshield with the driver, Mongoose swung his pistol up and put two bullets into his chest.

The bullets killed the man, but had no effect on the foot that was pressing on the gas. The vehicle sped through the intersection toward the market, scattering people and carts stationed in the market's overflow area. Held in place by the momentum of the car,[18] Mongoose bounced with the car as it bounded over the curb and into the low rail in front of a building housing a restaurant. It crashed into the steel gates at the front of the building, landing in the middle of the dining room amid tables and chairs. Mongoose emerged with a handful of cuts and some deep bruises.

Shotgun, being Shotgun, was right there as he walked from the building. "Kitchen open yet?"

"Food's good, but the service sucks," answered Mongoose. "You'll never get a table."

Shotgun checked the driver's body to see if there was any ID. It was clean, as was the glove compartment.

---

[18] A corollary of the little-known Newton Law, the Desperately in Motion.

Miraculously, no one except the driver had been hurt. The boys slipped away and we caught up with them two blocks away.

"What a disaster," said Garrett.

"Hell no," said Shotgun, who'd managed to snag a large orange on the way out. "Just your typical SNAFU—situation normal, all fucked up."

[IV]

Magoo already knew about the bank robbery, and not because Garrett was with me—he'd sent his people to watch the banks in town. The two assigned to ours arrived just after the mayhem.

He naturally bawled me out when I called to tell him what had happened. I didn't expect a pat on the back, but something north of a FU would have been in order.

"You're dismissed, Marcinko. The U.S. government appreciates your support. Don't let the door of the airplane hit you on the rear as you leave."

"I won't. But we're not through," I told him. "There's still the matter of getting the drugs."

"I don't need the drugs. We'll be watching the accounts. Thanks for your help."

He abruptly hung up.

In fact, he did still need my help. It wasn't just the fact that there'd be a lot more potential for intelligence when the ship landed, starting with the fact that we'd know which ship it was. I'd realized on the way back to our hotel that there probably weren't going to be any bank transfers, at least not of the wired variety. I hadn't interrupted a bank robbery; the men with the burkas had come to collect the down payment.

Duh.

It was just a theory, but a promising one. With Shunt now monitoring the accounts at the bank and looking for transfers, I set Trace and the boys hunting from the other direction: "Get IDs on the bank robbers, the car, anything else you can find. Report to me when I get to Mumbai."

"What do I do with Abdi?"

"He may be useful getting information. If not, pay him off and cut him loose. Help him get a bank account and get him a ticket to Mogadishu," I told her. "Or wherever he wants to go."

"What if he wants to go to Brooklyn?"

"Talk him out of that if you can."

Nothing interesting happened on my long-ass flight to India—in coach—so we'll stay with Trace and the boys in Djibouti.

Garrett volunteered that the local CIA station might be able to get information about Allah's Rule operations in Djibouti, and together they went to the embassy to see what they might discover. The chief of station was an affable sort, who led them to the SCIF (Sensitive Compartmented Information Facility, a room supposedly impervious to eavesdropping) and then proceeded to tell them that he had never heard of the organization. Garrett tried to salvage the situation by pumping the chief for general information, but this was mostly a waste of time as well.

On the way back to their hotel, Garrett obviously noticed Trace's foul mood and tried lifting it by filling her ears with sweet nothings. Or more accurately, he did what a lot of guys do when they see what they think is a promising romantic situation rapidly deteriorating—he started talking about himself. (Gentlemen: wrong thing to do.) This didn't exactly win Trace over, but it did push the conversation in a direction that Trace found useful, making it easy for her to pump him for data. He'd spent much of his time over the past few months in Pakistan, posing as a drug buyer for a French syndicate. In among mostly useless details, Trace managed to get a few questions in.

"What's with the prescription pills?" she asked. "Why are they smuggling them?"

"Good markup, steady customer base," said Garrett. "Plus, since they're medicine, they're not forbidden by the Koran. Unlike other drugs."

Garrett segued into a longer dissertation, during the course of which he mentioned that he had tracked the source of the drugs to a factory in Bangladesh.

"Dick should check it out," he said. "The agency can't do anything about it because of politics, but he could."

"I don't think he's interested in opening a pharmacy."

"He could track the drugs as they go to the Middle East, then turn the information over to Magoo. He'd be grateful. It would get Dick on his good side."

"Dick doesn't care about being on people's good side," said Trace. "And from what I've seen of Magoo, he doesn't have one."

Concerned that Mongoose's injuries were more severe than they looked, Trace ordered him to the clinic at the base. A navy corpsman looked over Mongoose, saw the small frog tattooed on his arm, and gave him the green light. The frogman tattoo is known inside the navy as a tribute to UDT (Underwater Demolition Teams), the dedicated predecessors to the SEALs. It's often worn by SEALs, and the corpsman jumped to the right conclusion that Mongoose had been a member of the Teams.

"You better be careful," the corpsman told him. "They're looking for people who were in town. Europeans. They say they robbed a bank."

"I'm not European," said Mongoose.

"You are to them. Filipino, yes?"

"Why?"

"Brother." The corpsman rolled up his sleeve and displayed an elaborate tattoo featuring the islands and the Filipino flag. "Goes with this one," he added, rolling up the other sleeve to show the U.S. flag and country.

"The American flag is a little higher on the shoulder, get it?" added the corpsman. He tilted his body, exaggerating the difference.

"Nice tats," admitted Mongoose.

The corpsman took out some antiseptic and began cleaning the cuts on Mongoose's face. I'm sure it stung like hell. I'm also sure Mongoose did everything he could to keep from wincing.

"There was a big accident in town," continued the corpsman. "A bank robbery. The police put out a bulletin looking for people."

"Oh yeah?"

"You wouldn't know anything about that, would you?" asked the corpsman.

"Not at all."

The corpsman retrieved some gauze from a cabinet and returned.

"There was an accident at the market," said the corpsman. "They're looking for a couple of white guys."

"I'd say my color's a little closer to brown than white," said Mongoose.

"White's a relative concept out here," said the corpsman.

He raised the gauze to Mongoose's head to start a wrap. Mongoose stopped him.

"In case somebody got a good look," said the corpsman. "And you've been here since six A.M., waiting to get in. Hell of a long line Thursdays."

"Damn long," said Mongoose.

They were now friends for life. The corpsman explained that the base security office had received the bulletins, and passed the information on to the medical people, just in case military personnel showed up with unexplained wounds.

"But yours are pretty much explained by that fall you took at the Giz very early this morning," noted the corpsman.

"Giz?"

"Topless bar. Off-limits to current military personnel. But since you're a civilian, you're in the clear."

Someone came to the door of the clinic room, calling the corpsman away. Mongoose pulled on his shirt. After a few minutes, he decided to go see what was up. He ambled down the hall, only to be intercepted by the returning corpsman.

"No big deal," said the sailor. "They brought the bank robbers. We're going to do the PM—postmortem. Autopsy. Find out what killed them."

Mongoose knew what killed them, as would anyone else lifting the cloth to take a look. But he kept the information to himself.

"Ever see an autopsy?" asked the corpsman.

"Uh . . ."

"Come on. It's fun. You cut up people and look inside. Very nice."

Mongoose's stomach suddenly turned queasy. He likes blowing things up, but doesn't care to study the results.

"Another time, man," he said. "I gotta go see a friend."

"Maybe later?"

"Uh, sure."

Mongoose slipped out a side door. Trace had left him off and told him to call for a ride when he needed to be picked up. He dialed her now, and found she was in an unusually buoyant mood.

"Where the hell have you been?" she asked. "They give you a brain transplant?"

"Nice talking to you, too," answered Mongoose.

(There may have been a few other words sprinkled in there, mostly of the Anglo-Saxon variety. Neither one seems to recall.)

"I have to take care of getting another backup car rented and some other logistics," said Trace. "I need you to go over to the police station and see if you can get their IDs."

"Why the police station?"

"Isn't that where they usually take bank robbers?"

"Not when they're dead. They're inside, down the hall, waiting for an autopsy."

Security at the clinic was pretty much typical of any medical facility anywhere in the world—once past a trivial check at the door, people generally assumed you belonged there as long as you acted like it. Put a surgical gown on, tuck a stethoscope into your pocket, and people will sooner ask what to do about a trick knee than demand ID.

Looking like you belonged in a room where autopsies are performed could be tricky, however, especially if your stomach turned even thinking of the procedure. Scrubs were easily found, as were a face mask and a hairnet, but Mongoose lingered in an adjoining clinic room, gathering his courage, settling his stomach, and trying to think of some other way he might get the IDs without having to see the bodies being cut up.

He must have a psychotic fear of straight lines. Jagged ones never seem to bother him.

He was steadying himself against a cabinet when a gravel-throated voice boomed behind him. "What the hell are you doing in here?"

Mongoose grabbed the nearest instrument. It happened to have a handle and, to Mongoose at least, looked a little like a grease gun without the hose feed or canister.

"I was just getting, uh, this," he said, mumbling as he turned around.

Gravel Throat turned out to be an incredibly good-looking American nurse, not quite thirty years old, who filled her scrubs in a way that should be outlawed. Petite in all the right places, she had a pair of blue eyes and blond hair that was pulled into a braided ponytail curling around her neck.

"Dr. Torrence sent you here?" Her voice was the exact opposite of her face and figure. The cabinets rattled as she spoke.

"I, uh—" Brave in the face of danger, Mongoose turned speechless in the face of great beauty. "New," he managed finally.

"Oh, I know you're new. You better get back to Torrence before she takes off your head."

"Yes, ma'am."

"What the hell does Torrence want with a uterus manipulator?" asked the gravel-throated beauty.

Mongoose shrugged.

"What's with the mask?"

Mongoose feigned a cough. "Gotta bad cold. Torrence, uh, she—"

"Well you better get back before she bites your head off, Jason. She's a bitch in heels."

Mongoose hurried past her, trying to decide whether her voice was too much of a turnoff. A few strides into the hall, he met another man in identical scrubs, moving purposely in his direction. For a moment he thought he was going to be stopped. Then he caught sight of the ID clipped to the man's pocket.

"Yo, you're Jason—the new guy, right?" he asked, pointing the uterus manipulator at him.

"Yeah, that's me. Just started a half hour ago. I know I was a little late but—"

"Take this to Dr. Torrence." He held the instrument out.

"To who?"

"Nobody warned you about Torrence?"

"Uh—"

"Bitch in heels? The woman doctor?"

"Oh, yeah, right. She's at the end of the hall, right?"

"Yup." Mongoose made a show of glancing at Jason's ID. "You don't have the dot on your ID."

"Huh?"

"It's a security marker. They change them every day. I had to leave mine because they're putting a new picture on it. I'm on my way over to get it now. Here," said Mongoose, holding out his palm. "I'll get your dot for you. Give me the ID."

"Well."

"You take the instrument to Torrence, I'll get the badge. I'll meet you back here in ten. Don't screw around with her, all right? She's the one person in this place you don't want to mess with." Mongoose put his lips together and gave him a knowing nod. "And you owe me. You got it?"

"Yeah, uh yeah. Thanks."

Two minutes later, Mongoose entered the room where the autopsy was taking place. The corpsman stood with a surgical saw in his hand, across the table from a short, Chinese-American doctor who was talking into a voice recorder. The dead man lay between them. He hadn't been cut up yet, but he didn't look particularly happy at the prospect. The two other bodies were behind them, waiting their turn.

The doctor looked over at Mongoose. Mongoose looked at his friend.

"You made it," said the corpsman.

Mongoose nodded. Once again he'd lost his voice, but this had nothing to do with love—he worried that if he opened his mouth, there'd be nothing holding back the contents of his stomach.

"This is a buddy of mine who wants to be a corpsman, Doc," the sailor said. "I thought this would be a good intro—make sure he can take it."

"As long as the dead man doesn't object."

This apparently was a joke, because the doctor and the corpsman began laughing uproariously.

The doctor began doing a play-by-play of the procedure, explaining in great detail what they were doing as he examined bullet wounds and judged their effect. Mongoose spent the entire time concentrating on keeping his teeth in proper autopsy position: together.

Bullet wounds recorded and examined, the doctor moved on to the next part of the autopsy—checking whether the dead man had been under the influence of drugs at the time of his death, looking for heart disease or other possible contributing factors . . .

"The silent killers," said the corpsman.

Another apparent autopsy joke. Their laughter was *almost* enough to wake the dead.

A few moments later, the doctor asked the corpsman for the saw.

At that point, Mongoose found it difficult to breathe. He retreated to a restroom at the rear of the room. The corpsman found him sitting on the floor some forty-five minutes later.

"You all right?" asked the sailor.

"I'm good," mumbled Mongoose. "Something I ate."

"Don't sweat it. You aren't the first SEAL I've met with a queasy stomach."

"Listen, I need to find out who they were."

"Huh?"

"It's a long story. You got IDs?"

"No. No one does. They're John Does. Police say they're not from the city. We're doing DNA samples. We'll run them through the military registry, do the whole routine. Maybe there's a match with a name in the database."

Even Mongoose, who has lost more than his share of money at the Kentucky Derby, knew the odds on that were astronomically poor.

"Damn."

"Send me an e-mail and I'll give you whatever information we pull out," said the corpsman. "Here's a clinic card—just use that e-mail at the bottom."

"Thanks."

"Word of advice," he added, backing toward the door. "Stay away from the fish next time you're planning on watching an autopsy. Tastes great, but smells like hell on the way out."

"I'll try to remember that," Mongoose managed.

[V]

Talking to Indian politicians is a lot like talking to American politicians. They nod their heads, smile wistfully, and then explain in a hundred and one different ways why they can't do what makes the most sense.

"Local prerogatives" was one of the buzz words that night, as the politicians attempted to explain why every district and state in India needed its own autonomous intelligence force, and therefore would have to continue with the byzantine non-communicative, no-command, and not-so-control system that was already in place. We may have a lot of duplication, turf protecting, and unnecessary bureaucracy in the United States, but the Indians made us look like rank amateurs when it comes to chaos and inefficiency.

But I've complained about all of this before.[19] So let's fast-forward through the endless cocktail party and the dull sub-cabinet meeting the next day. Junior and I were invited on a tour of some of the frontier areas, to see what sort of security improvements had been made since my last visit. Eager to get out of the red-taped halls of Mumbai, I accepted.

Adjust for the geography, and the border of India and Bangladesh will remind you a lot of the border between Mexico and the United States. Both are fairly porous and in many areas ruled by gangs that fear each other far more than they fear the legitimate authorities. Smuggling is a huge problem; all manner of goods are taken into Bangladesh from India, right up to livestock.

People searching for jobs come the other way. The Indian Border Security Force has orders to shoot to kill, but this doesn't stop thousands from trying. Most are just simply poor people searching for better lives; others are Muslim terrorists and spies who for various reasons find a border crossing more expedient here than in Pakistan.

Bangladesh is a multifaceted problem for India, complicated by history, geography, and religion. Poverty doesn't help, either. It used to be part of Pakistan, but gained its independence (with Indian help) in the early 1970s. It's heavily Muslim, subject to pretty horrific weather, and extremely poor.

Bangladesh sits like a cyst on India's right shoulder, surrounded on three sides by Indian states. Junior and I visited a post in Tripura, a smallish state in the east touched on three sides by Bangladesh. We went directly from the airport to the northwestern border, inspecting—I use the word loosely—

---

[19] Check out *Domino Theory.*

the double barbed-wire fence that runs along the boundary. A roll of razor wire was strung very deliberately between the two fences.

"Impossible to pass," claimed the major tasked as our guide. "We often find tigers dead in the middle."

I wasn't sure which claim was more fanciful, but I let them pass.

The fence was every bit as interesting as barbed-wire fences get, and I gratefully accepted the invitation for an early lunch. Junior mentioned that he had never seen a tiger, and wouldn't mind coming across one before eating.

"Sometimes, a mile or two further," said our guide. "On the other side of the fence. If you are interested, a tour can be arranged."

I suspect that Junior's real interest was in avoiding the luncheon, which was sure to be as scintillating as the barbed wire. Whatever. Within minutes, he was outfitted with a bike and two guards for an extended tour. They set out along the packed-dirt road skirting the fence, tinkling their bells every so often as they climbed over the hillside.

Having been cooped up in airplanes and cities for the past few days, Matt appreciated the exercise. The day was a little muggy, and the sun a little strong, but the fresh air and open path felt invigorating. After a mile or so, the border guards decided to show the American visitor what they could do, and began pedaling in earnest.

When Junior first came to us, he was a scrawny little tech specialist, a computer whiz nearly as proficient as Shunt without the peculiar habits. But his real goal was to become a full-fledged shooter. He has been working steadily, with the help of Trace and others, to learn the dark arts of warfare and to get himself into what we call "SEAL shape." He could still use a bit more meat on his bones, but he's made considerable progress—a real "blast from the past" that makes me prouder every day.

As soon as he realized that his guides were testing him, he began pumping his legs. Unencumbered by gear, he put his legs into overdrive. He caught them on a flat, then raced up a hill, cresting a good thirty yards ahead, and built on that lead as he headed downhill.

The road reached a dip after about a half mile, then angled to the left (and south) as it started up another hill. Junior was just reaching the low point when something shot out in front of him. It was small and low to the ground—and orange.

He hit the brakes, sure it was a tiger. The rear wheel flew out from under him, and Junior skidded into a semi-tumble against the fence—not particularly pleasant. He managed to slow himself just enough to avoid serious laceration, but got his clothes snagged and tangled.

He hunched down and began freeing himself, meanwhile glancing in the direction of the tiger.

Which wasn't a tiger, but a girl who had scampered through a nearby hole in the fence. She was crouched at the side of the dirt road, staring at him with eyes that seemed to take up half her face.

"Are you OK?" asked Junior as he unhooked the last prong from his shirt. "I'm sorry—I didn't see you."

The girl looked at Junior, screamed, and bolted away. He was shocked. I have that effect on people, but not Junior—he's a lot easier on the eyes, clearly taking after his mom.

"Wait," said Junior, rising.

A burst of automatic-weapons fire sent him diving to the ground. His first thought was that his two guides had made the same mistake he had. But when he turned to warn them he saw them approaching on their bikes, their INSAS assault rifles still strapped to their backs.

A fresh volley tore through the fence above him, pinging and ricocheting. Up on the right, about fifty yards into Bangladesh, a small crowd of people emerged from the heavy brush and dashed toward the hole in the barbed wire the little girl had used. Five or six men in shorts and black shirts ran several strides behind them, emptying assault rifles in their direction. With more chops than smarts, Junior jumped up and started yelling to the guards who'd been with him.

"Get them! Get them! Make them stop!" He pointed at the men on the other side of the border. "Get the bastards!"

The Indians pulled up on their bikes, dropping the vehicles beneath them as they pulled up their rifles and took aim—at the refugees who'd crossed over the border.

"What the *fuck*!" yelled Junior. "What are you doing!"

They didn't pay much attention to him—the men in the black T-shirts started directing their fire at the Indians, who scrambled for better positions. Except for the fence, there was no cover where they were, and so they retreated to a row of trees about twenty yards behind them.

With their pursuers distracted, the people who'd been running from the gunmen slipped under the fence and ran for the woods. The men in the black shirts split up; four followed while two stayed back. Junior was forgotten or missed in the confusion.

Being ignored is not one of Junior's favorite things. Violating the first law of tourism—never get involved in a foreign gunfight, especially when unarmed—he leapt to his feet and ran after the last man through the fence, tackling him a few strides from the trees. The man collapsed, his AK47 flying. Junior gave him two hard punches to the back of the neck and went for the gun.

Two hard punches to the back of the neck is one more than needed to incapacitate most people—if delivered to the right part of the neck. Apparently Junior missed the mark, for as he grabbed the rifle something grabbed his leg.

Then bit it.

Junior screamed as he fell, scooping up the rifle in the meantime—and getting a mouthful of dirt as he rolled to the ground, which ought to teach him a lesson about vocalizing on the battlefield.

He swung the rifle at his opponent, but despite a good bash to the face, the man's bicuspids remained firmly attached to the bottom of his calf. Junior reared back and pounded the tip of the barrel into the would-be cannibal's face. The muzzle strike collapsed the man's cheekbone and knocked him unconscious, but his bite was so fierce that when Junior pulled his leg free, a couple of teeth remained in his pant leg.

Bloody but uneaten, Junior looked around, trying to get his bearings. The Indian soldiers were shooting at the black shirts, who were prone and returning fire. Otherwise, everyone was in the woods, rushing through the thick foliage.

Cautiously, Junior began making his way toward the tree line. He paused a few feet in, unable to see either the gunmen or the people they were chasing. Finally, he spotted something bright against the dark brown floor of the woods a few yards away. It was the little girl he'd braked to avoid.

She looked up and spotted him, staring for a moment as if he were a space alien—which he might just as well have been, as far as she was concerned. The girl made a face, then started to run back into the trees.

"No, no, it's OK," Junior yelled, following. He found it difficult to duck through the branches, but managed to keep her in sight as she doubled back toward the fence.

The rifle fire had stopped. Concentrating on the child, Junior ran through the low brush at the edge of the woods, following up the embankment to the narrow road along the fence. Just as he closed to about five yards, he tripped and fell, sliding on his butt back onto the grass.

The girl screamed. He looked up but couldn't see her.

"I'm coming!" he shouted, and he began running toward her, moving in the direction of the hole in the fence. He glanced at the AK47, making sure it was ready.

The girl had snagged herself on the barbs of the fence a few feet from the hole. Trying to unhook herself, she'd only become more tangled.

"Relax, relax," said Junior, trying to calm her. "Ssshhh."

She cringed as he reached to try undoing her shirt from the hooks holding her. Tears were streaming down her cheeks.

"I'm not going to hurt you, honey," said Junior. "Shsssshhhh. Be quiet now."

Junior is in his early twenties, and his experience with children probably amounts to having watched the last installments of *Harry Potter* in a crowded theater. But he did his best to calm the child, talking to her in a quiet voice and trying as gently as possible to get her shirt undone. She was extremely jumpy, which didn't help matters—as he reached to unsnag her arm, she jerked, embedding one of the barbs in her back.

Her crying turned to a wail.

"All right, all right, relax," he pleaded. "Relax now. I'm going to help."

He put down the rifle and hovered over her, trying to work out the hooks without hurting her or getting her stuck worse. The girl's shrieks gradually lessened to whines, then to a series of soft, unsteady sobs.

"All right now, you're free," he told her, pulling the last barb away from her shirt. Prodding gently, he tapped her away from the fence. Suddenly, she leapt up into his arms.

"It's OK, it's OK," he told her.

But it wasn't, as Junior saw when he turned around.

The four gunmen who'd come across the border were standing a short distance away, their guns pointed at Junior and the girl.

Sometimes the best way to get out of a situation like that is to move boldly and forcefully. There was no way Junior could reach his gun, but he decided that didn't mean he was trapped.

"We're going back," said Junior, taking a step.

"No," said the tallest of the four men. He raised his rifle, making it clear that he had the girl's head in his sights. His English had a Bangladesh accent, though to Junior's untrained ear it sounded a lot like the Indian tongues he'd heard over the past day or so. "You come with us. That is what you will do now."

"I don't think so," insisted Junior, taking a step.

"We do."

The others raised their guns.

Junior didn't back down. He kept walking, leaving the gun behind, striding right for the four men. It was a gutsy thing to do, but then, I wouldn't have expected anything else.

Remarkably, two of the men stepped aside.

Junior kept his mouth tight, eyes hard, game-face firmly in place. He strode past the men.

"We'll be home soon," he whispered to the girl.

As the last word left his mouth, the butt of a rifle hit him across the back of the head, and sent him to the ground, unconscious.

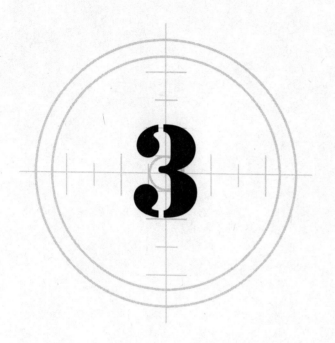

(1)

While all of this was going on, I was enjoying a festive lunch that included several different versions of beans, goat meat, and lamb. The spices improved with each serving. My hosts kept glancing at me from the corner of their eyes, trying to see if the chili and whatever other spices they had added would set my hair on fire. But the food was very tame; when you've had warm monkey brains (warm because the monkey is still squirming when you eat it) a few little chili peppers aren't going to bother you.

We were through the main courses and heading toward desserts when a young lieutenant walked briskly into the dining room to report that shots had been fired to the north. My hosts weren't particularly alarmed; gunfire along the border is an everyday occurrence. The commander ordered the lieutenant to organize a team to investigate.

"I wouldn't mind going with them," I said, getting up. "I need a little exercise after all that food."

For some reason this struck the commander as funny.

"You are exercising?" He patted his belly. Though not quite as fat as Buddha's, it was headed in that direction. "Exercise is for morning. After lunch, we will hear Captain Panchavati lecture on crossing numbers."

"I'd just as soon stretch my legs first," I said. Having already heard the captain lecture on general security measures just before the food arrived, I knew I'd need to do something to stay awake.

My legs didn't get much of a stretch—the lieutenant and two of his men headed to an eight-wheeled ATV in the lot maybe ten yards from the building where I'd been having lunch. The ATV looked like a swamp boat with wheels and no fan unit. Instead of a steering wheel it had a set of motorcycle-style handlebars. It wasn't exactly fast. Rumbling downhill we barely reached five miles an hour.

It didn't occur to me that Junior might be in any danger until we reached the hole under the fence. I saw bicycle marks on the road, and blood trailing across the dirt to the trees. Instantly I pulled out my sat phone. Junior didn't answer.

The lieutenant tried radioing the men who'd been with him, but also got no answer. He sent his men wading into the woods.

Tufts of clothing were hooked into the barbs near the fence, but it was impossible to tell who they belonged to. I began walking up along the fence line, training my ears to listen for human sounds—hushed voices, maybe, or better, footsteps through the brush.

Finally I heard something to the left, in trees beyond a short hill covered with thick weeds. Someone was running in my direction.

I ducked down and got ready to grab whoever it was. A white shirt shot out of the trees, running almost directly for me. It dodged left, then right, materializing into a person and pushing brush away as it went. When the runner was within five yards, I coiled myself, then sprang.

My knees had been battered during my African narco-pirate safari, but the pain had subsided to the point that I'd mostly forgotten about them. They apparently felt neglected, and gave me a sharp reminder as I sprang to grab the runner. I ignored them, concentrating on my target. He was a thin young man, so fragile that as I tackled him I thought I cracked half his bones.

His threadbare clothes didn't seem capable of holding a penny, let alone a weapon. He was so scrawny he looked like he'd hurt himself hitting me.

"Why are you running?" I demanded.

He just stared at me.

Something black flashed through the woods in the distance. It was one of the men who'd come over the border earlier, though at that point I had no idea who or even what it was. While my head was turned, the man I'd tackled jumped up and began running in the direction of the fence.

The man in black pulled his rifle up and began firing—probably at the runner, though the bullets came in my direction.

I started to get up, then fell immediately on my face as my knee gave way. That proved to be a good thing—either the man with the black shirt didn't see me or thought he'd killed me, because he ran directly toward me without stopping, intent on getting the other man. Just as he was passing, I threw out my arm and caught the back of his boot. He flew forward, tumbling into the bushes and losing the gun as he fell.

Had Murphy been on my side, he would have sent him into a tree. But that bastard has never been particularly friendly.

We both dove for the rifle. I grabbed it first, rolling it away from his grip. I lifted myself onto my left side, ready to shoot.

The man in the black shirt froze, fear in his eyes. My knee had me in a bad mood, but somehow I managed not to fire.

"Hands up," I told him.

He immediately complied.

The lieutenant I'd been with came trotting up from the road, where apparently he'd observed the entire encounter from a safe distance. He obviously has a real future as a C[2] officer.[20]

"Commander Marcinko—are you all right?" he asked. "You have captured a smuggler!"

He ran over to the man who had his hands up and punched him in the side of the head. Either the punch wasn't very hard or the man had a particularly high pain threshold, because the prisoner barely flinched. The lieutenant gave him a few more smacks, then a kick to his side. The prisoner took it stoically.

"Easy," I told the Indian. "You're going to hurt yourself."

"He is a criminal. A smuggler."

"What is he smuggling?" I asked.

"You name it, they bring it." The lieutenant yelled at the man in Bengali, the native language of Bangladesh. It's also commonly spoken on the Indian side of the border in Tripura.

The smuggler didn't answer. The lieutenant smacked him again, then hauled the man to his feet and began marching him toward the ATV.

A few minutes later, the lieutenant's two men emerged from the woods with Junior's escorts. The escorts told a greatly embellished tale of having been ambushed by dozens of black-shirted smugglers. The shirt color was significant, at least to the border guards, since it signaled that the men were part of a local gang known in English as the Shirkers. The leaders were Muslim deserters from the Indian army who had found refuge in Bangladesh.

I interrupted their tale of bravery—in their account, they'd each killed half a dozen before running out of ammo—to ask what had happened to Junior. They claimed they had seen him turning his bike around toward the base in fear.

"He should be there now," said the mouthier of the two. "He turned as soon as he saw them. Not a brave man."

Junior has his faults, but a lack of courage isn't one of them. I knew they were lying, even before I found his bike in the grass a short time later.

By then, more troops from the border guard station had arrived. While the lieutenant organized them into search parties, a sergeant with drooping eyebrows and thick forearms began asking the smuggler what he knew. The first two or three questions came in a calm voice; then the intensity level began to increase exponentially. By the sixth question, it was clear the man wasn't going to respond no matter how hard the words. The sergeant resorted to using his fists, first on the man's midsection, then on his face.

---

[20] Can't Cunt. You've been reading Rogue Warrior books for how long and you didn't know what that meant?

This didn't work either. If anything, it only seemed to stiffen his resolve not to say anything.

"Let me talk to him," I said, interrupting. "You're not going to get anywhere like that."

The sergeant was a little shorter than me, but wider—heavy without seeming fat. He blinked at me. Apparently no one had ever questioned his interrogation techniques.

"Commander, you should go back to camp," said the lieutenant. "We will carry on from here. We are used to these searches."

He pointed to the three groups he had organized, which were moving into the woods on the Indian side.

"If the smugglers are from Bangladesh, why the hell are you looking on this side of the border?" I asked. "Aren't they likely to have gone back over?"

The lieutenant smiled indulgently. "You do not understand our ways, Commander. We will see you back at the base."

While I was trying to make sense of the nonsensical, Junior was imprisoned in one of the gang's safe houses across the border. His captors had realized he was American, and while kidnapping was out of their line, they figured he would bring them a good amount of ransom if handled properly. With other things to worry about at the moment, they locked him with the goods they were planning to smuggle across the border after dark.

These goods happened to be poor Bangladeshis hoping to find work across the border, and willing to sell themselves into virtual slavery for it. A dozen men were packed into Junior's room, which measured roughly ten by twelve. They had been there for two days, waiting for their chance to get across the border. Women and children, including the little girl Junior had tried to rescue, were in the room next to them.

"Does anyone speak English?" Junior asked as soon as the door was closed behind him.

No one answered.

"English?" he asked again, raising his voice slightly. It was a small room, but no one seemed to hear him.

"English?" he repeated, this time even louder.

"Sshh," admonished one of the men. "Keep your voice down. Do not anger our jailers."

Junior lowered his voice to a whisper. "You can speak English?"

"Most of us can." The man, dark-skinned and skinny, looked about forty years old, with knotted fingers and deep wells around his eyes. "But reminding them of that is bad health. They think we are planning, like the others who left."

"How many got away?" asked another man, shorter and younger.

"I'm not sure," said Junior.

"They have some chained outside. Did you see them?"

Junior shook his head. He suspected that most if not all of the escapees were recaptured, but saying that felt too pessimistic.

The older man explained that most of the people had been in the house for several days. Tired of waiting, a few had hatched a plan to pry boards off the floor of the women's cell. The smugglers naturally objected, since that meant they wouldn't be paid.

Junior examined the walls and ceiling as the man talked. The three-room structure was made of clay bricks with a wood-shingle roof. The single window consisted of an opening filled by thin slats of wood—it wouldn't take much to break through them. Junior could see parts of the four other buildings in the small complex through the openings.

There was a commotion out in the courtyard. He craned his head but couldn't see.

"They're trying to decide what to do," said the older man. "They aren't sure whether to decide if he's dead or not."

"Who?"

"One of the guards. He was left behind in the gun battle. They think he is dead, shot—we could hear the gunfire. Weren't you there?"

"I was," admitted Junior. He wasn't sure how many details to give. "I didn't see anyone get shot."

The man listened some more.

"Are they going to look for him?" Junior asked.

The man shook his head.

"No. They are blaming the people who escaped. They are trying to decide whether to kill just the ones they returned, or all of us."

II

Less than a mile away as the crow flies, I was making a plan to find and then rescue my son. It was pretty damn clear that either the border guards had no clue, or weren't interested in putting themselves in danger to find him. And I sure as hell wasn't going to go meekly back to the outpost. The Indian commander assigned two men to escort me and the prisoner back. While they were pulling him to his feet, I took out my sat phone and called Shunt.

"Man, you know what time it is here?" he asked in a groggy voice.

"I need you to locate Junior."

"Uh, he's like, with you in India."

"Pull up the GPS locator map. I think he was kidnapped and taken across the border. Or he's lost somewhere in the woods."

"Hold on."

If I'd been in a better mood, I would have asked Shunt when he started sleeping at night—it's not like him. We don't break down our office costs by food items; if we did, I'm sure the coffee and caffeinated drink bill would look high enough to feed several third world countries.

"Just under a mile from you," he told me.

"I need you to send actual GPS coordinates to my phone," I said. "And stay on the line with me."

"Uh—"

"You got something better to do?"

"Not after I take a leak."

"Use an empty Coke can, Shunt. I need you on the line."

Back in his makeshift jail, Junior had just stepped away from the window when the door to the room flew open. Two of the black-shirt gangsters came in and began pushing the men out of the room. The first two were slow to realize what the men wanted; they were hurled against the wall on the other side of the threshold; after that, the others filed out as quickly as they could, more or less on their own power.

Junior ended up at the tail end of the line. The black shirt at the door held out his hand and said something in Bengali.

"You're to stay," said the man he'd been talking to.

"Where are they taking you?"

"Finally, to India to get some work." The man smiled. "Good luck."

Alone after the door was closed and locked, Junior went back to the window. He watched as two rows of refugees, men and women, were marched into the small compound. As soon as they stopped, the black shirts began opening fire.

Junior shouted and pounded helplessly on the slat window, which despite his earlier assessment failed to give way. The gunfire continued, drowning out his yells.

At the right side of the courtyard, he saw the little girl whom he'd unhooked from the fence. She was frozen, staring at the soldiers gunning down the others.

"Run!" yelled Junior. "Run!"

She looked in his direction, then bolted. At the same moment, bullets began slicing the ground near her.

"Son of a bitch!" yelled Junior. "Run!"

He punched the slat window. When it didn't budge, he spun and ran full speed at the door to the room, crashing into it and tumbling free, into the hallway.

"You, here," I said to the shorter of the two men who'd been assigned to escort me to the border guard camp. "Give me that gun."

The man opened his mouth to object. I snatched the rifle before he could talk. It was loaded with a twenty-round magazine. I held out my hand and demanded the rest of his supply—which amounted to a grand total of two more magazines.

"What are you doing?" asked the other man, a sergeant well past retirement age.

"My son is on the other side of the border. I'm going to go get him. Are you coming with me?"

The sergeant turned pale. "We have to escort the prisoner."

"Great—I'll take your ammo, too."

"I do not have a rifle."

"I will come," said the private who'd given up his gun. He still had a sidearm.

The sergeant started to object.

"You're welcome to try and stop me," I told him, heading toward the hole in the fence.

Junior bounced off the wall to his feet and charged down the small hallway to the empty front room. Sliding on his heels as he reached the front door, he grabbed at the handle and threw it open.

One of the black-shirted thugs was standing a few feet away, his back to the house. Junior bowled him over. Flailing wildly—his martial arts teachers would have been appalled—he knocked the guard unconscious and scooped up his rifle.

The gunfire in the courtyard had reached a crescendo, the metal rap of half a dozen guns echoing against the hills on both sides of the border. Junior ran like a wildman, barely breathing as he raised the gun and prepared to fire.

He halted just before the corner of the yard. The little girl lay at his feet, dead, her orange shirt soaked with blood.

There's nothing like the sound of gunfire in the distance to make a Rogue's heart go all pitter-patter. I quickened my pace, moving up along the side of a narrow but well-trodden trail that went nearly straight up a thirty-foot rise and led through a fallow farm field. The throb in my knee had faded, as if it couldn't quite keep up with me.

The same was true, though in this case literally, of the private who had come to help me. By the time I reached the field, he trailed a good twenty yards behind.

The field was open for about a hundred yards. I sprinted for the first ten, then dropped to a trot for the rest, the pain in my knee gradually catching up as my speed fell. I reached the woods and grabbed for my sat phone, wanting an update from Shunt.

"You're five hundred and fifty three meters away," he said. "I tried getting Junior on the phone, but he didn't answer."

"I know. I tried myself."

"You sound tired."

"Fuck you."

I pushed on through the trees. What had looked like a thick jungle from the field was actually a set of undulating hills with widely spaced trees. Bushes and smaller trees about a man's height filled in the gaps, but there was still plenty of room to move through.

The gunfire had stopped by the time I got close enough to see the cluster of houses where the bandits were camped. A wire livestock fence, its strands forming large rectangular boxes, enclosed the entire area. I could see part of what looked like a military vehicle parked just beyond the fence; rather than green it was painted black, the finish worn and full in sunlight.

The border guard who'd been following me slipped in behind me.

"What's your name?" I asked.

"Sil."

"Can you understand my accent?" I asked him.

"I understand."

He didn't sound convincing, but there wasn't any time to give him a competency exam.

"I'm going to move up to the fence and reconnoiter," I said, pointing to the area of the compound near the road, which was on our right. "I want you to move a little closer to the road. We don't shoot until I say so, all right?"

"Yes. Do not shoot until ordered."

"Make sure you can see me. If I wave to you, come forward. Got that?"

"Come forward with wave."

"Good."

Head low, I started trotting toward the fence. After having UAVs and satellite photos and laser dazzlers, this was a very old-school operation.

Modern's better. Though I would trade an army's worth of high-tech gadgets for a single SEAL any day of the week.

Screened by the truck, I ran up toward the compound, searching for a good vantage. I found one near the fence, where a row of bushes provided cover. Still, much of the view was blocked by the nearby building. Two or three men were standing out of sight. They sounded angry, but I had no idea what they were saying.

I turned and signaled to Sil. He made a little more noise running than I would have liked—there was something jangling in his pockets—but he reached the fence without attracting any attention.

"Can you hear what they are saying?" I asked.

"Yes." Sil listened for a few moments. "Bury the bodies."

That made me feel all warm and fuzzy.

"Come with me," I told him. "Stay low. Cover my back."

I moved along the fence, pausing a few feet from the entrance as the interior of the compound came into view. I saw a little more than half of the yard, which was empty except for two large feed troughs.

And bodies. A pair lay a few yards from the nearest trough. Neither of them looked like Junior, but that was small comfort.

Making sure Sil was behind me, I ran forward to the building nearest the entrance to the compound. Checking quickly through the slats and seeing no one there, I moved up to the corner, cleared the area in front of me, and then began moving down the side of the house.

Two men in black shirts walked over to the dead men, arguing.

I raised the rifle. Double-tap left, double-tap right.

Argument over.

I swung out to my right, looking for anyone else in the yard. A man came flying from the building I was watching. He was roughly Junior's size, and for a second my eyes saw what my mind wanted them to see—my son.

By the time I realized my mistake, the black shirt already had the barrel of his weapon pointed at me. A shot rang out; the man fell sideways, sliding onto the ground.

Sil had nailed him.

Three down, but how many to go?

There were more bodies, at least a dozen, on the far side of the compound, next to another of the buildings. I did my best to ignore them.

Nothing else moved. The place was quiet. I took out the sat phone to talk to Shunt.

"Where is he?"

"Twenty yards due east. I'm looking at a sat image from yesterday," he said. "You see the building?"

"Yeah, all right."

"What's going on?"

"I'm teaching the Bangladeshi to fish."

I looked at Sil, then pointed at myself and the building. "I'm going in. Cover me when I run. Then move up, cover the outside."

He gave me a thumbs-up, and I started to run.

The door to the building was on the right, angled away from my view. I went to the window, checked briefly but couldn't see much. Then I moved to the corner of the building.

There was a body on the ground. I could only see his legs; the pants were khaki, just like Junior's.

Damn.

Sil ran up behind me. Fighting emotion, I crouched down and began crawling on my haunches toward the body. After a few feet, I could see that he didn't have a shirt, and his coppery torso was darker than Junior's, and not as developed. He was one of the gang members, his upper body scarred in several places. He was still breathing.

Instinctively, I reached for my knife, only to remember that I wasn't carrying one. No problem. I put his neck in my arms and twisted.

Sil moved to the corner behind me. I went to the doorway and listened. I didn't hear anything.

"Junior," I said, as softly as I could. "Junior?"

Nothing.

I raised my voice a bit.

"Junior, it's me."

There was still nothing. I pushed in, gun ready, but at the same time aware that it might be Junior in my sights.

The room was empty. I moved around it left to right, hugging the walls until I reached the door to the short hallway and other rooms. I crouched down about as low as my knee could take without complaining.

Clear.

Something was on the floor a few feet away.

Junior's satellite phone. Murphy had pulled it from his pocket and dropped it on the ground as he ran from the room.

My heart was beating overtime, not because I was in a particularly large amount of danger; I've been in far worse situations. What was amping me up was the fact that I was looking for Junior. I told myself I would have been nervous about any member of my team, but I think I knew deep down that I was lying, or trying to.

Just as in SEAL Team Six, we add a shooter to the team by consensus—everybody in the room gets a say. Yes, as top dog I may have the biggest bark, but the team only works when everyone's a partner. You have to trust the person who's got your back. Junior had seen a lot of action with us, but he was still a probationary shooter, trying to work his way into field operations from support.

Until now, the questions about him were the same ones we ask of everyone: How's he going to react to pressure? What's his breaking point? Etc., etc.

What I hadn't done was ask myself the question: How would I react when he was in danger?

He'd been with us in tight spots before, yet somehow this one felt different. It was *my* reaction that was different. I was worried about him. I'd always treated him the same as everyone else—hell, I was probably harder on him. But I had to ask myself, even as I was figuring out where we would go next, could I deal with his getting hurt?

I'd rather lose my proverbial left nut than see one of my people hurt. In Junior's case, I couldn't even work the math for a trade.

There were still three more buildings to check.

"That building," I told Sil, pointing at the next one. "Same routine."

"I think camp empty," he said.

"We don't take it for granted," I told him. "Cover me."

The next building was larger than the others, but laid out roughly the same. The front room looked like a campground brought inside, with blankets and pillows on the floor and a small hibachi-like stove in the corner. There were some papers piled haphazardly near the wall, along with a laptop.

The rest of the rooms were used as sleeping quarters. The stench of sweat got thicker as I went, until in the last room I nearly choked with it. But the building was clear.

"Next one," I told Sil as I came outside.

He wasn't there.

"Sil," I growled, keeping my voice low. "Where the hell are you?"

I felt like I was in a teenager slasher movie, looking for my date. Backing against the front of the building, I slid over to the corner and peeked around. Sil was sitting on the ground, a big smile on his face.

A smile I knew too well. As I watched, his head flopped to the side. The rest of his body slid to the ground.

Bullets slammed into the building above my head. I threw myself down, hunkering into the dirt, unable to see where the shots were coming from, let alone who was doing the shooting.

The gunfire quickly stopped, the gunman trying for a better position. As he moved, I realized he must have been firing from the corner of the truck or the woods farther back.

I retreated on my belly to the corner of the building, then rolled around it, checking quickly to make sure I hadn't just blundered into someone's sights. The yard was clear. I could see all the way to the fence and the slight rise beyond it.

A burst of shots pinged into the dirt a few yards away. The gunman was at the corner of one of the buildings I hadn't checked. Then a second man appeared behind him, standing over the crouched figure and firing as well. I fired two bursts from my rifle, then rolled right, pushing to the side of the nearest building.

If I'd been in their position, I would have split up, with one circling around while the other held me in place with covering fire. I decided to head off the flanker, racing to the far end of the building just in time to see one of the gunmen running to my right about sixty feet away, trying to circle the long way around. He went down as I fired, diving to the ground. Unsure if I'd gotten him or not, I started moving toward him, but before I got there a wave of bullets from the other gunman drove me back.

Dead or not, the man I'd shot lay still on the ground. I decided to concentrate on the one I knew was alive. I went back along the building and dashed across to the place where I'd started, intending to either engage him from there or, if he had retreated, come around from that direction.

Sil's body lay slumped where I had left it. By now I was low on ammo for the rifle. So I took his pistol and began searching his body for spare magazine boxes.

As I did, I saw someone in a black shirt aiming an AK47 at me from near the truck.

(III)

It wasn't my life that flashed before my eyes at that moment, it was something far lighter and quicker, loud and white and then suddenly black, more than enough to blind me and throw me down to the ground.

The next thing I knew, Junior was standing over me.

Damn, I thought, *I am in heaven.*

Heaven? Me? Obviously, God has a very strong sense of humor.

"Dad. Up," said Junior. "There's still one of them in the compound."

"What the hell?"

"I threw the flash-bang a little too far. I needed to divert his attention."

"Who?"

He pointed to my right. "The guy I killed."

A bullet-ridden body lay to the right of me, just past the corner. Junior had seen him approaching and shot him. I couldn't have done better myself.

"There's one behind the back of this building," said Junior. "See if you can pin him down and I'll swing around the other way."

Junior ran off before I could stop him. It wasn't the worst idea in the world, though I would have preferred it if I was the one in motion, taking the bigger risk. I crawled back to the edge of the building. As soon as I ducked my head out at the bottom of the corner, bullets ripped into the wall. I pulled back quickly, then stuck the gun out and began firing maniacally, trying to draw his attention.

The tango was happy to comply. He fired several dozen shots. I couldn't quite hear if the gun had clicked empty, but poked out and fired anyway.

Boom . . . crash—Junior threw another grenade.

The dust had barely settled when I heard a bloodcurdling scream. If you can imagine what a Hound of Hell might sound like when someone steps on his tail, you'll have about half the noise I heard. The other half was several decibels higher and four times as fierce.

I got up and peered around the corner. Junior was smashing the barrel end of his gun into the black-shirted torso. There wasn't much left of the body when I got there, even though he couldn't have been more than forty feet away.

"He killed her. He shot her in cold blood." Tears were streaming down Junior's face as he raged. "The bastards gunned them all down like fucking paper dolls. Kids and everything."

He kept hitting the body, not stopping until I pulled him away.

"Keep your head," I yelled. "We haven't cleared the place."

"This motherfucker. This mother—"

"All right, all right, I get it. Let's go. We're going back."

"We have to bury them."

"Bury these guys?"

"The victims. The little girl."

"No, Junior. Man up now. We are getting *out* of here before we get killed. We're down to a pistol and whatever bullets are in that gun."

"I have one more mag."

"That's my point. The border patrol can send over troops. Come on."

He didn't entirely snap out of it, but he did regain enough of his senses to come with me as I tugged him toward the gate.

"You're hurt," he mumbled as we went down the path.

"No."

"You're limping."

"My knee's stiff. That's all."

He came over and put his shoulder under mine, helping me back toward the fence. I didn't really need his support, but it took his mind off the girl, and his anger.

The commander of the border guards gave me the usual business you'd expect from a C^2 officer, explaining how tricky the border situation was and how difficult dealing with the smugglers could be.

I wasn't in much of a mood to hear it, so I cut him off.

"We had to leave your man's body up there," I said. "Delhi will want him back. Get a patrol together and I'll show them where he is."

"We must call for permission," said the commander.

"If you do that, it'll take days. On the other hand, if you were trying to rescue a lost American visitor . . ."

Out of excuses, the commander smiled. He called the lieutenant I had met earlier and tasked him to lead the group back. A dozen men, the best of the troop, were mustered.

Junior stalked back and forth in the compound as they were gathering, restless. I've seen rabid dogs that were calmer. Finally we mounted up, with half the troop on bicycle and the rest divided in a pair of ATVs. The patrol was methodical to the point of madness, with scouts moving a short distance forward before the rest of the unit came up, and a flanking unit dismounting and moving parallel to the main group through the low jungle brush. The Indians formed up for an assault as they reached the border. Finding no opposition, they began moving toward the enemy camp. They secured the perimeter in what seemed like slow motion, then began taking down the compound building by building.

Junior and I stayed with the lieutenant. I'd remembered seeing a laptop in one of the buildings, and decided I would retrieve it; I didn't intend on alerting the Indians. The lieutenant barely paid attention to us, and it was easy to slip away as the last building was secured. I went back to the building that the smugglers had used as a headquarters, and walked to the wall where the laptop had been.

It was gone. So were the papers that had been there. Outside, the bodies of the smugglers had been retrieved as well.

The lieutenant organized a burial detail. Junior borrowed a shovel from one of the men, and buried the little girl himself.

The sun was starting to set by the time we got back. The commander wasn't much of a military leader, but he did have a good idea of how to treat guests—he invited us to his private hut for drinks before dinner. Once there, he produced gin. And not just any gin.

"I have heard that you are a fan," he said, whisking a bottle of Bombay Sapphire out from his cabinet. "Would you like it on the rocks?"

"As long as that means ice."

Junior insisted he would drink only water. He stayed with it as the commander and I went several rounds, trading stories and refills. You've heard most of the old war stories the commander pried out of me, so we'll jump back to Africa and Djibouti, where Trace and the boys were trying to fill in the gaps and wait for the call to cell phone Number 2 to tell them what to do.

[IV]

While for most normal human beings there was plenty to do, Trace considered the assignment as basically being "sit and twiddle your thumbs."

Actually, she had a more colorful idea of what her thumbs were doing, but we'll leave that out so as not to upset the librarians.

For the record, Shunt had infiltrated the bank's computer network with his usual aplomb, but all that really did was make it possible for us to use the ATM without withdrawal fees. There was no Allah's Rule account at the bank—a fact that was confirmed that afternoon, when the bank was held up a second time.

The second wave of robbers was bigger, and less merciful. They shot everyone in sight. Trace was retrieving Mongoose at the time, and though the CIA had suggested to its local counterparts that the bank be watched, no one seemed to have arrived in time to record the robbery, much less prevent it. Calls went out to watch all the local banks for deposits, even though the drug smugglers' attitude toward banks was pretty obvious at that point.

Why rob the bank? You ended up with the cash, and maybe a little bonus. There was no electronic transaction number or other data to trace. Marked bills could be disposed of elsewhere with impunity—it had been a relatively small down payment, after all.

Of course, you could also ask, why not skip the drug-smuggling racket and rob banks for a living?

Garrett, our CIA secret agent man, was providing a lot more cooperation than Magoo had promised—no doubt thanks to his extracurricular interest in Trace. The evening I left, they convened a debrief session at a mutually agreeable hotel bar.

"I got some more information on that prescription drug setup," said Garrett. "It's in Bangladesh. They have a shipment at sea right now. I don't think it's the same one, but you guys might want to check it out."

Talk about whispering sweet nothings in a girl's ear. Trace responded immediately.

"Why are you telling me this?" she asked.

"I—uh—well, I thought you might, you know, uh, be interested. The ship, uh, *Indiamotion*. Well, um, huh?"

Trace's interest had been drawn to a shifty-looking man with a beard sitting several tables away, speaking with two equally shifty-looking individuals. Garrett followed her gaze, then tapped her hand.

"You spotted him, huh?" said Garrett.

"Yes," said Trace.

"Hoshang Zal is the number-two guy in al-Quds. A real scumbag."

"Interesting."

Al-Quds is the export arm of the Iranian Revolution. Set up to help groups like Hezbollah, al-Quds (also called the Quds Force, Qods, Ghods, Gonad Rippers, and a variety of less flattering names) is charged with bringing the Iranian Islamic Revolution to other countries. While Israel has been the primary target of their beneficence, Quds has done its best to stir trouble up in other areas. They're a subset of the Iranian Revolutionary Guard, a group very much like our own Boy Scouts, if our Boy Scouts were demonic sociopathic psycho jobs.

No slur intended on the Boy Scouts, who are none of those things.

Hoshang Zal was the branch manager for the organization's Yemen operation, as Trace soon learned from Garrett. As such, he was actively directing operations in Yemen to undermine the legitimate government, back the rebels, and when possible, attack Westerners and their facilities. He hadn't been all that successful on the last count, mostly because any Westerner with any sense had left Yemen long ago. But he was high on the Christians in Action list of International Slimeballs.

"The main terror group in Yemen is al Qaeda in the Arabian Peninsula," noted young Mr. Garrett. "These guys have been trying to move in over the last several months. They've only been somewhat successful. They appeal to Shiites, and there aren't as many as there are Sunni."

Actually, the Shiite population runs about 42 percent, with Sunnis making up 55 percent of the overall census count. There are significant divisions within each subset—most Sunnis in Yemen are Shafi'i, for example, but other sects are represented—but for our purposes it's enough to know than Quds and al Qaeda hated each other only slightly less than they hated us.

"Why don't you take him out?" Trace asked.

"If he were in Yemen, we'd take him down straight away," said Garrett. "Drone strike, sniper, car accident—he'd be gone. But as long as he stays in Djibouti, we can't touch him."

"Why not?"

Garrett shrugged. The decision had been made many levels above him in the government food chain. In fact, the whole matter belonged in the very thick file labeled: *BS Restrictions in the War on Terror / Diplomacy Department*, with a mention also in the *Political Correctness* tab. While the CIA and Defense Department *can* make attacks on declared enemies of the

United States, and *can* help allies, no attack can be made if said enemies are *not* in the declared war zones. In other words, even if we know exactly what the bad guy is doing, even if we watch him do bad things, we can't get him if he's doing these things in most places of the world. Kind of like him yelling "Ollie-Ollie-osen-free" in freeze tag when you were a kid. And that's on top of a myriad of other requirements and regulations, an insane finding process involving everyone from the National Security Director to the White House janitor, and a decision-making process that appears to involve a dartboard.[21]

Garrett had played a small role in watching Hoshang in Djibouti a few months before, and plied Trace with various details over the course of two more drinks. Most of these details consisted of complaints about how his bosses refused to let him do anything about the bastard. How much of this was bravado designed to get Trace into bed is impossible to calculate, but enough of it was true that Trace went back to her hotel room (alone) and immediately called Shunt for information on Hoshang. After the requisite grouching about how overworked he was, Shunt found and forwarded a dossier on *Monsieur Hoshang Zal, le terroriste* (lifted from an intelligence agency not to be named) for her perusal.

The dossier confirmed Garrett's earlier assessment that Hoshang wasn't actually connected to our operation. Still, I doubt Trace finished translating the first paragraph before deciding to make Hoshang her pet project while killing time waiting for the drugs to land.

---

[21] The situation is somewhat more complicated than I'm detailing here, but that only means it's worse, not better. If you want to delve into it a bit, Google "Osama Moustafa Hassan Nasr" and "Abu Omarcheck" and read about the CIA agents and the operation in Italy that resulted in murder charges. Admittedly, this involved the Italian justice system, an oxymoron to be sure, but still . . .

[V]

This is not Somalia," insisted Abdi the next morning when Trace sat down with him and the boys to explain what she wanted to do. "You cannot buy explosives at the market."

"I don't know," said Mongoose. "Some of the stuff Shotgun's eating looked pretty explosive to me."

Shotgun smiled and continued chewing.

"We can make a small bomb with some mortar charges," said Mongoose, turning serious. He's one of our demo experts. "Or hell, I haven't used fertilizer in a long time."

"You are going to blow up innocent people?" sputtered Abdi. "You cannot, cannot do that."

"Relax," said Trace. "No one else is going to be hurt. Just the terrorist."

"How do you guarantee this?"

"We'll take care of it. Don't worry."

As Trace pointed out later, Abdi was undergoing a transformation. He'd started out pretty selfish, concerned only about himself and getting away with the most money he could manage. But now he was thinking about innocent people.

It wasn't the world's most dramatic development, but it was a start.

"Besides, an explosion is too obvious," added Trace. "Our friend here needs to die . . . artistically."

"Blowing his head off with a sixty would be artistic," said Shotgun, using slang to refer to a machine gun (after the M60). "The blood would splatter very nicely."

"Car bombs can be just as pretty," insisted Mongoose.

"I'm thinking of something more creative," said Trace, getting up from the table.

Bus service in Djibouti was erratic at best, but the drivers themselves were universally hailed for their professionalism. They unfailingly hit every stop, and always halted promptly for pedestrians in the streets. So as the battered city bus bore down on the man crossing the street, he paid it no mind, continuing across.

Until the bus sped up and veered directly for him.

The man glanced over his shoulder, then started to hurry across, tripping as he did. The bus loomed down. The man cringed. Suddenly, Abdi darted from the side of the street. Running all out, he dove and managed to push the man just out of reach of the bus's tire as it sped past.

"Ugh," said the man on the ground. It was Hoshang Zal—the Iranian agent.

"Are you OK?" asked Abdi in Somali.

Two men rushed from the other side before Hoshang could answer. One of them grabbed Abdi and began pulling him across the street.

"No—leave him. He save my life," said Hoshang in Arabic. "The Prophet, blessed be his name, must have sent him."

Two blocks away, the bus driver pulled against the curb, tossed open the door, and bounded down the steps, a bag of Twinkies in his hand. His stunned passengers—picked up at random after the bus left early from the garage on the other side of town—sat in shock.

"What took so long?" asked Mongoose, who was waiting with a pair of motorcycles a few yards away.

"Guy couldn't make up his mind where he was going," said Shotgun. "I must have circled that damn block a dozen times."

"Figures."

"Think we can stop and get some food somewhere? I just ate my last Twinkie."

A block away, Trace was listening to the eavesdropping device they had planted in Abdi's clothes. The Qud leader and his companions were talking in Arabic; the conversation was translated in real time by our computer system back in the States. The English was then piped as text to her iPad.

"Please," said Abdi in Somali. "I do not understand well what you are saying."

"You are not meant to understand," answered Hoshang in French.

"Uh?" Abdi shook his head. This time he wasn't pretending—unlike Arabic, which he could understand reasonably well, he couldn't speak French at all.

"Can you speak any English?" demanded Hoshang, frustrated.

"A little English, yes. Somali—that is my language."

"A tongue for dogs. Why do you not know Arabic?"

"I can say my prayers."

"Get rid of him," said one of the guards in Arabic. "Pay him. A few cents will change his world."

"Why are you in Djibouti?" asked Hoshang instead.

"I am for work."

"And you have it?"

Abdi shook his head. "I can do many things. I have worked in restaurants. I have driven cars. I went school and learned English and—"

Hoshang spit and said a few curse words in Arabic to the effect that schools were only palaces of propaganda where stupid fools were filled with the nonsense of Western lies. Abdi held out his hands, indicating he didn't understand; Hoshang repeated it, without the curses, in English.

"I had a good teacher," said Abdi. "Imam Muhammad Shirazi."

"Ah." Hoshang's voice lost its condescending tone. "You are a brother with al-Shirazi?"

"I am only a humble man," said Abdi.

"He seems more like al-Shabaab," said the henchman. "A spy against us."

In Somalia, al-Shabaab is an important Islamic militant group—assuming that's what we're calling murderers these days. The group, which probably has more foreigners in its leadership than native Somalis, is funded by al Qaeda. Its radical Sunni members are extremely hostile to Shi'ites, and presumably would be Hoshang's enemies.

"Are you with al-Shabaab?" said Abdi, pretending to be terror stricken. He stopped on the street, and took a step back. Hoshang grabbed his arm.

"Relax, brother, you are among friends, if Shirazi is your teacher."

"He is."

"You will stay with us, and we will reward you with a job," said Hoshang. "Come along to the harbor. I have to meet with someone."

Hoshang had recently received a text from his superiors instructing him to meet with a crewman of a ship that had just arrived from Greece. The man had information about a load of guns, which were to be included in a shipment of wheat bound for Ethiopia. We knew about the message because it had actually been sent by Shunt, who is as adept at breaking into texting systems as he is to e-mail.[22]

Hoshang and his men headed for an SUV Trace had identified earlier as his, thanks to a photo in the dossier. She'd already taken the precaution of putting a GPS transmitter under the chassis to make it easier to track.

But instead of getting into the SUV, they continued walking down the street. Worrying that Hoshang suspected he was being followed, Trace turned her car down another block, circling around.

"They're still on foot," she said.

Though small by Western standards, the houses that surrounded them on the block were considered middle class here. Built within the past two or

---

[22] We should also credit the afore-not-mentioned intelligence service, whose "borrowed" dossier included the information that helped Shunt make the proper connections.

three years, they looked like down-sized duplexes; in fact they were four-family units, with two full apartments back to back as well as side to side. Hoshang had a mistress who lived in a house at the end of the street, which Trace had under surveillance thanks to one of our video bugs.

The residents of this area were relatively prosperous, most with jobs at the port, the larger businesses in town, or the railroad that ran to Ethiopia. They didn't make much money by Western standards—a few hundred dollars a month at most—but they were far better off than their neighbors who lived in the slum just to the west, on the other side of the main road. While not the worst in the world—we'd seen some of those in India—the place was a collection of shanties, lean-tos, and makeshift tents. It, too, was only a few years old, bacterial mold on the side of a dump.

Shotgun and Mongoose drove their bikes off the main road, closing the gap with Hoshang to two blocks. The narrow streets and alleys were not ideal, even on a motorcycle—there was barely room to turn around, and it was too easy to get ambushed or cut off. But there was no choice; they couldn't leave Abdi on his own.

Even with Trace giving them directions, they were lost within a few minutes. People, women and children mostly, watched from outside the hovels, a few working very small pots over infinitesimal fires, but most just sitting either inside or out, staring blankly at the two foreigners as they passed. They were wearing helmets and the bikes were battered, but it was clear they were out of place.

The gap between them and Abdi increased. After a few minutes of trying to steer them closer, Trace gave up and had them back out to the wide street where they'd come in.

"Circle around to the north," she told them. "He must be using the narrow streets to lose any tails. Keep your distance."

Meanwhile, Hoshang led Abdi and the others to a small shack on the far side of the small slum. He pushed aside the blanket that covered the doorway and ducked his head to get through the low frame. Abdi started to follow, but one of the guards held his arm out to keep him back.

Hoshang and the guard came out a few moments later. The guard held what looked like a coat in his hands. Hoshang walked over to Abdi and smiled at him.

"Today, you are blessed," he said. He gestured to the other man. "Today you become a martyr. Put on the vest."

Abdi hesitated.

"Are you a believer or not?" said Hoshang calmly.

Abdi faced a choice: he could either take the suicide vest and hope he could somehow avoid detonating it, or he could prove he was a liar and be killed on the spot.

He took the vest.

"Damn," said Mongoose when Trace told him and Shotgun what was going on.

"Let's grab the bastards," said Shotgun. "The hell with making this look like an accident."

"How far away are you?" asked Trace.

"Six or seven blocks," said Mongoose.

"Tighten it up. They're on the north side of the ghetto—they're on regular streets now."

Mongoose and Shotgun got there just in time to see Abdi in the passenger seat of a Nissan pickup, eyes wide and a look of sheer terror on his face as the truck pulled away from the curb.

"Murphy's kicking our ass," muttered Mongoose.

"We ain't doing too bad a job ourselves," said Shotgun.

"Follow Abdi," said Trace. "I'll watch Hoshang."

"Should have just blown the bastard up," said Mongoose. "We'd be done by now, and Abdi'd be safe."

"Blowing shit up doesn't solve everything," said Shotgun.

"Just most things."

The boys followed the truck as it turned onto N2, the main highway that led to the waterfront. As they passed the soccer stadium, they worked out a plan.

"I'm going to ride up next to the driver and shoot him through the head," Mongoose told Shotgun. "You come around the other side and grab Abdi in case he jumps or whatever."

"Works for me. Think we should warn him?" Trace had given Abdi a cell phone, and Shotgun wanted to call him.

"Probably won't answer. But give it a shot."

"What if the driver has the phone, or Qud-shit[23]?"

"Just say 'duck,' nothing else."

"Yeah. Maybe I should quack."

In the truck, the sheer amount of sweat pouring off Abdi's body was matched only by the number of prayers that were passing through his lips. He practically bolted through the roof of the truck when his cell phone began to vibrate.

---

[23] The boys' lovingly applied nickname for Hoshang.

"What?" demanded the driver. He said it in Arabic, but the meaning was obvious.

"Ph-ph-ph—" Abdi reached into his pocket and held out the phone, which was still vibrating.

The driver gestured with his hand that Abdi should throw the phone out the window. Abdi answered it instead, speaking Somali.

"Duck!" said Shotgun. *"Duck!"*

Abdi turned to his left—just in time to see Mongoose pull parallel to the truck and raise his pistol.

Abdi pushed his head down. Mongoose fired point-blank into the driver's turned head.

The truck veered to the left, crossing into the oncoming lane. Clipped by a passing Nissan, it veered back, plowing across a narrow divider and into a traffic circle that formed one of the hubs of the downtown area. The front wheels struck the rounded curb marking off the circle, sending the truck headlong into the monument at the center—a bizarre, life-size sculpture of dancing dolphins.[24]

"Kick ass," yelled Shotgun approvingly.

The truck barreled over one of the metal mammals and continued across the traffic, hitting a large truck ferrying stone from a quarry before rebounding into the lot of a commercial building. Shotgun skidded around the dump truck and pulled next to the pickup as its radiator gave way with a huge burst of steam.

Abdi, in a state of shock, fumbled for the handle of the door. Shotgun, straddling his bike, yanked it open, then reached in and lifted the light-boned Somali out.

Mongoose had sped ahead and had to backtrack to the lot. When he got there, he put another round in the driver's head, just to be sure he was dead.

"We need to go," yelled Mongoose. Onlookers were gathering.

"Hold on to my back!" Shotgun barked to Abdi, plopping him onto the seat behind him.

"Go east," said Mongoose. "We'll circle back to the docks later."

"Aye, aye, captain," said Shotgun, jerking the bike around and setting off.

While the boys were playing motocross, Trace followed Hoshang and his remaining minion to the dock area. She drove to the Avenue General Galileni,[25] taking a left to scoot around yet another traffic circle. She drove

---

[24] I have no idea. I'm not an expert on art.

[25] French colonial officer and hero of World War I. By the way, the name was spelled wrong on Google Earth the last time I checked.

past a row of warehouse buildings, most large and gleaming, before spotting Hoshang getting out of his vehicle behind the last ship docked along the pier.

Though tempted to try and run him down, Trace decided he could easily escape by jumping into the water, and instead drove past, parking behind one of the large cargo holding facilities and getting out.

That took no more than thirty seconds, but in that time, Hoshang disappeared.

Three dozen or so men were working along the pier area, mostly coming and going from the ships. There were the usual assortment of crates, miscellaneous stacks of materials, and a pair of forklifts.

Actually, there were *four* forklifts, two more than she expected. Which greatly complicated matters.

Trace walked quickly to the nearest forklift. She reached under the dash, groping for the radio control she'd left earlier in the day.

It wasn't there. She had the wrong forklift.

Hiking the long skirt she'd worn to fit in with the locals, Trace trotted to the next one. A nearby worker shouted something to her. Trace ignored him, sliding into the seat and once more trying to locate the large boxy controller she'd taped under the dash.

No joy. Somewhere, Murphy giggled. How he had managed to slip two more forklifts onto the dock in the barely two hours since Trace and the boys had set things up is a mystery. But then again, so is everything about Murphy.

The man who'd yelled at her had gone to another forklift, started it, and was driving away. Trace realized *that* inevitably would be the one she wanted. But as she started to pursue him, she saw Hoshang walking down the gangplank of the ship on her right. She veered left, heading for a pile of crates as she formulated a new, simpler plan. She hooked the vehicle's front teeth into the bottom skid, backed up, then leaned to her right to see where her target had gone.

Behind another row of boxes. Still walking slowly, and alone.

Trace veered a little too sharply, and the forklift started to lean on two wheels. She quickly leaned back, but the disruption was enough to cause the crates she'd grabbed to slide off the forks. The top box slid from the stack, and the second followed. They exploded against the wharf's macadam, splattering their contents: several million marbles shot across the pier.

Trace put the little vehicle into reverse, then spun around. Hoshang was behind her by now, almost to his truck. Trace stepped on the gas, and the forklift jerked forward—then began skidding uncontrollably on the flood of marbles she had unleashed.

The scene was worthy of Buster Keaton, if not the Three Stooges, but Trace was not a film buff. The unstable forklift skidded sideways and then went over, forcing her to abandon ship. She landed on both feet, retrieved her pistol from beneath her skirt, and found herself facing the car. There was a moment, a very brief one, when Trace and the two occupants of the vehicle saw each other and stared.

That passed with Trace's first shot, taking the man in the passenger seat.

It was only after she pumped the second bullet into the man that she realized that he was the bodyguard, not Hoshang—the Iranian spymaster had decided to take the wheel himself.

Had he thrown the car into reverse and stepped on the gas, he could almost surely have escaped; Trace had come with no backup, and the path to the road was open. How long he might have lived after that, having pissed her off, is anyone's guess.

But once a psychotic killer, always a psychotic killer, and rather than trying to get away, Hoshang did what came naturally—he stepped on the gas and tried to run Trace over.

Trace got off a single shot as she threw herself out of the way, barely escaping the car's front fender. Her shot evidently missed, for the car continued to accelerate, its back end swerving, either because of the marbles or torque-steer caused by the acceleration.

Trace started to run after the vehicle, then saw a forklift approaching out of the corner of her eye. Apparently oblivious to what was going on—maybe things like this happen every day on the Djibouti docks—the driver continued along toward Trace, carrying a skid of shrink-wrapped boxes in front of him. Trace leapt up onto the cockpit area. Throwing the man off, she slipped into the seat and reached under the dash.

Her fingers found the transmitter, a radio-control they'd stolen for the nearby crane unit. (They'd hidden it there because they expected to have to split up, and weren't sure who would be using it.)

Controller in one hand, hem of her skirt in another, Trace hopped off the forklift and started running. Hoshang's car was already at the end of the pier, turning to the right.

Feeling herself starting to slip on the marbles, she pushed the button on the top right, ordering the crane holding the large metal crate to release its cargo.

Bull's-eye.

The crate fell directly onto Hoshang's car; he was crushed beneath a load of fermented pig parts, destined for South Africa. I'd be hard-pressed to think up a more fitting end.[26]

---

[26] I always thought bin Laden deserved to be decapitated, castrated, and covered in pig blood, then wrapped in pigskin in keeping with the tenets of his preaching.

[1]

Back in India, Junior and I spent a relatively quiet evening. Junior slept. I contemplated the healing properties of gin: good ol' Dr. Bombay, Healer Supreme!

We rose early the next day, just before six, and after a brief but intense PT, got ready to leave for the airport. We were just about to board the jeep when the Indian air force officer who was coordinating our transportation called to say the plane wouldn't be ready until the following morning due to "mechanical issues."

Junior went back inside to sleep. I decided to change back into my workout clothes and go for a run. I was just lacing up when Shunt buzzed my satellite phone.

"Remember all those Viagra ads I was tracking?" Shunt asked.

"No."

"You know where that stuff comes from? The drugs, not the spam."

"Hoboken."

"Close. Bangladesh. Trace didn't tell you?"

"Tell me which?"

Trace had passed the information about *Indiamotion* and the clandestine drug factory along to Shunt, telling him to see if he could verify it. He had, and more.

"It's pretty close to the border where you are now," explained Shunt. "They must smuggle just about everything over—your guards are probably getting a kickback. See, they set up in Bangladesh and sub out to legit and illegit places in India. No inspections, no taxes—the Indian government probably even knows about it, but by the time they get their act together and do something to shut it down, we'll be drinking Viagra with our orange juice."

"Shunt, is there some connection to anything we're doing?" I asked. "Or are you asking me to bring back some souvenirs?"

"Trace said that Garrett was hinting the CIA wanted someone to track the next shipment, and kind of implying we should do it. You know, out of the kindness of our hearts."

"Uh-huh."

"That's what I was thinking. But I ran these cross-checks against our databases, you know, see what kind of hits we got. And I left the bank database in the queue by accident. Guess what?"

"You know what time it is here?"

"The company in Hungary that's sending out all those illegal Viagra ads we've been getting was paid with an account from the American International Bank. That account was originally set up by a company in Nevada whose incorporators included Veep."

"Veep?"

"Even listed his bank address. Either Jason Redlands, vice president of the American International Bank, can't get it up, or he's hooked into the business big time."

I'll spare you the increasingly lame jokes on the male member that followed. Shunt reported that the company that established the account changed its name and registration a few weeks before, removing Redlands from any official registry. Shunt had found the original documents by searching archived information.

"So Veep has a company that sells illegal Viagra?" I asked.

"Looks like it."

I called and woke up Trace. It was a bit like poking a bear, but I wanted to trade info. I didn't mention the connection with Veep and the bank; I was more interested in *why* Garrett had passed along the information.

"I think he's trying to get in good with his boss," she said. "They think he screwed up by letting you rescue him. Magoo hates the sight of you."

"So he just let it slip?"

"He's definitely trying to get us interested. But he doesn't have much information."

I pumped her a bit more, but Trace didn't know anything more than I've said here. When I got off the phone, I considered the situation. According to Shunt and Garrett, there was no direct evidence that the factory was connected to Allah's Rule, or that the terrorists were anything other than random customers—if that. As for our friend Veep—it was an intriguing coincidence, but nothing more than that. Despite my fervent love of the slimy banker, his holier-than-thou sneer and endearingly condescending attitude, the evidence was slim that he was personally involved in illicit Viagra, except maybe as a customer.

Had my flight been ready, I might have ignored the whole thing. But with nothing to do, it seemed a shame not to at least take a look at the Bangladesh pill factory and see what was going on there. At only three miles away, barely enough to raise my pulse rate if I ran.

While I was waiting for Shunt to gather some more information and satellite photos of the plant, the lieutenant who'd gone across the border with us the day before came over and asked if I'd like to sit in on his interview with the captured black shirt. Thinking it might be educational, I agreed, and ambled over.

The prisoner was being held in a pit at the far side of the complex. The hole, about six by six feet and roughly square, was covered with a metal grate secured by three boulders so large they had to be pulled off with the help of an ATV. The hole was deep; the prisoner couldn't be seen from the surface. One of the guards threw a rope down and told him to pull himself up. His head emerged a few seconds later.

"We have questions," said the lieutenant in Bengali.

"What?"

"You will speak with them, or you will suffer greatly."

The lieutenant didn't translate that last line, but the look on the prisoner's face made it clear what he said. The prisoner was prodded toward a log on the ground nearby. The lieutenant and I sat on a second log facing him, the ashes of a fire between us. There were six border soldiers surrounding us, all with weapons aimed at the black shirt's head.

The prisoner kept blinking, trying to get his eyes used to the light. Yesterday he had seemed wiry and defiant. Today he looked more like a scared, undernourished kid. He told the lieutenant that he was twenty; I guessed immediately that he was exaggerating. The lieutenant began translating for me, asking his questions in Bengali and then English. He paraphrased the answers.

"What is your name?"

"My name is Tukai."

"Where were you born?"

Tukai shook his head. "I was told Rangpur."

"You were told?"

The man shrugged. Rangpur Division is the northernmost district of Bangladesh, until recently part of Rajshahi. Like most of the country, it's predominately Muslim, and in olden times played a significant role in the subcontinent's history—the Sannyasi revolution (the monks' rebellion) took place here in the eighteenth century. Today it's centered around one of the major cities in Bangladesh, with several colleges, a newspaper, TV and radio stations—all the things we'd take for granted in the West, but can seem like miracles in Bangladesh. Rangpur is not as poor as much of the country, but it's not the land of opportunity either.

Tukai journeyed to India for a job at fifteen. There he fell in with the wrong types—not that he put it that way—and eventually found his way here. He was an unimportant member of the gang, he said, a soldier who did what he was told, much like the lieutenant.

The lieutenant didn't like the remark, even though nothing was meant by it, and slapped him across the face.

The man took it stoically, falling back just enough to convince the lieutenant he had been hurt, but not quite so far that he lost his balance. He gave no overt sign of pain; I'm sure he was used to much worse.

"Let me ask some questions," I said. "If you'll translate."

"Of course."

"Tukai, I am interested in knowing what kind of things you bring across the border."

Tukai shrugged.

"People mostly?" I asked. "Like yesterday."

"I do what I am told," answered Tukai in English before the lieutenant translated.

"I know that many groups move drugs across the border, back and forth. I am wondering if you know about that."

"People bring what they want to bring," he said. "We simply help."

"Do you take drugs out of Bangladesh?" I asked.

He gave me a puzzled look. Before I could explain, Junior leapt over the log, rushed across, and grabbed Tukai by the front of his shirt. The look he gave him was unlike any look I'd seen from him before.

"Tell Dick what he wants to know or I'll tear you apart with my bare hands," he told him, his voice something like you'd imagine a wolf's would be.

Now if Trace had done that, I wouldn't have been particularly surprised. Or Mongoose. But Junior, God bless him, has neither the deportment nor the temperament of a sociopath. He has many fine qualities, but there's no touch of psychotic killer in his eyes. But the man standing over the smuggler clearly could have been a homicidal maniac. And in fact, when he put his left hand on the man's throat, he very nearly was.

"We move anything," said the man, stuttering. "Many things. Cloth. People. Drugs."

"What kind of drugs?" I asked.

"D-drugs."

"Let go of him, Junior."

Junior reluctantly complied. The prisoner slid a few feet away on the log.

"There's a drug factory near here," I told him. "A few miles from the border. Do you know where it is?"

"World Pharmaceutical." He garbled the syllables in "pharmaceutical" around, but it was clear what he meant.

"Do you take packages from there?" I asked. "Have you been there?"

"Yes. Yes—I will tell you how to get in. How the doors are. The l—locks."

"Would you take me there?"

The lieutenant shot me a glance. He'd been placid while Junior grabbed his prisoner; I suspect he secretly approved. But he wasn't about to look the other way while I took a stroll with his prisoner. And his boss would never approve.

"I, uh, will tell you how to get there," said the prisoner.

"Dick, he's one of the scum that killed the girl," said Junior. "We should kill him."

"Relax, Junior."

Junior's hands were flexing into fists. "I'll tear him apart with my bare hands. Say the word."

"Go take a shower," I told him.

Junior took a breath that seemed to enlarge his entire body. Then he stalked off.

Tukai sketched the layout of the factory on a notebook one of the lieutenant's men fetched. Once he did that, his will seemed to break, and he was considerably more forthcoming about the organization, its ties, and its plans, than he had been with the Indians. The smugglers had no connection with terrorist groups, he insisted; they were simply transporters, experts at getting things across the border.

I believed him; he was too scared to lie at that point. But the lieutenant pointed out that many smugglers, especially those near the Pakistan border and in the very far north, have links with al Qaeda and a myriad of other terror groups and organizations around the world.

"I think I'm going to take a walk now," I told him. "Good luck with your prisoner."

I checked back with Shunt, gathered a few things, then stopped by the tent where Junior had camped. He was sitting in a canvas chair, feet on a battered soccer ball. His expression as dark as I'd ever seen.

"Playing soccer?" I asked.

"No."

"Getting along with the guards?"

"Not really."

"Feeling antisocial?"

"Huh?"

"I'm going to take a walk after dinner," I told him, deciding that he had to stay home. "I'll be back."

"You going to check out that drug factory?"

"Yeah."

"I want to come." Junior sprang to his feet.

"You need to rest. You're too wound up about the girl," I added. "You need to get past that."

His eyes flashed with anger, pretty much confirming everything I'd said.

"I'm not going to lose my control."

"You already did."

"I didn't hit him."

"You wanted to."

"But I didn't."

"Stay here and keep the Indians company. They may get restless."

"Dad."

"Stay here."

He did. Reluctantly, I'm sure. But he stayed.

The pharmaceutical industry is a billion-dollar enterprise. As such, it employs some of the smartest people in the world. The manufacturing techniques for *many* drugs are very much up-to-the-minute: cleanrooms, high-tech production lines that look like science labs, miniature forests of test tubes and chemical containers. There is a supreme effort to maintain quality, involving constant safeguards and almost obsessive checks and balances.

Security is usually on par, especially at large multinational companies where trade secrets are highly valued and closely watched.

I didn't expect that would be the case here, and I wasn't disappointed. There were only two guards on duty, both at the entrance to the facility, which was surrounded by an eight-foot-high fence topped by barbed wire. Granted, the location meant it was unlikely to be targeted by anyone, including the tax collector. And heavy security would have probably drawn unwanted attention. But sometimes you wish people would present more of a challenge.

Even in the dusky twilight, getting past the fence was simple; all I had to do was put a pair of sharp-nosed wire cutters to appropriate use. I pushed the fence back and slipped through. I didn't have night glasses, but there was no need for them; the stars and moon gave plenty of light as I walked to the back door.

It was locked. Ordinarily this wouldn't have been a problem, but I didn't have my lock-picking tools with me, and there had been no acceptable substitutes at camp. So I took a more creative approach: I went to the trees, picked up a fallen limb, then hurled it through one of the windows.

I scurried back to the other side of the fence, expecting an alarm to ring. I didn't hear any, but soon a beam of light danced in the window closest to the front of the building. I grabbed some other branches and threw them over the fence near the window, then retreated into the shadows.

The guard and his flashlight made their way methodically through the building, checking each room until at last he came to the one broken by my tree branch. Discovering the branch, he turned on the light. It framed him as he examined the broken window. Opening it, he stuck his head out and looked down on the ground, then around toward the fence. Satisfied by the debris on the ground, he closed the window and retreated.

As soon as the light was off in the room, I ran to the building. I pushed the glass shards out of the bottom of the window, then snaked inside. I found myself in an empty storeroom.

The first order of business was to check for internal security devices. The window turned out to be wired; I gathered that the alarm must be silent—a slightly more high-tech flourish than I'd hoped for. Though it was a little late now, I popped my flashlight on to check for a motion detector (none), then checked the door for wiring (ditto).

The door opened into a small manufacturing area. Machines were grouped into different clusters; some were set off by drapes of sheer plastic, others were wide open. Computer workstations, mostly ganged in twos and threes, filled tables near every cluster. While there were a few shadows toward the edges of the room, LEDs on the machines provided enough of a glow for me to see easily.

There were no motion detectors or other security devices in the large room. Closets similar to the one I'd been in ran about halfway down the side. An enclosed vestibule sat at the front of the room, on the side where the guards were stationed. I went to it and cracked the door open.

Long and very narrow, the vestibule was empty. There were posters on the wall with Bengali writing—they looked like the sort of propaganda factory owners put up reminding workers to be careful, as if that were necessary in a place where becoming crippled is tantamount to condemning yourself to an early death.

The steel door on the opposite wall looked like it went to the outside. The guard post would be nearby, in a small shack separate from the building.

Moving back inside, I spotted a beam of light swinging through the darkness outside two of the far windows; the guard I'd seen earlier or maybe his partner was outside, checking to see what was going on. Most likely he would conclude that the branch had been blown into the window from one of the nearby trees.

And if he didn't—I planned to be gone by then.

Expecting to find an office where the records were kept, I discovered only a single desk a few feet from the rear door. There was a brand-new Dell computer at the side, with a modest display screen and a wired keyboard on the desktop. I booted it up, finger over the screen button so I could turn it off if I heard someone coming.

The machine booted into Windows 7 without asking for a password. A few clicks later I had an Internet connection. I typed in the URL of a site Shunt had set up and hit Return.

The site looked like a garden-variety page of porn, featuring your usual big bazookas and unprotected flanks. I moved the cursor to a sensitive area on the first picture and clicked.

A message appeared: Access denied. It wasn't really, though—it was a fake message that would be stored in the computer. Five seconds after I cleared the screen, Shunt was looking at the computer's hard drive, starting to download the data.

I went and looked around. The place was a druggist's wet dream—there were pills of every shape and size imaginable, identified only by bar codes. Large bottles were stacked neatly near some of the machines; boxes with other bottles were packed in different pyramids around other stations. The place could cure a thousand different diseases, I'm sure.

The far side of the room contained a cascading collection of metal containers, miniature silos of different chemicals. An area at the front contained shelves of more boxes and a few very large bottles, all with writing in English identifying what they were.

How good were the drugs that were being made here? The machines to mix and press the pills practically gleamed in the dim light, and there were no rats or other vermin in the place—present company excepted, of course. Would I buy my acetylsalicylic acid from here? Lansoprazole? Codeine? Xanax?

I'd gone back toward the front of the room when I heard the outer door opening. Ducking down, I hid behind a stack of boxes, slowing my breathing as the door opened.

This time the guard switched on the light. I squeezed my shoulders down, trying to make myself invisible. I took my pistol, in case that didn't work.

The guard mumbled to himself as he walked through the room. I leaned forward just enough to get a glimpse of him as he peered left and right. Satisfied that the room was empty, he came back and began working his way methodically down the small storerooms at the south side of the room, checking each one.

I sidled around, waiting for him to finish. But as he came out of the last one, he happened to glance to the back of the room. Something caught his eye: the computer screen, which I had neglected to turn off. He walked to the machine and began complaining loudly. I'm not sure what he was saying, but I would guess it was along the lines of *Those dipshit techies never remember to turn anything off.*

By the time he left the room five minutes later, my sat phone was shaking so hard it could have pounded a nail into my leg.

"What the hell is going on?" asked Shunt when I answered. "Why'd you turn the computer off? I wasn't done downloading."

"It wasn't me, it was a guard. How much time do you need?"

"A few minutes." I went to the computer and turned it back on. "Find anything good?"

"Some lists of people they do business with. Nothing jumped out at me. They also have the names of shipping agents they use. We can track through them if I don't get any other information."

"OK."

"Say, do you think you could pick up some codeine while you're there? I have a tooth that's bothering me."

"I'll cure it when I get back," I told him. "I have some rusty pliers that'll do the trick."

"Thanks."

I restored the connection. Shunt's program finished doing its dirty work in a few minutes and he placed a "rat" on the hard drive—a type of program that would share whatever happened on the computer with Shunt's network back home.

"We're done," he said.

I shut down the machine and started to take my leave. But as I cracked open the back door, light flooded in—enough light to shoot a movie. Closing it quickly, I retreated to the side room where I'd come in to see what was going on.

The guards had activated a set of floodlights surrounding the building. The lights weren't as much of a problem as the people in front of them were: the grounds were filled with workers, several of whom had chain saws. Apparently the guards' supervisor didn't want a repeat of the "accident" that had broken the window.

If he was sending people to take care of the trees, what about the window itself?

I made it out of the room just in time, ducking behind a set of machines as three men came in from the front. They were workmen, carrying tools and several very large panes of glass. The men were wearing lab coats—why that was necessary, I have no idea, but it did provide me with an easy means to escape. While they were inside the room, I skirted through the machinery, went over to the storeroom nearest the front, and selected the largest coat and cap I could find.

By that point, the window had been repaired. The men came out of the room and began examining the machines, making sure there was no damage. They were techies, not glaziers.

A quick wave to the two guards in the guardhouse on the left, and I was out.

Almost. One of the guards yelled to me in Bengali. I have no idea what he said, but I replied in a universal language all guys would understand: sweeping around, I mimed myself unzipping my pants and relieving myself, rocked my arms as if running, then spun and walked quickly into the woods.

Works every time.

The connection to Veep via the bank account was a thin reed. The fact that the unlicensed drug plant manufactured goods similar to those I was buying was an intriguing coincidence.

The fact that the cell phone I had taken the call on in Djibouti had been purchased by the same credit card that paid for a bill to the drug company—now *that* was interesting.

"It wasn't actually a bill to the drug company," Shunt said, correcting my paraphrase of what he'd just told me. "What they did was, they bought chemicals and then had them delivered to this office in Rangpur. That office is rented by the people who own the drug company. Got it?"

Shunt had a lot of information about the overall operation, thanks to his downloading of the hard drive on the administrator's machine. Among his choicest finds were e-mails sent to a man in Chittagong who acted as a shipping agent. The bootleg drugs apparently were shipped from the building right alongside other shipments to India. Once they reached the port, they were placed on a different ship, and from there, traveled to Africa, Europe, or the Middle East, wherever the buyer had specified.

That gave him a dozen leads to pursue. As he pursued them, he confirmed that the most recent shipment was aboard the *Indiamotion*, the same ship Garrett had mentioned. It was headed to Europe. He'd done some research on the company.

"Research" in this case being Shunt's word for breaking and entering.

"Pretty typical shipping company computer system," he told me. "They have this interface where their company officials and the ships' captains can check the position of all the ships. They think it's pretty innovative. Easy to break into, though."

"Which you did."

"Yeah. Wasn't very hard. *Indiamotion* is off the coast of Africa," said Shunt. "The boat's going through the canal up to Europe. If we could bug the boxes, we'd get a lot more information. I could coordinate arrivals with payments, maybe figure out the whole network. I don't know if it's an

Allah's Rule shipment," Shunt added. "But until I get more information, you know, it's what you always say—don't *ass*-u-me."

Shunt started babbling technical information and other things he'd been working on. I started to zone out—until something in the middle of his diatribe about 0s and 1s caught my attention.

". . . The shipping line's security is so easy to breach, that a bunch of people have done it. I put a tracker on, and guess whose computer has been used to access the company site?"

You can always tell when Shunt thinks he has earth-shattering information: he answers his questions with breathless answers.

"Veep." Shunt was hyperventilating. "His computer goes on that site regularly. He's checked that ship like two or three times this week."

"Veep?" I asked.

"We have that earlier connection, now this. There's got to be something up with him, right? I mean, not to ass-u-me, but, right? Right? Right?"

"What were the ports again?"

"Hang on."

I was thinking we could follow the shipments once they landed, but the logistics would be tricky—I'd have to set up in every port they were planning to land in. Meanwhile, we'd still have to set up for the Allah's Rule delivery, assuming it was a separate shipment.

No, it would be much smarter to visit the ship before it landed. And so a visit was arranged.

(II)

Forty-eight hours later, I stood behind a curtain at the rear of a 727, sucking on pure oxygen and waiting for a signal from the cockpit. We were flying right around 29,000 feet, following the general course taken by cargo flights from India to Djibouti—which made sense, as this was a commercial cargo plane on a scheduled run.

I wasn't going all the way to Djibouti. My destination was a speck in the ocean several hundred miles to the east.

Connections inside the Indian security forces—and a good amount of hard American currency—had helped make it possible for me to hitch a ride. And now as the lights flashed in the hold, it was time for me to take my leave.

I have fond memories of 727s stretching back to my days with Six. They tell me the aircraft are obsolete now, due to aging airframes, changing airline requirements, flight regulations, and unfortunate developments related to the price of fuel. Boeing stopped making the planes decades ago, and no major American passenger line I know of still uses them. But the engineers who designed them and the men and women who put them together knew what they were doing, and those that have been properly maintained still ply their trade around the world.

My enthusiasm isn't so much for their versatility and dependability, but rather the door at the back of the plane. It opens to a retractable set of stairs, famously used by D. B. Cooper over the northwest mountains in 1971 when he escaped with a bag of money. At SEAL Six we installed a metal slide over the stairs so we could expeditiously exit the whole team. The "laundry chute" strewed agents of mayhem across the sky.

I tumbled out of the plane into the slipstream, struggling to get my body into a frog-like position. Skydiving is a lot like riding a bike—you never forget how to do it.

Then again, it's not a big deal if you do. You *will* land. One way or the other. After all, you don't really fall through the sky—the earth just comes up to meet you.

Quickly.

Junior was not with me. I had sent him back to the States the day before. I told him I needed him to help Danny as he set up surveillance on Veep, which was true enough. We'd need someone with high-tech skills to monitor bugs and whatever electronic intelligence we gathered.

I'd also told Danny to keep an eye on him, and gave him a quick rundown of what had happened.

I can't say that Junior was happy to be going home, and he would have been even angrier if I'd told him that I was jumping from the plane—he had night-qualified for parachute jumps a few weeks before, and undoubtedly would have loved the chance to strut his stuff.

But I was concerned about him. His outburst at the border camp, and the effect the little girl's death had on him, weren't good. He was still wearing his heart on his sleeve. Even at SEAL Team Six, I didn't expect my people to be automatons without emotion. But they had to be able to control it. I didn't like what I'd seen from Junior.

The perils of *parenthood:* Was I being too hard on him because he was my son? Was the real issue the fact that I was worried he would be hurt, or worse? Was I the problem, not him?

Those thoughts crossed my mind as I plummeted downward. My position was marked on the visor in my helmet, which included handy little arrows to show me where to go. The unit could even give me advice on how to correct my course, if asked. Made by my friends at Innovate Technologies, the unit came with a money-back guarantee—if it sent me more than thirty meters off-course, the price of the helmet would be refunded.

My estate would no doubt be overjoyed. I had a similar guarantee from the parachute company; put them together and half my funeral would be paid for.

I was feeling awfully cold, even with the thermal layer and wet suit. Nothing like plunging through several thousand feet at terminal velocity to chill your blood.

A few more technical notes on the helmet while I'm falling: from the stern, it looks a lot like your basic military-style A-Bravo half-shell. It's black, lightweight, and has the basic four-point suspension with a Bungee Molle fastener. Come around the side and you start to see some differences. There are small but noticeable wedges above the ear area for the embedded antennas. The helmet shield is made of a substance similar to the Gorilla Glass found in iPhones and other electronic gizmos. Gorilla Glass—made by the fine folks at Corning in New York—uses a special ion-exchange process to make the surface hard to scratch or break. In the helmet, there's an LCD layer sandwiched inside to provide the displays. The LCDs are embedded and arranged in a way that you can still see reasonably well through the visor.

That will change in the next version, where the image will be synthetic, provided by small cameras at the top of the helmet—basically you'll be watching a movie of your life, not only in living color, but in infrared and whatever other imaging system occurs to the geeks at Innovate Technologies. And I suppose if you're bored on the long trip down, you can always catch Netflix or Hulu.

"Prepare to engage," said a voice in the helmet. It sounded English—the engineers at Innovate apparently believed men would pay more attention to a girl with an accent . . . or they were married, and accustomed to taking directions from a female.

I checked the screen. I was coming down toward four thousand feet. She was right on time.

"Three seconds. Two . . ."

At 3,800 feet, I pulled the ripcord. An instant later—

Ugh . . . !!!

The sound you heard was the tightening of my body harness against the tender morsels of my anatomy, resulting in a plaintive cry from all of my future generations.

Better than the alternative, certainly, since it meant that my parachute had correctly deployed. I did a quick check above, making sure I had good cells, then got down to some serious navigating. I was no longer a brick— I was a certifiable flying man, moving with purpose and some amount of grace toward the red triangle that appeared in my helmet.

The triangle was homing in on a radio signal from the small boat I was heading for. I've made over 110 night jumps, enough to lose count but not to lose the memory of each one. They're all the same, and different—you remember the tugs and the way the wind kicked you, the spray of water when you landed, or the time Murphy played with the lines.

Tonight was an easy one, with no wind to speak of, or at least not enough to interfere with me as I glided toward the radar signal. I was just passing fifteen hundred feet when an almost imperceptible light flashed ahead of me—Shotgun and Mongoose were watching from the boat, and gave me the high sign.

Sure now that I had the course set, I turned to the next problem—a water landing. The boat the boys were in was too small for me to touch down on, which meant I had to hit the waves next to them. Land on the waves when you're not quite ready for them, and you might as well be landing on concrete.

Actually, concrete is a little better.

Because it was dark, I had little depth perception—at night, depth perception over water is nil, since there are no horizontal reference points to gauge height against. Thirty feet off the water looks the same as three hundred feet. So I had to rely on the helmet to know when I was going to hit, er, touch down. In theory, that was great—a high-tech visual aid to assist in what is one of the trickier problems of a night jump. But the best theory takes quite a bit of practice to become a reality, and it had been several months since I'd last jumped with the helmet. So I got my feet out a second or two early, then wondered what the hell was going on when I didn't splash when I thought I would splash.

A second later I did "walk" into the ocean, a little off-balance, but down at least, and only a few yards from the Zodiac I was aiming at.

You've heard of a paper trail; I had a nylon trail streaming after me. My first order of business was to shed it, slit it so there'd be no air pockets, and then bundle it up to be weighted down and sunk as shark bait. I worked quickly, not because I was afraid of being seen, but because I didn't want to spend more time in the water than necessary.

The Indian Ocean is the world's warmest sea, with surface temperatures that have been measured at just under 37 degrees centigrade. But the average human being's temperature is 0.5 degrees higher, and even on the hottest day in the warmest part of the ocean, everything around you is cooler than you are. Thermodynamics being what they are, your body tries to accommodate the temperature difference by warming up the rest of the world; sooner or later, you'll freeze your butt off.

"Hey, now, Dick, about time you dropped in," said Shotgun, adding a few choice words of greeting, mostly of the four-letter variety.

Mongoose, meanwhile, leaned over the side and helped pull me into the small craft.

"Target is five miles away," he told me as I settled in. "They're just chugging along. We can catch them easy."

"Want some licorice?" asked Shotgun.

"No saltwater taffy?"

"Damn. I should have thought of that."

We set a course for the ship. The boys filled me in on recent developments, such as they were, as well as the latest on what was going on with the ship.

According to the company records, it was bound for passage in the Suez Canal, and from there to ports in Greece, Cyprus, and France. Our plan was to get aboard, find the shipment, and put some bugs in it. Then we'd hop back on the Zodiac and return to Djibouti.

It wasn't clear whether this was my shipment or not. It might be, and that was one reason I wanted to tag it. But even if it wasn't, following it would give us more information about the smuggling network, and potentially more data on connections with the bank, our friend Veep, and Allah's Rule. It would also keep us at least one step ahead of the Christians in Action, who as far as we could tell didn't know about the shipment or the connection to Bangladesh.

The craft we were using was not your plain vanilla Zodiac, if there is such a thing. Longtime readers—and shouldn't you all be?—will remember my good friend Steve Seigel,[27] aka "Indian Jew," among other embroidered titles. Steve is now CEO of Zodiac North America, and despite admonishments to the contrary, continues to associate with riffraff like yours truly. Even more incredibly, he has opened the doors of the factory and its R&D department to Red Cell International. It's an arrangement that benefits us both—we get to play with their newest toys; they get to see what they can do in real-world situations.

Clearly, I have the better end of the deal.

The craft Steve's people had loaned us featured a motor that made use of a new fuel technology. Combined with technological improvements related to the hull, it had a tremendous range and a decent speed, without sacrificing anything in the way of seaworthiness—assuming you didn't mind getting wet.

Even so, we couldn't carry enough fuel and still have room for weapons and ourselves. Because of that, we'd arranged to be refueled in the morning, with a helo drop courtesy of Trace. Assuming she could tear herself away from Garrett for a few hours.

A navy operation would choose from a variety of tools to find the target; everything from satellites to small UAVs could be employed to track down the needle in the haystack. All we had was Shunt's access to the company computer system, a pair of infrared glasses, and a small marine radar unit. Shunt got us into the general vicinity, but a night fog rendered the IR practically useless. The radar, however, came through. Made by Raymarine, it had roughly a fifty-nautical-mile range, and we found the cargo ship with no trouble.

I wish I could say that about our approach. Murphy was working overtime as Mongoose plotted to take us up into the ship's wake, where we would be especially difficult to detect. The wind, which had been nonexistent when I jumped, had gradually whipped itself into a frenzy. That diminished the fog, but the whitecaps rose so high that it felt like the bow was being pummeled.

"Weather report said this was supposed to hold off for another couple of hours," groused Mongoose, struggling to keep us on course. I'm not sure that Noah could have done a better job against the sudden tempest. A sea

---

[27] Commander Seigel's résumé is too long to reprint here, but one of the big bullet points is SEAL Team Six, where he distinguished himself as a man among men. Check out *The Real Team* for a list of achievements—and know that even those thirty pages barely scratch the surface.

squall literally materialized from nowhere, constructing itself from a momentary depression or whatever it is the meteorologists use to explain Murphy's various whims.

In one way, the sudden surge was good news—it meant there would be less of a chance that anyone would see us coming aboard, let alone be on deck when we climbed up. But we still had to get there, and for a good half hour that seemed to be an impossible mission. A blind man climbing Mount Everest on his hands and knees would have made more progress than we did.

The worst of the storm suddenly slipped past, and Mongoose found himself struggling to keep us from ramming the side of the ship. He pulled us alongside the stern of the heaving monster, bucking the waves as Shotgun and I prepared to go aboard.

There are a number of ways to get onto a ship at sea clandestinely. The easiest is to find a line trailing off the stern or one of the sides. It sounds ridiculously inept, but more often than not someone aboard has forgotten to square away a line (or rope, for you landlubbers). The line inevitably ends up trailing off through the water, a veritable escalator to the deck. But the sailors aboard the *Indiamotion*—our target ship's name—were operating under the supervision of a competent master and mate; nothing dangled off the side.

Shotgun took a collapsible aluminum pole from the side of the boat and began uncollapsing it, extending the base and adding a similar pole until he had a veritable Empire State Building of tubular aluminum in his hands. At the tip we rigged a hook and a thin but strong line, and as our little rigid-hulled boat bounced in the water, Shotgun tried to lasso the line onto the ship above.

Indiamotion was a medium-sized vessel that could be used for bulk carrying and containers, though it carried most of its cargo in the latter on this voyage. The ship had a relatively low gunwale amidships, and the three rails gave us plenty to aim at. However, the waves not only affected Shotgun's judgment but his balance in the boat, and he had a hell of a time getting his hook into position. The pole clanked and clattered until finally a good nudge from the waves—or Murphy—sent Shotgun flailing backward. He just managed to keep himself from the drink.

The same could not be said for the pole.

I fished it and the line out while he cursed at Mongoose for not keeping the boat steadier. This led to a terse debate about the fine points of seamanship. In the meantime, I took matters into my own hands—I grabbed the grappling hook, made sure our line was clear, and pretended I was a cowboy.

I got the hook around the rail and a post on the first try.

"All aboard," I yelled at Shotgun.

"You lucky son of a bitch."

"Skill," I told him, swinging up on the line.

Murphy must have heard me bragging. With my first pull the ship lifted suddenly and our boat ducked down. I smacked my right knee against the side. It felt like I'd been kneecapped with a sledgehammer. It was all I could do to hang on.

"You goin' up, or what?" yelled Shotgun behind me.

I grappled my way to the deck, falling rather than climbing over the rail. Sucking some serious wind, I righted myself, got my MP5 into position, and scanned fore and aft to make sure we hadn't been spotted.

I almost wished we had. Shooting someone would have taken the edge off my pain.

Shotgun popped his head over the rail and came aboard. I moved across the deck to a spar connected to the cargo crane. Pulling off my waterproof ruck, I took out a small package wrapped in plastic. Cutting the covering away revealed what looked like a slightly oversized pack of off-brand cigarettes wrapped in a thin filament wire. The wire was an antenna. I twisted it around the spar and taped the box beneath it on the side opposite the deck, hidden from view. The box held a satellite radio scanner, which would pick off radio frequencies used on the ship and transmit them back to Shunt, literally phoning them over our own circuits. Once he had the frequencies, he could then use our equipment to monitor the transmissions.[28] There was also a GPS sending unit in the box, which would help us keep track of the ship independently of the shipping company's system.

I tested the setup by using my phone to call Shunt.

"Strong coms," he told me. "They're not talking to anyone at the moment."

"Let me know if you hear anything good."

"Will do."

I took a few steps back to make sure the wire and device were hard to spot. Shotgun, watching the deck, gave me a thumbs-up between bites of his Twinkie.

---

[28] Since this all happened in real time, there was a bit of a lag with the first transmission and the interception, and we always lost a bit of the conversation the first time a different frequency was used. And because it used commercial sat frequencies, our system was relatively easy to detect, unlike the much more expensive bugs the Christians in Action and folks at No Such Agency routinely employ. Our method was cheaper, though.

"Sea spray adds a little flavor," he said, unwrapping another.

"Put down the food and let's find the container with our drugs," I told him.

"Aye, aye, Cap," he said, stuffing the snack cake in his mouth.

Not only was *Indiamotion* a relatively modest-sized vessel, but according to the documents that Shunt had tracked down, she was carrying only eleven containers. We had the serial number of the one with the drugs, thanks also to his detective work. More importantly—since I suspected that it might have been switched—Shunt had managed to track down the origin of nine of the other ten containers and determined that none of them had originated in India. He had numbers and even color descriptions for all of them. Worst-case scenario, we could tag the two remaining containers and follow each to its destination.

Or so I thought.

"Say, Dick, I'm not the greatest at counting," said Shotgun as we moved toward the bow. "But I'm thinking there's more than a dozen containers here. Like, a lot more."

Over sixty, in fact. Either the ship had taken on cargo that didn't appear on its records—imagine that.

Or we were on the wrong ship.

The name was right, at least. While I called Shunt and told him to re-check his data, Shotgun began scrambling up the stacked containers, inspecting each one. The rain and waves made it difficult to hang on, and it was slow going. The ship's running lights shed little light on the containers, and Shotgun had to be as discreet as possible using the flashlight attached to his wrist.

"That's the right one, Dick," said Shunt. "Listen, an Italian navy vessel just hailed them. They're only a couple of miles west."

"They ask to board?"

"Negative. But it sounds like they're going to come real close."

I told Mongoose over the radio to turn on the radar and track them. He also moved the Zodiac to the other side of the ship.

"How long are you going to be?" he asked.

"We're going as fast as we can. Slip away if you have to. Just make sure you're not seen."

"Roger that."

Fifteen minutes passed. Shotgun found two of the containers Shunt had said were *not* ours, which at least confirmed that any mistake he'd made was consistent. But our container was nowhere to be seen.

"A thousand to go," he said.

"Don't exaggerate," I told him. "I'll take the next row."

"With that knee?"

"My knee's fine."

"You're limping."

"Nah."

"That cursing before was just celebrating how happy you felt."

"Something like that."

The cargo containers were stacked with about four feet between the rows, and it was easy enough to walk between them and check out the bottom containers. Ours was not among them.

Metal pipes ran straight up and down the fronts of most of the containers, giving me handholds to use to climb. I picked one in the middle and began hoisting myself up. The rain made the pole slippery, and the soles of my sodden athletic shoes (what us old-timers used to call tennis shoes or sneakers) felt as if they'd been greased. The ship's heaving didn't help. I finally managed to get to the top of the crate, and shined my wrist light on the serial number of the container at the top.

Not my container.

I worked my way up to the next container.

No joy.

Had the ship been steadier, I might have tried moving across sideways as Shotgun had done. But all this motion and the rain that was kicking up again made for a Murphy party waiting to happen. I backed down to the deck, then moved to the next crate.

"It's none of the ones on bottom of the next row," Shotgun told me. "But I did find two of the ones on Shunt's list. Maybe we should check above them."

"Good idea."

"Wanna Twinkie?"

"No thanks."

"Last one."

"Shame."

We moved around the corner to the next row. Shotgun scrambled up the side of the cargo like he was bounding up an escalator.

Show-off.

He was fast, but he had just as much trouble reading the serial numbers on the crates as I did. They were scratched and in some cases obscured with grease and graffiti. He'd gotten about a third of the way through when I heard a very loud crash followed by a scraping sound coming from somewhere aft on the ship.

Ships in even a light storm are not exactly places of serene quietude. To hear *anything* above the ocean and the steady thump of the vessel's power plants meant it was really loud. And loud sounds on a ship are uniformly bad sounds.

My first thought was that one of the cargo containers had come un-moored. I quick-checked the ones where Shotgun was climbing, then went out along the rail to see the others. The containers left a narrow passage along the starboard side of the ship; the scraping noise echoed loudly against the wall of metal, and any second I thought I was either going to be crushed or thrown out to sea.

But neither happened. The containers seemed secure.

Finally I saw what it was: a large metal whaleboat had come off its divots and was hanging against the side of the forward superstructure, flapping like a loose shutter with the wind and the waves. The boat hung by a single line at the bow, and besides clanging it was doing a good bit of damage to the ship's superstructure. Sooner or later, the crew was going to have to deal with it.

Make that sooner, rather than later—a door a few feet from the dan-gling boat opened, its yellow light obvious in the blackness. Two figures emerged, took a look, then retreated.

I backed around to Shotgun, telling him what I'd found over the radio as I went.

"Maybe they'll just cut it loose," he said.

"Not likely. The boat's probably more valuable to the ship's company than the crew."

That wasn't a joke.

"Should we hide?" he asked.

I glanced around. There wasn't much of anywhere to hide. But as long as they were only dealing with the boat, there wasn't a need—we were well out of their vision.

I told Shotgun to stay put and went back around the side, intending to keep an eye on the crew and the boat. Turning the corner, I saw a pair of men in slickers coming down the ladder and heading in my direction. The captain, wisely concerned that his cargo might come loose and create a *real* problem, had detailed a party to investigate and make sure all of the con-tainers were secured.

(III)

I'm sure the sailors were every bit as unhappy about their assignment as I was. But that wasn't of much comfort.

I slipped through the open space between the container rows to the other side of the ship. Two men were coming along that side as well, and in fact had made a little better progress.

Retreating, I joined Shotgun halfway up the container stack. He'd curled his arm around a metal pipe and looked a bit like a gorilla—not least of all because he had pulled a banana out of his backpack and was munching it.

"Hungry?" he asked.

"We have sailors coming to inspect the containers," I told him. "How the hell can you eat?"

He just shrugged.

We could avoid the sailors by climbing to the very top of the containers, but that would expose us to anyone on the bridge. As bad as the lighting was, we'd still be pretty obvious up there. And hiding on the deck wasn't much safer. We could go over the side, but even then we'd be risking a chance of being seen.

"We'll hide in one of the containers," I told him. "You have the picks, right?"

"Uh-huh."

He reached into his fanny pack and pulled out the small kit. I'm much better at picking locks than he is. Larceny is in my blood; his is filled with cholesterol.

I scanned the nearby containers to see which would be the easiest to get into. There are some very high-tech locks out there these days, with fancy electronic gizmos that alert the owners when they've been tampered with. Even the less sophisticated models can be tricky to get around, at least if you're in a hurry. The two nearest containers had what looked like Enforcer locks, electromagnetic models that would be a pain to tamper with. I skipped them, clambering up to a more battered model that had an old-fashioned steel wire loop and key lock. The steel would have given the wire cutters we had with us a hard time, but the lock itself was easy to pick.

Or would have been, if I could have done it without hanging off the container in the rain while the ship started rolling at an unhealthy rate.

I fumbled badly with the tools, my hands getting colder and wetter by the second. Shotgun came over and leaned over me, providing a little shelter. Finally, the pins gave, and I slipped the lock apart. The whole process might have taken only a dozen seconds, but it seemed as if it had lasted a full hour. What happened next was nearly instantaneous: I undid the latch, and Shotgun pulled the right door open.

And swung out on the pipe as the ship lurched. The door was wide open, easily visible. Murphy was having his little tease. Just as I reached to grab the door back, the ship bucked and the panel came flying toward me. As I ducked, it reversed course, smacking Shotgun against the front of the next container.

Better him than me.

He kicked himself away from the container, reaching his hand toward me as he swung in. I grabbed it and pulled him into the interior of the container. He squeezed past me; I wedged my foot against the opening and held the door in place, a narrow crack of very dim twilight filtering through from the ship's lights.

"What are we going to do if they come up and lock it?" asked Shotgun, squirreling back around.

"We push the door out and clobber them," I told him. As much as I wanted to complete our mission without being detected, I wasn't about to spend the next two days locked in a cargo container with Shotgun.

I leaned over and peered through the crack. There just wasn't enough light to see to the deck, and so I had no idea how the search was progressing. Meanwhile, Shotgun began a search of his own.

"Oh my God!" I heard him say in a barely muffled voice. "These are boxes of peanuts. I *love* peanuts. And cashews! And look at this—dried apricots."

He'd stumbled on a culinary nirvana, or at least the trail-mix version.

We spent about twenty minutes in the cargo container, probably about fifteen minutes more than we needed to. The metal interfered with our radios, and I couldn't get Mongoose or Shunt. Not that they would have been helpful: Shunt didn't have eyes-on, and Mongoose had pulled the Zodiac far enough away to keep from being spotted. Finally I slipped the door open and looked around, clambering down to the deck while Shotgun filled his ruck and every pocket he had with goodies.

The crewmen who'd been sent to deal with the whaleboat were still at it, trying to secure it to its divots on the side of the superstructure. From where I was standing at the edge of the cargo area, the proceedings looked a lot like an outtake from a Three Stooges movie, with Emil Stika as a guest star. The two men would raise the boat up, then lose it as the ship lurched. They weren't quite strong enough to get the job done.

I was tempted to send Shotgun over to help them. But I don't like to bother the boy while he's eating.

Meanwhile, the Italian destroyer had drawn near the port side of the *Indiamotion*. Mongoose was now nearly two miles away, with the ship between him and the Italians. He was worried about fuel; fighting the storm had meant burning more than we'd planned.

"We're going to be a while longer," I told him, glancing in the direction of the Italian ship, whose mast loomed between the containers. We had to be careful moving around the port side of the carrier because it was so close. "What the hell are the Italians doing, anyway?"

"I don't know. Shunt said they were radioing back and forth for a bit, warning them about pirates and talking about soccer," said Mongoose.

If the container was aboard, it was in the row closest to the bridge— about par for the way our luck was running. I scanned the bottom while Shotgun, trailing nuts and dried fruit, started to climb.

I found another of Shunt's containers, but not the one we wanted. One of the containers on the far side of the ship was slightly undersized, and because of the way the lights fell, there was a shadow where the space was. Shotgun used this to climb up. I lost sight of him for a few moments. The next thing I knew, a war cry pierced my eardrum.

"Found one," he said.

"Good. Plant the tracker and move on."

"Yeah, OK. Still got the rest of the row to check for the other. But you know, we went through all this trouble—don't you think we should crack it open and take a look?"

"Guns, plant the device."

"Shunt says the Italians are sending a boat over," warned Mongoose. "They just radioed that they want to see the papers."

In the interests of protecting my readers with sensitive ears, I've deleted the page and a half of curses that followed in real time.

Shotgun planted the tracker, then dropped to the deck and met me in the space between the containers. I didn't want to risk hiding in one now—it was one thing to surprise unarmed sailors, and quite another to take on a boarding party, even if they were Italian.

I considered abandoning ship. But we were still one container short. And given everything we'd been through already, there was no way I was settling for a fifty-fifty chance of success.

We hid in a space roughly a foot and a half wide between containers in the third row. It was a tight squeeze even for my girlish figure. Shotgun had to hold his breath for the entire hour or so it took the Italians to check the papers. By the time they scrambled back to their destroyer, the sun was edging at the horizon.

"Gonna be one of those last three," said Shotgun, when we snuck back to the row of containers. "Gotta be."

"Which one do you think it is?" I asked.

Shotgun pointed.

I told him to try the one farthest from that.

Bingo.

What we'd planned as a thirty-minute operation had taken nearly five hours. Both of us were pretty damn tired, thirsty, and hungry. And we still had to get off the ship without being seen.

Mongoose had gone north, cutting his power to preserve fuel. He was more than five miles away when I called him.

"Radio us when you're two miles off," I told him. "We'll slip over the side and swim to you."

"That's a long swim."

"I can handle it."

"I don't know about Shotgun."

"Don't worry about me," he boasted. "I can float."

Mongoose cursed. "Radar is picking up something else out ahead of you."

"Another NATO ship?"

"No, no, too small."

"How small?"

"Size of a longboat, a little bigger. High prow."

I crawled out to the gunwale and moved forward toward the bow. When I got there, I spotted a black blur moving along the edge of the water, just visible against the lightening blue of the sky.

Pirates. Speeding in our direction.

[IV]

If you're thinking there are entirely too many pirates in these waters, I completely agree. The bastards ought to be keelhauled where they live.

On the other hand, you might argue that the pirates were none of our business, and that in some ways their arrival was beneficial—they would provide the perfect cover for leaving the ship. But consider: I had just spent half the night setting up a shipment so I could track it into Europe. If the ship was parked off the coast of Somalia for a few months, I was going to be twiddling my thumbs for an awful long time.

Someone on the bridge had obviously spotted the approaching boat as well, for the ship began to speed up. You've probably heard that small parties of armed guards are being put on some ships to fight off pirates; this wasn't one of them. Nor did it appear that the crew was armed—two seamen came out on the starboard deck and set up a fire hose, preparing to soak their enemies.

The captain radioed the Italian destroyer, but it had sped to a call to the south. The Italians didn't have a helo with them; they told the captain they would check their distress call and then return as quickly as they could, but not to expect them before an hour. The captain's response was appropriately vulgar.

The pirate vessel was a high-prowed longboat originally designed for fishing; it was open and sturdy, though not particularly exceptional. What were exceptional were the two outboard motors on the stern—each looked big enough to propel a locomotive up Mount Everest. The crewmen aimed their fire hose as the boat swung in a circle to come alongside the ship on the starboard side. The burst of water pushed the prow sideways, and for a moment I thought the crew had successfully fended off the attack. But the pirates weren't going to give up that easily. Two men rose and returned fire, shooting with lead rather than water.

Even so, the bullets didn't seem to faze the sailors. The grenade launcher was a different story. They fled as the man at the bow rose with the RPG. The sailor barely managed to get into the superstructure before the projectile exploded against its side.

No longer being harassed, the pirates pulled in close; one threw a grappling hook around the rail.

"Stand by to repel boarders," I told Shotgun, creeping forward.

A head popped up over the rail, turned in our direction—then disappeared, no doubt because of the bullet I put into its nose.

The pirates responded by moving off and firing their guns at the bridge. It was an impressive display of firepower, the spray of bullets taking out the large plates of glass with stupendous clatter.

It was also a handy diversion—the pirates were so concentrated on the bridge that they didn't see Shotgun or me lean over the rail and take aim.

Strike that—one man did. But the last thing he saw was a bullet from my MP5 as it zeroed in on his skull.

I have no idea what the other eight saw. It would have been roughly as pretty. The boat's hull had been pierced in more than a dozen places, and it began settling immediately.

"Stow your gun and let's go," I told Shotgun, straightening. "We're going over the side."

We swam, floated, and swam some more for nearly a half hour as the freighter disappeared behind us. Finally Mongoose appeared in the distance, the bow of the Zodiac a welcome smile on the waves.

Once we were aboard, I had him radio the captain on the channel the Italians had used. He claimed that a NATO anti-pirate force had just taken care of the pirates, and I wished him well.

Oddly, the radio failed as soon as the captain began asking questions.

Four hours later, our fuel gone, a helicopter appeared on the horizon. It was Trace, right on time. Within an hour we were fully refueled and heading toward Djibouti.

Trace met us when we landed later that evening with typically warm greetings.

"What the hell took you assholes so long?" she yelled as we waded up the mudflat that stood in place of a beach southeast of the airport.

"If we'd known you were waiting, we would have gone slower," answered Shotgun.

Trace responded with a hearty round of tender endearments and suggestions for Shotgun's physical improvement, most of which were anatomically impossible. We pulled the Zodiac into the back of the pickup she'd rented, then headed across the dunes to the highway, and from there to a warehouse near the port. We'd amassed a good amount of equipment and storing it was problematic.

Sometime later we assembled in a briefing room—aka, the hotel bar—and began debriefing properly, assessing the recuperative powers of cold German beer. Shotgun chatted up one of the waitresses—a comely lass who was from Ireland—while Mongoose went over to the pool table and began showing his skill at knocking defenseless balls silly.

Trace and I discussed Junior and a myriad of other topics, including how many people we would need in place when the ship docked in Europe. My plan now was to follow the trailers, identify the main players, flesh out the bank connection, and turn the information over to the bank's board of directors.

"You think Veep's involved?" asked Trace.

"Up to his sneering smile."

"Why not give the information to Garrett?" asked Trace. "Make him look good."

A certain tone in her voice made it clear she'd taken a shine to young Mr. Garrett. I said nothing: I learned long ago that interfering in *affaires de cœur* is a good way to piss off people. Or in the case of Trace Dahlgren, get your throat slit. Which is better than your balls, as you serious Rogue Warrior fans always remember.

"The agency's goals are not our goals here," I told her. "We have to keep him at arm's distance."

Was that a blush I saw on her cheek? The lighting was too dim to tell. Trace left a few minutes later to keep an appointment—the word "date" is expressly forbidden—with said Garrett. She was under strict orders not to tell him that we had taken his advice and visited *Indiamotion*. I'm sure she found plenty else to do.

I meditated further on the situation with the help of timely communiques and background material from Danny in the States.

I also had occasion to check on the progress of our containers: still aboard ship, which was making its way toward Aden.

Aden?

"Looks like it, Dick," said Shunt, who was looking at it on his computer plot. "Check it on the iPad. That's what we wrote the app for."

I swiped and typed, getting my password into the overpriced tablet computer, then tapped the little picture to bring up the tracking app. A few seconds later, I saw that Shunt was right—the ship was on a beeline for Aden, a major port in southern Yemen.

"Is that a scheduled stop?" I asked Shunt.

"Negative. And there's been no traffic about it either."

"Can the company track it?"

"Their system isn't particularly precise, but it will be obvious if they stay around for a while, say to unload something. Why wouldn't this be listed?"

"Same reason seven-eighths of the containers aren't," I told him. "And even more."

The fact that the ship was making a side trip to Aden didn't meant that our cargo containers were getting off there. But if they were, tracking them was going to be much more difficult than following them through Europe. If they were bound for customers in the Middle East it would still be worthwhile tracking them, just more of a pain. I'd already had my share of fun and joy on the Arabian peninsula.

I was cogitating on what to do next when Trace returned from her rendezvous. I was frankly surprised to see her back in the bar, even though several hours had passed—I thought her assignation would have required considerably more time.

"Garrett's on his way to France," she announced. "They have information on where the ship is going. Marseilles."

Trace pronounced the name of France's most important Mediterranean port with an air of triumph, as if it wouldn't have been the most obvious place for the ship to land.

"You're sure?" I asked.

"He said they intercepted a message to the ship just before he and I had dinner. I drove him to the airport."

Hmmm.

"They know the ship?" I asked.

"Yes."

"What's the name?"

"He didn't say."

"He didn't? Did you ask?"

"He just wouldn't say."

"How much do you like him?" I asked.

Trace's face colored. "Why?"

"Just wondering."

"I'm fine, Dick. He didn't say. Is it our ship?"

"If so, he's lying."

Trace's eyes narrowed, but she remained quiet.

"Our ship is a few hours out of Aden," I told her, showing her the iPad. "Unscheduled stop."

"I'll slit his balls off if he's leading me on," she said, starting to rise.

"Let's just take this one step at a time."

"I will cut his balls off," she repeated. There was enough conviction in her voice that I pushed my own legs together, and didn't move until she was across the room.

[V]

I didn't need Murphy to tell me that the containers we'd marked would almost certainly be offloaded in the worst possible place for us to track, and so when Shunt reported that they were being moved at the dock in Aden, Trace, Mongoose, Abdi, and I were waiting to catch a plane at the Djibouti airport.

Aden had a colorful history as a British colonial city, but if Americans know it at all, it's as the port where the attack on the USS *Cole* took place in 2000. That was an al Qaeda production,[29] one that got a lot of attention from everyone in the world . . . except the United States, which sent FBI agents to investigate, then let them be browbeaten away by rifle-waving Yemen soldiers when they landed at the airport. This at a time when the entire Yemen military could be defeated by a Boy Scout troop from New Jersey.

The attack on the *Cole* brought al Qaeda to the attention of many Americans, but this was far from their first attack in the area. In 1992, al Qaeda operatives detonated a bomb at the Gold Mohur Hotel in Aden. They were aiming for U.S. servicemen, supposedly; they killed an Austrian tourist and a Yemen citizen.

Why did they want to attack Americans? Because Americans were trying to bring food aid to Somalia.[30] Apparently trying to keep starving people from dying is a crime against Islam if you're a member of al Qaeda.

I brought Abdi with us to help with our cover; we were international businessmen with vague plans to stay for a week. Americans are not particularly welcome in most parts of Yemen, and not knowing which parts we were going to, we adopted identities that had nothing to do with the good ol' USA. Trace's Indian background is adaptable to a variety of nationalities, and my beard has helped me pass as Arab before, especially with the aid of the proper clothes. With his swarthy Filipino face, Mongoose could

---

[29] A U.S. court ruled that the attack could not have been carried out without the help of Sudan, and awarded a judgment against the government there. Personally, I would have added the Yemen government to the docket, and the award I would have awarded would have been paid in blood.

Yemen eventually arrested some possible plotters, but all were soon released. Rumor has it that a few have since met other fates.

[30] In case you're wondering, the battle we refer to as *Black Hawk Down* takes place the following year, and was part of a different operation, or "mission shift" in militarese.

probably have passed as an Arab—until he opened his mouth. To avoid that problem, we presented him as a Filipino labor broker, anxious to hook up with companies in the port area. That made him the boss—Trace was his Filipino secretary, while Abdi and I were flunkies with various abilities, mostly unspoken. It was worth the sneers from Mongoose just to see him in a suit and tie.

Shotgun, about as white as Wonder Bread, stayed in Djibouti.

Aden was packed with spies, domestic and otherwise. Two members of the national police tailed us from the airport, and another with a camera snapped our photo as we came into the hotel. Which was probably unnecessary, since I'm sure the hotel transmitted copies of our passports to the local police and intelligence apparatus within a few seconds of our signing the registry. At least two people in the lobby were using their cell phones to take clandestine pictures of everyone who came in, and I spotted a fellow in the corner pretending to read a newspaper two days old.

Our GPS system, accessed via the iPad, showed the two containers next to each other in a lot near the water. The mapping was accurate to about a foot, but it didn't supply real-time imagery; it was possible that the sensors had been discovered and moved. So I needed to get there and examine the scene with my Mark 1 Eyeballs.

If there was time, I'd take a look at any other containers that were plucked off as well. Maybe they were just dried fruit and nuts, or maybe they were something fruits and nuts would find useful in a shooting war.

Squared away at the hotel—we also had a pair of secret reservations elsewhere as backup—we headed to the pier on the north side of Al-Ma'ala, the rocky tip of the arm of the bay protecting the interior. There was no security to speak of—though anyone approaching on foot would be taking his life in his hands, as the locals drove with the abandon of Frenchmen on holiday.

Warehouses larger than most of the ships and barges lined the far end of the pier. We'd rented a Mercedes E280—1,328 euros per week, plus gas, a complete ripoff. Mongoose drove, taking us into the holding lots around a stream of kamikaze truck drivers. He got us out to the staging area near the end of the pier just in time to see the first of our trailers exiting past us.

Container number two was just being hitched.

"I thought you said they'd stay on the docks for at least a day," said Trace. Her tone could be best described as sarcastic.

"Take us back to the other car," I told Mongoose. "We'll split up. Abdi will come with me."

The other car was a Ssangyong Kyron, an *almost* SUV made by the Korean company Ssangyong. Mechanically, the car was typical of effective but not flashy Korean workmanship. But it was so small Abdi and I rubbed shoulders in the front seat.

The trucks drove west. After dropping us off, Mongoose and Trace raced ahead on the highway, and found that there were four other trailers besides the ones we'd tagged, all traveling relatively close together. Wary of being spotted, Trace got about a half mile ahead of the lead vehicle, and kept pace with the help of the tracking program.

We caught up near Ta'izz (or Taiz as some in the West spell it). This is an incredibly densely packed city in southwestern Yemen, built in and around mountains. The city itself is some 1,400 meters above sea level, high enough that my ears popped on the climb.

The streets were quiet and dusty. Yemen roads in general are about on par with the rest of those in the Middle East, which is to say they suck. But outside the city, the highways were decently paved, occasionally featuring three lanes (mostly empty) in each direction. There were no military patrols or checkpoints, and the hardest part of the drive was staying awake.

Abdi and I swapped places about a mile outside of Ta'izz. I needed to make some calls and arrange for weapons—the trucks' sudden departure meant we had no gear. I got on the phone with Danny back home, to see if he could arrange to have one of our "friends" find us some weapons and meet us along the way.

We have friends everywhere. Some are more friendly than others.

"Where do you think they're headed?" asked Danny, trying to figure out where we might set up the rendezvous.

"Saudi border," I said. "Drive up the side of the Red Sea, maybe go through all the way to Turkey and then into Europe from there."

"I think you're looking at local stops. Otherwise why land in Yemen? Why not just offload in Turkey."

"They want to avoid any customs inspectors."

"Easy to bribe them. Cheaper, too."

"Maybe the answer has to do with what's in the other containers," I told him. "Prescription drugs are one thing. Guns and ammo another. Al Qaeda's pretty active in Yemen."

"Could be. I'll get back to you once I have things set up."

The next two hours passed slowly. We stopped for gas, paying 175 Yemen rials per liter, a price set by the government. That's a little less than a dollar, or roughly three bucks a gallon. I may fill up there all the time.

Danny called me back north of Al Hudaydah. He'd arranged for a rendezvous a few miles over the Saudi border.

"If you end up staying inside Yemen for the night," he added, "then

Ahmed[31] can get south and hook you up. But it's probably better to wait until past the border. You can get through right on the highway, without worrying about being searched."

The crossing to the north near Al Tuwal was well guarded and extremely bureaucratic. Most likely we could get guns through, but Danny was right; there'd be no sense taking the chance. Especially since the trucks were driving along as free and easy as if they were going through Indiana.

As we skirted around Az Zaydiya and continued north, Trace got on the radio and asked what I thought we should do about getting food.

"We can wait for them to stop," I told her.

"They should have stopped by now, if they were stopping," she told me. "Mongoose is getting hungry."

"Be grateful Shotgun's not with you."

"He'd at least have something to munch on."

"Go on ahead a little and see if you can find some place to stop," I told her.

"Where? It's not like they have McD's at every exit."

I checked the map. There was a small city about ten miles ahead of her. "Stop there. Just don't take too long. We'll close the gap in the meantime."

Trace and Mongoose pulled off the highway at a small hut selling local food. They uploaded fresh videos of the trucks as they passed, hoping Shunt might get some more information. They were still getting the food when we passed.

There was generally a good queue at the border customs station, and it might be possible to pose as customs men and make a personal inspection there. To do that, we'd need some information about Saudi routines, and specifics on the station. I was just about to call Danny to see what he could get when I looked at the iPad and noticed the tracking map showed our two vehicles suddenly going in different directions.

That was inconvenient.

"Are you seeing this?" asked Trace a few seconds later.

"Yeah. They just split up below al Ma'ras." I looked at the map. The lead truck was heading east, back into the hills in the direction of a city named Hajjah. The other was still going up the coast.

"You stay with the vehicle going up the coast," I told Trace. "We'll go east."

I had Abdi speed up to close the distance between our little SUV and the truck, unsure whether there were more vehicles with it. The road was well

---

[31] No, of course that's not his name. He came to us via an associate who works in Virginia, who also can't be named. He knows who he is.

paved, but it curved violently with the sides of the hill. North of Hajjah it became particularly treacherous, angling sharply. The sides of the road were filled with rocks from landslides.

After about five miles, the truck turned off the highway and the road narrowed further. The mountains around us were sprinkled with little green specks—large bushes and small trees—that stood out against the dreary brown and dark yellow of the sandy hillsides. The valleys were lined with small fields. Crooked hamlets backed up into the hills. They were small and old. Occasionally there would be a new brick building near the street. Korean compacts, haphazardly parked, jutted half into the road in front of high stone walls. The macadam gradually disappeared into hard-packed dirt.

If we were going to Saudi Arabia, we were sure taking the long way there. Abdi closed the distance between us until I could see the dust cloud in front.

I was beginning to think I'd chosen the wrong truck to follow when the phone rang. I went to answer it, then realized it wasn't my sat phone.

It was the phone Shire Jama had given us. The one that wasn't supposed to be used until the shipment arrived in Europe.

"Yes?" I said.

"We are under—attack. New arrangements—"

There was a loud explosion in the background, then a softer pop. The phone went dead.

The car suddenly stopped. I looked at Abdi. He was pointing ahead.

"Truck, Dick. They've stopped."

In the middle of the road.

"What is going on?" asked Abdi.

The answer was supplied by a man with an AK47 near the front of the truck. I thought he was the driver or a helper, but then realized he was approaching the cab from a pickup truck blocking the roadway ten or twenty yards up. He fired a few rounds into the air, then pointed at the windshield. Apparently he didn't like the response he got, for he lowered his aim and fired directly into the passenger compartment.

"Throw us into reverse," I told Abdi, planning one of those evasive J maneuvers security drivers and James Garner are so fond of. But as I swung around to check the rear, I discovered our exit was cut off by not one but two pickups, which together had blocked the narrow mountain road.

There was a .50 cal machine gun in the back of one of them. A man with a grenade launcher stood in the other.

"This would be SNAFU, yes?" said Abdi.

"You could call it that," I answered, throwing my hands up as a gunman started to approach.

[1]

Abdi gave the man at the window our cover story, claiming that we had been separated from our boss, who was driving to the border to check on Filipino contract workers.

The man was confused, but it was clear that they had set up here for the truck and his orders didn't include killing bystanders. We were ordered out of the car, quickly frisked, then told to stand on the side of the road.

"We'll need to know the area so we can find our way back," I told Abdi. I wanted to give him something to focus his mind on rather than the danger we were in. "Stick to our story."

He nodded grimly.

There were a dozen gunmen, not counting the drivers. They were dressed in typical Arab peasant clothes, long dirty white shirts and loose-fitting trousers. They wore head scarves wrapped to obscure their faces. A few had knives tucked into their belts; two or three had hand grenades and bandoliers as well. They pulled the bodies from the truck and one man got in the cab. Another man took our car, and slowly the two vehicles set out behind one of the pickups. The man who had come to our window prodded us to follow on foot, in front of the rest of the troop.

I kept looking to the sides of the road, sizing up possible escape routes. Running for it didn't make sense, at least not at the moment. There was still at least an hour to go until sunset, and the starkness of the hills nearby meant the gunmen would have an easy shot.

Trace and Mongoose would know soon enough that something had happened, as would Shunt, who would track my phone. The first order of business was to stay alive, and until I saw at least even odds, running for it made no sense.

After we'd gone a few hundred yards, the truck turned down a narrow dirt lane on the left. We followed. A terraced field stepped down the hill to the right, and for a moment I thought of making a break for it. But Abdi was walking a little ahead of me, and I didn't want to leave him behind—he'd be an easy target.

A thick wall rose at a curve in the road a short distance ahead. Two men in Arab garb with AKs stood on the road. Someone in the lead pickup shouted a greeting. A wrought-iron gate was pulled back, and our little convoy turned into a small compound etched into the side of the hill.

There were five buildings spread over a space of about four acres. Besides the guards I'd seen at the road, there were two guard posts at the corners of the road looking down the valley. They had an impressive view across the valley to a stretch of dark desert many miles away.

Two vans were waiting in the center of the compound. I didn't see what was going on—the man who'd radioed for instructions barked and the gunmen who'd been behind us prodded us toward a one-story building built into the south side of the wall about ten yards from the road. It appeared to be used as a stable; bits of straw clung to the floor, and it smelled like Shotgun after a long workout.

"What will happen to us, Mr. Dick?" asked Abdi.

"We'll get out."

"How?"

"Haven't figured it out yet."

"You will find a way?"

I nodded.

"I wish I could be like you. My uncle was that way, too. He always knew."

I inspected our new digs. While the sun hadn't set yet, there was only a small window in the building, and it was fairly dark. There were no lights to turn on that I could see.

The window looked to be our obvious exit. Two rows of bricks broke the open space into three almost equal parts. Take those away, and we could get through easily—and since the hut was built into the perimeter wall, once through we'd be free.

The problem was getting through the bricks. They were old but they were thick. I didn't have a knife or any other tools—our captors had seen to that—and trying to scratch the base away with my fingernails would take a long, long time.

"How do you know?" asked Abdi as I stared at the bricks.

"How do I know what?"

"To do—how do you know what to do?"

"Sometimes I don't," I confessed. "But you always try."

"Yes. My uncle said that."

"He was a wise man."

I looked down at the floor. It was made of boards nailed into crossbeams. The nails were old-style wedges: miniature chisels. All I had to do was pry one out.

"Find a loose board," I told Abdi.

I explained a little of what I wanted to do. He dropped to his knees and began searching with me.

"Why a restaurant in Mogadishu?" said Abdi out of the blue.

"What do you mean?"

"Why did my uncle open the restaurant there? Why not America? Or at least Cairo. Alexandria. He could have gone to Egypt."

Egypt as the Promised Land is a difficult concept to get your mind around, even in 1012 BC, but I knew what he meant.

"Your uncle wanted to stay and help your family," I told Abdi. "He believed in the country where he'd been born. That's why he was still in Mogadishu."

"I should stay there. To help the family now." He reached to the board in front of him. "This nail is loose."

I took the nail and went back to the window. The nail was small and a bit dull, but it made decent progress against the old mud of the brick. I had a good slice across the base a half inch deep when we heard voices outside the door. I stuck the nail in the crevice and stepped away just as the door opened.

Two men came into the house. One was the man who had been in charge of the team that took us prisoner. The other was younger, skinnier, with only a bare beard; he was dressed in Western trousers and a T-shirt.

"You are an American," said the younger man in English. He was so thin that his arms could have been made of wire.

"I have an Egyptian passport," I told him. I could tell from his expression that wasn't going to work, so I continued. "But I am Italian by birth. My mother was Egyptian, my father a soldier." I repeated it in Italian, mostly to establish that Skinnyboy didn't speak the language.

"You are American," he insisted.

"You have my passport." They had taken it earlier.

"Passports are not worth the paper they are printed with."

I shrugged. He was right, given the outrageous price of paper these days. The other man grinned. "You will fetch good money, American."

"Come," said Skinnyboy. "The leader wishes to meet you."

The other man barred Abdi as he started to follow.

"He's with me," I said.

"He is of no concern to you," said the young man.

"I don't want him harmed. He's my friend."

The young man smirked. "Americans always try to protect others." He shook his head, as if this were the worst failing in the world.

"You'll pay if you harm him," I promised.

Skinnyboy laughed. "We don't harm fellow Muslims. Only infidels. It's your life you should worry about. Not his."

The truck and the men who'd taken it had disappeared. In their place were a pair of Mercedes sedans and a half-dozen guards, all in Western-style clothes except for the scarves that made it hard to see more than their eyes. Dressed in black cotton pants and wearing blazers over button-down shirts, they could have been running security at a politician's campaign event, rather than watching some Middle East terror wannabe.

We walked past them and down a set of wide steps that led around a fountain to the main house. The building was a two-story structure covered with stucco. I wouldn't call it a mansion, but compared to the structures we'd passed on the road, it was opulent. Most importantly, it didn't smell like shit.

Two more guards, these in pinstriped business suits, were outside the door. They stiffened as we approached, but said nothing. A guard inside opened the door just as I reached it. The door opened onto a hallway about ten feet deep and another sixteen wide. Beyond it was a large room where a man in a long robe sat on a divan holding court. Four other men, these in ill-fitting and wrinkled business suits, stood near him, addressing him in Arabic. Well into their fifties and sixties, the men were so engrossed in their conversation that they didn't even glance in our direction.

"Wait," hissed Skinnyboy, stopping me at the doorway.

I'd seen the man in the robe before. He was Mohammad Abu al-Yasur— one of the key operatives of al Qaeda. He was instantly recognizable by a long scar on his cheek, which extended to his beard. He'd gotten the scar during fighting in Iraq—the man had gotten around over the past decade and a half.

Once a close associate of Ayman al-Zawahiri—the man most Western-ers believe succeeded Osama bin Goatfucker—al-Yasur was considered the number-two man in the organization by a number of experts, including the Christians in Action. I'm not sure the CIA has ever met an al Qaeda member they *didn't* think was the number-two person in the organization. But al-Yasur definitely was high up, and according to the Pakistanis was a link between the funding arm of al Qaeda and the organization's most ac-tive unit, al Qaeda in the Arabian Peninsula.

And the Paks would be in a position to know, don't you think?

I stood more or less at attention—probably less than more—waiting for my audience with his holyshitiness. It had been a while since I saw the dos-sier, but as I recalled he had begun his career in Turkey, helping a pair of youngsters blow themselves up in Beyoğlu, a section of Istanbul frequented by many tourists. As it happened, the two young men succeeded in killing only themselves, but it was a start.

Al-Yasur's next plot was to blow up a ferry in the Bosporus, which is the neck of water that separates Istanbul between Europe and Asia. The police broke that plan up (with a little unacknowledged help from the Christians in Action). The aspiring mass murderer decided to take the hint and move

(II)

...ove to tell you about the operation in great detail, explaining how the ...m took down the compound without incurring a casualty of their .... I'd love to describe the way they silently took care of the posted look-...s, incapacitated the guards, and stormed all of the buildings in the com-...and.

I can't, though, and not because I'm sworn to secrecy. I didn't see any of .. I didn't hear much of it either. I'd no sooner thrown Abdi to the ground than the door blew open. The flash-bang grenades were still going off. The grenades are non-lethal—well, I wouldn't want to swallow one—but render most people deaf, dumb, and blind long enough to be subdued. Before I could even cough, two SEALs trussed me like a lamb waiting for the butcher. Cuffed hand and foot with flexcuffs, I was rolled next to Abdi.

I expressed my gratitude freely.

"You such-and-sos," I yelled, using words other than the ones my editor has supplied here. "What the *hell* do you think you're doing?"

"Commander Marcinko, please relax," said one of the SEALs in a slow-Georgian drawl that would have tenderized a slab of beef on a roasting spit. "We'll let you all go once the area is secure."

"What the hell did you tie us up for?"

"I'm sorry, but we're under orders to treat everyone like they're hostile," continued the SEAL. "Even you, Commander Marcinko."

"How do you know who I am?"

I didn't get an answer. Securing noncombatants *is* standard operating procedure, and it wasn't as if we were manhandled or ill-treated. But cuffing us was a bit over the top, especially since they knew who I was.

After we'd been on the floor for twenty minutes or so, I heard two or three sets of boots come into the building. A voice that could *only* belong to a chief petty officer barked.

"You can *let* that asshole Marrr-*chink*-O up," he growled. "I don't think even *he* could screw this up at this point."

I grinned. The chief[32] was an acquaintance whom I'd raised practically as a baby. When I first met him, he was a squirrely-looking preteen looking

---

[32] Given that he has somehow swindled the navy into thinking that he is ultra important and remains on active duty, I'm not going to use his real name. You can call him
Chief Asshole if you want. Just duck when you say it. Better yet, run.

on, seeking greener pastures in places like Kenya and the Sudan. Eventually he found his way to Iraq, from there to Afghanistan and bin Goat-fucker's palace in Pakistan. He had no fixed base after that, though he spent a lot of time in Yemen.

"So who is this American?" he said finally, turning to me. His English, though heavily accented, was fluent.

"*Sono Italiano,*" I answered. I switched back to English. "I'm Italian."

"There are no Italians in Yemen."

"Then I must not be here. I'll be going."

Skinnyboy didn't have much of a sense of humor. He grabbed my arm and squeezed it, probably thinking that the pressure would hurt. But I've met two-year-olds with tighter grips.

Naturally, I winced. No sense letting him know what a wimp he was.

"Where in America do you come from?" asked al-Yasur.

"Rome." I started talking in Italian again, wheeling off a travelogue of the great sites of the eternal city, all prisons, all including special treatments for Muhammad's chosen idiots, of which his highness in front of me was one. Obviously he didn't understand a word of it.

"Your French is not very convincing," he said when I finished.

"That's because it's Italian."

He waved his hand, dismissing me. Except that he wasn't sending me away—he just wanted me in a position where I couldn't talk. This was accomplished by the guards. One came up and gave me a kidney punch. The other took me in a choke hold and coaxed me toward the floor.

Unlike Skinnyboy, this guard had real power. His forearms were thicker than telephone poles, and the press of his knee against my back as I went down felt like a crowbar. My legs buckled, and I had to use my hands to keep myself steady.

My right knee reminded me it had been taking a lot of abuse lately. My left knee wasn't crazy about its recent past either.

"The Christians are a dog's race," said al-Yasur. "You have degenerated even further from the Jews. This is to be expected. The seed of the bad tree becomes an even worse tree as time goes on."

The imam was off to the races. For the next fifteen minutes he talked about the downward evolution of the human race due to the influence of Christianity. In his worldview, every ill known to man could be blamed on or traced to a Christian: poverty, illness, the success of *American Idol*.

I suppressed a yawn, then several more. I can see why alcohol is banned in Muslim countries—half a beer and I would have been snoozing on the floor. Finally, one of his assistants leaned in close to him, and whispered something in his ear.

Al-Yasur looked at me. "I have to teach this evening. You've heard the text. I have a mind to take you with me, as an example. Though I'm sure the mosque walls would tremble to have an infidel between them."

Skinnyboy said something in Arabic. Imam responded. Apparently they were talking about what to do with me, because presently the guards took hold of my arms and marched me back to the little hut.

I was disappointed not to be guest of honor at the mosque. I'd been looking forward to making the roof fall in.

Abdi had been talking with one of the guards while I was gone. The man was a Nigerian, and had lived in Mogadishu briefly. He claimed to have seen Abdi's uncle's restaurant, though Abdi thought that unlikely.

"He is a stranger in Yemen," Abdi told me. "All of them are. He was brought here for the fight. They knew the trucks were coming weeks ago, and have been planning ever since."

"Why?"

"He didn't say. There were bad men in charge—that was his excuse. They had to be killed. Even the driver."

"Why?"

"There are conflicts—he is too low to understand or know much."

Abdi was right on that score, and he'd made a fairly good assessment of the situation. Bringing in bodyguards from outside of Yemen meant, or at least implied, that al-Yasur didn't trust the people in his own country, which in turn meant there was a power struggle going on. But that information wasn't of immediate use.

"What are they planning to do with us?" I asked Abdi.

"You, for ransom. Me . . ." He put his lips together. "We have no money," he said tightly. "Maybe—they kill me."

"Don't worry about a ransom. It's not going to come to that. If it were a question of money, I'd pay. But we'll be gone before they even figure out who to contact."

"How?"

I went to the window and took the nail out of the crack where I'd put it. "Start scoring the edge of the mortar here where the brick meets the window. I'll find another nail."

Abdi took the nail eagerly. As mindless as the task was, it filled him with hope, and he dug at the brick.

Two hours later, enough of the mortar had been loosened that I was able to push it out. Unfortunately, I pushed a little too hard—the brick tumbled onto the ground before I could grab it.

The hole it left wasn't quite large en[ough] let alone me, so we went to work on the n[ext] moon out; it gave us enough light to see wha[t] thing beyond the wall remained pretty much i[n] like maniacal ants, scraping and scraping on both fingers and hands knotted. Needing a break, I put [it] over toward the door, flexing my fingers and arm. T[he] quiet since the departure of the imam and his entoura[ge] fore; under other circumstances I might have welcome[d] of the countryside.

I had just put my ear against the door, thinking I wou[ld] guards, when I heard a dull humming sound in the distance, so[unded like] a vacuum cleaner with a muffler on it. I'd heard it before some[where] couldn't quite place it.

In a flash, I realized what was going on.

"Down!" I yelled to Abdi, running over and throwing him to the [floor.] "Down!"

There was another flash, and the room exploded. SEAL Team Six ha[d] decided to pay a visit.

for advice on how to get into the SEALs. I took him under my wing, offered encouragement and the occasional kick in the seat of wisdom as he progressed. Despite my help, he had not only managed to become a member of the Teams and then DEVGRU, but had actually thrived. Some people are born to achieve no matter what handicaps they labor under.

We exchanged a few terms of endearment after my bonds were cut and I was raised to my feet. The chief tried to claim that I owed him money from a bet gone bad at our last social encounter. I countered that I had in fact paid; it wasn't my fault that he had decided not to grab the money from the G-string in which it had been placed.

"Who's your friend?" he asked, pointing at Abdi.

"My terp," I told him. "We needed a Somalian. He's done a good job."

"Take the terp outside," Chief told the others. "Grab a cigarette break."

"Chief, none of us smoke."

"Then *burr-ache* something else."

The house was quickly vacated.

"Damn new guys," griped Chief. "I gotta teach them some vices."

"How did you know I was here?"

"Can't say." Chief winked at me. "Have to talk to the head shed on that one."

"You are the head shed."

"Marcinko, you curse me like that again, I'm going to have to do something about it." He lowered his voice. "Can't say. The walls have ears here."

"Who's in charge of the operation?"

"Lieutenant *Colby* would be the officer in charge here. Whole operation is actually under the domain of—"

"Wait, don't tell me." I should have seen this coming two thousand miles ago. "It's a CIA operation with a guy who wears thick glasses and squints a lot?"

"Magoo," said Chief. "Never seen a man whose last name fits him better in person. You've met?"

The SEALs had come for al-Yasur. The operation had been planned for months, ever since the Christians in Action intercepted communications indicating that the old-line elements of al Qaeda were planning on shaking up the drug trade and reinforcing their role in al Qaeda in the Arabian Peninsula at the same time. They saw prescription drugs as a profitable loophole in Islamic law, and intended to move the operation in that direction. There had been resistance, however—some of it probably instigated by the CIA itself. In any event, the agency had seen the conflict as an opportunity to get al-Yasur.

Was my presence a coincidence?

Ha. And Santa Claus just wanders down a billion chimneys every Christmas.

Upon hearing the plans to get al-Yasur in Yemen, the current administration balked. They had just concluded a major diplomatic pact with Yemen and Saudi Arabia, and feared that the raid in Yemen would start a diplomatic firestorm. The Saudi situation was especially touchy. If the Saudi princes might raise the sort of hell the Pakistani MPs had raised after Osama was brought to justice, the result might be an oil embargo and serious damage to the world economy—and the president's chances of reelection.

"No raid in Yemen," the administration directed.

Which threatened to torpedo the whole project, until someone at the CIA came up with the notion that while "arresting" a bad guy would be bad publicity, "rescuing" an American would be the opposite. The plan was back on, as long as they could find an American to rescue.

Guess who.

"I was set up from the beginning?" I asked Chief.

There may have been a few other verbs and adjectives used, but that was the gist.

"Three weeks ago, someone started talking about you."

"Magoo?"

"I heard it came from someone higher. But . . ."

"Higher" meant only one person to me—the admiral. His was exactly the sort of devious mind that would think nothing of putting an American citizen in a dangerous situation to save a few thousand lives.

I admired him for it. In his position I'm sure I would have done the same. I also wanted to kick his ass for not telling me what was going on.

Murphy, though, had thrown Six a curveball. The imam had left a while before and not returned, messing up their plans to assassinate him.

I mean, to coax him into freely surrendering and repenting the error of his ways.

Unsure where he was, they had hidden themselves in the house and outside the compound, waiting for him to return. The problem was, they couldn't wait all night. They needed to be out of Yemen and on their rendezvous vessel within two hours, or there was a good chance they were going to swim home. SEALs do like to swim, but it was a bit much even for them.

"Lieutenant's trying to get permission to move," said Chief. "We've got it narrowed down to three places. But we had to drop off some personnel when we lost one of the helos coming in, so we can't get to all three. We can get two. Murphy's working overtime tonight."

"I know where he went," I said.

"You do?"

"He's giving the Sermon on the Mount at a local mosque. He gave me a private preview."

"No shit?"

"I wouldn't shit you. You're my favorite turd."

Chief shook his head. "Such a mouth."

"Let me talk to the lieutenant."

"Yeah, all right. But listen. You might want to salute. He's got a bit of a hard-on for you."

That wasn't meant as a compliment, let alone a reference to his sexual preferences. While Yours Truly is long gone from the active rolls, the legend lives on, and continues to piss off a decent percentage of the brass.

Mom would be so proud.

I didn't salute. I did call him "Lieutenant." He was equally pleasant.

"What the hell do you want, Mar-*chink*-o?" he said when I walked in the door. Was it a coincidence that he was standing in the same spot where al-Yasur had lectured me a few hours before?

In fact, now that I think about it, there was a bit of a resemblance.

"It's pronounced 'Marcinko,' Lieutenant," said Chief. "Soft c."

"That's not all that's soft around here. What the hell do you want, Mar-*chink*-o?"

"I know where the imam went."

The lieutenant's mood changed instantly. Now I was his best friend.

Well, not quite.

"Damn it," sputtered the lieutenant. "Are you going to diddle around all day, or you going to open up the flytrap you call a mouth and share your information?"

"He went to preach at a mosque. He left about two hours ago. He may still be talking. He's pretty long-winded."

"Son of a bitch."

"You can't find the mosque?"

"Oh, I have a pretty good guess which one it would be. It's just off-limits."

Chief explained that the mission had been approved by "the highest levels." That approval—some might call it interference—included a long list of THOU SHALT NOTs.

At the top of the list was THOU SHALT NOT GO INTO A MOSQUE.

"I don't think that's much of a problem," I said. "If you know where the mosque is."

"Listen, Mar-*chink*-o." The lieutenant's tone suggested I was more than a little dense. "I don't go around disobeying orders."

"Who says you're disobeying orders?"

"You're suggesting we go into a mosque. My ass will be court-martialed faster than you can say Leavenworth."

"You're not going into the mosque. I am."

III

The word "dubious" does not begin to describe the lieutenant's attitude toward my proposal. He dismissed it, waving his hand at me and telling Chief to get me out of his sight. Chief escorted me from the building apologetically.

"We've been training on this one for a while," he told me. "The lieutenant has been on the top team tracking al-Yasur. He was in Pakistan a while back, and we almost got him there. We were going after him in Africa, but at the last minute someone tipped him off. And a sandstorm screwed up another mission."

"Nine lives, huh?"

"He's got more than that."

"Your lieutenant been in charge of every operation?" I asked.

"Every one. Unluckiest son of a bitch in the navy." Chief rubbed his chin. He had a scar there that I recognized—he'd gotten it in a bar fight during his first leave. It was then that he knew he had made the right career choice, or so he claimed.

"Your ROEs are what screwed you," I pointed out. "But we can fix that. Send me there, I'll drag him out, and then you can do the rest. Or you can claim I was being held there. That was the original plan, right?"

"Not in a mosque. We were reasonably sure where you'd be. Place has been under surveillance for months. There's only one other safe house along the route the truck takes. We trained on that one, too."

"You know that, the lieutenant knows that, but nobody else does. And screw the mosque crap. They're used by terrorists and crooks all the time. They have no right to sanctuary."

"I'm with you, Dick. But it's not my call."

He walked me back to the building where I'd been kept prisoner.

"If I was in charge," said Chief, taking a cigarette from his tac vest, "and I said you could go for it, what would you do?"

"Well, I'd go into the mosque," I said in my best old-timer's voice as I bent and held my back, "I'd go into the mosque to pray and make sure my prayers were answered."

A half hour later, with their time on the ground already over an hour, the lieutenant concluded that the operation to arrest al-Yasur was a bust, and ordered a full evac of the premises. The helos were just taking off when a fresh call came in:

An American citizen was in deep shit nearby.

"I cannot ignore an American citizen in danger," declared the lieutenant. "Turn these helos around."

That was the way the press eventually reported it. Events on the ground may have been slightly different.

[IV]

0155, on the ground in northern Yemen

A stranger pauses to remove his shoes outside the mosque in the small city of Te'h'run. The mosque is nearly as old as the city itself, which was a trading post in the hills before the Ottoman Empire conquered the known world. It is a good-sized building, with a large, open area where the men pray. Women are not allowed into the prayer area proper, and must content themselves with one of the porches, which are closed to the elements but open to the main hall via an arched wall.

Lit by candle, the place is filled with more shadows than light. But this doesn't bother the speaker, who has been talking now for more than two hours, and looks as if he can talk for several more.

The mosque is attached to a school, which has played a key role in the continuing struggle of the faithful as they seek to undo the horrible injustices imposed by the Infidel West and its audaciously evil plan to poison Islam. The preacher notes all of this, meeting with nods of approval from the crowd. About three dozen men sit or kneel on the floor nearby. A few have eyes nearly closed, but most of the rest are at absolute, rapt attention.

The stranger, an old man whose body is worn with the fatigue of age, proceeds to the door. The guard looks at him suspiciously, then points to his ear. The old man pulls out the hearing aid and shows it to the guard. It is an old device and does not work well. The guard inspects it, then finally hands it back to the man, who shambles in to join the others.

0205, on the ground in Yemen

The old man moves to the back of the small crowd, walking uneasily. His breath failing, he clutches at his chest and stumbles across the open space of the large room toward a row of benches. They are near the entrance to the reception area and a small kitchen and classrooms. If any of the other congregants see him, none make a move to help.

The imam's voice rises as his denouncement of the Americans continues. This has been a long day for him, but his speech invigorates him. He knows he could speak forever if he wishes. It is very late, however. The local imam hosting him insisted on his meeting some promising students before

giving his talk. And then there was a long reception in the outer room before he could begin.

Outside, the stars are shining brightly, their light pushing away the occasional thin wisps of clouds. The air in the low mountains is crisp but not
unpleasant.

0209, on the ground in Yemen

Strength restored and no longer wheezing, the old man rises and walks slowly
toward the rest of the congregation. A few members of the audience glance
in his direction. Some of the younger members suppress giggles; they have
seen scores of these old-timers struggling in at odd hours, nodding and
mumbling to themselves, more crazy than inspired. A few others look on in
admiration, hoping that the one true creator of the universe, praise be his
unmentioned name, might grant them similar strength and faith when they
reach such an advanced age.

The old man catches the imam's eye. The gray beard looks very familiar
to the teacher. Very, very familiar. Change it to black, take away some of
the creases, subtract a decade or two, perhaps three, and the man would
look very much like the Italian prisoner the brothers had taken earlier.

A coincidence surely.

The imam turns his gaze elsewhere, his fervor increasing.

0210, on the ground in Yemen

Someone at the side of the audience smells smoke. He turns around just in
time to see flames bursting from the door of the kitchen.

"Fire!" yells the man in Arabic. "النار"

The others turn and stare. The imam continues speaking for a few moments more. Then he realizes what is going on.

"We must leave quickly," he tells them all calmly. "My men will deal
with it. Everyone else, follow me."

His words calm the rising sense of panic. The audience rises and begins
moving toward the door. The guards, meanwhile, rush toward the fire, even
as fresh flares shoot from the doorway. A chemical smell begins to permeate
the large hall. Smoke curls out the back. What begins as a light mist of gray
quickly mushrooms into something far more sinister—a blanket of black
rolls from the rear of the hall as the fire begins to rage.

The imam urges his followers to come with him. He stops at the door and waves them on like a flagger at a NASCAR race. The old man, tottering unsteadily, grabs his arm for balance.

The imam pats it, then helps him to the door. The old man mumbles incoherently, but nods his head fervently, bowed low toward the ground.

0213, on the ground in Yemen

The back room of the mosque explodes, sending flames and smoke cascading outward. The imam, worried now, tries to push off the old man and run ahead. But the old man's fingers are like pliers, firmly gripping the imam.

"We will get outside the gate," says the imam, perhaps recognizing that he has little choice—in his panic, the old man has gained energy and is literally dragging him along toward the gate, twenty yards away.

The wrought-iron bars loom on both sides of the walk. The imam reaches for the gate on the left side as they approach, wanting to steady himself as he lets go of the old man.

But the old man doesn't let go. The imam feels himself being pulled forward, then flying through the air, landing in a tumble on the rock staircase.

The old man collapses on him as he hits the ground. The old man laughs.

"Move, cockbreath, and I'll have the pleasure of killing you with my bare hands."

Not particularly poetic, but I'd had a long day.

At about the time I was pouncing on al-Yasur, four or five flash-bangs exploded at the wall behind me—just *outside* the mosque precincts.

People started to run. There was confusion. Disorder. Gunshots. I grabbed the imam by the hand and strolled with him down to the road. His hand happened to be behind his back. Very possibly he was screaming at this point, though surely not in pain. It was a very pleasurable stroll.

I would be very happy to report that he suffered an accident, that a bullet fired by one of his guards struck him in the temple and took him down, or that he tripped over an untied shoelace and fell headlong into a very sharp and perfectly placed rock.

Alas, Chief and two other SEAL Team Six members stepped from the shadows and grabbed the imam before any of that could happen. Ten minutes later, we were aboard a helo, en route to the Indian Ocean.

[V]

When SEAL Team Six took out Osama bin Goatfucker, the "prize" was eventually brought aboard an aircraft carrier—at least according to the official story. Al-Yasur didn't rate a flattop. All he got was a (former) boomer submarine, which surfaced at precisely 0315 to receive the party of SEALs and their prize.[33]

There was one other critical difference: al-Yasur was alive. He wasn't talking too much, but given his natural inclinations, I think that was only a matter of time.

Abdi and I were along for the first part of the ride. I have to say, it's been a while since I was aboard a submarine, and even longer since I ran an operation from one. (You'll enjoy my book *Red Cell*; the description of that operation starts around page 229 in the paperback version. You'll have to use the search function if you have an e-book.)

They didn't ask me for my ID when I boarded, though given some of my history with submarines when I worked with Red Cell (I stole one), I wouldn't have been surprised to see my photo, post-office style, pasted inside the conning tower with the words "Don't Let This Man Aboard." A petty officer hustled me down to sick bay for a quick medical check, then returned me to the galley, where Abdi was already enjoying the submarine coffee—always stronger than any other coffee known to man.

The SEALs had disappeared into a specially designated space to debrief and rest. Abdi and I were given bunks to share or "hot bunk" with sailors aboard—they hadn't been expecting us and there wasn't room for special accommodations with all the SEALs aboard.

Not feeling particularly tired, and knowing we would only be aboard the sub for a few hours, I took advantage of an offer of a tour from the COB, or chief of the boat, the senior enlisted man on the submarine. This included a visit to the forward torpedo room, always a personal highlight, though I must say the chief watched me especially carefully near the "fish"—maybe he thought I was going to try sticking one in my pocket and walking off with it.

---

[33] I'm not supposed to mention the name of the submarine, or even the fact that it was a member of the Ohio class—oops—which was modified partly to facilitate SEAL missions. The submarine now carries Tomahawk missiles rather than Tridents, so it retains one hell of a punch.

There was a lot on the boat to admire. A good deal had changed since the last time I'd played tourist below the waves. The helmsman worked at a station that looked several times more complicated than the average rocket cockpit. I even got a chance to look through the periscope, which is basically a glorified camera these days.

"Nothing up there except a few naked mermaids," I reported.

While SEALs have operated off of submarines pretty much since the teams were formed, things have changed quite a bit since the old days when yours truly was trying to figure out whether he was allowed to "flush" while the boat was blowing its sanitaries. (NO!!!) The submarines are larger, or at least seem that way, though I'd admit that's a relative term and couldn't blame anyone for feeling claustrophobic once the hatch is secured. The procedure for getting SEALs to shore is a lot easier and less fatiguing—a serious plus. But other things never change—there's no going aft where the nuclear power plants do their work, for example, and there's no escaping the knowledge that if things get catastrophic and the sub loses its bubble, the rest of your day is going to be very, very bad.

Since I mentioned Red Cell and my stint as a submarine thief earlier, I should probably mention that security aboard the boats has improved over the years. But again, there are limits to everything—human limits, especially. Here's a simple one that we can discuss without giving away the family jewels, just so you understand what the navy, and by extension all of us, is up against:

Having two crews—"blue and gold"—to keep the submarines deployed as much as possible makes very good sense. But that means that even though the submarine may get the benefit of a Red Cell–style (or other security) exercise, only one of the crews actually gets the experience.

Worse, we've generally found that maybe 10 percent of the sailors (or other humans and close relatives) *remember* what they were taught during an exercise. So if you're not constantly, constantly, constantly training, the odds are almost overwhelmingly against you.

One of the *good* things that I've noticed is common among crews with high security ratings: there's a lot of communication going on. Partly this is because the commander encourages it; he or now she sets up a culture that gets people talking together and comparing notes. And I noticed a lot of contact on the sub I was on.

I worry, though. A lot of elite people—and here I have to include submariners in general, since they are definitely an elite—lack some of the social graces that permit ready verbal exchange. In short, they're a tribe that includes a lot of brainy geeks . . . and introverts. Add our current propensity to text and use other nonpersonal forms of communication, and I worry that future generations won't have trained enough or exchanged enough general knowledge to properly guard our most precious assets. The pressure is really going on the navy leadership to keep communication lines open, and as always to train our people to deal not just with their jobs, but things that will prevent them from their jobs.

Like tangos stealing a sub.

End of lecture. Back to the mayhem.

The vans I'd spotted in the compound had been tracked by a stealthy UAV and followed as they drove north toward the Saudi border. About a half hour after the team entered the compound, a separate unit of Rangers, which had been deployed as a backup reaction force and came all the way from Kuwait, stopped the trucks on a mountain highway north of the compound. Besides prescription drugs, they found a good amount of pure heroin and hashish.

Trace and Shotgun, meanwhile, had followed the second cargo container to the customs station at the northeastern corner of Yemen. She arranged to keep the driver busy while Shotgun took a look inside.

He probably hoped to find something similar to what we'd found aboard the ship—a day's supply of dried fruit and nuts. Instead, the trailer turned out to include an even bigger load of prescription drugs than we'd grabbed. Besides enough Viagra to increase Europe's birth rate by 200 percent, there were cartons of synthetic morphine and a few crates of an Oxycodone knock-off as well.

All were listed as "ceramics" on the shipping papers. It's amazing what they're doing with cups and saucers these days.

Shortly after my tour ended, the chief came to fetch me. "Lieutenant wants a word."

He didn't appear happy. Neither did the lieutenant.

"You have to get your story straight," he told me when I entered the wardroom where he was waiting. He said this the way most people say things of that sort—pointing his finger at me and jabbing it repeatedly.

"I don't have a story."

"Which is what?"

"I found al-Yasur on the ground outside the mosque. I jumped on him. You jumped on me."

"You were *rescued*," Chief prompted.

"Definitely rescued," I agreed.

The lieutenant nodded tentatively.

"And you knew nothing of the operation at the camp?"

"Which camp?" I said innocently. "I'm supposed to put in an appearance at a Boy Scout camp this month. Is that what you're talking about? I love doing that—there's nothing like corrupting kids at an impressionable age."

The lieutenant smirked, clearly more relaxed.

"Thirsty?" asked Chief, walking over to the sideboard near the coffee machine.

"I've had my share of coffee," I told him.

"I wasn't talking about coffee," he said, opening the cabinet. "I understand this stuff cures all sorts of ailments."

He held up a bottle of Bombay Sapphire.

"Doctor, pour me some medicine."

I was on my second glass when Chief told me Magoo wanted to talk.

"That's nice. I don't want to talk to him."

"Don't be an asshole, Marcinko," said the lieutenant. I think that was the first time he pronounced my name correctly since we'd met. Maybe he had a guy crush.

"If I thought I could carry on a conversation with that part of my anatomy," I told him, "I would gladly talk to him."

"He wants to go over a few things," said Chief. "Just to make sure we're all on the same page."

"You and I already did that."

"We don't need the media making this into a big bullshit thing," said the lieutenant.

"Who says the media is going to find out?" I asked. "This is a DEVGRU operation—it's classified. No one talks about it."

"Man, you are *old*-fashioned," said Chief, escorting me back to the wardroom.

I found Abdi there, wide awake. He'd been given a tour as well, though slightly modified to avoid revealing sensitive information.

"Mr. Dick. Coffee?" he asked, getting up to go over to the coffee machine.

"No thanks. I have my own." I had brought a mug with the doc's elixir from my meeting.

Abdi began telling me about his tour, which had obviously impressed him greatly. Every fourth or fifth word that left his mouth was an adjective that meant "incredible." I don't think I've heard anyone wax that poetic without using four-letter words in quite some time.

"Maybe you should do a submarine theme," I told him. "They don't have many of those in Brooklyn. If you could get a location near the old Navy Yard—"

"I am not going to Brooklyn," he said. "I have decided to stay in Moga-dishu. My family needs me."

Maybe it was just the light, but Abdi seemed to have aged about a decade in the few short days we'd been together. And the age fit him well.

"I see what you were telling me," he continued. "If I want to honor my uncle, I should try to do what he would have told me to do."

I'm not sure that was exactly my message, but I can't say that I disagreed with it.

Westerners often feel an impulse to rush into places like Somalia—or Yemen for that matter—and straighten out their screwed-up crap. It's very American to want to fix things. It's part of the Christian spirit, *Help thy neighbor* and all that. But the real solutions come from the people who live there.

What's that old saying? *Give a man a fish, and you feed him for a day—teach him to fish, and he'll eat forever?*

To that I would add: you can't teach the bastard anything if he doesn't want to learn. And if he does want to learn, then you can't hold him back.

Abdi's country was and remains a hellhole. It's still a place none of us would want to live. But the kid has the balls to try to make it better, and for that, I salute him. It was, in fact, a very American thing to do.

We talked for a while about his uncle, and about his plans for improving the restaurant. I guess I'm getting soft in my old age, because I promised to visit the place the next time I'm in Mogadishu. As long as he doesn't offer me meatloaf.

I amused myself for the next few hours by getting workout pointers from some of the young bucks in Six. They say you can't teach an old dog new tricks, but you sure can make him sweat his butt off.

There's a common misunderstanding about SEALs and special opera-tions troops in general. A lot of the public thinks these guys are seven feet tall and built like gorillas. That's simply not true, and even among the small group I was with there was a wide variety of physical types.

They were *all* in great shape, however. Frankly, I think the new genera-tion knows so much more about nutrition, health, working out, etc., that they're better physically than we were when I started Six. Of course, I think some of us graybeards could use our heads in a way that would even things out, but then you probably expect me to say that. I'm just glad I managed to stay on the right side of these boys throughout the op.

I was recovering from my workout back in the wardroom, consulting with the good Dr. Bombay, when Chief appeared and gave me the "come hither" sign. I followed him topside, discovering to my surprise that the sun on, seeking greener pastures in places like Kenya and the Sudan. Eventually he found his way to Iraq, from there to Afghanistan and bin Goatfucker's palace in Pakistan. He had no fixed base after that, though he spent a lot of time in Yemen.

"So who is this American?" he said finally, turning to me. His English, though heavily accented, was fluent.

"*Sono Italiano*," I answered. I switched back to English. "I'm Italian."

"There are no Italians in Yemen."

"Then I must not be here. I'll be going."

Skinnyboy didn't have much of a sense of humor. He grabbed my arm and squeezed it, probably thinking that the pressure would hurt. But I've met two-year-olds with tighter grips.

Naturally, I winced. No sense letting him know what a wimp he was.

"Where in America do you come from?" asked al-Yasur.

"Rome." I started talking in Italian again, wheeling off a travelogue of the great sites of the eternal city, all prisons, all including special treatments for Muhammad's chosen idiots, of which his highness in front of me was one. Obviously he didn't understand a word of it.

"Your French is not very convincing," he said when I finished.

"That's because it's Italian."

He waved his hand, dismissing me. Except that he wasn't sending me away—he just wanted me in a position where I couldn't talk. This was accomplished by the guards. One came up and gave me a kidney punch. The other took me in a choke hold and coaxed me toward the floor.

Unlike Skinnyboy, this guard had real power. His forearms were thicker than telephone poles, and the press of his knee against my back as I went down felt like a crowbar. My legs buckled, and I had to use my hands to keep myself steady.

My right knee reminded me it had been taking a lot of abuse lately. My left knee wasn't crazy about its recent past either.

"The Christians are a dog's race," said al-Yasur. "You have degenerated even further from the Jews. This is to be expected. The seed of the bad tree becomes an even worse tree as time goes on."

The imam was off to the races. For the next fifteen minutes he talked about the downward evolution of the human race due to the influence of Christianity. In his worldview, every ill known to man could be blamed on or traced to a Christian: poverty, illness, the success of *American Idol*.

I suppressed a yawn, then several more. I can see why alcohol is banned in Muslim countries—half a beer and I would have been snoozing on the floor. Finally, one of his assistants leaned in close to him, and whispered something in his ear.

Al-Yasur looked at me. "I have to teach this evening. You've heard the text. I have a mind to take you with me, as an example. Though I'm sure the mosque walls would tremble to have an infidel between them."

Skinnyboy said something in Arabic. Imam responded. Apparently they were talking about what to do with me, because presently the guards took hold of my arms and marched me back to the little hut.

I was disappointed not to be guest of honor at the mosque. I'd been looking forward to making the roof fall in.

Abdi had been talking with one of the guards while I was gone. The man was a Nigerian, and had lived in Mogadishu briefly. He claimed to have seen Abdi's uncle's restaurant, though Abdi thought that unlikely.

"He is a stranger in Yemen," Abdi told me. "All of them are. He was brought here for the fight. They knew the trucks were coming weeks ago, and have been planning ever since."

"Why?"

"He didn't say. There were bad men in charge—that was his excuse. They had to be killed. Even the driver."

"Why?"

"There are conflicts—he is too low to understand or know much."

Abdi was right on that score, and he'd made a fairly good assessment of the situation. Bringing in bodyguards from outside of Yemen meant, or at least implied, that al-Yasur didn't trust the people in his own country, which in turn meant there was a power struggle going on. But that information wasn't of immediate use.

"What are they planning to do with us?" I asked Abdi.

"You, for ransom. Me . . ." He put his lips together. "We have no money," he said tightly. "Maybe—they kill me."

"Don't worry about a ransom. It's not going to come to that. If it were a question of money, I'd pay. But we'll be gone before they even figure out who to contact."

"How?"

I went to the window and took the nail out of the crack where I'd put it. "Start scoring the edge of the mortar here where the brick meets the window. I'll find another nail."

Abdi took the nail eagerly. As mindless as the task was, it filled him with hope, and he dug at the brick.

Two hours later, enough of the mortar had been loosened that I was able to push it out. Unfortunately, I pushed a little too hard—the brick tumbled onto the ground before I could grab it.

The hole it left wasn't quite large enough for Abdi to squeeze through, let alone me, so we went to work on the next brick. There was a sliver of a moon out; it gave us enough light to see what we were doing, though everything beyond the wall remained pretty much in shadow. Abdi and I worked like maniacal ants, scraping and scraping on both sides of the brick until our fingers and hands knotted. Needing a break, I put my nail down and walked over toward the door, flexing my fingers and arm. The compound had been quiet since the departure of the imam and his entourage about an hour before; under other circumstances I might have welcomed the peaceful bliss of the countryside.

I had just put my ear against the door, thinking I would listen for the guards, when I heard a dull humming sound in the distance, something like a vacuum cleaner with a muffler on it. I'd heard it before somewhere, but couldn't quite place it.

In a flash, I realized what was going on.

"Down!" I yelled to Abdi, running over and throwing him to the floor. "Down!"

There was another flash, and the room exploded. SEAL Team Six had decided to pay a visit.

[II]

I'd love to tell you about the operation in great detail, explaining how the team took down the compound without incurring a casualty of their own. I'd love to describe the way they silently took care of the posted look-outs, incapacitated the guards, and stormed all of the buildings in the compound.

I can't, though, and not because I'm sworn to secrecy. I didn't see any of it. I didn't hear much of it either. I'd no sooner thrown Abdi to the ground than the door blew open. The flash-bang grenades were still going off. The grenades are non-lethal—well, I wouldn't want to swallow one—but render most people deaf, dumb, and blind long enough to be subdued. Before I could even cough, two SEALs trussed me like a lamb waiting for the butcher. Cuffed hand and foot with flexcuffs, I was rolled next to Abdi.

I expressed my gratitude freely.

"You such-and-sos," I yelled, using words other than the ones my editor has supplied here. "What the *hell* do you think you're doing?"

"Commander Marcinko, please relax," said one of the SEALs in a slow-Georgian drawl that would have tenderized a slab of beef on a roasting spit. "We'll let you all go once the area is secure."

"What the hell did you tie us up for?"

"I'm sorry, but we're under orders to treat everyone like they're hostile," continued the SEAL. "Even you, Commander Marcinko."

"How do you know who I am?"

I didn't get an answer. Securing noncombatants *is* standard operating procedure, and it wasn't as if we were manhandled or ill-treated. But cuffing us was a bit over the top, especially since they knew who I was.

After we'd been on the floor for twenty minutes or so, I heard two or three sets of boots come into the building. A voice that could *only* belong to a chief petty officer barked.

"You can *let* that asshole Marrr-*chink*-O up," he growled. "I don't think even *he* could screw this up at this point."

I grinned. The chief[32] was an acquaintance whom I'd raised practically as a baby. When I first met him, he was a squirrely-looking preteen looking

---

[32] Given that he has somehow swindled the navy into thinking that he is ultra important and remains on active duty, I'm not going to use his real name. You can call him Chief Asshole if you want. Just duck when you say it. Better yet, run.

had just popped over the horizon. I thought we'd been under the water much longer.

The sea air was crisp, the water calm. A small party of sailors were on the deck of the submarine below the fin. Most prominent were two safety divers, who were standing by in case anyone slipped.

Including al-Yasur, who was surrounded by SEALs. A pair of sailors stood a short distance away, holding M16s. For a moment, I thought I'd been brought up to watch a makeshift firing squad, and considered how much I might bid to take one of the gunmen's places.

Then I heard the sound of approaching helicopters.

"You're letting this scumbag go?" I asked Chief.

"Not exactly."

"Can't he just slip into the water?"

Chief's frown told me he thought that would be an excellent idea.

"Orders," said the lieutenant, coming up from below.

"Where is he going?"

The lieutenant shook his head. He didn't know precisely, only that he had been ordered to transfer custody.

"What happens if I grab a gun and shoot him myself?" I asked.

"We pin a medal on you," said the lieutenant. "Then we arrest you and throw you in jail for the rest of your life."

It was a tempting deal, but there was no time to pull it off. The helos came in and al-Yasur was bundled off. From what I understand, he was transferred to a foreign government, where he is supposed to stand trial for a variety of crimes. At last report, he's still in prison awaiting trial.

Hopefully that means someone will administer some jail justice very soon.

PART THREE
SCORCHED EARTH

There is something in corruption which, like a jaundiced eye,
transfers the color of itself to the object it looks upon,
and sees everything stained and impure.

—THOMAS PAINE,
THE AMERICAN CRISIS, 1776–1783

[1]

A little over an hour later, we landed on the aircraft carrier USS *Reagan*, which was patrolling farther north in the Arabian Sea. I was looking forward to a tour of the hangar deck—I've never seen a jet fighter I didn't like, and a few minutes with the bomb loaders is a tonic for anyone's soul—but unfortunately there was no time for a tour or talk. I was hustled aboard a C-2 Greyhound headed for Riyadh. I had a great view of the tail end of the plane—for some reason, the seats in the aircraft faced backward ("aft" for you nautical souls). Maybe that was to make it harder for the passengers to rush the flight crew if the flight was too bumpy. Or maybe it was to make it easier to kick obnoxious passengers out.

I was strapped in about the third row from the back, the only passenger, when Danny called on the sat phone. He told me I was famous—the SEALs had just rescued me in Yemen.

"And how did they do that?" I asked.

"Apparently you were kidnapped while sightseeing," he said. "The word went out, and the navy came to the rescue. Couldn't let the father of SEAL Team Six suffer, et cetera, et cetera, et cetera. They haven't officially identified the unit that grabbed you, but everyone knows who it was, nod-nod, wink-wink. Great human interest story. Blah-blah-blah."

It was a good story, so good in fact that it left out al-Yasur, the power struggle, drugs, and the money trail. By the time I returned to the States two days later, the story had been enhanced, emboldened, and embroidered. Everyone but the White House janitor took credit for rescuing me. Everyone except for Six, which did the real work. Sound familiar?

Hello, *Good Morning America* and Bill O'Reilly. I was victim and father figure rolled into one.

The president wanted to have lunch. I respectfully declined, citing a prior engagement. You know how important teeth cleanings are.

Abdi returned to Mogadishu. The money we forwarded to his account at the bank there has been put to good use expanding the restaurant.

Unfortunately, there's no guarantee that he will be successful, let alone that the city or country he lives in will survive the painful hell it's going through.

But then I'm told there are no guarantees in life except for death and taxes.

It took me about a week to get past the hubbub, and even then it only died down because one of the Kardashians was rumored to have punched out the favorite on *American Idol*. It was at that point that I arranged to have cock-tails with the admiral.

Our sessions are always informal, and always held at locales where nei-ther of us is likely to be recognized—God forbid the world knew that the head of the CIA deigns to talk to Demo Dick.

This session was held at a bar about thirty minutes away from Rogue Manor. The place had a heavy firemen theme, which may have been why it was called Firemen's Bar. That may also explain why it had a ladder truck in the middle of the main barroom.

The admiral was lucky it wasn't a pumper; I would have used it to hose him down. He came expecting trouble—usually he travels to our sessions alone, but in this case he had two of his bodyguard types sitting at a table within eyesight, undoubtedly with orders to shoot to kill if things got out of hand.

"I know what you're thinking, Dick," he said as he walked behind the truck to get to the table where I was waiting. "You weren't a patsy. We might have used you, but—"

"*Might?*"

"Possibly."

"You lied to me."

"No. I withheld key information. Very different."

"Fuck you very much."

Our waitress approached. The strategically placed suspenders were cute, but I thought the fire helmet a bit much. The admiral ordered a light beer. I went with another Bombay Sapphire.

"You have to admit, you got yourself involved," said the admiral. "I didn't send you there. Magoo was very careful in what he let out. I knew if we laid out a few crumbs, you'd fill in the blanks. You put everything together. Tell me this: if I'd asked you to set up al-Yasur, would you have?"

"That's not the point."

"Sure it is. You went to rescue Garrett Taylor because you felt you owed his old man."

"Was that part of your setup?"

"Hell no. You ruined that. Magoo wanted to rake you over the coals for that. I suggested that we come up with a way to use it. He did. You should be thanking him."

"Tell him not to hold his breath."

The waitress returned with our drinks and a large platter of the bar's snack specialties—Pick-axe Pretzels, Five-Alarm Chili, Blazing Nachos, you get the drill.

"The owner loves your books," whispered the waitress as she set them down. "So does my boyfriend."

"Thanks."

"See? You should be thanking me," said the admiral. "Think of all the money I've saved you in bar tabs alone. Hell, you'll never have to pay for a meal in this country again."

"Garrett set me up?" I asked.

"No. Garrett passed along information that was legit, that he thought was legit, from Magoo. Magoo knew he'd talk—Mr. Garrett clearly has the hots for one of your people. Trace Dahlgren, I assume. He doesn't go for guys."

Having the hots for one of the guys would have been a lot safer. Trace was convinced he'd used her. I wouldn't want to be his life insurance agent.[34]

"If you were sure I would have helped, why didn't you ask?"

"Because knowing you, Dick, you would have left nothing to chance. And that means that instead of spending the past week smiling knowingly but admitting nothing at diplomatic receptions, the State Department would have been fending off a dozen UN resolutions and on my butt about the Geneva Convention."

"That's the one that says prisoners are allowed one beer a week, right?"

He didn't think that was very funny. "Why are you complaining? You got you all sorts of publicity."

"I don't need publicity in my line of work."

"Bull. It helps you sell books. It helps your company. Besides, it gave you a chance to work with SEAL Team Six—you've been telling people you're a proud papa, and here was some proof."

"Making me look like a dumb tourist who stumbled into trouble didn't exactly boost my image."

"Who believes that? Every blog I've seen hints that you were on some sort of top-secret mission, which we'd all read about in your next book. Right? Right?"

It took two more refills and another plate of nachos before we agreed to disagree. My actual purpose in coming to the meeting was to find out if the bank had been involved in the admiral's little plan to take out al-Yasur. His comments to that point seemed to say no. Of course, having just been

---

[34] A late addendum: apparently the two have made up. I'm not sure what sort of ritual was involved, but Trace assures me they are now "friends." Look for young Mr. Garrett to make an appearance in future episodes.

played, I couldn't trust anything the admiral said or implied. We talked in generalities for a while, then he surprised me.

"We've been having trouble with some of our operations in the region," said Jones, swirling his drink. "Almost as if al Qaeda and the other bad actors have been tipped off."

"Is your operation compromised?"

"I don't think so. But that was another reason we had to be . . . circumspect in your case."

"I assume you're trying to figure out what's going on," I told him.

"You might say that."

"And you don't need help from me."

"Internal matter. But it is nice to know there's someone outside the agency I can count on."

That's about as close as the admiral has ever come—and will ever come—to a compliment. My feelings were somewhat assuaged by his offer to pay for our expenses in Africa as a token of his gratitude. And of course he did the usual contract dangling—the next job would be bigger, better, bloodier, etc.

"What about the drug operation?" I asked.

"We hit all the connections to Allah's Rule. Most of them weren't part of the movement."

"You're calling it a movement now?"

"A bowel movement." He smiled. "See? I can make a Rogue Warrior joke. Maybe I'll write my own books."

The bootleg factory in Bangladesh had been shut down as well. The admiral wasn't particularly interested in the prescription drug angle. As far as he was concerned, medicine in the States cost too much money, and the only losers were the pharmaceutical companies, who deserved to lose. He didn't see the terrorists as a big beneficiary, another point on which we disagreed.

I made a few hints about the bank, but didn't get explicit enough for him to figure it out. By the time we said good-bye, we were back to our relationship of friendly antagonism.

I called Veep later that afternoon and gave him a preliminary report, noting that the CIA had closed down Allah's Rule and therefore "tentatively" it looked like there were no other compromised bank accounts. He was happy to hear that—so happy that he promised to cut Red Cell International a check immediately.

"You can hold off until the final report's done," I told him. "We still have some t's to dot and i's to cross."

It pained me to say that, and not just because I was purposely making a bad joke to divert his attention from the fact that I was arranging to remain in the bank's employ. Turning down a promise of cash in hand is only slightly less painful than one of Mongoose's kicks to the throat.

Nor did we have anything in the offing that would guarantee to increase our fee. Ten days of trying to penetrate the bank's computer records had failed to get Shunt any tangible evidence of embezzlement. Shunt had also gone nowhere with his attempts to make connections to the drug company.

But the connection between the bank and Allah's Rule still bugged me. While I'd made a case to the admiral that I wasn't altruistic and that I didn't do things because they were the right thing to do, in this case, Red Cell International was continuing to look into the American International Bank because : . . . it was the right thing to do.

In the past, terror organizations became what the accountants call "cost effective" by necessity—they spend very little to blow up very much. The USS *Cole* bombing is a good example. Depending on how you figure it, the average U.S. Navy destroyer costs in the area of $1.8 billion to build and launch. The average speedboat capable of carrying some seven hundred pounds of explosive runs two hundred thousand if it's fresh out of the show-room, waxed and shined. A terrorist on a budget can pick something up for much less. The cost of explosives *might* be as high as twenty bucks a pound if you use the good stuff.

The human cost multiplier is even more ferocious—figure two bombers in the boat, against seventeen dead aboard the *Cole*, with another thirty-nine injured.

The math is fierce. But what happens if you give the terrorists a lot more money than they're used to operating with. They're not going to spend the money on building a big destroyer; they're going to stick with what they know, and buy a lot more speedboats.

You were worried about Freddie Mac going bankrupt or the euro collapsing?

It's one thing for terrorists to use a drug network to fund their operation; there are inherent risks involved, and police agencies have another way of getting at them. But working with a bank to stabilize and extend their finances could put tangos, al Qaeda affiliated or not, in an entirely new category.

Flip the problem around: imagine a banker with his own private terror group. Oh wait, that's what Congress is for.

Admittedly, I didn't have any real evidence. Banks have been duped by drug dealers since rolling papers were invented, and terrorists have used them to move money since the silk trade. So when Shunt hit a cyber-brick wall and Danny suggested we follow our bank security expert in hopes that something would turn up, I agreed. The day before my meeting with the admiral, I'd told Danny we'd follow Veep for a week and then reevaluate.

Danny put together a mix of some of our younger bulls to man the surveillance squad. Among the people he wanted to use was Junior.

I wasn't entirely sure of Junior's mental state, given what I had seen in Bangladesh. I talked with Danny extensively about what had gone on and what I had seen. The crux of the conversations was a question both simple and devilishly tricky: Did Junior belong as a shooter, or should he be moved to the bank bench?

Personnel evaluations are never handled by just one person. While I have the final call—the "buck stops here" theorem—it takes a number of people to really get a good perspective not just on how someone is performing, but how they fit in with the group. Knowing their mental state and how they may (or may not) handle stress is absolutely critical to a smoothly operating team, and it's not something that one person can decide. I've learned to rely on people like Danny, Trace, and Doc for their opinions.

Of course, every so often they give the green light to fruitcakes like Shotgun and Mongoose, but none of us are perfect.

Danny's assessment was that Junior had changed—he was quieter, more to himself. What that really meant in terms of dealing with pressure remained to be seen.

"Let him work with me for a while," suggested Danny. "There'll be some pressure, but it won't be life or death. I'll watch him closely, stick nearby, and we'll see how he does. I think he'd be more relaxed with me than with you. No father-son thing."

I couldn't argue with any of that, and in fact I thought it was a good idea. But when I told Junior about it over the phone, he reacted as if he were being fired.

"You're pulling me out of the field," were the first words out of his mouth. These were followed by a string of adjectives and adverbs that aren't included in most grammar school dictionaries.

"I'm not pulling you out," I told him. "Danny needs help."

"I was supposed to go on an op with Sean[35] in Iran," he said. "You're taking me off that to do this."

"This is where I need you."

"At home. Under your thumb. Send Mongoose or Shotgun."

"You're under Danny's thumb. And you're still a trainee. You're still

---

[35] Sean Mako, one of our best team leaders. The mission in Iran proceeded; maybe I'll write about it someday. Then again, maybe not.

learning the ropes. Don't go comparing yourself to people who have more experience."

"I've been on ops. Important ops. If it weren't for me, Cuba would have been a total goatfuck. India—we would never have figured that out.[36] So I'm more than just a new guy. I've earned something. More than just hanging out trailing people. Damn, Dad—that's gofer work."

I let him vent for a while. I don't want anyone on the team who doesn't want to be in the middle of the action, and following a banker around New York City isn't exactly the bleeding edge. But dissent has its limits; Red Cell International is *not* a democracy.

"I need you to work with Danny. End of story."

"You think I lost my cool because of what happened with that kid and the guard," said Junior. He was so mad he was having trouble getting the words out of his mouth. "You think I can't handle pressure. That bastard deserved to die. I did what you would have done."

He said a few other things, most of which I'm sure he'd rather not share with the rest of the world. I didn't say anything else, except good-bye when he was done. At the end of the day, Junior did as he was told, and went to work with Danny, and Red Cell International spent the next few days watching the head of bank security go to work every day.

If you've ever stood in a freshly painted room and watched the paint dry, you'll know exactly how exciting those days were. Until Veep managed to lose track of Danny and Junior while they were tailing him.

---

[36] More on Cuba can be seen in *Seize the Day*; *Domino Theory* details (some of) the India action he's referring to. He had a point, but only to a degree.

[II]

V eep was in his New York office, yelling at various and sundry underlings for failings real and imagined. We were listening in, thanks to
the vibrations on the office window. Those vibrations were being measured
by a laser device aimed at said window from the roof of a condominium two
blocks away, but in direct eye-line with our target's office. The condo
building was still under construction, and Danny had pulled some strings
with the New York Police Department to get access. We had a team there
24/7 monitoring the system, though we could have opted for a completely
automated setup.

(For the technically inclined, here's how the laser device works. Imagine
a drum: every time it's struck, the skin vibrates and produces a sound.
Drums are set up to take advantage of that vibration, turning it into something pleasing to the ear, unless of course it's being struck by a five-year-old
at six o'clock in the morning, or a member of a rap band. Windows are like
that drum skin, though since they're not set up to produce pleasing sound,
the vibrations are so small they are usually unnoticed. The laser device simply measures those vibrations, and its related equipment translates them back
into sound. The physics are straightforward, though extremely precise; the
gear measures with great precision the amount that the window moves. In
real life, things can get very complicated, however. First off, the thickness
of the glass, especially on commercial buildings where the architects are
trying to minimize heat loss and gain, lessens the amount of vibrations. The
angle of the beam can distort the measurements. And anything that inter-
feres with the beam—rain is a killer, and dust and dirt don't help—adds another difficulty factor. All of these things can be compensated for, to greater
or lesser degrees. Our biggest worry was that the beam would be somehow
observed—hit the window at the wrong place, and an unexpected reflection
could temporarily blind someone on the inside, giving away the operation.
And then there was the possibility of being seen, though we disguised the
unit as a piece of work equipment.)

Danny and Junior were down on the street, Danny at a coffee shop next
door to the entrance to the bank building, and Junior playing tourist a little
farther up the block. A little past twelve, the audio man called down and
said it sounded like Veep was going for lunch.

"Just called for his limo," Bobby Lewis told Danny.

"All right. Junior, I'll bring up the car. You hang on the street. Get the tag ready."

"On it."

The tag was a GPS tracking device. The units make it easy to follow someone, but they're also relatively easy to detect. So we followed a regular routine to minimize that: we would place one on Veep's car just before he got in, then remove it after Veep returned to his home base. This way, by the time the car returned to its garage in New Jersey, or even gassed up on the West Side, it was clean.

We'd practiced this routine several times, and in fact had watched Veep go to lunch just the day before, so nothing seemed unusual. Junior bought a newspaper from the vendor right next to the spot on the sidewalk where the limo would drive up.

The limo arrived, Junior crossed the street, tagging the car as he went. Veep exited the building about a minute later, walked toward the waiting limo and its open door—then veered quickly right and hopped into a cab that had just stopped to discharge its passenger. The cab sped off before Junior could get across the street to put another tag on.

The first thing he did was curse. The next thing he did was go to the backup plan. As he started walking toward the end of the block, he put his hand into his pocket and took out a small Hummingbird UAV, one of the devices manufactured by our friends at Forward Research. He activated it with his thumb, then as he reached the curb let it sail.

The bird-sized UAV climbed about twenty feet and then began circling in a preprogrammed orbit above the street. Junior took out his iPhone and called up the control app. A few seconds later, the screen showed a video being sent from the bird. He tapped a truck at the top of the screen; the Hummingbird changed course and began following the truck.

His next task was to find the cab. There were three within range of the video camera. Any one of them, Junior decided, could be the right one.

Problem.

Junior started running in the direction the cabs were taking. Danny, meanwhile, was wondering what was going on. He had retrieved his car and, not having heard from Junior, was driving toward the building where the limo was still waiting.

"He got into a cab," said Junior, finally calling him on the radio to tell him what was going on. "Crown Vic. Trying to find it."

"He's not in the limo?"

"Negative. I launched."

"You got him?"

"Working on it. He's on William Street."

Junior could see the cabs ahead, stopped for a light. At ground level, the cabs were easier to identify, and Junior immediately ruled out the Toyota Sienna van. But the other two were Ford Crown Vics.

He ran up the street, hoping to get close enough to look into the cab and ID the passenger. But before he could get there, the light changed and the traffic started to move.

The cabs were heading north in the direction of Fulton Street. If you're familiar with downtown Manhattan, that's the area of the South Street Seaport. It's also a place where you can get onto the FDR Drive or take the Brooklyn Bridge to Brooklyn; either choice would make the cab hard to follow. They're also heading in completely different directions.

As the two vehicles neared Fulton, Junior decided they'd inevitably split up, and so he double-tapped the lead cab on the Hummingbird screen. This directed the tiny UAV to land on the cab, where it continued transmitting its signal. It was an elegant solution.

"I landed the bird on the lead cab. I'll try to tag the other," he told Danny, breaking into a full sprint.

Racing down the sidewalk in New York City is the sort of activity that tends to attract attention, and as he got close to Fulton, Junior passed a squad car with two police officers. The one in the driver's seat rolled down his window and started to yell at him, but he ignored them.

The cab was several car lengths away, turning left—and then stopping as its passenger got out.

Veep.

Junior slammed on the brakes, dropping immediately to a walk and turning to avoid Veep's gaze.

The cops, meanwhile, had thrown on their lights and were bearing down. Junior looked over his shoulder and saw Veep hurrying down the nearby subway entrance. Junior set out after him, not quite running, but not walking either.

The police followed as he bolted down the stairs into the station. They were convinced he was running from them.

Junior leapt off the bottom step and ran toward the turnstile. He saw Veep just on the other side, hurrying for the arriving train. With a hop, skip, and a jump that would have made an Olympic hurdler proud, Junior went over the turnstile and got onto the train just as the door closed. He watched through the window as one of the cops rushed up to the turnstiles, an angry look on his face.

Junior had boarded an A train heading uptown. He was fairly familiar with the subway system, having spent several years here in school and having worked out in Queens with Veep, so he knew that there were many stops in the downtown area. Veep would have a lot of chances to get away.

The bank security expert was in the car ahead of him, and while Junior didn't want to make it too obvious that he was following him, he couldn't afford to let him get too far out of sight. Junior watched through the door at the head of the car. He couldn't see Veep, but he could see the door at the other end of the car. If it opened, he decided, he'd walk into the next car and risk being seen—it would be easy for Veep to work his way several cars ahead, making it harder for Junior to see him exiting.

Maybe a minute or so later, they stopped at Chambers Street. Junior got out of the car, glancing down the platform and hoping to spot Veep if he left. At the same time, he pulled off the sweatshirt he'd been wearing. He started walking up toward the next car door, staying just to the left of the passenger flow. When he didn't see Veep, he darted toward the doors, dropping his sweatshirt as he ran. The doors squeezed in on him, but he made it.

He turned around and saw Veep staring at him from the seat across the way.

Junior smiled, mumbled something about just making it, and moved farther into the car, holding on to one of the metal poles.

While he'd tried to vary his appearance by losing the sweatshirt, he couldn't be sure that Veep hadn't seen him earlier. There was nothing to be done about it now, though. Junior sat in his seat, trying to decide what to do if Veep moved or got off.

Under ordinary circumstances, we would have had someone else in the car, not to mention a team on the street above. But Danny was still tracking the taxi the Hummingbird had landed on, and Junior wouldn't be able to talk to him until he went above ground. Junior simply had to stay with Veep until someone else could get close.

Junior asked himself, *What would the counterintuitive thing be to do here?*

Or, to be more precise: *What would Dad do?*

He lifted his gaze toward Veep, who had already adopted the standard New York City subway stare into blank space.

"Didn't think I was going to make it," he told Veep. "I thought I was going to get squeezed."

Veep didn't respond. The train stopped at Canal. Junior waited, tense, as a flood of people moved into the car. Veep didn't move. The seat next to him remained open as the train started from the station.

Junior got up, walked across the aisle, and slid in.

"I love New York," he told Veep. "Been so long since I been here though."

Veep remained silent. Junior thought of slipping a GPS sending unit into his pocket, but reasoned that it would be easily found. Searching for something to talk about, Junior hit on Occupy Wall Street, a topic surely dear to the heart of any banker.

"I was looking for those Occupy people," he said. "I was hoping for a rally. You're a ninety-nine percenter, right? Right? You're part of the ninety-nine."

Veep's body, already stiff, tightened even more. Junior kept up the prattle through three more stops. Then he gave up his seat for a pregnant woman and stood right in front of Veep, talking to her about her child. (Girl; eight months; first child; no name yet.)

Two stops later, an old lady came on and stood in the crowded aisle. Junior nudged Veep and suggested he give up his seat.

Veep gave him a death glare. It didn't much bother Junior—he was used to much worse from Trace.

The old lady remained standing.

As the train approached Penn Station, Veep got up and walked to the door. Junior said something to the old lady, watching Veep from the corner of his eye.

Veep left as soon as the doors opened.

Junior waited a second, then smacked his head.

"This is my stop!" he shouted, and he ducked out, hustling after his mark.

Penn Station is a nexus for Amtrak and local commuter trains to New Jersey and Long Island; there are also two subway lines that use it. Junior lost sight of Veep going up the stairs, and as he rushed to follow he worried that he had completely lost him. But he soon spotted the bank security expert heading toward the stairs that exit onto Seventh Avenue.

Junior had another GPS locator and figured that he would have to tag a taxi if Veep got into the cab line on the east side of Penn Plaza, the direction he was heading. But after reaching the street, Veep walked north past the cab line. At Thirty-sixth, he crossed the street and went into Keen Steakhouse, a venerable restaurant and bar that has specialized in red meat since 1885.

By now, Danny knew that he had tracked the wrong cab. Still downtown, he had started north as soon as the GPS indicator in Junior's phone showed he was above ground. He'd been trying to get Junior both by radio and phone for several minutes.

"Where the hell are you?" asked Danny when Junior's phone finally came back on line. The low-intercept radio was too far away to work with all the obstructions in the city.

"I'm leaning up against a building on Thirty-sixth Street," he told Danny. "Place called Keens."

"Yeah, all right. Gonna take me a while."

"Take your time," said Junior. He glanced at his watch. As he looked up, he saw a man in a dark Windbreaker and a baseball cap trot across the street.

It was Magoo.

Magoo went straight in, past the little reception area and its collection of clay pipes, down the single step to the dining room. Junior, trailing behind, saw him locate Veep in a banquette toward the rear of the room. He backed out before being seen.

Why was the CIA supervisory officer meeting with a bank security head in New York City? Probably not to discuss whether he could get a toaster with his new checking account. But the lunchroom was full when Danny arrived a few minutes later, and there was no way to get a bug close enough to hear what was going on. Danny settled for a few clandestine photos, then planted two small video bugs to cover the area, in case someone else decided to join them.

They dined alone, Veep on the mutton, Magoo sticking with a steak. The limo reappeared about forty-five minutes later, and Veep got in it. By then, Danny had called in reinforcements to trail him.

Rather than leaving, Magoo got up and went into the bar room. Danny called Junior and told him to get a better look. Sporting a new sweatshirt and baseball cap bought at a tourist shop around the corner, Junior spotted Magoo sitting at the far end of the bar near the small chalkboard that held the day's trivia questions. He was working a smartphone, poking furiously at the screen.

Junior ordered a Guinness and settled in. He considered slipping an audio bug under the counter along the wall behind Magoo, but the place was so noisy it was unlikely it would pick up much. He decided it wasn't worth the risk of calling attention to himself.

Magoo drank slowly—Scotch neat. He swirled the glass between every sip, as if he were trying to blend various ingredients. A half hour later, he still had half the drink left. He swirled one more time, took the tiniest taste, then got up to leave. Junior threw a twenty on the bar for his half-finished beer, and ran out in time to see Magoo getting into a cab.

One thing you have to know about New York: there is never, ever a cab when you want it. And yet Murphy had so far arranged for two at precisely the worst times for my boy.

But this time, Murph was generous—a truck pulled out ahead of the cab down the street. As the cabbie blasted his horn, Junior snuck up behind it, slipped the spare GPS broadcaster unit on the back fender, and continued walking.

Naturally, there were no cabs nearby. Junior stood at the intersection of Thirty-sixth and Sixth with his hand up, until a black livery car pulled over.

"Where you goin'?" asked the man at the wheel. He was a white guy with a Bronx accent so thick you could roll spaghetti around it.

"Downtown," said Junior, simply guessing. The iPhone locator app showed Magoo's cab was stuck in traffic only two blocks away, still on Thirty-sixth.

"Forty bucks," said the driver. By that point, Junior had already opened the back door. He reached forward and dropped three twenties on the passenger side of the Lincoln's split bench at the front.

"Where downtown, bub?" said the driver.

"Jeez, you know. I forget." Junior glanced at the iPhone. Traffic was moving again; the cab was headed for the FDR Drive. "Head over to the FDR."

"Where is it we're going?" asked the driver. He had a definite edge in his voice.

Junior dropped three more twenties on the seat. "I'll tell you when I'm sure. I'm getting some new texts here. We're not doing anything illegal."

"You got that right."

Thirty minutes and six more twenties later, the limo driver pulled up in front of Terminal Building One at John F. Kennedy Airport.

"You shoulda tol' me ya was goin' to da airport in da first place, 'stead of makin' a game out of it," said the driver. "Woulda saved ya some dough."

"I like to play games," said Junior, hopping out of the car.

Magoo had a ten-minute head start. The security line was long, but not quite long enough: he was nowhere to be found.

Junior took out his sat phone and called Shunt.

"I need a reservation on a plane that leaves from Terminal One at Kennedy soon," he told him. "I need to get past security and check the gates out."

"Terminal One?"

Junior started reading off the names of the airlines that used the terminal. "Aer Lingus, Alitalia, Delta . . ."

"Man, I hate Delta. They always lose my luggage."

"I just need to get past security and check out the gates."

"I'm on it."

Five minutes later, Junior flashed his iPhone for the TSA people, who blinked at it then walked him through a machine to examine his privates.

Not finding anything beyond the normal equipment, they released him and his shoes into the bowels of the terminal.

He checked every gate, and finally succeeded in spotting Magoo as he boarded an Alitalia flight for Milan. Judging from the line, he was toward the back of the plane, in coach. Good to see our government employees economizing.

"He's not listed on the passenger manifest," Shunt reported as Junior watched them check through the last passenger.

"Get me a ticket," Junior told him.

"Plane's booked. Even first class."

"Get me something that I can use to get on board," Junior said. "Then I'll find out what seat he's in, and we can get his ID."

"What are you talking about?"

"Just get me past the attendant. I know you can do it."

"You're going to fly to Milan? Dick'll have a fit."

"Just get me a ticket. Dupe somebody's. Upload it now."

Junior ran to the gate, waving his phone at the attendant who was just about to shut the door to the boarding tunnel.

"I just made it," he said, trying to push past.

"Wait, sir. I have to scan your phone."

"Here, here," said Junior, shoving it toward her face. Then he started away.

"I need to *scan* it."

"I can't miss this plane."

"You're not going to miss it," she insisted. "It won't leave the gate for another ten minutes, at least."

Junior held the phone steady just long enough for her to position her scanner, then he turned and raced down the tunnel. The woman yelled after him that the machine hadn't accepted the scan, but he already had a good enough lead that he reached the cabin door before she could alert the attendants. He hustled in, moving quickly through first class—no Magoo—then into the back, moving all the way to row forty before spotting Magoo in a middle seat.

Obviously the CIA operative hadn't pulled any strings for that seat.

"Excuse me, sir," said one of the stewardesses. She had an Italian accent and very shapely legs that were highlighted by a tight miniskirt.

"Yes?" answered Junior, having trouble putting his tongue back into his mouth.

"Where is your seat? The captain needs you to sit so we can back from the terminal."

"Uh—"

He glanced at the phone. "Seat, uh, 12B."

"Sir, you're up in business class." She gave him a smile Mona Lisa would have killed for.

"Is that where you are?" Junior asked.

"We service the entire airplane."

"I'm looking forward to that."

Of course, there was someone already in seat 12B. By now the gate clerk had come aboard, and a discussion on how the computer could possibly have made this mix-up had begun.

Before seeing the stewardess—Gina—Junior had planned to simply step out and settle for some sort of refund. Now he wasn't so sure. The seat was occupied by a man in his mid-fifties, who had a wedding ring and a serious paunch.

Clearly, Junior deserved the seat more.

"I really do have to get to Milan," he said.

"We can offer one of you a voucher for another free trip," suggested the gate attendant, who was now under pressure to remove one of the passengers or the plane would miss its departure slot.

"That's hardly compensation," said the other man indignantly. "And I'm not giving up my seat for anyone."

"Maybe I could stand."

Junior glanced at Gina. She gave him a disapproving look.

"Just kidding," he said quickly.

"How about first class on the next flight out, a voucher for two more flights, and a thousand-euro voucher," said the gate attendant.

"I'll take it," said Junior, looking at Gina. "As long as I get your cell number."

Whatever else you can say about him, he's a chip off the old Rogue.

(III)

Veep returned to his office and went about his daily routine. Magoo flew to Italy. Junior—with the phone number and the promise of dinner at a time and place to be decided—went back and reported to Danny.

Shunt and his team went back to trying to piece together different information, starting with the alias that our CIA friend had used to get a ticket. That led them to the credit card he had used to buy the tickets—a card issued by Veep's bank to a Terrence Jonlable of Jersey City.

Was the agency using the bank to construct phony identities for its officers and agents?[37]

The agency did use a lot of banks, and had various means of camouflaging its officers' identities and hiding its intentions. Fake credit cards are one—but generally the addresses aren't fake as well, since the bills have to go somewhere and eventually be paid. The address in Terrence Jonlable's records was well out in the Hudson River. Yet the account was current.

If the airline computer was to be believed, Magoo had landed in New York barely an hour before the meeting. So he'd come here pretty much only for that meeting. It wasn't out of line for a CIA officer, even one of Magoo's stature, to fly undercover on a commercial airline. Or to have a meeting with an official of a bank narco-terrorists had used. But why all the secrecy?

Maybe Veep thought the terrorists were following him. Somebody *was* following him, after all: us.

Still.

"Stay on Veep," I told Danny when he reported what had happened. "Get more people if you need them."

"Will do."

I was in Washington, D.C., when I took Danny's call, engaged in one of my favorite pastimes—nodding thankfully at people as they sent over drinks from the bar. I was attending a conference on international security, and was taking a little walk to get ready for my keynote address on Afghanistan. Inside, coffee was just being delivered to the tables after dessert. The

---

[37] Legal counsel advises that the CIA absolutely does NOT do this, nor does any branch of the U.S. government engage in illegal fraud. (Legal fraud, of course, is a different matter.) You should treat these scurrilous allegations as COMPLETE and TOTAL fiction.

warm-up speaker was doing his best to encourage everyone to take the high-test; those sipping decaf were dropping like flies as he droned on. A mid-level muckety-muck at Foggy Bottom, he was speaking about how far the Afghan army had come, painting President Hamid Karzai as George Washington in a kaftan.

Walking back into the room, I could tell this was going to be another one of those occasions where I'd be as popular as a skunk at a church picnic. I was tempted to start my speech with the words "Horse swaggle." But being a very moderate and temperate man, I began with the much calmer and more deliberate "Bullshit, bullshit, and more bullshit."

That pretty much summed up what I thought and probably would have been sufficient for most of the people in the room, but I had been paid for fifty full minutes. I therefore felt obliged to continue, fleshing out my observations with facts that ought to have been self-evident to anyone with a sixth-grade reading level, which admittedly doesn't include 80 percent of civil servants.

"Karzai needs us but hates us," I said. "He needs us to fund his government, and to use as a whipping boy when things go wrong, which they do practically every day over there. Bucks and blame—that's our role."

I saw a few of the older men reach to protect their wallets.

"The administration has a plan to completely withdraw and let the Afghans protect the country," I continued. "That will work about as well as letting a three-year-old drive the family SUV on the Autobahn."

I suggested that we would have to keep special operations troops in the country for quite a while. Though we might *say* they were operating with the locals, the truth is they wouldn't. They didn't want the locals to interfere, and didn't trust them to keep their mouths shut. For their part, the local troops would be happy to stay out of the way—they didn't want to die. Roughly the same thing had happened in Iraq.

All in all, it was one of the more obvious speeches I've given on Afghanistan in the past decade. Outside the Beltway, people would have been throwing shoes at me, ordering me to tell them something new.

But here in Washington, D.C., the land where common sense goes to die, you would have thought that I told a kindergarten class that there is no Santa Claus. I did receive a healthy round of applause—from the waitstaff. On the bright side, there were no questions in the session that followed. And while no one sent over any more free drinks, no one waylaid me at the door with their latest get-rich-quick scheme either.

Get-*them*-rich, of course.

I was halfway to my car when my cell phone rang. It was Shunt, who made an offer I couldn't refuse:

"Wanna buy some Viagra cheap?"

We exchanged a few jokes about who was the one really lacking in that department—for a nerd, he can give as good as he gets. Then he got serious.

"You know that factory you and Junior visited in Bangladesh?" asked Shunt.

"Sure. The agency closed it down two weeks ago."

"Not really. The Indians stopped a boat off their western coastline yesterday with freshly made prescription pills from the same place."

"How do you know that?" I asked.

"Oh, well, you see, the Interpol computer network uses this security protocol that was written in the 1980s and—"

"Tell me about the drugs, Shunt. Skip how you got into the computer systems."

"But that's the fun part."

The drugs had been field tested for their ingredients. According to Shunt, the Interpol lab that analyzed them found the same impurities in them that were in the capsules confiscated in our haul. The impurities were like fingerprints. They were unique to the factory where they were made.

"Is it possible that these were already in transit?" I asked.

"Maybe, but I had accounted for all of the earlier shipments. The ship had sailed from Lahore. The drugs were in a container, which I tracked to a place about thirty miles north. My guess is that they moved the factory."

"You sure you have the right truck?"

"The people that own the tractor unit that drove the container to the shipyard are the same people who own the ones that drove yours," said Shunt. "And, uh, I backtracked some of their payments, all electronic transfers. That wasn't easy. You know the W32.Mubla worm? You might have known it as Fus.worm. Well, I took that idea—"

"Give me the results."

"The account that paid the transport company is held at Veep's bank."

"Tell me something I couldn't guess."

"I took the lab report and used those impurities to do a simple search against police records," said Shunt. "And I think some of the drugs are being sold in the U.S."

Ten hours later, I turned my rented BMW past a graffiti-strewn two-story building at the edge of Liberty City, Miami, heading toward the back lot of a large apartment building a block away.

Liberty City is named after what's touted as the first federal housing project in the South, Liberty Square. Erected in 1933 in hopes of relieving overcrowded and hell-like conditions in nearby Overtown, the area did well after the Depression and World War II, when it hosted a growing black middle class. But that changed in the 1960s, and while there have been various efforts to clean up the place and even some progress, it's still not the first place you would want to look for housing. My white face was surely the only one around for blocks, especially at that hour of night.

I was on my way to a meeting with a person ID'ed only as "Granny" by the head of the local DEA[38] office. He'd provided a personal briefing thanks to a call from a top field agent I'll only call Narco. If you read *Blood Lies*, you met him in Mexico. Narco and I did some subsequent business, and he owes me even more favors since the adventures described in that book. Coincidentally, he recently received a promotion and is now working in Florida, though how that figures as a step up I've yet to figure out.

Given that the Allah's Rule network had been shut down—something confirmed not only by the admiral but by Fat Tony's death and the arrest of a number of people in Bangladesh and Yemen—you would think that the people on the far end of the pipeline would be looking for either a new supplier or trying to cut back. But Granny was supposedly looking to expand; my source at the DEA had said she was putting out feelers for more business as recently as a day ago.

Posing as a drug dealer from up north, I'd used a connection Danny had in the Miami police department to reach out to an informer named Lion and set up a meeting with Granny. I was surprised when Lion said we could meet that very night, and now as I was driving down the block, alone, I had a strong suspicion I'd been set up.

I had backups less than sixty seconds away, but I was alone in the car and only lightly armed, considering the area and time of night. All I had was my PK on my hip, an MP5 between the seats, and a couple of shotguns in the trunk.

Plus a pair of grenades under the seat. But they were for emergency use only.

The directions took me to a long driveway covered in shadows. One of my guys—JJ—had just run up the block on his motorcycle, checking it out, and Mongoose was sitting in a car in the next parking lot over, slouched in the seat.

"Gotta guy stepping out of the building," said JJ, turning around on his bike. "Be sober, be vigilant; because your adversary the devil, as a roaring lion, walketh about seeking whom he may devour. First Peter, verse eight."

---

[38] DEA=Dickheads, Eunuchs, and Assholes. Otherwise known as the Drug Enforcement Administration.

Short and stocky, JJ is a former marine recon member who grew up in Jacksonville, Florida, but went to school in Miami. He's as black as night, and as you undoubtedly just realized, a bit of a fanatic when it comes to quoting from the Bible.

I spotted the man he'd mentioned and slowed, lowering my window. The man approached the car.

"Lion?" I asked.

He pulled open the door and got in. "Go."

"Where?"

"Just drive. I'll tell you where we gotta go. People follow me all the time."

From what Danny's friend had told me, I expected that Lion would be a low-level drug dealer and user, a guy in a hoodie with his pants falling to his ankles. The Hispanic sitting next to me was wearing an expensive silk suit and smelled vaguely of cologne. He was in his forties, tall, thin, and nervous; if he had a weapon on him it was small and well hidden.

"You're a friend of Coke's, right?" he asked. Coke was the street name of Danny's friend.

"Otherwise I wouldn't be here," I said.

"Just checkin'. Take a right."

He had me make a series of turns through shadowy neighborhoods. Here and there, a man or woman would be standing near a corner, but for the most part the streets were deserted. JJ and the others followed a few blocks behind, tracking with the help of a bug and a GPS locator. We'd also rigged a video bug in the radio. The view was fish-eyed and hard to see on the iPads, but they could hear everything we said loud and clear.

"You're a white guy, which is good," Lion told me. "Granny likes white guys."

"I'm not here for sex."

"You wouldn't want sex with Granny. Take a left."

We drove a few more blocks. I'm not sure if we could have shaken a tail, but the turns got me confused.

"Listen, I need you to put a good word in for me with Coke, all right?" said Lion. "Because my trial is comin' up, and I can't afford to be—I can't go to jail, right. And I can't lose my law license."

"You're a lawyer?"

Evidently the question insulted him, and he shut up almost completely after that, except to give directions. He had me get onto I-95, heading north. At that point, he started getting restless again.

"Can't this crate go any faster?" he asked. "BMWs are supposed to be quick. What'd you do, use regular gas or something?"

"We don't want to get stopped."

"Around here, you go the speed limit, you get stopped. Speed up."

I held steady at sixty, more intent on making sure my people were close by than calming his nerves. Off the highway again, we headed toward the ocean, then entered a development nestled inside a golf course.

Or maybe it was the other way around—the golf course hugged a cluster of McMansions, all lit with floodlights to show off their stucco facades and exotic landscape plantings.

"Stop here," he told me. "Right here, in the street. Don't park. Just stop the car and get out. Keep the engine running."

"What about you?"

"I'm coming. Don't do anything weird. Better leave your little machine gun."

I did. As I got out, two men dressed in black tracksuits came out from around the back of the house on my left. They were carrying what proved to be Uzis.

"Up against the car," barked one.

We went through the frisking routine. The man who checked me was fairly professional, finding the PK without giving me a wedgie. He tossed the gun in the car. Lion wasn't carrying.

"That an MP5 you got in the car?" asked the other man after checking the interior.

"That's right," I told him.

"Nice."

"You're not slumming yourself."

"That way." He pointed me toward the house diagonally across from the yard they'd come out of. The middle of the three garage doors opened as we approached. Two other men in tracksuits stepped out, Uzis framed in the dull light of a single interior bulb. They gave Lion and me grim looks, then waved us inside.

We walked between two pimped and freshly waxed Cadillac Escalades; the fumes of carnauba were so thick a spark would set the whole place ablaze. A raised wooden platform framed the door at the back of the garage; a man in a sport coat stood in front of the two-step staircase leading to it.

"You the buyer?" he said to me, pointing.

"I hope to be."

"Hands." He gave me a perfunctory frisk. "Go."

He stepped aside and let me pass, but blocked Lion.

The door opened. A man with an electric scanning device stood on the inside threshold.

"Phone?" he asked.

"In my pocket."

"Give it here."

He stepped over to the side of the hall and put the phone down into a large metal box. Then he waved the detector around my body.

"You're clean," he said.

"What about my phone?"

"You get that back when you leave. It won't work in here anyway."

He put a lid on the box. It was large and bulky; I suspect that it used isolated copper foil to create an electronic barrier to listening devices. A bank of electronic equipment was discreetly tucked under the table; I suspect that one of the devices was a cell phone jammer.

"Go to the end of the hall."

Another man in a suit was waiting for me there. I'll say this for the illegal drug trade: it sure does employ a lot of people.

"Inside," said the man, pointing to the room to his right. He had his hands together in front of him; his manner suggested that he worked in a funeral home during the day.

The room was a fair-sized living room, well appointed with Colonial-style furniture, fancy plants, and a large, slow-moving overhead fan. Light came from a fancy glass-base lamp on a black-lacquer Chinese cabinet near the side of the room.

Granny was sitting in an armless chair at the far end of the room.

"So you want pills?" she asked.

Contrary to what I'd expected, Granny *was* a granny. I won't call her elderly, but I'd be willing to bet she remembered when horses rode down Main Street.

"I represent some people in New Jersey," I started.

Granny put up her hand. "Stop. I don't want to know anything except how you're going to pay."

"Cash."

"Too much trouble," she said. "We work with bank transfers. If I decide to do business, we'll explain."

"Banks can be traced."

"We have ways of fixing that."

"How?"

"We'll handle it. Tell me what you want to buy."

I gave her a shopping list, with Percodan at the top. I "accidentally" mentioned Viagra twice, though in retrospect that probably wasn't necessary. Granny listened placidly; we could have been talking about yarns and knitting needles.

"We're interested in a long-term relationship," I told her. "I can handle whatever you can get."

"I've made some inquiries," she said. "You're in Hoboken?"

"And Jersey City."

"You have competition there."

"That's not really a problem."

She had done some homework, which was good—Danny had woven a tight background story, using the actual names of a Mafia-affiliated group in the two New Jersey cities along the Hudson. He'd also managed to give me a rap sheet, so I wasn't surprised when Granny asked if I enjoyed stealing cars.

"Way in the past," I told her. "Misspent youth."

"You look familiar," she said. "Have I seen you somewhere? Maybe on TV?"

"I haven't made *America's Most Wanted* yet," I said lightly. "And I don't intend on it."

She let the matter drop. We discussed some details about where the drugs would be picked up—she could deliver, which was preferable for me.

"I will decide in three days," she told me finally. "You will give me a phone number where you can be reached. We will not meet again. Ever."

"That's a disappointment," I told her, rising. "But I'll live with it."

I got my cell phone back at the door.

"Don't turn it on until you're in the car," said the man in the suit as he handed it over.

I kept the phone in my hand as I walked out to the driveway. Lion was standing there, practically hopping from foot to foot. I'd say he wanted to get out of there quickly.

I, on the other hand, wanted to take my time. I slipped my thumb on the power button to the phone as we neared the road, then stopped to tie my shoe.

The phone sprang to life. I waited for a few seconds, glancing in the direction of the car.

It wouldn't have taken too much skill to set up the cell phone to ignite a car bomb. Fortunately, no one had.

"You comin'?" asked Lion impatiently.

"Keep your shirt on."

"Jeez."

He marched toward the car. By now, Trace would have launched a UAV and would be watching from nearby. If there was a problem, she would have sent a message while I was inside. I glanced at the face of the phone. No calls, no texts, no nothing.

Lion slammed the door after getting in. He glared at me as I walked slowly over.

I waited until I was back on the highway before calling Trace.

"No one touched the car," she said. "You're not being followed."

"It went well," I said. "I'll talk to you when I get back to New Jersey."

I hung up before she could ask what I was talking about.

"Where should I drop you off?" I asked Lion.

"Ninth Ave. takeout place. I'll show you."

The route back was direct. I let Lion out, then drove six or seven blocks to a convenience store. JJ pulled up a minute later. I walked into the store; he followed, meeting me near the chips.

"Direct me in the path of your commands, for there I find delight," he declared. "Psalm 119:35."

"Scan the car for bugs. And give me your cell."

I called Trace and told her to follow Lion.

"Already on it," she said.

JJ met me inside a few minutes later. "Tracking device under the front seat. Want me to move it?"

"No, we'll use it," I told him. "Track me—if I'm followed, text me."

"In this way—"

"No more Bible tonight, JJ. Save it for the Sabbath."

"Exodus," he muttered as he left.

The tracking device was primitive by our standards, about the size of a pack of cigarettes. Since according to the video from the UAV no one had gone near the car while I was in with Granny, we assumed it must have come from Lion.

Leaving it in place, I drove down to South Miami to a hotel where Trace had reserved a room. I went upstairs, clunked some things around, then went down to the bar. Within a half hour, two lugs had shown up. One went and retrieved the tracking device from the BMW; the other came into the hotel and looked around for me.

It was one of the men in the tracksuits who'd frisked me on the way in. I had a good view thanks to the video bug I'd planted at the doorway. I sat at the far end of the bar, pretending to fiddle with my phone, as he got a table close to the front.

What were they up to? Checking my bona fides, I figured, since it would have been easy to take me out at Granny's and there hadn't been enough time since then for them to decide they didn't like the cut of my dungarees. In that case, it would be easy to help them along. I waited a few minutes, ordered another drink, then went over to the booth directly behind my friend's. I took out my cell phone and called Trace. For the next ten minutes, I discussed the logistics of the drug arrangement. By the time I hung up, tracksuit boy had a full rundown of our plans.

He left the bar shortly after I finished the phone call. In the meantime, his friend had been upstairs checking my room. Among other things, the thug had discovered the spare pistol magazine I'd left in the overnight bag: giving us his fingerprints, in case we needed them.

"I'm watching him tidying up now," said JJ, who was tied into the feed from a bug I'd left in the room. "Doesn't look like he remembers which way your bag was facing."

"That makes two of us."

"Should I follow them?"

"I don't think that's necessary. I'll meet you at the Grant."

That was a hotel in a much nicer part of Miami where we'd reserved rooms. I finished my beer, threw two twenties on the bar as a tip, and went out to the lobby. As I walked through the door, I noticed two men in dark suits standing by the registration desk. One of them made eye contact. His face seemed to light up, as if he'd just recognized me.

At that precise moment, a hand clamped on my right shoulder. A knee caught me in the back and I felt myself being pushed to the ground.

"You're under arrest, scumbag," hissed a voice in my ear. "Anything you say can and will be used against you in a court of law."

[IV]

At least my cover story was working.

My first thought was that it was part of a show arranged by the DEA to improve my bona fides with the drug ring and talk to me at the same time. So I played along, complaining about the handcuffs and bitching about being pushed into the backseat of the plainclothes car waiting outside the hotel, while being just compliant enough to avoid getting thrashed.

Trace and the others held back, knowing from the car registrations that these were real cops. We headed to a building used by a local drug task force, with its own security, apparently chosen to make it more difficult for any spies in the department to leak information. There was an underground garage with a private elevator; I was hustled unceremoniously inside and taken upstairs through darkened corridors to an interrogation room.

Remember those old movies where the bad-guy cop comes in and shines a bright light in the face of the criminal before slapping him around a bit? Then the good-guy cop comes in and offers a cigarette?

These guys tried the modern version, but I'm afraid it doesn't have quite the same sting. The bad-guy cop came in and tortured me with a minute description of what had happened on *Dancing with the Stars* the night before, then the good-guy cop entered and offered me a fresh Starbucks latte.

Maybe I have the good-guy/bad-guy thing turned around. In any event, the officers looked like identical twins, both blond-haired and blue-eyed, deeply tanned, wearing golf shirts, chinos, and a little too much aftershave. I felt like I had stumbled into a slightly updated version of *Miami Vice*, cleaned up for the young adult crowd and following a script written by the most politically correct screenwriter in Hollyweird.

"Now, we're going to record this," said good-guy. "When you see that little red light over there, then we are recording you."

"Some of this may be uncomfortable," said bad-guy.

"Is the air-conditioning OK?" asked good-guy. "We can turn it down if you want."

Finally they got down to business, asking what I knew about Granny. Their politically correct interrogation techniques had obviously been developed with the help of the FBI, or as we affectionately call it, the Fucked-up

Bunch of Idiots.[39] I kept expecting a *real* cop to come in and, if not rough me up, at least ask some pointed questions about what I was up to.

About an hour into the interrogation—if I can use that term loosely—my lawyer arrived. She marched into the interrogation room, escorted by several members of the task force, all of whom seemed to be having trouble breathing.

Trace in a miniskirt does that to people. She demanded to know what the charges were; they supplied half a dozen, all misdemeanors, ranging from loitering to vandalism—someone had kicked over a planter on the way out.

In the end, I was handed an appearance ticket on the vandalism charge and the others were forgotten. I was still puzzled by what was going on when Trace handed me a piece of paper as we got into the cab she'd called to take us to our hotel.

THEY HAVE A WIRETAP WARRANT. ROOM AND PHONES BUGGED. THEY WERE STALLING TO GET IT SET UP.

"They could have played a little harder," I groused. Trace shot me a shut-up look—she thought maybe the cabbie was part of their operation, like the bodyguards who had checked me out. Granny apparently was the focus of quite a lot of work by the task force, which seemed to be a few days if not hours from shutting her down.

Unfortunately, the local task force and the DEA did not get along, so when Danny tried using his DEA sources to get information, there was little to be had. He tried talking to the task force directly, but made no inroads.

"You threw them for a loop," he told me a few hours later, after I'd napped and recovered from my horrible ordeal at the hands of the police. "There is one positive—they see the connection to the New Jersey mob as a reason to delay their bust. They want big headlines. They're burning up the phone lines north. That may give us a couple of more days to fill in the details."

Danny knew this because Shunt had infiltrated their communications and computer system. As far as we could tell, they had no information on the connection with the bank; we'd already figured out the account that was being used, and had the fake addresses and IDs. But they did have one vital piece of information that we didn't—they had figured out how Granny's network was receiving the drugs.

---

[39] No offense intended, of course. At least not more than necessary.

Which is a roundabout explanation of why I found myself two days later in Toulon, southern France, heading for the Hotel Général Leclerc, an establishment that had been awarded three stars by Michelin in its heyday.

That heyday had been during the 1970s, but from the look of the place, I wouldn't have been surprised if it had coincided with the Lascaux cave paintings. Paint peeled from the walls in the lobby, the marble floors were scuffed and missing about half their tiles, and even with the windows open and a stiff breeze, the reception area smelled like day-old beer.

The hotel did have its charms, however. One was an absolute rock-bottom price on rooms—thirty euros a night, which included a continental breakfast. Said breakfast consisted of stale croissants and rancid butter, but free is free.

Another was the five o'clock senior citizen special in the dining room, which offered a full prix fixe meal complete with wine for only ten euros. The food wasn't particularly good, but the wine was all you could drink.

As you may gather, the place was a magnet for budget travelers, and it was especially attractive to senior citizens, who were courted with a number of other amenities, starting with the vintage music that played in the lobby. Besides dyeing my hair gray and putting a definite lean in my back, I picked up a pair of grandpa blue jeans and a rosewood cane to fit in.

"*Bonjour,*" said the desk clerk as I poked my way across the lobby to his station. He looked to be about the age of the average patron, namely eighty.

"I have a reservation," I said, handing over my passport. "Julio Julio."

He checked his list—a hand-written roll in an old-fashioned book.

"*Oui,* very good, *monsieur.*" He smiled. The hotel may have been down on its heels, but the old-fashioned service was top rate. "And you will be with us for just the night?"

"I have a reservation on the *Bon Voyage,*" I told him.

"Ah, leaving in the morning." He had a light French accent, and his English tilted more toward the States than Britain, which is atypical. "We have a number of guests with the same plans. You will require a taxi in the morning?"

"*Oui.*"

He smiled indulgently at my use of French. Our business concluded, I headed for the elevator at the side of the lobby, and from there to my room on the fourth floor.

How and why did we get from Florida to a port in southern France? And what does any of this have to do with terrorists, prescription drugs, and crooked bankers?

Two months before, Granny had been basically a part-timer, supplying fellow oldsters with the odd baggie of pot every few days. Some of her customers were reformed hippies who'd never given up a taste of the weed. Most of the others used it as a painkiller for various ailments and cancer treatments. Talking to them, Granny realized there was a burgeoning market for something a little stronger than weed. She made some inquiries, and eventually hooked up with a German who was visiting Miami. The German had just started buying from the Allah's Rule on Earth network. He didn't know about the connection with al Qaeda, though I suspect he didn't ask many questions about the possibility either.

That much came from the files Shunt had infiltrated. Danny had then used his Interpol connections to track the German, who was no longer in the United States. In fact, he was no longer among us at all—he had been incarcerated in Egypt a few weeks before, apparently at the request of the CIA. According to the security forces there, he died while trying to escape jail.

At least they know how to do *some* things right.

The German had been replaced by a French Arab, not identified in the local task force records and apparently unknown to Interpol as well. He had consolidated and moved the operation, and was looking to expand, having indicated to Granny that he could supply considerably more drugs if she wanted.

How were the drugs getting into the States? The task force had photographed two pickups at a cruise ship dock in Miami. Presumably because they weren't interested in or didn't have the resources to make arrests overseas, that's as far as their investigation went. But Shunt's magic fingers and Danny's golden tongue had brought us to Toulon and Hotel Général Leclerc.

After checking into my room, I hit the shower, freshened up, and went down to dinner. It was early, but the room was packed. The maître d' came over and with a tsk-tsk apologized that he had no immediate offerings for *monsieur*.

"If you would prefer to wait at *ze* bar, I will send *ze* girl to get you when the table she is ready." He sounded like a dead ringer for Pepé Le Pew in a Bugs Bunny cartoon.

"Where is ze bar?" I asked.

"You go zis way and zat."

I found the bar and bellied up, ordering a wine: Bourdeaux, Chateau Coquin 2003. I was waiting for it to arrive when a good-looking young woman brushed against my arm. The glass in her hand tipped toward the floor. I caught it with my right hand; with my left I settled her onto the bar stool next to me.

"Oh, thanks to you," she said. Her English was lightly accented with French and heavily with drink. She had trouble focusing her eyes, which were hazel and very dilated.

I gave her the glass back. "You should be careful," I told her. "You don't want to spill it on your dress."

"Oh no, that would be tragedy." She crossed her legs and smoothed the silky material. The hem made a sharp line above her knees. She tilted her head to the side, letting her shoulder-length hair hang down.

Nice effect. Even if she hadn't been about a third of the age of everyone else in the place, she would have been the prettiest thing there. Her chin narrowed a little too much, but it was the sort of flaw easily forgotten.

"You are very kind," she said to me. "Very nice. American?"

"American, *oui*."

"And you speak the French." She took a sip from her glass, finishing the small amount of wine.

"What are you drinking?" I asked, offering to refill.

"Le Monde Chateau 2007. Eeetz wonderful."

I had the bartender get her another glass, and had mine refilled. We made some light conversation; she claimed to work as a tour guide, specializing in the sights.

"I'll bet," I told her.

She had come south with a group from Paris, but now was on her own for the night; she would return home the next morning.

"I like the American tourists the best. You are all so handsome and gentleman. Not like the French. French men—they are all very arrogant, yes? But paper tigers. They do not know how to treat a woman."

"It takes practice," I allowed.

"I am jest waiting for the table," she told me, slipping off the stool. "But I am not so hungry now. Maybe I will go down the street instead to my hotel to bed. Good night."

I caught her as she started to stumble. Being a gentleman, I naturally decided that I would have to shepherd her to her destination. By the time we reached it, she was barely conscious. I escorted her upstairs to her room.

Somewhere between the hall and the door, the wine I had drunk went to my head. The next thing I knew, I was sitting on the floor of her room. The bed was unmade; the room empty.

Not the usual effect I have on women.

There was a knock on the door. Before I could get up, two policemen burst in, guns in hand. One yelled at me in French not to move; the other went and checked the bathroom.

"*Merde!*" he yelled. "Send for an ambulance!"

The other policeman left me and ran to his friend. This was my cue to make my own exit. I jumped up and ran through the door—only to be tripped in the hall. I got my hands out in front of me and broke the fall, but something hit the back of my head as I started to get up. Everything went black.

This time I stayed down for quite a while, and when I woke up, I was in my room at the Hotel Général Leclerc. A large man in a trench coat was shaking me. As I jerked awake, I almost belted him before I got control of my reflexes.

He smiled, but stepped back nonetheless.

"Monsieur Julio, nice for us that you join us, no?" The speaker was a light-complexioned Arab, sitting in a chair at the foot of the bed. A long, shallow scar ran down the right side of his face, tracing a semicircle below his cheekbone. Scarface looked to be in his mid-thirties; he had an assured look about him. He was dressed in loose white pants and a long, baggy white shirt; toss in a floppy hat and we could have been on a plantation.

"What's going on?" I pushed myself up on my elbows, still disoriented.

"Relax. We have liberated you from the police." Scarface smiled, then nodded at the gorilla who had woken me, dismissing him. "My friend will wait in the hall. Not that I believe you will be giving me any trouble, eh?"

"What is it you want?" I asked.

"I want to help you. You are in trouble with the police. I can make it go away."

"What trouble with the police?"

He gave me the disapproving stare a father might show a five-year-old caught with his hand in the cookie jar. "Your temper got the better of you with that girl. She is no more. A shame."

"What? I didn't do anything to her."

"The police will have a different opinion. And you ran away." Scarface shook his head. "But I can make it better for you."

"How?"

"It is not easy to take care of these things in France. But once you are on the ship, then—poof." He snapped his fingers.

"I didn't do anything."

"Well, if that is your attitude." He took out his cell phone. "I remember the police number, eight—"

"How much is it going to cost?"

"For?" He didn't play the naïve innocent too well; it was too much against type.

"To get me out of this," I said. "What do I pay you?"

"Pay? Nothing. You just do a little favor for me. Nothing that will even bother you." Scarface rose. "Your passport and papers are on the dresser. Your bags are packed. Another bag will meet you at the dock. Do not be late for the ship, or I cannot say what might happen."

[V]

I glanced at my watch. The ship was due to leave its pier in an hour.

My bags were packed, and at least as far as I could tell, in good shape. That was more than I could say for my head—it felt like I'd been kicked by a bull. Among the papers on the top of the dresser was one showing that my room had been paid in full. There was a boarding pass for the ship, made out to the name Timothy Leary. The passport was in the same name.

At least my new friends had a sense of humor. My real passport was missing, obviously another incentive toward cooperating.

Downstairs, the last of the guests who'd been waiting for the cruise ship were finishing up breakfast. I went directly outside, where a row of taxis was waiting at the curb. Ten minutes later, I walked out along the pier where the *Bon Voyage* was waiting and made my way to the covered gangplank.

Naval history buffs will recognize Toulon harbor as the place where the French fleet scuttled itself in November 1942, after Hitler decided he could no longer trust Vichy France. The Americans had invaded Africa at the beginning of the month, and when French Africa went over meekly to the Allies, Hitler had reason to worry that the ships in Toulon and environs might follow. The German 7th Panzer Division was tasked with charging into the port and seizing the fleet.[40] As the armor swarmed the streets and dock area, the French seamen went to work, holding off the tanks with their guns long enough to destroy some seventy-seven ships, including three battleships and seven cruisers.

Strange to count blowing up your own ships as one of the great victories of a war, but that's the way it went for the French in World War II.

The ghosts of the old ships haunted the foggy harbor as I went up the gangplank, poking my rosewood cane between the boards. A rather distinguished-looking sailor met me about halfway up and grabbed my bag. Two more large and much younger porters swooped in behind me, practically curtsying as they escorted me onto the ship. My name—Leary—was quickly found on the manifest, and another member of the crew, this one a woman, appeared at my right hand and helped me find my way to my cabin.

---

[40] The British had already destroyed the most advanced French warships, but the remaining force was still potent.

"The rest of your baggage arrived earlier," said the woman. "It is in your cabin."

"I'm so glad it made it," I told her.

I inspected my new baggage after she left. There were some clothes, a couple of souvenirs, a stuffed bear—and a lifetime supply of synthetic codeine, along with enough fake Viagra to triple the birth rate of a small African nation.

And just in case I was thinking of throwing them overboard, Scarface knocked on my door about two minutes after I unzipped the bag. He was alone, though I'm sure at least one of his goons was nearby. He'd changed from white to a trendy striped polo and khakis; I liked the other style better.

"I am so glad you make it aboard," he told me. "As for your instructions— all you must do is enjoy your voyage. Eat, drink, play your shuffleboard."

"What about these extra bags?"

"Nothing should happen to them. When you are ready to disembark, the porter will come. You say nothing."

"Customs."

"I will worry about customs. I am taking this cruise myself. To relax." His grin was crooked—evidently his mother had never warned him to floss. "At the terminal you can go home. You will have your proper passport. It will be as if nothing happened."

"The girl?"

He waved his hand. "Taken care of."

"What if I don't cooperate?" I said.

"The ocean is a very wide and deep place," he said. "If the suitcases you are bringing are molested, it will be very, very bad for you. Enjoy your cruise."

This was how the network was getting their drugs to the United States: pushing them across in small batches, mixed in with luggage belonging to people you'd never expect. My bag included a set of prescriptions. According to the documentation, I was carrying exactly enough painkillers for myself and my wife to last a year—exactly the amount the prescriptions said. The same was true for the sexual "enhancer." The worst a customs agent could do was confiscate the drugs for further investigation.

I had no way of knowing how many of my fellow passengers had been blackmailed as I was. But there were a lot of anxious glances around the swimming pool that afternoon.

[VI]

While I was enjoying unusually balmy weather in the Atlantic, Trace and the boys were keeping tabs on Granny's operation. Day One, Day Two, and Day Three—all went by without much out of the ordinary, at least if you assume an octogenarian running a drug business is ordinary. Worried about tipping Granny off, and with two men already inside the organization, the task force had a very light surveillance plan: they had taken over a house near the highway that covered the only road into the development, and from there could keep track of the traffic in and out. Granny's phone lines were also tapped, and everything she did on the computer was duplicated at the task force headquarters—which meant that Shunt was seeing it as well.

We were worried that if the task force moved in, Scarface and whoever else was connected to him might pull the plug, making it difficult for us to get more information. The fact that Scarface was on the ship made me hope we might be in for a bonanza—maybe he would stay in the United States and contact Veep. I located his cabin and set up some bugging devices the first night out of port. He was arrogant, though not entirely stupid—the cabin wasn't guarded, but it was also devoid of any electronic devices. If Granny were busted, he'd be on his guard even more.

I didn't trust the task force enough to alert them to what was going on. Given that their e-mails indicated they were trying to gather information about "Hoboken Harry" (apparently my new *nom de druggee*), I decided we would hold off on that risk until there was no other option.

Up in New York, Danny and the rest of the surveillance operation continued to watch Veep. They, too, had a run of boring days. As far as they could tell, Veep didn't contact our friend Mr. Magoo, let alone the smuggling ring or Granny. And aside from that one adventure on the subway, he didn't stray out of his routine.

Which apparently led Junior to ask himself, What would Dad do in this situation?

The answer he came up with was break into Veep's New York City apartment.

Not a bad answer, except that he didn't bother to tell Danny. And his timing could have been a lot better.

Veep's condo unit was on the nineteenth floor of a thirty-seven-floor high-rise on the East Side of Manhattan. Junior realized that Veep would have had all sorts of security precautions. So the first thing Junior did was turn up the heat. Literally.

The building was equipped with thermostats that could be adjusted online—a little factoid Shunt had uncovered during a routine Google search, when a *New York Times* real estate story about the building and its $8 million units popped up. Junior put his computer skills to use, hacking into the thermostat interface and setting the temp in Veep's apartment up to ninety. Unfortunately for the other residents of the building, the programming dictated that he interfere with all the thermostats on the particular code block pertaining to that building; otherwise, the change would have been noticed by anyone running a diagnostic.[41]

The building maintenance staff called for assistance about two hours later, after repeated efforts failed to lower the temperature. Junior showed up within ten minutes, double-parking his step-van in front of the building. He went in carrying a pair of toolboxes and whistling a tune.

One of the maintenance people and a security goon met him in the lobby and accompanied him to the first thermostat, tucked into a frond-filled alcove near the elevator. It took him about ten minutes to set up his diagnostic laptop and get the face of the thermostat off.

"Blew out a circuit," he told the maintenance person after pretending to run a few checks. "You have a power surge in the building?"

The man gave the answer all New York maintenance people are trained to give: *Dunno.*

"Let's spot-check another," said Junior. "Take me up to floor eighteen."

"Why eighteen?" asked the security goon.

"Because it's in the middle. You have to balance air-conditioning systems or they don't work. The velocity of the air as it comes through the system is equal to the coefficient of the squared diameter of the passage. It's actually a principle of physics. One of the Newtonian laws of air velocity."

"They're all separate units," said the maintenance man.

"Precisely." Junior was in fine BS form. "The differential between the various floors is evened out at the mid-state. If we go back to Sir Isaac Newton."

"Just fix the damn thing," snapped the security goon. "And make it quick. More people will be home soon. They're going to be pissed."

They went up to the eighteenth floor via the service elevator. It happened

---

[41] There were actually thirty-five apartments in the building. Add in the lobby, which had its own system, and you see that Junior screwed up two thermostats *not* in that building. We apologize for the inconvenience.

that the nanny and her two charges here were home; Junior insisted that the rambunctious three- and four-year-olds be kept out of his way as he checked each room for airflow. The security goon was happy to help out—the nanny was extremely good-looking—and with the maintenance man working as a gofer, Junior quickly completed his true mission—planting bugs in the ventilation system under each room of the apartment above.

Veep might discover the bugs if he swept his apartment with a bug detector. But the fact that there were two kids' bedrooms below him, each equipped with a baby monitor, would confuse even the most sophisticated devices.

Junior hadn't known for sure that there were monitors in the apartment. He'd chosen it because bugging Veep's condo would be too obvious, and the shafts here were close enough to pick up most conversations above anyway. But when he saw them he realized luck was running strong in his direction. He used his iPhone to reset the thermostats, fiddled with the one in the apartment, and, after a few not-so-discreet glimpses of the nanny and her prodigious endowments, decided his job was finished.

"Should work now," he told the maintenance man. "Should we go?"

"About time you're done," said the security goon, who nonetheless had a difficult time tearing himself away from the apartment.

They went down through the main elevator. Junior was feeling pretty good about himself, and practically floated into the hallway—until he looked through the double glass doors at the front of the foyer and saw a small van pulling up behind his.

He had neglected to phone the actual air-conditioning company and cancel the emergency call. This ordinarily wouldn't have been a problem in New York City, where typically no tradesman answers an emergency call in less than forty-eight hours. But somehow Murphy had stepped in and managed to find the one conscientious service company in the five boroughs, and then canceled a series of other calls nearby, freeing the serviceman.

Junior decided his best bet was to hustle past the doorman and intercept the technician. He put his head down and his feet moving, gathering steam as he went. He pushed through the first set of doors and went at the outer set with his back, waving good-bye in a smooth dance that would have made Fred Astaire proud.

As poetic as the move might have been, it also meant that he didn't see the man coming into the building until he had bowled him over. And when Junior reached down to help him up, he realized it wasn't the serviceman at all—it was Veep.

"Watch where you're going," stuttered Veep.

Junior let go of his hand and turned quickly—too quickly, as he bumped into the legitimate serviceman, who was portly enough to bounce Junior to the curb.

"Don't I know you?" said Veep.

"Just a problem with the lobby thermostat," said Junior to the other tradesman, scurrying to his truck. "All done."

Veep took a couple of steps toward him, trying to get a better view. Junior hopped in his truck and pulled away. He headed down the block, running the light and barely missing a cab before getting far enough away that he could relax.

Or at least think he could.

"What have you been up to on your afternoon off?" Danny asked Junior when he reported to him an hour later.

"I decided to take a little initiative," said Junior.

"By bugging Veep's condo?"

"Actually, the unit just below." Junior was so proud of himself he practically sang. "He won't be able to find the bugs."

Danny pulled over his iPad and brought up a media player. He tapped the arrow, and a hushed voice began playing over the static. It had been computer-enhanced, but it was still a little difficult to hear.

"I'm pretty sure I'm being followed. We may have to go scorched earth."

Danny hit pause.

"Veep," said Junior.

Danny nodded. "Why would he think he's being followed?"

"I don't know. I'm not following him. I mean, you took me off. I've been working the mike."

"And bugging his apartment." Danny slid his finger along the timeline at the bottom of the file window, until he located a section later on. He hit Play again.

"I need a Class One scan of my apartment and office," said Veep's voice.

"I bumped into him on the way out," said Junior. "I was going to mention it."

"Why the hell did you go there in the first place?"

"I just—you always tell me to show initiative. I was just doing that."

"Initiative is not a synonym for being stupid."

Junior had a response that, even for a Rogue Warrior book, was unprintable.

Before Danny could answer, his sat phone buzzed with a call from Shunt.

"I just intercepted a text," said Shunt. "The task force is moving in on Granny."

"Warn Trace. We don't want them to hit the place until the bank transfers go through."

"Already on it. But you better hurry if you're going to call the task force commander. He's on his way down there personally to supervise."

[1]

Shotgun had been stationed near the highway, manning a motorcycle and munching on a pair of Hostess Twinkies, when Trace put out the order to slow the police down until Danny could get a hold of the task force chief. He shoved the cakes into his mouth, wiped his fingers on his pants leg—always classy, that Shotgun—and gunned the Wide Glide Harley to life. Then he strapped on his helmet and set out. (Shotgun didn't need to wear a helmet—as long as you're over twenty-one and have ten thousand dollars in medical insurance, you're good in Florida to go without—but in this case his customized helmet served several purposes: there was a radio unit inside, and it also had an embedded GPS map that could be worked via voice command.)

The task group was driving into the development via a pair of unmarked nine-passenger vans. The plain vanilla-colored vehicles were just coming off the highway when Shotgun spotted them in the yellowish triangles of the streetlights illuminating the ramp. He peppered his throttle to gain on the rear vehicle, reaching at the same time into his jacket for a .22 Walther GSP Expert, a precision pistol preferred by marksmen for popping targets . . . or rear tires, which is what Shotgun popped here.

He tucked the gun back into his jacket and started to pass on the left. But a moving van had just turned onto the street, and Shotgun found the headlights bearing down on him. He veered left, crossing the lane and jumping the curb onto a sidewalk. Starting to brake, he found his way blocked by a child's bicycle ahead. He veered to miss it, sending the Harley onto a freshly-watered lawn. Shotgun applied a little too much English to the handlebars trying to steer back, and the bike slid out from under him.

Down the street, Mongoose was sitting in a set of bushes, waiting as backup. He had a modified .22 caliber rifle equipped with disintegrating carbon-fiber flechette rounds. Nearly as hard as steel, the small rounds shredded the tires within seconds. As the van skidded to a stop, Mongoose retreated behind the house, through the backyard, and to the next street, where he hopped into a pickup and drove toward Granny's house, where Trace was waiting.

While Shotgun manhandled the Harley upright, the officers in the van piled out a few yards down. Drawn from the state trooper tactical response team and dressed in full body armor and helmets, they weren't sure what had happened with their truck, but when they spotted the motorcycle on the nearby front yard they decided its operator should be sequestered on general principles.

Two of the troopers began running in Shotgun's direction. They looked a bit like Storm Troopers from *Star Wars*, a movie Shotgun has never particularly liked. He gunned the bike down the street, only to find a ninety-degree turn where he thought a straightaway would be. He tried braking but it was too late; when he hit the curb this time he separated from the bike, flying in a tumble all the way to the garage door of the nearest house.

Several blocks away, Trace heard a helicopter flying in the direction of Granny's house. Unsure whether it was part of the task force or not, she tried to reach Danny on the radio for clarification. But Danny was talking to the task force head, and wouldn't interrupt the call. With the helo closing in, Trace used a flashing laser device to ward off the pilots. The laser wasn't quite strong enough to blind the pilot, but the dazzler made it difficult for him to see, and he immediately diverted back to the airport.

The task force chief's initial response to Danny was something along the lines of *Who the hell do you think you're talking to?* He calmed down somewhat as Danny recited the names of half a dozen mutual acquaintances, including Narc's. Fortunately for us, the agent was a legend in anti-drug circles, and mentioning his name got the chief's attention.

"We need you to call off the raid on Granny," said Danny. "I'll explain the reasons in person tomorrow, but I need you to call it off right now."

"How the hell do you know what we're doing?"

"We're watching the property right now," said Danny. "She has a major drug shipment coming in from Europe in a few days, and we need to track it."

"You're with the feds?"

"Not exactly."

That was actually a better answer than *yes*, given the relationship between the task force and the DEA, but it wasn't so much better that it got instant cooperation. In fact, it took Danny another two or three minutes to persuade the chief to call his men back.

Which should have ended the operation right there, at least temporarily. But Murphy had other plans.

Oblivious to what was going on a few blocks away, Granny decided that she wanted to slip out for a midnight snack. Over the protests of one of her bodyguards—one of the undercover agents who had been slipped in by the task force—she got into her SUV. As she sometimes did, Granny insisted on driving; all the bodyguards could do was go along.

"McDonald's, next stop," she told them.

She'd barely gone two blocks when she heard the siren of an ambulance, which had been called by the homeowner whose lawn Shotgun had plowed into. Granny continued on toward the highway. The siren probably made her slightly nervous, and the sight of armed men milling in the road a few blocks from the highway couldn't have made her any more comfortable.

The bodyguard-double agent had knocked out the right brake light on the vehicle earlier that evening, to make it easier to spot and identify. Unfortunately, its absence attracted the attention of a traffic patrol just after she got on the highway. The officer hit his lights. Granny sped up. She lost him long enough to reach the next exit. But the officer had radioed ahead, and a patrol cruiser was parked across the intersection below the highway, blocking her off. Within seconds, her car was blocked front and back.

The bodyguard in the passenger seat pulled out his pistol. The man in the backseat, the planted agent from the task force, decided things had gone too far. He, too, took out his gun—and did a double-tap against the back of the other man's head.

"You're under arrest, Granny," he told her, pointing the gun at her.

"I guess this means I'm not getting my Big Mac," said Granny as she was led from the vehicle in handcuffs.

S hotgun rendezvoused with Mongoose not too long after his tumble, and we were also able to recover the Harley, once we straightened things out with the task force. Holding Granny on flight to avoid prosecution of a traffic violation would have been difficult, even in Florida, so the task force went ahead and filed drug charges against her.

A few hours later, someone called Veep from a phone booth in Italy, leaving an automated text-to-voice message on his answering machine. The message was short, and we had no idea what it meant, or even if it was actually meant for Veep: "Scorched Earth."

We heard the message thanks to the bugs Junior had placed. Shunt eventually tracked the call to the phone booth, but that was as far as the trail went. Veep came home a few hours later and didn't seem to react, deleting the call along with a half-dozen others. When he went to work the next morning, he acted as if nothing had happened.

Something had, but we were damned if we could figure out what.

Junior had earned himself a time-out from Danny. Even though the information we'd gotten from the bugs had helped us immensely, we couldn't afford to have someone freelancing in the middle of an op. Danny now conceded that his original decision not to bug the complex was wrong. But that didn't excuse Junior for going ahead and doing it on his own. A properly planned and executed op would have succeeded just as well, without taking the chance of tipping off Veep.

From being the golden-haired boy—not literally, since his hair is black— Junior had become a problem child. The fact that he was my son made things worse: not only couldn't I cut him slack I wouldn't cut anyone else, but I couldn't even appear to give him special treatment. Frankly, I felt a little betrayed—he of all people should know that the highest standards were expected of him. In the past, he'd always gone the extra mile, militantly insisting that no one cut him any extra slack or give him any break because his dad was in charge. But what the hell was I supposed to make of what he was doing now?

I knew one thing—I'd have given him a good, swift kick in the seat of his intelligence if he was nearby.

But I was far away, in the middle of the Atlantic, basking on the sun deck of the *Bon Voyage*. The cruise ship had an air of restrained elegance, though you didn't have to chip too hard at the surface to get at something a little chintzier. The central ballroom had mahogany-paneled walls and a large crystal chandelier at its center; four smaller chandeliers flanked its sides. The rug was so thick and soft you could walk barefoot through it and swear you were walking through a field of the softest grass in the world. The dining rooms were equally plush, though there were noticeable differences between the "king class" and the "knights class": the tables in the upper division's De Gaulle Room sat fewer people though with more room at each than either the Louis XIV or Joan of Arc Rooms; the velvet on the seatbacks was a little plusher, and the nightly specials always included some variation of caviar.

Walking through the passages to the cabins, you could be forgiven for thinking you'd been thrust back into some golden age of opulence. Of course, that golden age included a recreation room with a state-of-the-art pool table—no matter how the ship bucked, the balls stayed put, thanks to a gyroscope mechanism. It also included just about every boutique clothing store known to man, or I should say woman. Fountains, three different inside bars and a fourth on deck (not counting the cocktail wagon), and small jazz combos cemented the impression that you were among the privileged in a floating paradise.

By the second day, however, you started to notice things like wallpaper that didn't quite match at the seams, silver glitter paint that no longer glittered, edges of curtains that were as frayed as an old sailor's bellbottoms. The sticks used for shuffleboard had chipped handles, and no matter which bar you tried, they tended to go overboard on the ice, no pun intended.

Bug planted, I devoted most of my time to sight-seeing, of which there was quite a lot to be accomplished in the pool area. While a good portion of the passengers were elderly, there was a small but strategic contingent in the mid-twenty to mid-thirty range, and a pleasing proportion were of the female persuasion. String bikinis were making a serious comeback, and you had to get out early to get the best spot.

One afternoon not long after the raid on Granny's, I returned from lunch and settled into an excellent perch close to both the bar and the pool. I'd just begun sipping from my drink when a steward approached.

"Commander Julio?" he asked.

"Yes?"

"The captain asks if you would honor him with a visit to the bridge."

I hesitated. I had just spotted a very real threat to the ship's safety, namely a twenty-something blonde in a Wicked Weasel bathing suit that seemed more imagined than real. But seeing that the five lifeguards on duty were clearly alert to the threat, I decided to go along to the bridge.

The time on the ship had allowed my knees to recover from the knock-ings they'd received, and I had to suppress the urge to spring up the ladder[42] to the bridge as I walked, reminding myself that I was playing the role of an eightyish pensioner. The steward went ahead and opened the door as I caned my way upward, ushering me onto the space.

If there were bits and pieces of the ship's décor that were somewhat dated, the bridge was decidedly not. It was refreshing to see that the cruise line had put serious money into the command area—I suspect the board of directors includes more than a few former sea captains. The bridge had a rail at the back of the console area, most likely so that it could accommodate visitors during VIP tours. But then again, the entire space was larger than a number of minesweepers I've seen. The center navigational console looked like something out of *Star Wars*, with an array of configurable flat screens that read out every possible vital sign. A large panel plotted our position; there were accompanying radar and sonar displays demonstrating that the nearby ocean was our own. There was no paper to be seen anywhere; each crewman, from captain to second lookout, had a tablet-type computer, which tied directly into the ship's command data systems.

The area forward from the console was divided into two separate sec-tions that stepped down from the console deck; even Shotgun could have stood in front of the captain's chair and not blocked his view. Doors at star-board and port opened onto the flying bridge, which extended around the superstructure like the porch on an old Victorian building.

The captain rose from his well-padded leather chair as I came in. He cut a good figure—full head of gray hair, the slightest suggestion of whiskers, a strong gait. He was only of average height, and I doubt he would tip the scale over 150, but he seemed larger in his uniform. He'd shortened his name from Adolf to Alf, and like many of the crew, was Swedish by birth. He shook my hand as if I were an old friend.

"Well, old-timer, what do you think of our bridge?" His words had a slight lilt to them, betraying his first language.

"Very nice," I told him.

"Like the navy ships you commanded?"

"I never had the honor of command." I didn't think he was testing my cover story—he seemed too affable—but just in case, I reminded him what I had said during dinner the night before. My highest shipboard role was as exec, an able and strenuous number two, but not the main fiddle.

---

[42] I'm calling it a ladder only because it was on a ship. Even in the crew areas, the *Bon Voyage's* interior looked more like a hotel than a garbage scow, and the ladder would have served well as the main staircase in a four-star establishment.

"You were on a destroyer, though?" said the captain, remembering.

"Early in my career, aye. A bit different than this."

He smiled proudly, and began showing me the different stations. Though there was a helmsman, the ship was currently running on autopilot; I wondered how the man kept himself awake.

"Soon, they won't need a crew," the captain said wistfully. "Just program the computer and voilà. You will arrive."

"I don't think I'd like to be on a ship like that."

"I would not have expected many things when I started."

The captain introduced me to the rest of the bridge crew. Like him, most were Swedish—it seemed almost a requirement for advancement in the upper ranks of the company, even though the firm was not itself headquartered in Scandinavia. The next-largest contingent of officers was Filipino, which was appropriate since the largest portion of the crewmen had come from the islands. A polyglot of different nationalities made up the rest.

The captain had first served as a crewman aboard a liner in 1969; he liked the experience and went to a training school, joining another line as a junior officer. He'd been with this company for more than a decade, but wasn't yet senior enough to command their *best* ships—something that rankled him just below the surface. Still, he relished his vessel; his sunburned face beamed with pride as he took me to the forward windows and had me look across the deck.

"Quite a ship," I told him.

"Would you like a turn at the wheel?"

"Love it."

The "wheel" consisted of a large pistol-grip controller, more like something you'd find in a spaceship than a ship. I wouldn't have been surprised if it was just for show, but the bow did move a degree or two to port as I steered.

"Now watch the effect of the autopilot," said the captain. He tapped a few buttons and gave the control back to the computer. The *Bon Voyage* moved ever so gently back to starboard.

"Impressive."

"You look tired," said the captain.

"Just my knees acting up."

"Have a seat, have a seat."

He gestured toward the chair next to his. I thanked him and sat down. He picked up a walkie-talkie and began speaking to a member of his crew.

I rested the cane against the console panel and slid back in the chair.

It was comfortable—so comfortable, I could have fallen asleep. And maybe I would have, except for the loud explosion that went off right behind me.

The shock wave rattled the bridge. I grabbed at the armrest to keep from falling. When I looked up, two men had materialized in front of me, both holding sawed-off shotguns.

"The ship is under our command!" one of them yelled. "Do as we say! Do not be foolish!"

His voice was familiar, but until he took a step closer, I didn't realize who it was: Scarface.

The captain pulled himself off the deck where he'd fallen from the shock of the explosion. Grabbing the edge of the console, he steadied himself.

"This is my ship," he growled. "I am in command here."

Scarface answered by pulling the trigger, scattering a good part of the captain's skull across the bridge.

"We are in full command," he said in a strangely calm, even understated voice. "Anyone who resists will be killed, as he was."

(III)

After being dressed down by Danny, Junior headed over to our e-head-quarters in Queens, New York, sharing his misery with Shunt. They'd been friends before either worked for Red Cell International, and being the same age—assuming Shunt *has* an actual age—had a lot of things in common besides their techno-prowess.

As Shunt tells the story, Junior wanted to get back in Danny's good graces, and was desperate for some sort of plan that would take him there. Shunt, meanwhile, had his hands full trying to figure out what Veep's "Scorched Earth" message referred to. Junior started to help.

They wasted a lot of time tracking the phone booth and then cracking the European phone company to look for parallels or other calls. Eventually, Junior started doing random searches and discovered a Twitter account named TWT345 that contained exactly two messages: one, back two months before, was simply the word "Sending."

The second was "Scorched Earth."

There must have been hundreds of messages with those words in them, but the tweet was unique for two reasons: one, that was the only thing in the message, and two, it happened within a few minutes of Veep's phone call.

More interesting, at least to Junior, Twitter account TWT345 had no real followers. The six accounts "following" TWT345 were all spambots, which sent out advertisements but didn't actually read anything sent to them. TWT345 was the proverbial tree falling in the forest that no one was around to hear.

(For those of you who have better things to do with your lives than play with Twitter, the service works like this: once a user signs up for an account, he or she can send messages—called "tweets"—to anyone who has subscribed to receive their messages. That is called "following." Followers can "retweet" or repeat messages, which basically means forwarding the message to the people who follow them. More on Twitter: each message can be no longer than 140 characters. If you think of it as a semi-closed system for sending text messages to a list of people, you have the basic idea.)

The account could have been used to communicate basic information without being noticed by the authorities, but from what Junior could tell, no one else had noticed it either. Then he realized that tweets could be re-trieved through searches instead of subscriptions. Someone doing a regular search would see the tweet without having to subscribe to the specific account. No subscription, no record, no way to track.

Or, no easy way to track. The Twitter servers had records of the searches; all Junior had to do was break into the system and retrieve them. That took him several hours, but once there, a few minutes of downloading and examining search strings revealed that TWT345 had been searched every half hour over the past two weeks by two different computer users.

While the identity of the users themselves was hidden, the service providers were not. One user was in Europe, the other in Washington, D.C. Knowing that backtracking to the actual person could be difficult, especially in Europe, Shunt prioritized the Washington, D.C., user and began digging into the service. He discovered that the same computer had been searching Google for days, looking for plans to the Capitol and the Supreme Court Building, both of which had been mentioned in the intercepts that Junior had looked at weeks before.

Just a coincidence, surely—but Junior found that the computer had accessed a Web e-mail address, and was able to tease out the account. And the e-mail account had received the following message from a heretofore unused Gmail account about a half hour after Veep got his phone call: *Initiate Scorched Earth.*

There were a lot of connections and a few cyber jumps in that chain, and I can't blame Danny for telling Shunt it was all very tenuous. He told Shunt partly because Junior was still working, and partly because Junior hoped Danny would be more receptive if the information came from him.

"Maybe we ought to tell Homeland Security just in case," said Shunt.

"They get a million of these alerts every day," said Danny. "This would be just one more bit of noise. It's a convoluted coincidence, Shunt. I'm surprised at you."

"Dick always says he doesn't believe in coincidences."

"Neither do I. But this is definitely one."

Danny's doubts made Shunt doubt the connections as well, and if he hadn't received a phone call from Karen Fairchild, he might have forgotten the whole thing. Karen had heard a bit of what had happened with Junior and was concerned about him; she'd called his cell phone without getting an answer.

Junior was standing a few feet from Shunt when she called, sipping a Diet Coke, about the only sustenance he'd had in the past twenty-four hours. Shunt answered loudly, greeting Karen and glancing at Junior. But Junior waved him off, not wanting to talk.

"He's gone out for a soda, I think," said Shunt, searching for something to say. "Wants to get a Big Gulp while they're still legal. Mayor's outlawing big sodas."

"I've never seen Junior drink more than half a can at a sitting," said Karen.

"Yeah." Shunt searched for something to say. He had a feeling Karen knew he was lying. "I, uh—did Danny talk to you about Scorched Earth? We intercepted this weird message. It was a tweet, sent in the open. But we think it's a code."

Karen listened as Shunt explained.

"Interesting," she told him when he was done. "It's probably not related, but the CIA just sent a bulletin to Homeland Security suggesting we up the alert status in D.C."

"Really?"

"We get these alerts every few days," she told him. "They're always nothing. But just in case—can you send me what you have?"

"It's on its way."

Three and a half hours later, Junior got off an Acela Express at Union Station in Washington, D.C. The station was crowded with commuters—and National Guardsmen, police officers, and bomb-sniffing dogs, all called out because of the alert that had originated with the CIA and been passed on to the authorities by Homeland (in)Security. The entire city was on extra-high alert, ready to deal with the suspected terrorist attack.

Actually, no. That's what Junior expected. That's what a *reasonable* person might expect when a government agency is investigating a bona fide terror threat. But in fact there were no dogs, no Guardsmen, no chemical sniffers. The only policemen Junior saw in the station area were at the restaurant outside the train platform, joking with a waitress.

As Karen had said, alerts from the CIA came so often that they were routinely ignored. It was a modern-day variation on the story of the boy who called wolf.

Confused, maybe a little disappointed, Junior walked to the Capitol building. Bomb-detecting dogs patrolled near the street, augmenting chemical sniffers placed near the steps that could pick up trace amounts of plastic explosives. But this was more or less routine, and things were relaxed otherwise. Junior made a wide circuit of the area near the Capitol and the nearby Mall, wondering why he didn't spot any heavy-duty precautions.

The more he walked, the angrier he became. He was sure he and Shunt had fallen on a major plot against Washington, D.C., and equally convinced that no one was taking it seriously.

Junior had come to D.C. with the name of the Internet provider whose system had been used to access the Internet to search for the Twitter message. In order to identify the customer, he needed to access the company's records, coordinating them with the log-on data. The company was inefficient, old-fashioned, or security conscious (take your pick), but the customer records were not kept on the same servers Junior had accessed, and it appeared that they could only be accessed by someone with administrative rights on the system at the company's administrative offices. Doing that implies illegal activity, and so perhaps it's best that I don't know exactly how he managed to discover the customer's name and address. Surely it's a coincidence that he has recently been spotted several times since with one of the computer system operators, a heavily tattooed lass who could easily pass for a Suicide Girl.[43]

The address was in the Trinidad section, one of the less savory areas of the city—not quite as bad as the Congressional office buildings or the lobbyists' lairs on Jay Street, though sketchy nonetheless. The subscriber's name was Robert Jones—a good American name, one easily faked, though Junior pretended not to know this when he knocked on the door of the house, a renovated row house a couple of blocks over from the firehouse.

As the door opened, Junior caught the sweet scent of a burning substance that was *not* tobacco. Out stepped a young white man with dreadlocks and irises that could have held a coffee cup.

"What up?" he asked.

"I'm looking for Robert Jones," said Junior.

"What up?" White Rasta repeated.

"Robert Jones?"

"He ain't here."

"You sure?"

"You mean the landlord, right? Mr. Jones. Like, who we pay rent to."

"He doesn't live here?"

"No way." White Rasta gave him a dreamy smile. "We're all in college, man. We don't own, like, buildings."

"Really? Does Jones live upstairs?"

"On the third floor, you mean? We have like, two floors. The girls live on the third floor." White Rasta winked, or tried to. His facial muscles were so sedated by the herbs he'd been imbibing that the lids never made it to the bottom. When he winked, his eyes looked like those donut pillows they give hemorrhoid patients.

"Who else lives here?" Junior asked.

---

[43] If you don't know who they are, I'm not going to be the one to corrupt you. But if you're thinking *Playboy* for the Goth set, you're not too far off.

"You a cop?"

"Hell no. I'm just looking for Jones." Junior stepped past White Rasta and poked his head inside the door. "He owes me money."

"I don't know where he's at."

"I really, really need his cash. You know what I mean? You're a friend of his?"

"No way, bro. Listen, I'd help you if I could."

"Where do you send your rent?" asked Junior.

"Oh yeah. Good idea. Come on."

While not fancy, the exterior of the building presented a tidy appearance to the world: thick paint over solid bricks, the weathering around the edges adding dignity and solid middle-class value. The interior, though, was dorm-room lite, with second- and thirdhand furniture cluttering the living room, bicycles and bike parts lining the hallway, shoes and clothes littering various parts of the floor. Junior followed White Rasta to the kitchen, where the strong herbal scent gave way to something halfway between garlic and a cat that had been in heat for far too long.

"How many people live here?" asked Junior.

"Big, huh?" White Rasta opened one of the kitchen drawers, where the communal records were kept in a three-section notebook. He plopped it onto the least-stained portion of the counter and began flipping through it.

"Mind if I use the bathroom?" asked Junior, who wanted a pretext to search the place.

"Just bring it back when you're done." White Rasta giggled as if this was the funniest thing anyone had ever said since the debut of *Saturday Night Live*.

Junior went down the hall, peeked into the bathroom—it reminded him of an Indian slum, though not as tidy—then proceeded through the house, taking stock. All three of the bedrooms were upstairs, and all were conveniently if temporarily unoccupied. He found a notebook with a name in the first: Habib. In the second, some court papers demanded Robert MacLeroy to appear for a traffic summons. In the last, which the sweet scent identified as White Rasta's, an exam in organic chemistry was headed by the name "Terrence Jonlable."

He'd scored a 98. Maybe the herb does help the brain function.

"I got the address," said White Rasta when Junior returned. "Where'd you go?"

"I was looking for a bathroom that was on the clean side."

"I usually go off the back porch." White Rasta handed Junior a brown paper bag with Jones's address on it.

"Did you say your name was Terry?" asked Junior, taking the paper.

"Terrence."

"Oh yeah, I'm sorry. So you guys all go to school?"

"Yup."

"You're in like, organic chem, right?" Junior asked.

"Yeah. Crazy, far-out class, huh? Some of those tests are bummers. I only got a ninety-eight on the last one. I'm thinking I might have to study."

"What's your major?"

"Pre-med. You're familiar. Yeah. You're in organic?"

"No, no. I'm just looking for Jones and the money he owes me."

"That's his address."

"He welched on my deposit," said Junior. "He owes two months. And I need the cash, you know?"

"What a prick."

"What a prick." Junior sized him up. "Do you have a credit card?"

"Credit card?" White Rasta rolled his eyes so far back in his head Junior thought he'd collapse. "I'm capitalistic system, dude."

"No credit card?"

"No way, man. Besides, you get one of those cards, you gotta watch for fraud and stuff. All sorts of illegal activity goin' on there."

"Yeah. I'd be careful if I were you." Junior glanced around. "You live with a couple of other guys?"

"Two, yeah. Far-out dudes. Habs and Bobby. Bobby is like super into his bike. And his girl, like, they're always together and I expect them home soon. But, uh—"

"We had the same deal," said Junior. "Three guys. Except I was the only one who put up the deposit money. Now I'm screwed."

"Bummer."

Junior poked a bit, asking White Rasta about his roommates, trying to get more information on who they were. But his interviewee's vacant stare held him off. Finally White Rasta asked if he wanted to "imbibe."

"Gotta pass," said Junior, holding up the paper bag with Jones's address. "Say, when do your roommates come home?"

"Huh? Like, why?"

"I was thinking maybe if we all went over together—you know, if I had a little muscle with me."

"Dude, you're buff. Bobby and Habs—they couldn't scare a fly."

"Strength in numbers?"

"I heard about that. Hey listen, I gotta do some homework for Abstract,[44] like field automorphisms, man. You sure you don't want some weed?"

---

[44] Abstract Geometry, judging from the assignment.

"No thanks."

Back outside, Junior considered his options. Not being a member of the U.S. government, he'd concluded that his most likely suspect was Habib, or "Habs," as White Rasta called him. But he couldn't rule the other room-mates out, nor even any of the neighbors, if they had Wi-Fi. Pretending to have a phone call, he paused near the front stoop and took out his iPhone. Firing up the connection panel, he found that the apartment did in fact have Wi-Fi (TeamRoom was its handle; the girls on the third floor apparently preferring the more prosaic though equally appropriate LadiesNet). The router was using WPA2-PSK encryption—decent, though far from impenetrable.

Junior took a short walk around the block, checking to see how many other Wi-Fi connections were nearby. He stopped counting at fifty; half had no security at all. The fact that there were so many open connections in the area indirectly reinforced Junior's belief that he was on the right track. Since it was so much easier to use a different connection, he reasoned, anyone who wanted to throw an investigator off would use one of those. The operator probably didn't realize he could be tracked so easily, or believed that the method they were using to communicate was so arcane that no one would ever figure it out, let alone trace it.

Ducking into a basement entrance to a three-story walk-up just barely in eyesight of the house, Junior considered his options. He'd pretty much ruled out White Rasta as a suspect; though clearly highly intelligent, he just didn't have the destroy-the-world vibe Junior thought he was looking for. So that meant buttonholing the other occupants—or better, stealing their laptops.

Junior was trying to decide how he might do that when he saw a skinny, dark-complexioned man walking down the street, a backpack slung over one shoulder.

Habib?

The man jogged up the steps into the house and was gone before Junior could get close. He walked past the house, continuing down the block toward the corner. Just as he turned it, he saw a man and a woman, both in their early twenties, approaching. The man was pushing a bicycle.

Junior decided to take a chance that this was the other roommate. He waited until they were a little closer, then stopped and did a double-take.

"Hey, Bobby, right?" he said to the man.

"Huh?"

"Bobby MacLeroy, right? Weren't you in my orientation? And at that party, uh—"

"I don't remember, man." MacLeroy curled his arm around his girl-friend's.

"No prob. How's it goin'? You livin' with uh, Conner? In the dorms, right?"

"I live down the street."

"Oh yeah, yeah, with that dude, uh—Terrence? Always smokin' pot? Right? But he's genius smart."

"You know Terrence?"

"Everybody in pre-med knows Terrence. He's getting perfect grades in Organic. He's a legend. You guys got the place by yourselves?"

"Transfer student's with us. Who are you again?"

"Matty. Remember?"

"Uh, vaguely. Kind of a blur, you know?"

"Believe me, I know." Junior focused on the girl for the first time. She had red, curly hair, and if she stepped on a scale, wouldn't have tipped it past ninety pounds, fully dressed. Which she was, in enough layers of sweaters and shirts to keep an Eskimo warm.

"We gotta get goin'," said MacLeroy.

"Maybe we'll party some time," said Junior.

"Uh, yeah, sure." MacLeroy sounded about as convincing as a life-long Republican swearing his willingness to vote for Obama in the next election.

Junior went swiftly to the end of the block, then leaned back to make sure the pair were in fact going to the house. They were. And just as he was about to go back to his hiding spot, he saw Habib come trotting down the steps, backpack on his shoulder.

Junior waited until Habib was at the end of the block, then started following, making sure to leave roughly a block and a half of gap between them. He closed the distance as they neared the college campus, expecting that Habib would go into one of the buildings there. But instead, he walked a zigzag path across H Street toward Union Station. Junior worried that Habib would take an Amtrak, which required a pre-purchased ticket. But Habib headed for the Metro entrance.

Junior didn't have a card. The line at the machines was just long enough for him lose Habib, and after getting his card he had to guess which way he was headed. He guessed toward the Capitol area, then had to bolt to the platform as the train pulled in. But by the time he reached it, the doors had closed. He pounded but it was too late; the train jerked forward, out of the station.

Cursing, he turned around, trying to decide what to do. As he did, he spotted someone at the far end of the opposite platform, moving down to the very edge of the station where the tracks entered the tunnel.

The man had a backpack, but from this distance and with his back turned, Junior couldn't be sure that it was Habib. The man reached the end of the platform, glanced quickly over his shoulder, then hopped down and began walking along the tracks.

Junior decided to follow.

[IV]

B ack aboard the *Bon Voyage*, six men joined the other two on the bridge. We were shepherded into a large chart room immediately aft of the command area. While there were charts on one side of the large table that filled the center of the space, the captain primarily used this area to brief his officers. His quarters were through a door on the aft bulkhead; next to the door sat a console with a com set and a computer setup. Two of our guards trashed the gear, then went inside the captain's cabin and broke up the equipment there. They hunted inside the captain's desk and chests, retrieving and breaking open a strongbox that contained a pistol and some cash. They took the gun, left the money.

The bridge crew gathered at one side of the table and began to whisper among themselves, but before long the man who had shot the captain reappeared with two other hijackers and grabbed the second mate, who'd come up on the bridge just before it was stormed. Wearing what looked like typical crewmen's clothes, the men made no attempt to hide their faces—a very bad sign, I thought.

Scarface came in. He must have recognized me, but didn't bother to acknowledge me. He spoke in clipped, quick English, saying that we were to keep quiet and not cause trouble, or we would face the same fate as the captain.

He left us and began barking orders at the others, who hopped around to different stations on the bridge. They'd been among us the whole time, a few as passengers, others as crewmen. It wasn't hard to get low-level jobs on the ship, given the industry's penchant for low-wage, bottom-rung workers.

"You'll never get a ransom," sputtered the helmsman.

Scarface smirked. Somehow I'm always lucky enough to find myself among scumbags with a sense of twisted humor.

As soon as the hijackers left with the mate, the crew began discussing the situation among themselves in Swedish, debating whether a distress signal had been sent from somewhere else in the ship. The captain's death had shocked them; a few were close to tears, their lips and hands occasionally trembling. I went to the window and watched the men now occupying the bridge. They worked almost as smoothly as the regular crew had, looking over the various instruments and controls and making only slight adjustments.

"What are you looking at, old-timer?" asked the helmsman, coming over. I could barely understand what he was saying through his accent.

"I was watching them. They know what they're doing." I pointed. "Are they changing course?"

"Oh yes. You can see that we have moved a few degrees north." He pointed at the large screen. "Soon, the company will attempt to contact them. Every move that is made, it is radioed back. Some deviation is always allowed, but this will be more than enough to have questions raised."

I figured that they would have answers ready, enough to hold the company off for a while at least. Instead of mentioning this, I asked if he could guess where we might be headed.

The helmsman shook his head. "Too many places to say."

I went over to the charts and rolled them out, trying to solve the puzzle for myself. When the others saw what I was doing, they came over and looked on. The helmsman took more of an interest, and studied the chart more intently. Finally he leaned over and traced a course with his finger.

"On this heading," he said, "we will go to Maryland."

"Norfolk?" asked another of the crew.

The helmsman answered in Swedish. I could give the answer myself—if the ship stayed its course, it would go right up the Chesapeake Bay. If alerted, the navy could intercept it. But what would happen then? If the hijackers started killing people aboard, would the navy try and retake the ship?

It would be the right thing to do, but who would have the guts to make that call? I didn't see the president—or any politician—giving the order, at least not until things were clearly desperate. And stopping the ship without gunfire would not be an easy matter, if the hijackers knew what they were doing.

The second mate returned about an hour after he left. His thin face had grown longer and more bleached.

"They've planted explosives all over," he said, using English. "They must have smuggled them in with the cargo."

"Where are the passengers?" I asked.

The question surprised not only him but the others. They didn't think an old man should be worried about anything but himself.

"They are locked in their cabins," said the mate. "With no food—I don't know what the hijackers are thinking."

The *Bon Voyage* was neither the largest nor most popular cruise ship on the seven seas; I'd estimate that about half of the cabins were vacant. Still, there were several hundred passengers aboard. The crew would add another hundred or so, depending on how many were actually hijackers. That was a lot of people to keep under control, even if a good number were senior citizens.

Actually, senior citizens might be even harder to control. Take the one wandering to the bridge from below, mumbling to himself. One of the hijackers jumped up abruptly, grabbing his submachine gun and pointing at the intruder. The old man's waxed handlebar moustache twitched, then drooped as he backed against the window of the chart room.

I went to the door and grabbed hold of him, pulling him toward us.

"It's OK, it's OK," I said. The poor old man was slobbering, drool running off his chin. "He's just demented. Probably Alzheimer's."

The crewman with the gun barked at me, but I ignored him, throwing the door closed and helping the man to a seat. He mumbled something at his shoes, then raised his gaze in my direction.

"You took your damn time getting here," I told him.

He blinked his eyes and smiled, immediately throwing off the persona of fool that had served him so well. But even as a plank holder of SEAL Team Six, Albert "Doc" Tremblay always had an intelligent look about him.

As I've often told him, he's living proof that appearances can be deceiving.

"It's a big ship," complained Doc.

"You couldn't find the bridge?"

"I had trouble getting out of the bar."

"Story of your life."

As seasoned readers, friends, and hangers-on well know, Doc has been an employee of Red Cell International pretty much since our inception. Besides being an excellent corpsman and a natural-born leader, he was born with a golden tongue. Everyone has heard of the salesman who could sell ice to an Eskimo. Doc would add a refrigerator and a lifetime maintenance plan. Then he would start working on an air-conditioning unit.

He'd used that talent to wheedle his way through the lighter part of the hijackers' perimeter, getting past the guard who initially took him and about two dozen people hostage by claiming that he had left his medicine in a friend's cabin. Allowed to go and get it, he quickly slipped away. When the guard picket became a little thicker, he began play-acting with the Alzheimer's bit.

"Saved time," he explained. "I didn't feel like talking much anymore. My Arabic's rusty."

"We'll send you to Libya next month for a refresher course."

"Did you get the device in?" Doc whispered as we sized up the men on the bridge through the window.

"It's there. All we have to do is go below and activate it. We'll run the ship from there."

"They won't be happy."

"I hope not."

"Storm blowing in from the south." Doc gestured at the large fist of black hugging the horizon. Like most cruise ships, the *Bon Voyage* was built to minimize roll in rough waters, but she was starting to feel the heaves. "Looks like a rough night ahead."

"In more ways than one. Let's get moving."

Our first task was to get out of the bridge area. My plan for this followed time-tested Rogue Warrior doctrine: Keep It Simple, Stupid, otherwise known as KISS. I found a bobbie pin on the floor, waited until no one was watching, then jimmied the pathetically primitive lock on the door between the chart room and the captain's quarters. As Doc slid inside, I looked back at my fellow hostages.

"I can't explain now," I told them. "OK?"

One by one, they nodded.

The captain's quarters were spartan. There were no personal mementos, and except for the clothes neatly hung in the open closet, barely a sign that anyone lived here. You could have bounced a quarter off the bed and caught it in your teeth.

Doc's knees groaned as he knelt near the door to the corridor. Mine groaned in sympathy.

"I'll just have a look. *Damn*," he hissed, closing the door quickly.

There were two guards in the passage, a few feet away.

"We can rush them," suggested Doc.

"Then they'll know something's up," I told him. "Best to go back to Plan B."

"We're already on B, aren't we?"

"More like D."

Ten minutes later, one of our fellow hostages began pounding on the window, screaming to our captors in Swedish. I'm not exactly sure what he was saying, but the words "heart attack" come to mind.

Doc was on the deck, having clutched his chest as he went down. I thought he was hamming it up a bit much, until one of the others dropped to their knee and started pressing on his chest. I had to step in quickly before she attempted mouth-to-mouth—Doc's wife Donna would never have forgiven me.

The hijackers ignored the pounding for a short while, but eventually one of the men came over and yelled at them to stop. The hostages yelled back in Swedish.

"I need to take this man to sick bay," I said, hopping up. "He needs to go to sick bay."

The others chimed in. The hijacker raised his voice; they did as well. He raised his gun; they backed from the window, but continued to scream. Finally, our captor waved at me and said one word: "Out."

I got Doc in a fireman's hold—there was a collective gasp from the others, sure that the old gent would break his back—then staggered out on the bridge. I'm not saying Doc has put on a few pounds since his navy days, but I was certainly wondering if my health insurance would cover hernia repairs. But at least that diverted my attention from the pain and agitation in my mending knees.

The hijacker led us into the passageway and yelled something to the men there. They frowned, but one of them started walking ahead of me, apparently having been designated as my guide to the sick bay, or Shipboard Clinic, as the signs said.

I didn't mind that he made me carry Doc by myself, but it was inconvenient for him to stay with us the entire way. When we arrived, we found the clinic guarded by two other hijackers. The medical staff had been confined to the clinic area, which consisted of a largish compartment and two smaller offices, along with an isolation area at the far end filled with a dozen beds. A doctor met us as we came in, and immediately walked me to a gurney near the far bulkhead.

"What is wrong?" asked the doctor. His English had a Spanish accent, or maybe it was the other way around.

"Heart attack," I told him.

The physician practically crossed his eyes, then began examining Doc.

"Hmmmm," he muttered, frowning at the blood pressure cuff as he held his stethoscope to Doc's pulse.

"It's a ruse," I whispered, knowing that Doc's got the vitals of a thirty-year-old and worried that the physician would give us away.

The doctor gave me a worried glance. "To lie—"

"We lie or we die," I said.

He winced. But then he called one of the nurses over, and asked for a needle.

"Saline," he whispered, adding in Spanish that he just needed to reassure the patient, who would be fine. He was playing along.

I glanced over at the two lugs near the entrance. They were paying a lot of attention to the two nurses who were looking after a pair of patients lying on cots nearby.

"Do you have morphine?" I asked the doctor. "I want to knock the two guards out."

"I have something much better than that. Come."

He told the nurse who'd gone for the syringe of saltwater to watch Doc carefully, then walked me to one of the offices. He took a key from a chain around his neck and opened one of the cabinets.

"We use this in case we are dealing with one of the animals in the hold," he said, pulling a box off a bottom shelf. It was filled with vials. "It works very quickly."

"Great," I said, taking the vials.

"You have to be very careful. It's very potent."

"Needles?"

He went over to his desk and opened the bottom drawer. It looked like a heroin junkie's wet dream, stacked with hypo setups. He helped me fix up two doses, and once again repeated his cautions.

"I can use as many of these as you have," I told him. "Do you have something I can carry them in?"

"Only a medical bag."

"That'll do."

I went over to the door and grabbed his spare white lab coat. I was just contemplating how to take down the two lugs at the same time when they provided the solution for me: one of the men came over to see what the doctor was doing in his office.

The guard didn't speak English very well, and between his limited vocabulary and the doctor's lush accent, they didn't communicate very well. The doctor explained that he was worried about an outbreak of a disease among passengers—something very contagious and similar to scarlet fever. He had looked it up in the thick book on his desk, right here. The guard said he could not stay in the room and must return to the others.

I sidestepped closer to the door, trying to get behind the guard. He glanced at me, but went back to haranguing the doctor, who was jabbing at the open page.

"Come outside *now*." The guard raised his weapon, insisting.

"Look at these lab results," said the doctor, pointing. "An epidemic. We may all die."

"I do not care about this. Come. Come."

That sounded like an invitation to me. I took the syringe and jabbed it into his gluteus maximus, which was rather more maximus than gluteus. Unfortunately, my technique was somewhat lacking—I didn't get the plunger in on the first jab, and the lug turned to me with murderous eyes.

"'Scuse me, sweetie," I lisped—then took him out the old-fashioned way, with a left cross to the chin. He fell back, landing on the deck—pushing the plunger in the rest of the way.

He rolled to his right, then fell back, completely unconscious. I grabbed him under the arms and dragged him behind the desk while the physician closed the door.

"You don't need to get them in the butt," advised the doctor. "It works fastest if you get them in the neck. Just make sure to push the whole dose in."

"I'll do better next time. Do you have keys to the rest of the ship?"

"No."

"A master key? Anything like that?"

He didn't.

"We're going to leave as soon as I take out the other guard," I told him. "You stay here. Pretend nothing has happened. If you can, hide the bodies somehow and keep them sedated."

"I would throw them in the sea if I could."

That seemed a slight contradiction of the Hippocratic Oath, but who was I to point that out?

"Don't take any unnecessary risks," I said. "It may take us a while before we regain control of the ship."

"It's just you two? Against a ship full of hijackers? There must be two dozen at least. All fully armed."

"I know the odds are unfair," I said. "But they should have thought about that before they decided to play."

The other guard had begun talking to one of the nurses, a pretty Scandinavian woman with a forest of blond hair and hips that would dizzy a deer. She glanced at the physician and me as we came out. The doctor nodded ever so slightly, and the next thing I knew, the nurse had her arms around the guard and her lips at his face. I strode forward swiftly, hypo ready to strike, when the lug suddenly dropped to the deck. The nurse administered a swift, very therapeutic kick to the neck. He didn't move after that.

"He's a pig," said the woman, revealing her own syringe from behind her back. "I need mouthwash—the strongest we have."

Doc sprang up from the gurney, a medical miracle in the making.

"Keep them sedated," I told the others. "We may be back. Don't worry if we're not."

I grabbed a stethoscope and hustled out into the passage, with Doc trailing behind me. We headed aft, looking for the ladders that would take us down to the engine room. Once there, we would commandeer one of the computers and use it to link to the device I had planted below the console on the bridge. Once activated, it would give us complete control of the ship's mechanical systems.

I had explored the ship thoroughly since boarding, and had located not one but two different ways to get from this deck to the compartment in question. The first was guarded by one of the hijackers; we spotted him as we turned the corner and managed to scurry back just in time. Worried that he would be missed if we incapacitated him, Doc and I backed away quickly.

"We have to go back to the gym," I told Doc. "We can get down from there."

"Which way is that?"

I'd forgotten. I walked down the passage to the directional sign at the corridor intersection. The gym wasn't listed, but the video amusement center was, and it was close to the gym.

"Left," I told Doc, just as a whirring sound began filling the passage ahead.

"What do you think the noise is?" asked Doc.

"A motor or something. Let's not worry about it. Come on."

"Halt!" yelled a voice behind us.

I glanced back and saw that the hijacker who'd shouted was at the far end of the hall.

"Go," I told Doc, pushing him down the passage at the left.

We started to run, then stopped abruptly as another hijacker turned the corner ahead. He was holding an AK47.

"Shit," muttered Doc.

Behind us, the second hijacker had just turned the corner. He was holding a pistol.

"I think they want us to stop," said Doc.

"Where are your cabins?" demanded the man with the AK47. He appeared Arab, but his English was clear and precise, with a discernible American accent. "How did you get out?"

"I'm the doctor. I am supposed to be in sick bay. I need this man and am taking him to the medical ward," I said. "We have a patient who is having a seizure. I have permission from your commander. Doc is a specialist in seizures."

It wasn't too much of a lie, actually. Doc was great at seizing things.

"You will go back to your rooms." The hijacker glanced down the corridor at his companion. The man stopped, as if warned to keep his distance.

"You don't understand," I told the thug. "The man will die."

He raised his weapon. "And you will die now if you don't do as I say."

[V]

We started down the passage toward the man with the assault rifle. He backed up to the intersection, making sure to leave plenty of space between us—there was no way either Doc or I could get close enough to grab his gun, let alone jab him with the hypodermic. He looked like he would put up a good fight—he was taller than me and a bit broader at the shoulders. The guy behind us wouldn't be much easier, and he stayed even farther away.

I stopped at the crossway of the two corridors. A man was waxing the deck with a large machine about three-quarters of the way down on the right.

"Cabin's that way," I said.

"Go," said our jailer, who was now behind us. In our younger days we might have tried sprinting for it at that point—not because we were more energetic, but because we were more foolish. There was no way we could get a lead big enough to outrun bullets, but when you're young and full of vim and vigor, sometimes you think you can do anything.

"Watch your feet. It's slippery," I told Doc. "Fresh wax."

"I can smell it."

You have to admire dedication to duty. Here the ship had just been taken over, and yet a crew member was still hard at work, shining the deck.

The man with the AK behind us was not among the admirers. He started haranguing the worker in Spanish, asking why he wasn't in his quarters as all crewmen were supposed to be. When his words failed to have an effect, he switched to English. The worker still didn't react.

"Do you hear me?" demanded AK.

"Oh, I hear you," said the worker, raising his arm to reveal a Taser. "It's just that I'm not listening."

He fired. The dart sped across the space and hit the hijacker in the forehead. Fifty thousand volts shot through the thin wires between the dart and gun. AK shook like a leaf in a hurricane.

Tasers are great weapons for their intended purpose—incapacitating civilians in a dangerous but nonlethal situation. The problem with them, though, is that they tend to be single-use; most do not let you fire multiple times within a few seconds. That meant there was nothing to turn on the hijacker with the pistol as he raised his gun. But he couldn't get the shot off—the floor-waxing machine whipped down the corridor, charging like a bull, its long handle slapping either side of the bulkhead. The thug jumped but he couldn't get high enough; his leg hit the machine and he fell off-balance. The gun flew down the passage, but he was trapped as he fell, the waxer disk grabbing his pant leg and chewing it like a pit bull gone mad. He struggled, but instead of freeing himself, got his arm caught. As his shirt sleeve tightened around the whisk of the disk, his face was pulled in and the machine chewed at his skin.

I hopped over and pulled the waxer back while Doc retrieved the hijacker's gun. The man made a weak effort to get up; a shove of the machine into his forehead put him down for good.

"You finally screwed enough nurses that you turned into one," said the man who'd been waxing the deck.

"I'm a doctor," I told him.

"A quack, maybe." It was Larry "Bullet Head" Barret.[45] Larry—no relation to Danny—is a Six plank holder and an expert in the various black arts of special operations. Like Doc, he'd slipped aboard to help me.

"Since when are you working maintenance?" Doc asked after the two men exchanged their usual terms of endearment.

"Somebody had to find a way to save your sorry ass," Larry told him. He had spotted the machine in the corridor as he was being herded into his cabin. After slipping out a short time later, he grabbed the machine as cover. Another hijacker, also hit with the stun gun, had donated the uniform. Unfortunately the man hadn't been armed.

"That was my last cartridge for the Taser," he told me after we finished tying and gagging the hijackers. A pair of tranquilizer doses from my store of vials put them both down for the count, and we dragged them over to a nearby maintenance closet. It was a tight squeeze, but they didn't seem to mind.

"You have the radios?" I asked. Larry had been tasked to sneak our com gear aboard.

"Lost it when they threw me into my cabin. Goon saw the gym bag, looked in, and took it away." Larry glanced at Doc and saw how his moustache was twitching downward. "Sorry. It was kind of a Murphy event."

Larry took a mop from the closet and soaked up enough blood so there wasn't an obvious trail. We left the bucket and mop against the bulkhead at the far end of the corridor.

"You take the pistol," I told Larry, handing Doc the rifle AK had been

---

[45] You can read about Larry and some of his real-life exploits in *The Real Team*. Besides "Bullet Head," he's known as one of the "gold dust twins," the other being Frank Phillips, another associate to whom I'm deeply indebted.

carrying. "Wait at the top of the passage while we go down to the engine room. You make sure no one comes down until we have the place secure."

"Sounds good," said Larry.

"Which way is the gym?"

"Up past the barber shop and Victoria's Secret Lounge."

"Damn. I must have missed that," said Doc as we made our way forward. The cabins we passed were filled with passengers locked in by the electronic key system. Larry and Doc had broken out of their cabins thanks to a handy device concocted by Shunt.[46] (I had one packed away in my bags as a backup.) We'd release them once we had control of the ship; for now, the cabins were the safest place for them.

The gym was a large room enclosed by glass on three sides, with a variety of exercise equipment that would rival any Gold's Gym on the mainland. The upper walls were plastered with video screens, so you could sweat and watch your favorite reality show at the same time. We were just about to go in when Doc suddenly stopped and held up his hand.

"Someone's coming," he said. "Two guys at least."

"Into the workout room," I said.

The one wall that wasn't glass was covered with a mirror. Hiding inside was impossible.

"Jockeys or boxers?" I asked Larry.

"Boxers, always."

"Strip and work out."

Doc had already started to do so, mounting a treadmill not far from the door. The assault rifle was on the deck nearby, out of immediate sight.

"Medicine ball," I told Larry, moving over to the rack where they were kept.

"Man, I haven't used one of these in years," he said, examining the rack.

Medicine balls are an old-school exercise tool, about the size of the dodge balls you used to play with when you were a kid. Made of rubber, they come in different weights from two to twelve pounds. Larry picked up a ten-pounder and threw it at my abdomen.

The damn thing nearly took my breath away.

I threw it back. He must have really been hitting the crunches before joining us in France, because he stopped the ball without a problem.

The door swung open and two hijackers walked in. They were light-skinned Arabs wearing khakis, dressed like bona fide security personnel. They yelled at us in Arabic, telling us to get on the floor. We ignored them.

---

[46] The device is also useful for getting in and out of hotel rooms without leaving a record—maybe a few Secret Service agents are in the market for one.

"You dogs will get to rooms!" yelled one of the men. He had a dimpled chin, kind of like Kirk Douglas.[47] He didn't look much like Kirk, though, and I'm sure the real Douglas would have kicked his sorry ass with one hand tied behind his back. "Dogs!" he yelled when none of us responded.

"Are you talking to us?" I asked innocently. "What language are you speaking?"

Dimple-chin understood enough English to realize that I wasn't kissing up to him. He pointed the rifle at me and repeated something to the effect that we were ignorant dog infidels and should get on our knees and pray before we died.

"If you want to play catch, that's fine," I said, throwing the medicine ball at him.

His natural reflex was to raise the rifle and fire at the ball. He was a good shot—he hit it almost dead on, changing its trajectory so that it fell to the side. But he was so focused on it that he didn't notice the ball Larry threw at his ear. Dimple-chin sped backward into a rack of dumbbells, poetic justice I guess.

Dimple-chin's smooth-faced companion was caught flat-footed by the rapid flight of the balls across the room. He blinked a few times, not sure what was going on or what to do about it. By the time he finally raised his gun in our direction, Doc had retrieved his AK47 and put it to good and fast use.

He left a bit of a mess, though. Both men turned out to be quite the bleeders.

We pulled the bodies across the deck, hiding them behind the recumbent bikes. Anyone entering the gym would see them, not to mention the blood, but there was little we could do about that. Worried that the gunfire would bring unwanted attention, we hustled down the passage to the "crew only" door that led to the lower portions of the ship.

Unlike the main "public" sections, the architecture here was plain and functional; a lot of steel, exposed piping, and enough wires to keep Shunt happy for years. The shaft itself was well lit, and there was plenty of light to see as we descended. More than enough, as it turned out, to spot the man standing at the bottom of the stairwell with a light machine gun. He was extremely well illuminated. I could have counted the freckles on his forehead, if he'd had any.

"Sharkman, day late and a dollar short, as usual," he bellowed. "Damn good thing Doc and Larry are with you, or you'd never have gotten here."

---

[47] Youngsters: Kirk Douglas was an American movie star and former navy man, injured during combat in WWII. His real name was Issur Danielovitch. He played a badass and he was a badass.

It was Denny Chalker,[48] a Six plank owner and the last of my compadres who had snuck aboard the ship to help.

There wasn't time to conduct the usual greeting ceremony with its elaborate exchange of pleasantries, so I just gave him the finger and asked for a sitrep.

"Control room, two decks down," he said. "Two tangos inside. One looks like he's pretty well trained. Another. Eh. He wouldn't be able to fix a straight rum in a bar."

There was a passage one deck below that would take us aft to the engine room; Chalker had found three entrances.

"Door at the stern is our best bet. They have at least two tangos in the engine compartment, but I wasn't able to get a good look. There may be more. They move around—tough to say exactly where they'll be. Some discipline; I'm guessing they've been practicing for a while, but I don't think they have lot of experience overall."

I sent Doc with him to watch the control room while Larry and I went to the engine compartment.

Time hadn't exactly stood still since the various gardens of delight we served in as young bucks, but what we lacked in youth we made up for in wisdom. Back then, we didn't realize how idiotic and dumb some of the things we did were. Now we were wise: we knew what we were doing was dumb.

Maybe not dumb, but definitely risky. The door to the compartment was open. Chalker peeked around the hatchway, then ducked inside, tiptoeing to the platform where the ship's five diesel engines sat. These weren't the engines you'd find in an oversized pickup or even that tri-axle dump truck you've had your eyes on. The power plants were about the size of a compact car, and were dressed politely in painted aluminum risers and well-ordered steel headers that made them look like the freezer section of a fancy ice-cream place. The compartment was neat and clean, gleaming from the light, and tidier than the lunch counter at an old-fashioned five-and-dime at closing time. The usual odors of bilge and fuel were overwhelmed by a perfume of fresh paint. The motors weren't even that loud, for ship's engines, though if we'd wanted to talk, Larry and I would have had to yell into each other's ears.

We communicated the old-fashioned way, pointing and using hand signals we'd honed back in Six—*advance, halt, cut this bastard's balls off.*

I didn't have a knife, so I settled for locking my arms around the hi-

---

[48] You can get his full background and details on his stint with Six in *The Real Team.* Denny spends a lot of time in Eastern Europe on business these days, and luckily for me happened to be on his way home from a sojourn there when I called him for help.

jacker's neck and choking him into unconsciousness. He had wandered around from the far side of the engine, oblivious to us as we crept forward in the direction of the control room.

The engines were arranged two by two, with the middle engine paired with a turbine rather than a conventional diesel motor. This was used to cut emissions in port and could also be tapped to give extra power. I was just drawing near its rocket-ship-like housing when I heard someone yelling a few feet away. I dropped to my knees. A goon in blue coveralls was coming down the platform ahead, looking for the man we'd just knocked out.

I retreated around the rear of the turbine cowling, then moved up to a large twist of pipes, which hid me from view. The goon walked toward the stern, passing me on the other side. But he stopped after a step or two, sensing something was wrong. He yelled again—I assume it was Arabic, though I couldn't make it out over the engine noise—then turned to his left and started coming around the front of the turbine. I could just see the top of his helmet as he approached.

I readied the AK. I preferred not using the gun, since even with the engine noise there was a chance it could be heard in the nearby control space. But I wasn't going to let him grab me either. I took a breath, finger steady on the trigger. His helmet bobbed and weaved as he came toward me. I got ready to fire, planning to hit him as his head came over the top of the cowling.

Double-tap only. As much as I loved tattooing an enemy, the less sound the better.

Suddenly the helmet pivoted. A loud hiss rose over the heavy drum of the motors, and steam erupted over the deck. I leapt up, thinking the engine had broken somehow—a suitable trick for Murphy.

But it wasn't Murphy, it was Larry. He'd broken off one of the hoses and was applying its pressurized hot water and steam to the exterior of our helmeted hijacker.

I imagine he was screaming. I couldn't hear over the rush of the steam and the engine sounds. I circled back around the engine and grabbed the hijacker's rifle off the deck where it had fallen. The metal was so hot I nearly burned my fingers off my hand.

The hijacker had stopped screaming and progressed to shuddering in thermal-induced shock. The spray had been strong enough to tear the top of his coveralls, exposing his back to the stream. His flesh was bright purple.

"You can turn it off," I told Larry.

"I can't," he said. "I pulled it out of the connection."

"It's going to burn your hands."

"This handle piece is insulated," said Larry. "The whole pipe is insulated pretty well. Look how narrow the inside is. That's why the spray's so strong."

He managed to secure the hose between a quartet of pipes that ran along the nearby engine, but not before spraying water over much of the compartment. A thick cloud of steam hissed above as the hose continued to vent. The air thickened and within seconds it seemed as if we were in the middle of a cloud.

"Up to the control room. Quick," I yelled through the fog.

Larry was already ahead of me, scrambling up the ladder to the platform that rose over the last set of engines at the forward area of the compartment. I could barely see the large windows of the control room.

Larry cursed, then dropped to his knees.

"What?" I started to ask. Then bullets began raining from the forward area of the compartment.

Chalker's estimate of how many men were in the control room was off by a factor of three, at least—alerted by the steam, a half-dozen goons had come out of the space at the end of the engine compartment and were standing along the pipe-railing of the scaffold-like walkways flanking the forward sides of the engine room.

"A real goat-fuck," muttered Larry as I ducked in behind him. "Just like old times."

[VI]

While we were out of the direct line of fire, we couldn't see our attackers. Besides the pipe-flanked and mesh-covered catwalk they were standing on, the goons were protected by a small forest of heavy hooks and chains, part of the crane mechanism used to move heavy parts for repairs.

"I say we go old school," said Larry. "Charge straight ahead."

"Since when is getting killed old school?" I answered.

"Those dorks can't shoot straight."

"There's enough of them—one will get lucky."

"Well, what are we going to do, Skip? Wait for Doc and Chalker? They're not supposed to move until they see us in the control room."

"I'm thinking of an aerial attack," I told him. "Along with artillery."

Precisely two minutes later, Larry sprayed covering fire while I retreated back down the motor platform. When I reached the last row, I tucked and rolled across the platform, dropped down to the deck, and began making my way forward along the starboard side. Steam was continuing to pour from the hose, but it was too high to camouflage me. I stayed as low as I could manage as I came in sight of the forward railing where the hijackers had clustered.

Three men, two in blue coveralls and a third in khaki, were huddled behind a thicket of pipes running from the deck to the upper reaches of the ship. Their guns were pointed roughly in the direction of Larry, who was trying to keep their attention without running out of ammo.

There was so much water vapor in the compartment that it started to rain. My hands were already sopping wet, and I was worried about losing my grip on the rifle. I wiped them one at a time on my pants, which made them marginally drier, then stepped out and quickly took aim at my target—the water pipes running along the top of the catwalk where my enemies were huddled.

My plan was simple—I'd shoot through the pipes, releasing a spray of steam similar to the one that Larry had used to lay out the other hijacker earlier. As the gunmen scrambled backward, I would hustle to the crane controls and move the chains in on them. There was a long pipe boom that looked like it could be lowered and swung directly into them.

But just as I stepped out, the ship's bow pushed into a massive dip, then immediately bucked upward. I lost my balance and fell flat on my back.

Luckily, the hijackers were also shaken by the wave and stumbled on the catwalk. And just like in the old days, Larry stepped up and took charge. He took aim at the pipe and did my job for me. A new spray of water and steam engulfed the hijacker goons.

I got to my feet and bolted to the nearby control panel. Pushing the safety cage from the power switch, I yanked hard on the master control for the arm, expecting it to swing down toward the deck. But the mechanism was arranged differently than any overhead cargo controller I'd worked before, and instead of dropping, the boom began riding its tracks toward the stern. I reversed its course quickly, and pushed the other lever, thinking it would lower the pipe. Instead, this made the pipe go marginally faster. Spotting a slider at the far end, I pushed that. The pipe ratcheted toward the top of the compartment, squealing with a loud clank as it hit its stops. I reversed it, then barely ducked in time as the chains that were attached to the boom swung in my direction.

The ship pitched again, and I found myself flying forward on the deck, sliding against the casing of the machine; the chains and their large hooks and pulleys crashed downward, then wrapped themselves against the rails of the catwalk. Two of the hijackers fell off the opposite end as they tried to escape, slipping on the wet metal; the third was caught in the tangle of chains.

Larry reloaded and began dueling with the remaining hijackers. Hoping to get them from the side, I scrambled toward the ladder to the catwalk. I was about halfway up when the ship nosed down hard again, mashing my face into a tread and smashing my hand and gun on the side. Being a modern ship, the *Bon Voyage* was undoubtedly equipped with active and passive stabilizing systems, but the inexperienced crew either wasn't employing the gear properly or the storm was simply too much for them. The motion continued, sending loose material—and bodies— sliding across the compartment. I finally managed to get up to the top catwalk. Seeing the men firing at Larry through the steam, I dropped the first, winged the second, and then it was my turn to be surprised as the rifle jammed.

Kalashnikovs never, ever jam. Say what you want about the Russians, but they know how to make good, extremely simple weapons. I had the pleasure of meeting Mikhail Kalashnikov while performing a job for the Department of Justice in St. Petersburg a year ago. Two huge rooms in the Artillery Museum there are devoted to his work; you could spend hours there. The general was feisty and colorful; he reminded me of our own Navy Admiral Rickover: smart and cocky.

So:

Kalashnikovs never jam.

And yet, this one did. It was my *second* AK47 jamming in a little more than a week. What are the odds? And how does Murphy play them so dramatically?

The hijacker stared at me. I looked at him. I prayed for another sharp dive of the bow or a hard rock to port and swing to starboard, but we were in a momentary lull.

The raghead calmly lifted his rifle and pointed in my direction. I tried to take a step back, but my way was blocked by the rail. The bastard grinned and squinted his eye to focus his aim through the iron sights.

His head exploded before he could press the trigger. Doc had come down through the control room.

"You owe me a beer," snapped Doc. "And dry-cleaning money. I got gore on the cuff of my pants."

"That's why you should never wear cuffs," said Larry, trotting up.

"Did you power up the remote?" I asked Doc.

"No."

"Well, turn it on and let's take over the ship."

"There's something you have to see first."

Hearing what they suspected were gunshots above the hum of the engines, Chalker and Doc had entered the control room and quickly dispatched the hijackers to their private paradise. There was surprisingly little blood on the control consoles, which made sorting out the high-tech screens and control widgets that much easier.

But even if it had been drenched in blood, one unit would have stood out immediately—a suitcase-sized box of radio transmitters that were set up as detonators. The hijackers had apparently placed plastique explosive charges around the ship.

"That's easy to deal with," I said, inspecting it. It was homemade from several remote radio controllers, clever but not overly innovative. An ambitious thirteen-year-old with a screwdriver and soldering iron could have done the same. "We'll just power it down and decommission it."

"That's what I thought," said Doc. "Then I found this."

He led me across the compartment to another console used to monitor the turbine. The panel at its base was loose. Doc pulled it away—gingerly.

"Two packets of Czech C4," he said, pointing down at a small but extremely powerful bomb. "Vintage stuff. Looks like it's wired right."

The most interesting—or alarming—part of the bomb wasn't the radio connection that would allow it to be detonated from a distance, but the extra circuitry to a watch face.

"Timer backup," said Doc. "I'm just guessing, but I think those numbers mean we have about twenty hours to the failsafe boom time. That gets us to the coast and a little beyond. But check this out." Doc bent down. "There's a second timer wired into the master circuitry. It's set for twenty seconds. And it has its own battery. It's another failsafe—a tamper safety. Boom if somebody tries to disable it and does the wrong thing. To get rid of it you'll have to know what you're doing."

"That leaves you dumb ol' bastards out," said Larry, strutting over. "Let me take a look."

He bent down and examined it. The frowns grew deeper the longer he stared.

"I need a penknife. A beer wouldn't hurt either."

Doc supplied the penknife. No beer was available. Just as well, though—Larry has been "dry" for well over ten years. Truly a miracle when you consider how long he's been working with me: he survived SEAL Two, SEAL Six, Red Cell, and Red Cell International. (Rest assured, he does more than just hang around getting into trouble with yours truly; he's a partner in his own company, Training Resources International, or TRI, where he works on anything that goes *boom*.)

Larry gently pried two small and tightly twisted wires apart at the edge of the circuit board. I felt my heart jump into my throat as the knife slipped and Larry winced, and picked up the knife.

"No boom, no foul," he said. "I'll try again. Hold your breath and pray. Not you, Dick," he added. "God hears you praying he may have a heart attack."

Larry flicked his wrist. The knife point jerked against the wire. There was a spark.

Then nothing.

Not the *big* nothing. Just . . . nothing.

"Whew," said Doc. He laughed. "See? Nothing to it."

"Yeah—nothing," said Larry sarcastically. He showed us the second clock face—it had counted down to thirteen.

"The problem isn't dealing with the bombs," Larry explained, rising with the device in his hand. "The problem is finding them all. From the looks of that panel, there could be as many as a hundred of the damn things. Miss the wrong one, and one of those turd brains who took over the ship can put a pretty good-sized hole in it. These can be detonated by any radio device that knows the frequency, and I'm sure they have more than one."

I went over to the control console. Besides the array of instruments and devices for checking every system on the ship, there were also displays that duplicated the navigational units up in the wheelhouse. We could see not only our present position, but where we had been, and, more importantly, where we were going. I rechecked the course. We were still on the same line we'd been on earlier.

"Norfolk," said Doc, looking over my shoulder. "Blow the ship and block the channel."

"Mmmm. Failsafe won't go off for a few hours beyond that."

"Gives them a margin for error."

Sinking the cruise ship near the harbor at Norfolk would certainly cause a serious pain in the rumpus for the navy, but that wasn't the way these types generally thought. They liked flash and sparkle, along with civilian casualties.

Economic disruptions. Panic that leveraged the damage of the event itself.

Headlines.

Like the sort you would get if you went past Norfolk and kept going all the way to the Liquefied Natural Gas Port at Cove Point.

Blow the ship up at the right spot, and you might get a nice flare that could be captured for any number of prime-time news shows around the world. You'd also generate lasting publicity. Plans to expand the port were already controversial, and you could bet that an "event" would live on in the hearts and minds of many for decades. It would be another Three Mile Island—and not coincidentally, a free advertisement for al Qaeda and its far-flung worshipers.

To say nothing of the innocent lives that would be lost in the process.

"Could be," said Doc. "Either way, we have to stop it. And that's one hell of a storm we're steering into," he added, pointing at the huge red ball on the screen of the monitor to the right. "These waves we're getting are only at the leading edge."

As if to punctuate his weather analysis, the ship tilted abruptly forward. I grabbed the metal handhold nearby and held on as we pitched back the other way.

"Jackasses probably learned to sail in the air farce," mocked Larry.

I had thought we'd disable the bridge control, radio for help, then take out the hijackers in small groups. But radioing or interfering with the controls would tip them off that we were here. Better to go after them systematically until they realized we were here.

It sounded like a good plan as the words came out of my mouth. But what's the old saw about battle plans? They become obsolete the moment the first gunshot is fired.

This one didn't even last that long.

"Two guys coming down the ladder," said Chalker, ducking into the control room. "They're only armed with pistols, but one of them has a walkie-talkie."

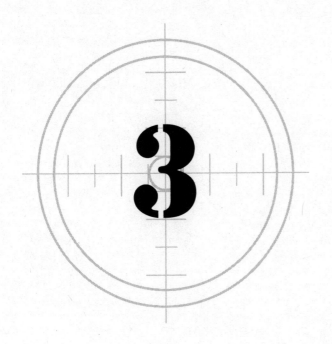

Doc joined Chalker at the door, while Larry and I retreated back into the engine compartment, aiming to circle around and attack from the corridor. We moved quickly, but by the time we reached the compartment, Doc had already grabbed one of the hijackers as he came into the control room. The other had been shot through the neck by Chalker.

"Did he use the radio?" I asked Doc.

"I don't think so. They'll figure something's up soon enough, though. It's squawking with Chinese."

"Arabic," said Larry, taking the radio. "They're asking what's going on."

"Can you answer?" I asked him.

"My Arabic's not going to sound that good," said Larry. "It's hard to sound like these guys. That's the first thing you learn in language school."

"Make it sound muffled," suggested Doc. "Better 'n nothin'."

We went into the engine room and gave it a try. With Doc making static noises in the background, Larry told the others that things were OK.

The other person on the line immediately asked where he was. Even louder static practically drowned out Larry's answer that he was on the dog deck.

Dog deck?

"I thought it would confuse them," he explained.

We moved the bodies into the engine room then returned to the control area to figure out what to do next. We could systematically go through the ship, but to do that effectively we'd have to leave the control room. Larry said he thought he could disable it without making it obvious. I told him to get to work on it.

"We need reinforcements," said Doc, staring at the walkie-talkie. "What about the rest of the crew? Not all of them could have been plants. If we can find them, at least a few would be able to help us, don't you think?"

"Hell, some of the passengers could help, too," said Larry.

"Most of them are over the hill," said Doc.

"No farther than you."

Doc blinked. I'm sure in his head he's still twenty years old.

It wasn't ideal, but it was the best option we had.

"It's not a bad idea," I told the others. "As long as we do it the right way."

"I agree," said Larry. "It has to be planned out and executed just right."

"Hell," groused Doc, "why start now?"

[II]

Back in Washington, D.C., Junior had followed Habib—or rather, someone he was pretty sure was Habib—down into the bowels of the Metro system.

If you've ever been to the nation's capital and taken the trains there, you know that the stations are large concrete tunnels done in a modern design. Beauty is in the eye of the beholder, and I would never wax eloquent over a bunch of train tracks and aggregate, but the design attempts to remove the claustrophobic sense you can get underground.

The walkways along the side of the tracks in the tunnels are another story. They're narrow, uneven, and without rails in many places. When a train shoots by, the wind feels like it's going to sweep you below any second.

Two trains passed before Junior finally spotted a figure walking ahead, hugging the side of the tunnel wall with outstretched hands and moving extremely slowly. Junior guessed that he'd been spooked by the trains that had passed—a rather rational response.

Junior stopped at a railing, waiting for the man to get a little farther ahead. He crouched, hoping the light on the wall ahead wouldn't show where he was. He needn't have worried, as the man kept moving forward, albeit at a snail's pace. Staring down at the tracks, Junior debated whether to continue. He'd been moving south in the direction of the Capitol stop, but he had no idea how far he had gone or how close the next station was. The man might not be Habib after all; he could just be a homeless derelict, looking for a place to flop for the night.

Something scurried down the middle of the tracks, running past him before ducking into the blackness farther on. Junior's first thought was that it was a small dog. Then he realized it was a rat.

A slight but growing vibration announced that another train was coming. Junior wrapped his arms around the rail, then hung on as the light from the train grew, sweeping the narrow confines of the tunnel ahead, catching a dip and bend to the left. The rush of the train as it passed seemed to take all sound from his ears. He tightened his grip on the rail even though the last car was disappearing around the bend.

Only when the ledge below him stopped trembling did Junior stand up. He looked down the tunnel, but couldn't see the figure he'd been following. Unsure what else to do, Junior began walking in that direction. The tracks were dark again, but there was enough light from the steel sconces on the wall to illuminate the narrow walkway ahead.

The man was gone.

Junior walked faster, bracing himself for the sight of the man's body severed on the tracks. But he hadn't fallen. There was an alcove on the right just ahead of the bend; behind it a set of transformers were nestled behind a fence. A metal door sat across from the fence.

Junior put his ear against the jamb, but could hear nothing through the block walls. He opened the door slowly, crouching behind the metal. A dim ray of light spilled onto the ground. He looked for shadows, saw none, then eased inside to a small landing with a metal stairway leading downward. He closed the door as gently as he could behind him and descended, holding his breath.

Two flights later, he came to an open workshop area. The place looked like a cross between a bomb shelter and an old salvage shop, with railroad parts and assorted machinery. It smelled heavily of oil and metal shavings. Three of the four walls were lined with shelves; the last featured a *Playboy* centerfold that looked older than I was.

Miss October still had it, though.

The room itself wasn't lit, but a faint light came through an open door-way diagonally across from the one Junior had entered. He slipped across the room, then flattened himself against a shelf next to the door, listening as the people in the room beyond talked.

He heard three voices. They weren't speaking English, but the voices were so muffled that Junior couldn't be sure what language it was. They spoke for a few minutes; then suddenly there was silence.

He barely managed to get behind the workbench in the first room before Habib walked through. Junior caught a glimpse of him in the light, then ducked down, waiting until he heard the man's feet on the steps above. Then he slipped into the room where the men had been talking.

Lit by a pair of yellow lights, the room was filled with dusty soda and snack machines. Two were open. Unlike the others, they were new and clean. A pair of toolboxes were tucked on the side. Junior looked at the machines but couldn't see anything special about them, aside from the fact that they didn't seem to belong with the others.

Beyond the other door was a foyer area flanked by a large service elevator and a door leading to a stairwell. As Junior opened the door to the stairs, he heard the elevator descending. He pushed inside, and watched through the narrow glass window as two men walked into the adjacent room. They returned a moment later carrying the two tool cases he'd seen, along with a handcart that had two heavy-looking boxes.

Junior moved back as the elevator doors closed, afraid they would glance in his direction and see him. But nothing looked nefarious—he seemed to have stumbled onto a late-night work crew. There were a dozen reasons Habib might have come to talk to them, and none had anything to do with a terrorist attack or even drugs.

Not wanting to walk along the side of the train tracks again, Junior decided to take the stairs. He expected that there would be a door out within a flight or two, but instead he went up eight sets before he came to a landing. The small window in the door showed that it opened into the basement of a large building; there were lights and a distant, beige wall across the wide expanse.

Junior hesitated, took a deep breath, then pushed the crash bar boldly, striding out as if he knew exactly where he was. He was standing in a large empty hall, part of an underground complex. The hall was large, long, and empty. Its floors were polished concrete, painted a dull but unscuffed gray—not fancy, but far different than those he'd been in downstairs. The tunnel was used by workers to get from one part of the government complex to another.

Junior had no idea where he was, and even less of a notion on how to get out. The elevator across from him gave him no clue. Faced with a choice— left or right?—he went right. One hundred feet, two hundred feet—the hallway was empty. Junior passed two large desks, which looked like they might be used as security checkpoints, but they didn't appear to have been used in years.

At the far end of the hall a metal gate partially blocked the way. Junior could hear voices and some noises inside, but the area dipped down and he couldn't see anything beyond the metal gate. Slowing as he got closer to the gate, Junior spotted a hallway to the left just in front of the gate. There were more elevators there, along with doors to a pair of stairwells. Three vending machines stood across from them. With the voice growing louder, Junior ducked down the hall, moving to the far side behind the third machine.

He heard two men come out from behind the gate. They stopped near the intersection with the main hallway. One said something softly in Arabic—or at least what Junior thought was Arabic. He didn't understand a word.

The men walked on, back in the direction of the stairs Junior had come up from. He waited a few minutes, then went out to the fence. It had been pushed closed but not latched. He started to push it open, but then heard someone coming and retreated back to the hall where he'd hidden earlier.

The man whistled as he walked. He clattered as well—Junior suspected it was a security guard. He thought of coming out from his hiding place and telling the guard—what, though?

The whistling grew louder. The whistler came over and used one of the machines to buy a soda. Then he went to the machine where Junior was hiding and made another selection for a snack. Junior saw his uniform pant leg—and a holster.

A candy bar or something similar plunked down in the machine. The guard started whistling again, walking back into the building. Junior went across to the stairwell, pushed through, and jogged up the steps. The door was glass; there was a guard at a desk a few feet away, watching a baseball game on a small television.

Go, Junior told himself, and go he did, pushing through and walking quickly to the door.

"Night," he called over his shoulder to the guard, raising his hand as he went.

If the guard even noticed him, Junior couldn't say.

Outside, he was surprised to find himself on the side of the Supreme Court Building.

What the hell was going on?

That was the same question Karen Fairchild asked when he showed up at her door an hour later.

"What happened with you and Dick? And with Danny?" she asked. "What's going on?"

Karen has a certain way about her—a no-nonsense, get-to-the-point stare. And yet her voice isn't harsh, and her tone somehow seems to suggest that whatever the problem, she'll help work it out. After a swat to the head, of course.

She didn't swat Junior. He mumbled something to the effect that he was confused himself.

She took a better look at him. Disheveled wouldn't quite cover it. "Have you eaten dinner?"

He shook his head.

"Come in, then. I'll put on some pasta. Go take a shower—I'll find you some spare clothes. You'll eat, and then we'll talk."

[III]

Out in the Atlantic, Larry and I were making our way to the bridge; Chalker and Doc were en route to the main passenger cabins, aiming to search for the crew and any able-bodied passengers who wanted to help. We had a limited number of arms—just the captured rifles and pistols. We now had four ship's radios. Using them would tip off the hijackers, and though we worked out a primitive code, we were reluctant to use them. We could hear the hijackers' chatter on them, but it was of limited value, since they rarely used English and the talk was fairly garbled.

By now it was morning. The storm's intensity had increased, and besides the wind and waves, the portholes we passed were as dark as if it had been midnight. Every so often we saw a faint blip of lightning through the glass. At points I felt a bit like a cross-country skier working his way through the foothills of the Alps.

We reached the main deck without seeing anyone, and were just about to cut through the dark-paneled Amusement Salon to the main staircase when we heard voices in the corridor. Larry and I ducked into the salon, crouching between the vintage Pac-Man game and Terror Arcade as four hijackers stalked past.

"Four against two," said Larry, getting up. "Hardly seems fair."

"Since when did we start fighting fair?"

"Guns or not?"

"Fire hose," I said. "Guns are backup."

I ran over to the bulkhead near the passage, where a fire hose hung. I pulled the hose down and grabbed the trigger, intending to knock them down with the spray and take them by hand.

During a drill on the first day we sailed, I watched the crew have some fun pushing each other around with a jet of water that could take paint off a wall. But that was then, and this was now: I've seen more powerful streams on Baby Wet Me dolls.

You can make the rest of the metaphor yourself. Fortunately, Larry was right behind. He took down the four goons before they got a chance to make fun of the piddle of my hose.

"So much for saving ammo, and being quiet, huh?" said Larry, checking the bodies.

They had two rifles between them, and each had a spare magazine. It was better than nothing. We pulled the bodies back into the amusement center, hiding them behind a bank of games that included Sgt. Slaughter and Winged Fury. Then we continued down the corridor. We had no sooner reached the grand staircase on Amuse Deck when a trio of hijackers appeared. Clearly alerted by our earlier gunfire, they had their guns up and were ready for us, firing a hail of bullets as we backtracked for cover.

We ducked into the Louis XIV Dining Room. The bow dipped as we entered, and the tables and chairs, which had gathered themselves aft, rushed forward like the bulls in Pamplona, Spain. We ducked as best we could, sliding to the floor near the bandstand as the tangos fired from the passage and bullets began sailing into the room. Chandeliers began breaking, and bits of the mirrored ceiling exploded downward in a hail of glass.

Suddenly the bow of the big liner stopped descending, hesitating at the bottom of the mammoth wave she'd entered. The ship heeled backward, bucking her bow upward and sending the room's furniture back across the room. We threw ourselves to the side, then began firing at the men at the doorway as they struggled to keep from following the furniture.

As the last one fell, I realized we were being fired on from behind. Two more hijackers had come in from the doorway on the aft side of the room. Taking cover behind a settee, they began peppering us with gunfire from pistols. Larry and I dropped to the deck, then crawled uphill toward the door as the ship shifted again. Apparently this made the tangos think we'd been hit; they stopped firing and began working up the side of the room, looking for us as the ship heeled backward. I grabbed a chair as it slid by, rose, then ran with the tilt of the ship toward the nearest hijacker, less than ten feet away. Off-balance and surprised, he got off a few ill-aimed shots before I threw the chair at him, puncturing his larynx.

Messy business.

Larry took out the other man the old-fashioned way, firing at him as the tango slid back between two tables.

"I forgot how much fun this was," said Larry, getting to his feet.

We made it to the main staircase without finding any more exchanges of lead, but going through the Arc de Triomphe Bar just about broke Larry's heart. The tables here were secured to the floor—always a wise idea for a bar, even on land—but the ship's bucking had sent bottles scattering against each other, with lamentable results. The place reeked of alcohol—a not un-pleasant smell to be sure, unless you considered where it rose from.

Looking over the place, we found charges on the bulkhead pillars that sat on either end of the bar proper. If blown, the charges would take down not only the bar but the deck above. Hit enough spots like this, and the ship would implode from the top, falling in on itself.

"We'll get to them later," I told Larry as he began inspecting one of the bundles. "Let's take the bridge first."

Glass crunched under our feet as we ran to the sliding doors that led out to what was called The Porch, an exposed deck at the far end of the bar area. We passed the magic pool table as we went; the balls sat perfectly on the green-felt top.

As I opened the door, I saw a shadow bent in the light ahead. It was one of the hijackers, seasick, emptying the contents of his stomach over the nearby rail. I took pity on him, and raced to relieve him of his discomfort.

Granted, he did have a few other worries as he went over the rail, but being seasick was no longer one of them.

No good deed goes unpunished, and mine was swiftly rewarded when the man's companion, holding on to a stanchion nearby, spotted me and started firing. I retreated back into the bar area through the doors. He made the mistake of following, giving Larry an easy shot as he came through the door.

"I *really* forgot how much fun this was," said Larry, hopping down and leading the way toward the bridge.

Meanwhile. Doc and Chalker reached the passenger area and began liberating passengers and crew. Among the first people they found was a sailor who had been working in the lower hold when the hijackers took over the ship. He had seen where about a dozen of the bombs were placed. Doc decided that they should split up; he sent Chalker ahead to continue freeing people, while he went below with the crewman to find and defuse as many bombs as possible.

We had no code for this, and Doc didn't think it was smart to break radio silence to tell me about it.

I remembered the goons in the main passage behind the bridge, and guessed that there would be more guarding the doors that came in directly from the lower deck. From what I could recall, though, there had been no one watching the flying bridge, and with this storm intensifying, it was unlikely that someone would be out on it. So that was the logical place for us to attack.

The problem would be getting through the doors quickly. They were secured from the inside by a deadbolt handle. We could always break the glass if they were locked, but that would take time and we'd lose the element of surprise.

So Larry suggested we blow the doors down.

We went back to the bar and dismantled the bombs. Taking them apart took about ten minutes. Larry had them reconfigured in two.

I didn't get the nickname "Demo Dick" by going light on explosives, but even I recognize the fact that you can have too much of a good thing when it comes to C4 and its cousins Semtex, PE4, and plastique in general. So I didn't object to Larry's cutting down the bricks. Still, there was a bit of guesswork involved, and the truth is neither Larry nor I wanted to err on the side of too little. Nothing would be more ego-flattening than Failure to Eradicate.

We split up, each with our own little bomb, and went to separate sides of the ship. Under other circumstances, getting into position would have been easy—there were ladders on either side of the upper deck that led to the extensions of the gridwork on the outside of the bridge. But the raging and unpredictable waves made it hard work, and a little nerve-wracking. Plastic explosives are very stable—throw some in a fire and there won't be an explosion. In fact, you might even have used it to heat your C-rations, if you were of a certain age. But the stuff *does* ignite when subjected to heavy shock. Would falling a few stories to a lower deck qualify? I didn't want to find out.

By the time I got to the bridge level, my shins were battered and bashed from the edges of the ladder. I was wetter than squid at a hundred fathoms. I checked my watch—one minute to detonation.

I crawled out on the deck, and placed the bomb against the bottom of the steel-and-glass hatchway. Then I got out the knife I'd grabbed from the dining area, checked my watch, felt my short hairs get shorter, and flicked my wrist to break the wire that was preventing the backup clock from counting down.

Seconds started draining. For some reason I got a little fussy and positioned the timer piece on the block and its igniting cap, then retreated down the ladder. About halfway down the sky lit with lightning, the clouds putting out a pyrotechnical show to rival many a Fourth of July celebration.

As I hit the landing, I glanced at my watch, then looked up at the bridge—just in time to see the block of C4 slide off the deck and down the steps.

Instinct kicked in: the wrong instinct. Running would have been the *smart* thing to do. Instead, I threw myself forward, spread out like a wide receiver at the goal line.

I caught the bomb in my hands.

Somewhere, Murphy was grinning.

Five seconds were on the timer. Four . . .

I threw the bomb upward, more or less in the direction of the bridge. There was no time to duck.

The shock wave probably pushed me down or back, but the ship was bucking so badly that I honestly never felt it. I leapt up the ladder, helped by the movement of the ship. The gun was in my hands, and I was on full automatic. How exactly I got to the middle of the wheelhouse I have no idea. All I remember is running through a torrent of rain into a thick cloud of vaporized metal and plastic. There was a body on the deck to my right, and a stunned hijacker at the console directly in front of me, blood streaming from the side of his face.

"I got these guys!" yelled Larry, over on the starboard side of the bridge. There were two bodies on the deck near him.

I scanned around, looking for the rest of the hijackers. A single man stood near the door to the conference space, a submachine gun in his hand.

I recognized him immediately—it was Scarface, the man who'd "hired" me to transport the drugs to America.

"You!" he yelled.

There was a crack of lightning—or maybe it was a flash-bang. The next moment, everything went dark.

(IV)

Junior spilled his guts—figuratively—to Karen over dinner. By the time he was done, she had a good picture of everything that had happened.

"You're going to have to settle things with Dick on your own," she told him. "He's not going to treat you any differently than he would treat Trace or Shotgun or one of the newer guys."

"I don't want him to," Junior blurted. "I just want to be—I wanted to be treated fairly."

"Fairly? By your standards or his?"

If this was a movie, Junior would nod pensively, get up and embrace Karen, then fly out to meet me. The music would rise, and we'd sail into the sunset together.

But this wasn't a movie, and Junior's reaction wasn't anything like what a Hollywood screenwriter would have proposed.

"I'm tired of getting treated like crap because I'm his bastard son," said Junior.

He pounded his fist on the table. Karen stared at him.

"That table has been in my family for five generations," she said. "You break it, you're in trouble with me."

"Sorry," he said weakly.

"I can't help you with Dick," she told him. "Or Danny. You have to talk to them yourself. But I think I know what's going on at the Court. Grab your things and come with me."

Four hours later, Junior and Karen sat in the back of a Homeland Security mobile command center—essentially a dorked-up van—and watched from a remote feed as a clandestine bomb-removal team began inspecting the vending machines.

The bombs were removed in short order, several hours before the Court Building was due to open. What the Justices might term "a vigorous debate" ensued on whether to keep the affair a secret or not. Karen and her department wanted the matter kept quiet so they could capture the perpetrator. The bombs were to be detonated by a radio device, which meant that one of the plotters would soon be in the vicinity and therefore easy to catch. The other side of the argument was equally logical: if someone had missed a bomb, the consequences would be severe. There's a lot of pretty stone and marble in that building.

There were other considerations. Information was bound to leak out, despite Karen and her bosses' best attempts at keeping a lid on it. The FBI's special counterterrorism task force was already involved, and the Capitol Police, while not knowing the exact details, had been told enough that any stray comment would alert the plotters.

The FBI had Habib's apartment under surveillance, and was digging into his life online. As were we: armed with his connection to the college, Shunt and his magic minions had dug up more information on him. A Facebook page belonging to his girlfriend yielded a number of tidbits, including his probable location: her apartment, two blocks from the Orange Line out in Roslyn. A surveillance team was sent there, and around the time the Chief Justice phoned Karen to insist in nonjudicial terms that the building be shut and the alert made public, the FBI surveillance team sent a message via secure text that they had spotted a young male leaving the building.

The walk of shame had begun, in more ways than one.

Karen passed the Chief Judge up to her boss, then turned to Junior, who was staring at the monitors at the side of the van.

"I'm going to lose this argument," she told him, getting up. "They'll shut down the building. But the text I just got says the team spotted someone they think is Habib. Come on with me."

By the time Karen and Junior reached her car, Habib had gone into the subway, heading back toward the city. Karen drove in the direction of Habib's apartment.

"Maybe he's going to the building," said Junior. "That's this direction."

"It might be," admitted Karen. She knew from what Shunt had already supplied that Habib was more a messenger, some sort of conduit between whoever was supplying the material and support and the actual perpetrators. In such a case, it was unlikely that he would be the one pushing the button, though of course she couldn't rule it out. Still, there's no intelligence quite up to the level of female intuition, and even I trust her sixth sense much more than I do anything coming out of Langley.

They were nearing Habib's block when a new text came in—Habib had changed trains and was now on the Blue Line, heading south.

"Airport," said Junior.

"Yes," said Karen, her intuition panning out. "Let's get there."

It was early, so the usual crush of traffic wasn't in their way. Still, they were several miles away when Habib got off the train at the Ronald Reagan airport.

Karen called her TSA[49] liaison.

---

[49] Officially known as the Transportation Safety Administration, some know it best as the Tortured Sanity Administration. That's the clean version.

"We're going to need a no-fly restriction on someone," she told him. "But we want to wait to pick him up at the very last minute, at the gate."

Karen gave him more details, including his name and passport number, along with a description and the name of the FBI task force agent who was coordinating the surveillance team.

"Did you just get this information?" asked her liaison.

"Why?"

"Because we got an alert about this guy from the CIA literally five minutes before you called."

"From who?"

"Special desk."

"Which?"

"Terror 2." It was in-house shorthand for an overseas watch group.

"You have a name with that?"

"They don't come with names."

Karen knew she could find out, but at the moment had more immediate things to do. She contacted the supervisor of the surveillance team as they neared the airport, asking which terminal Habib was in.

"Not in a terminal," he told her. "Looks like he's heading toward the parking garage."

"Which one?"

"B."

The surveillance team theorized that he had hidden a car there, which seemed to be confirmed a few minutes later when the TSA reported that his name wasn't on the passenger list of any plane taking off in the next twenty-four hours.

"I have the young man who spotted him yesterday in the car with me," Karen told the team leader. "I'm going to drive through the garage and see if he recognizes him."

"Whoa, I don't think that's a good idea."

"He's with Dick Marcinko's outfit," said Karen. "He's been watching him for a while now."

"Karen, it's you I'm worried about."

"I can take care of myself."

"Ma'am."

That was exactly the wrong tone to take with her. "We're coming up to the entrance."

The agent on the other end of the line took a long breath. "As long as you keep your distance," he said, accepting what was obviously a fait accompli. "We don't know if he's dangerous. And he doesn't know he's being followed."

"Understood. We'll park and move on." Karen turned to Junior and pointed to the glove compartment. "I have another pistol," she told him. "Take it just in case."

They were just pulling into the lane to get into the garage when a dark Impala cut them off.

"Is that a bureau car?" Karen asked her FBI contact.

"Which?"

"The one that just cut in front of me."

"Negative. What's going on?"

"Nothing. Just an asshole late for his flight," muttered Karen. She got her ticket and drove into the garage, passing one of the surveillance teams. She followed around the aisles, driving slowly. The lot had been closed for overnight maintenance, and the full aisles near the entrance quickly gave way to sparsely populated and then completely empty rows.

"We're going to stick out," Junior said.

"We'll stop at the level below the roof."

"That's the Impala," said Junior, pointing as the other car disappeared up the next ramp.

Karen slowed down, giving the other car a good lead. They came up to the level directly below the roof. There were only two other cars there, and neither one was the Impala.

"Gotta be meeting them," said Junior. "Or it's the FBI moving in. It looked official."

"There was only one person in the car. They usually travel in twos." Karen pulled the car into a spot near the ramp, turning it around so she could get out directly onto the roadway, then radioed the surveillance team.

"Yeah, we agree," said the supervisor before she could say anything. "Got to be a meeting. Did you get the plate number?"

"Negative. It was an Impala."

"We're trying to look at recent rentals, but there are a ton of those things. I'm sending someone over to the roof of C, to try to get a closer look, maybe a plate."

"We're going to come back down," said Karen. "There are no other cars near us, and I'm afraid—"

Karen stopped talking as a pair of gunshots echoed above. Junior jumped out of the car, pistol first. The radio exploded with curses and traffic. Another vehicle raced up from the bottom, as did two of the FBI task force team that had been shadowing Habib.

Junior ran to the stairway to the top level. He took the stairs two at a time, leaping onto the top level and racing across the roof.

A man was leaning over a body about ten feet away. He dropped something, then straightened immediately.

Junior skidded to a knee.

"Drop your gun!" he yelled.

"Whoa, whoa, whoa," replied the man. He held his hands out. "Calm down now. Calm down."

"Get away from the body. What did you drop?"

"I didn't drop anything."

"You're Magoo," said Junior. "CIA."

Magoo still had his pistol in his hand. He started to move it in Junior's direction.

Junior fired. He hit him in the shoulder—he was actually aiming for his head—and Magoo fell backward, dropping the gun.

"CIA, CIA," gasped Magoo, unleashing a stream of curses as the FBI team swarmed around him and Junior. "I have a terror suspect—I shot a terror suspect. Damn. Damn, why the hell did you guys hit me. There's a plot—they're going to blow up a national building. Damn. Your kid shot me. Your guy shot me."

"He planted that gun," said Junior, pointing to the pistol Magoo had tossed down.

Habib, meanwhile, lay bleeding from a pair of bullet holes to the head. By the time Karen reached the roof, one of the FBI agents had retrieved a sweatshirt from his car and put it over his mangled head.

"Ambulance is on the way," said one of the FBI agents, pointing to Magoo. She could already hear the siren in the distance. "I don't think it's life-threatening. We gave him first aid."

"Right."

"A lot of people are going to have questions about your shooter," he said.

"I understand."

"CIA officer says he picked up the gun, then realized he shouldn't have," added the agent. "It was a mistake."

"I don't think so," said Karen. She glanced around, then realized that Junior had run off. "Damn it."

"Something wrong?"

"Just your typical SNAFU," she told the agent wearily.

[V]

I stood on the bridge of the *Bon Voyage*. The world around me was dark. My ears were filled with the guttural howl of the ocean. My first thought was that I was on my way back to the womb—a poetic way of saying that some bastard had blown up the bridge and I was on my way to my just reward.

But then I realized it was nothing so dramatic as all that: Murphy had just turned off the lights. A bolt of lightning had struck the *Bon Voyage*, wiping out the main power circuits. This is not particularly easy to do, and our friend Murphy had undoubtedly stayed up for days on end figuring on how to deliver the bolts that took it down. Then again, given all the lightning that was flashing around us, maybe the odds were with him all the time.

My bearings back in an instant, I started moving toward the chart room when someone hit me from the side and I went down. It was one of the hijackers. Severely wounded by Larry, the man had staggered with the roll of the ship and fallen against me and then to the deck. By the time I figured that out and got to my feet, Scarface was escaping through the captain's quarters.

I started after him as the emergency lighting system began flickering on and off. A sharp flash of light and loud boom drove me back—Scarface or one of his guards had thrown a flash-bang to cover his retreat.

Behind me, Larry was rallying the bridge crew to the controls. They got the auxiliary power on and took over, changing course south and radioing an SOS.

In his haste to get off the bridge alive, Scarface had abandoned a backpack with gear. Besides a pistol and some spare ammo, there was a radio remote control and a sheaf of papers. In with the papers were diagrams of the ship with Xs in various compartments, along with numbers.

"Gotta be where they put the bombs," said Larry. "Look. Even tells you how many there are in each compartment. Four in that bar we were in—two to a post."

Besides the bridge, they had concentrated on two levels—the one with the bar area that we'd found, and the lowest deck where the engines were. Though the simplistic maps didn't detail the precise location in each compartment, just knowing which places to look made things easier.

Three dozen spots, including the bridge.

"Bring them to a central location, and I'll disable them together," Larry told the mate. "You don't have to be too gentle with them, as long as you don't break the wires."

Larry decided that the safest place to dismantle them would be on the top deck at the center of the ship, where presumably the blast would do the least structural damage. There would still be an awful lot of explosive in one place, but he was the expert and I wasn't about to argue with him. The mate detailed two of his crew to search for them, then sent another crewman to look for more help. Larry and I left guns and ammo, and went to follow Scarface.

We could tell from the radios that Scarface was moving toward the stern of the ship, but it wasn't clear who was with him.

Doc and Chalker were listening to the same transmissions. Doc set up an ambush in the Front Office, a space used on the port side of the ship to welcome passengers and deal with administrative matters. We were close enough to hear the gunfire as we ran aft, though it was a deck above us. Larry and I waited until it had died down to go up to the corridor adjacent to the Front Office.

"Doc!" I yelled as we neared the space. "It's me."

"Who the hell else would you be?" he growled from inside.

There were eight bodies on the deck and the nearby furniture. Seven were hijackers, the eighth one of the crewmen who had joined Doc. The poor slob had been shot by the bastards as they came down a narrow spiral staircase at the corner of the Front Office. His death was not in vain: once the hijackers had shot him, they thought they were clear, and ran across toward the corridor where we'd come in and where Doc had an easy shot from behind the administrator's long desk.

"We have more crewmen above," Doc told me. "Chalker's organizing them into search parties. We have the extra arms."

"How many more hijackers?"

"Not too many, if at all," said Doc. "There hasn't been any traffic on the radio since this bunch came through."

I told Doc to go down to the engine room to make sure that the hijackers didn't try retaking it. Once he was sure it was secured, he could bring the bombs up to the rendezvous point. Larry gave him the papers that showed which compartments they'd been planted in.

"Hell, I'll just disarm the damn things in place," said Doc. "You're not the only one who knows how to blow shit up."

"The idea is that they *don't* blow up," I snapped.

"Ha-ha."

Actually, I had full confidence in Doc, who if anything is more careful than I. Larry and I resumed our search. Within a few minutes we came across another group of crew members and passengers, all unarmed.

"I don't have weapons for you," I told them. "Your safest bet would be to go back to your cabins."

"The hell with that," said one of the passengers, a gray-haired senior who was their unofficial spokesman. "We'll tear these bastards apart with our bare hands."

That was a sentiment I could appreciate. Still, I didn't want them to get hurt—or get in the way. I decided to have them search out the rest of the bombs in the public areas of the ship. Larry would go and start disarming the bombs.

"You're going to track Scarface by yourself?" asked Larry.

"I think we better neutralize the bombs quickly," I told him. "Scarface isn't going anywhere—he can't get off the ship. But maybe he's got another detonator somewhere."

"He'd have blown us up already."

"Maybe not. We have the main one. He's going for the backup."

"I don't know."

"Go. Come back and join me once the rest of the bombs are disabled. There are only eight up here."

"Not counting the four in the GalleyPlex." Larry tapped the papers that showed where they were.

"Save that for last. I'll radio you with the word 'casino' when I'm about to go in. Give me an ETA when you hear it."

"OK."

"If you don't get back to me, I'll assume I'm on my own."

"If I don't get back to you, you will be."

The next forty minutes passed slowly, as I checked through the public areas amidships, gradually working my way toward the stern and the large GalleyPlex.

I met Chalker and his motley band of rescued crewmen and passengers on the pool deck, in the enclosed space overlooking *une piscine*. The ship wasn't jerking around nearly as wildly as it had earlier, but it was still moving enough to get miniature whitecaps on the pool surface. I told him to get below and help Doc secure the engine room and finish locating the explosives. He gave me a thumbs-up and herded his people to one of the service passageways.

The rain was coming down even harder now. The ship was on auxiliary power, and here and there some of the backup lights weren't working. Even in the areas that were, the lighting was dim until I came to the passage outside the casino. The casino and GalleyPlex had its own dedicated backup generator, and it was going full bore. The place looked like Times Square on New Year's Eve.

I made the radio call. "Casino."

"Five," responded Larry.

"Engines," said Doc, checking in from the control compartment next to the engine room. He and his band had encountered two more hijackers along the way; both were now dead. Doc and company were now working to try and get the power back on line.

It was pretty clear that Scarface and whoever was with him were the only miscreants left. But even if he didn't have another detonator, the ship was large enough that he could hide for days, and maybe even run an effective guerilla war against us until help came. So I decided that the best way to forestall that was to flush him out, and the best way to do *that* was to let him think he was outsmarting me.

"Doc, this is Dick Marcinko," I said over the radio. "I'm going into the GalleyPlex through the starboard side entrance. I'll cross over to port, then come down and meet you."

Doc must have realized what I was up to, because he didn't radio back. That or he concluded I'd completely lost my mind.

I got down on my knees and eased through the open portal into the casino—on the port side, of course. Crawling down a row of one-armed bandits, I made my way to the roulette table at the end. I was just peeking out to get a view of the door when Scarface's amplified voice filled the hall.

"So who is this Richard Marcinko, I ask myself. An egotist from America." Scarface's French accent added just the right touch of sarcasm to his English. "Why is it that I do not know him? Because he is an ant to be crushed, and nothing more."

Ow.

Checking my six to make sure I wasn't being flanked, I crossed behind the roulette table and moved up to the archway separating the casino deck from the steps that led down to the GalleyPlex. The furniture normally arranged around the deck had tumbled into a massive jam on the starboard side of the space, leaving most of the deck open. At first glance, I thought Scarface was hiding in the tumble, but when his voice boomed again, I realized he was on the highest balcony at the stern. He had a microphone, a gun, and two female passengers, whom he'd flex-cuffed to the railing.

"A gray-haired egotist warrior," he yelled, practically laughing.

"It's a dye job," I shouted back.

There was a whistle behind me. Larry and four liberated crewmen had arrived to back me up. I retreated to explain what was going on.

"We have all of the bombs that were on the upper decks neutralized," he told me. "Except for the ones in here. That's six bombs. Enough to put an iceberg-sized hole in the stern."

"They should all be above the waterline," I said. "Doc's working on the ones below."

"Even if Doc finishes, we can't take a risk, Dick. Some of the bomb clusters we found were doubled and tripled up. That much explosive—if it does any sort of structural damage to the boat, we're going down. Hell, look at the way the rain is pounding those windows. The waves are reaching the second tier. We might go down on our own."

"Where do you think the bombs are?"

"Against the bulkheads to blow open the ship so it can't be fixed or patched quickly. The idea was to cave it in. Here they might just be trying blow a big hole. At least they're easy to spot. They're too big to hide, mostly."

"I didn't see any in the casino," I told Larry.

"Let me have a look."

Larry scanned the most obvious places without finding anything. Then we went to the archway and looked into the GalleyPlex. After a few moments of thought, Larry decided that most of the bombs must be tied to the base of the large ribs at the side of the space—four on the port side, and two to starboard. Sure enough, I spotted what looked like a big black box at the base of the nearest rib. When I say big, I mean large—it was suitcase-sized.

"Could be over a hundred pounds of plastic in there, easy," said Larry. "Maybe two hundred or three. Big, big hole."

"Yeah, I agree with that."

"I can get them if you can distract him," Larry promised. "There are doors next to each one. All I need to do is sneak in from the door, undo the tape that attaches them to the wall, then take them back out into the passage."

"You're sure they're going to be taped? What if they're chained?" I couldn't see all the way to the base.

"The ones below were taped."

The plan made sense—especially since I didn't have a better one.

"I'll backtrack out, and get into position," he said. "When you see me at the doorway, start distracting him."

"Go."

Now all I had to do was figure out how to distract Scarface.

"So what are you doing, Scarface?" I yelled. "What is it you want?"

"You're going to give me the ship back." He was obviously in deep denial.

"What are you going to do with it?"

"If you don't give it back to me, I'm going to blow it up. Otherwise, I will get a ransom."

"How are you going to blow it up?"

"We've planted charges through the entire ship. Who are you, Marcinko? CIA? You're obviously not the old codger I took you for."

CIA? Bite your tongue.

"I'm just Dick," I answered. "No one special. Why do you want to blow up the ship?"

"We are committed warriors of God," said Scarface.

"I thought you were French."

"I am from Algiers." He launched into a far too brief and unfortunately sincere explanation of his Islamic beliefs, and how blowing up the ship would redeem his soul and grant him virgins in the afterlife.

"Was that your plan when you came aboard?" I asked. "Why smuggle the drugs on?"

"These are not details that concern you. It's enough to know what we are going to do now."

I suspected that destroying the ship was a contingency plan, to be enacted if things went sour. But Scarface didn't seem in the mood to answer questions along those lines. Larry still hadn't appeared at the doorway; I needed to keep my tango friend talking.

"How are you going to blow us up?" I asked Scarface.

He raised his right hand, showing me the spare radio unit.

"Why do you want to die?" I asked, spotting Larry near the doorway.

"You think of death as an end. It is only a beginning."

He may have been a fanatical terrorist, but Scarface had a (relatively) rational explanation of why death would not be a bad thing, and how Paradise awaited him. I suspect, though, that he was willing to expound on it at length because he didn't truly believe it—if he did, he'd surely have put his finger to the button immediately. He was talking to gin up his courage. But his diatribe had another effect—Larry snuck in and began taking down the bombs. By the time Scarface ended his lecture on the afterlife, Larry had finished dismantling the fourth and last bomb on the port side of the GalleyPlex.

Two more to go.

As Larry disappeared, I worked my way toward the center of the atrium, using the small garden in the middle for cover. Peering from between the fronds of the ferns and fake rocks, I faced Scarface and his two prisoners head-on. The windows were dark behind them, but every so often lightning slashed across the sky. It was a real Dr. Frankenstein effect, very ominous.

I looked to starboard, expecting Larry to duck into the forward doorway. Instead, he appeared at the one closer to the stern. He had his hands up. Two tangos were behind him. One had an AK47; the other an RPG launcher.

They started walking him into the atrium. I began to retreat, but Scarface yelled down.

"Join your friend," he said. "Or I blow the ship now."

I dropped back to my knee and took out the radio, pressing down the talk button.

"How can you blow up the ship from the GalleyPlex?" I yelled.

"Drop the radio," answered Scarface. "That's quite enough."

I had the AK in my other hand. I thought I could nail Scarface before he could detonate the bombs. But his goons would kill Larry.

"Drop the radio and the rifle," said Scarface, moving around on the balcony for a better view. "Come."

"Do all your men know you're killing them as well?"

"They are committed Muslims."

"Nice. Ready to die?" I looked at the two men holding their guns on Larry. They didn't look either devout or resigned to death; they looked stoned on khat or something stronger.

"Drop the radio and the gun!" yelled Scarface.

I rose, then let the radio fall to the deck. Doc would have heard all he needed to hear by now.

"The gun," said Scarface.

"I think I'll hold on to that for a bit. It seems to me we have a standoff."

"You have nothing I want, old man."

"If I shoot you, you won't get to blow anything up." I held the gun about half mast, pointing downward but ready. I walked slowly toward Larry. The two tangos holding him stopped and looked up at Scarface.

"Stop where you are, or I'll kill my hostages," shouted Scarface.

"You're going to kill us all anyway," I said. "What difference does it make?"

Scarface pointed the gun at the head of one of the women. Then he pointed it at me. I couldn't have prayed for a better opportunity.

I threw myself at Larry and the two men behind him. Larry, seeing the glint in my eyes, ducked, and the man on his right stepped back out of the way. I managed to get the one with the grenade launcher square in the midsection, and we both rolled to the deck. Larry grabbed the other and flipped him over his shoulder, wrestling him to the deck. I kicked my gunman in the head, then scrambled to the grenade launcher as two gunshots echoed through the large space.

Scarface was pointing the gun directly at me.

[VI]

There were two bombs in the GalleyPlex. Larry had one in his hands. The other was about ten feet from me, taped to a thick post that ran to the ceiling of the space.

Did I run to it? Did I pull it from the pier?

I must have, though I have no memory of doing that. Nor do I remember, except very, very vaguely, dodging through the open door into the corridor that surrounded the atrium.

I do remember, vividly, the wind as it hit me, howling from an unsecured door far behind me and pushing me toward the stern and its glass panels. And, while I can't honestly swear that I saw this, when I think back the digits "0-2" flash in my brain.

The timer, telling me it was time to let go.

One step, two—I wasn't going to make it. I ran anyway, tucking the bomb under my arm like a college halfback anxious to score. There was a door dead ahead. I hit the crash bar with my left hand, and with my right launched the bomb out into the storm.

A second later, I found myself propelled backward, sailing back into the passageway. My skull slammed against a partition at the bend in the corridor. I blacked out, this time for real.

"I will see you in Paradise," he yelled, reaching into his pocket for the detonator.

The RPG launcher in my hands was primed and ready to launch. So I fired.

I wish I could say I was a better shot. I aimed for the head. I missed.

But not by that much. The head of the grenade caught Scarface full in the chest, and the force took him, his gun, and the detonator through the glass window directly behind him.

The glass shattered with a roar. Rain began pouring in. I swear a bolt of lightning shot through the window as the thunder pealed. I glanced over at Larry. He looked at me.

Larry started to laugh. So did I.

"A close one," he yelled, walking toward the bomb nearest us. "Damn, Sharkman, you always make it tight. I've forgotten how much fun this is."

"Only when we win," I said.

"So? You gonna put this in one of your books?"

"Maybe."

"Spell my name right," he laughed, taking hold of the bomb pack. This was a smaller one, about the shape and weight of a day pack. He yanked it from its girder and examined the trigger mechanism.

"Holy shit!" he yelled. "It's armed—and counting down!"

EPILOGUE

ALL IN THE FAMILY

You must be able to underwrite the honest mistakes of your subordinates
if you wish to develop their initiative and experience.

—GENERAL BRUCE C. CLARKE

Encourage and listen well to the words of your subordinates.
It is well-known that gold lies hidden underground.

—NABESHIMA NAOSHIGE (1538–1618) IN WILSON,
IDEALS OF THE SAMURAI, 1982

Given the same amount of intelligence, timidity will do
a thousand times more damage in war than audacity.

—MAJOR GENERAL CARL VON CLAUSEWITZ, *ON WAR*

[1]

I came to some hours later, in one of the ship's bars. Doc had turned it into an overflow sick bay, moving mattresses in and helping the ship's doctor and regular medical staff tend to the several dozen[50] people who'd been injured in the takeover or the subsequent liberation. Doc claimed that the location of the bar made it the safest and most stable place on the ship. I suspect he chose it because it was convenient to one of the best medical cures known to man, namely Bombay Sapphire.

By that time, the worst of the storm had passed, and the sun was poking out between the last of the clouds. We were firmly in control of the *Bon Voyage*. Not only had all of the bombs been recovered and disarmed, but we had also found nineteen passengers who'd been blackmailed as I was into carrying prescription drugs back to America. Together we could have put Rite Aid out of business inside a month.

A navy team was en route to help secure the ship and make sure all the bad guys had been eliminated. The advance members were arriving just as I was getting my butt out of bed.

Yes, they were SEALs. And yes, they were members of that unit whose name we are not allowed to say, but which the entire world knows as SEAL Team Six. Doc, Larry, and Chalker were on deck to greet them as they fast-roped aboard. Rumor has it that they were disappointed that they didn't get to execute their takedown plan, but if so, they were too professional to let on. They went to work clearing the ship—no new hijackers or bombs were found—then, relaxing just a bit, began conversing and comparing notes with some of their predecessors.

I would have enjoyed the fun myself, but alas, I had work to do, catching up with Danny, Shunt, and Karen before calling in old favors to get a ride back to the States.

This is the boring part of the story, where I talk about hoisting myself up into helicopters, transferring to ships, and finally riding with the air farce, which is good for some great put-downs—though as the narrator's prerogative I only print the ones I make, not their comebacks. So we'll skip the fourteen or sixteen hours' worth of travel, the three naps I took, and

---

[50] Six hijackers were among the injured; the rest were dead, or so well hidden on the ship that we never found them.

even the fine shape of the female air farce sergeant who got me onto the right plane and even fluffed my pillow for me on the flight.

Instead, we'll head out to New York's Kennedy Airport, where Danny has arrived to pick me up.

"No Junior?" I asked, following him and the limo driver to the car.

Danny shook his head. Both he and Karen had already filled me in on his flight from the parking deck, as well as everything that had led up to it.

"You hear from him at all?" I asked.

"Not a word. Part of me wants to find him and kick him in the ass," added Danny. "And the other slap him on the back and buy him a beer."

"He probably could use both."

"What are you going to do to him?" Danny asked.

"I don't know."

I honestly wasn't sure. We could definitely use him in the organization— clearly he had skills we needed and spirit we prized. But we also needed people with level heads under *all* circumstances. And Junior had demonstrated that he wasn't always able to control his temper. Maybe I was too hard on him because he was my son, but that didn't excuse his going AWOL. Or the rest.

I followed Danny across the parking area toward a black limo. The trunk opened as we approached. Danny took my small bag, plopped it in, and then removed a briefcase from the trunk. "Here you go. Everything's set."

"How are we on time?"

"Tight, but we'll make it. Assuming the traffic cooperates."

"Since when has that ever happened in New York?"

"We'll call the cavalry if necessary."

Actually, Danny had something better than cavalry—a little electronic device used by certain police officials to automatically change traffic lights. It didn't help us much on the Van Wyck Expressway (the name is the definition of an oxymoron), but once in Manhattan the device shaved a good ten minutes off our travel time. That put us ahead of schedule, allowing me and Danny to be standing in front of the elevator when Veep arrived at his office.

"How long have you known Magoo?" were the first words out of my mouth.

He blinked. The rest of the people in the elevator moved past, trying not to make their stares too obvious.

"Actually, I know the answer," I said when Veep didn't answer. "He was first appointed to the task force in May 2010, but it wasn't until the summer that he started focusing on Allah's Rule. He learned about the impending power struggle a little later. By that time, he had already sketched out the drug smuggling network. The thing I don't know is at what point he decided to set up his own. That's when he got you involved. Was it legit at first? Did he tell you you'd be doing your patriotic duty, helping the government watch terrorists by setting up and monitoring their accounts? At some point soon, though, you must have figured out what Magoo really had in mind, because you didn't tell anyone else at the bank. So maybe you were skimming those accounts yourself from the get-go."

"I have no idea what you're talking about, Marcinko," said Veep. "What are you doing here?"

"It took a while for Shunt to figure out how the money was being routed. The donations came through the local bank branch. Which you authorized. That was why those records had to be destroyed in Berlin."

"I haven't a clue what you're talking about," he said, finally starting to move. "If you'll excuse me, I have work to do today."

Danny and I followed him into the office suite. The guard there nodded at Danny so subtly that Veep missed it.

"What are you doing in here?" thundered Veep as we followed him inside. "This is my office. Get out. Make an appointment."

"I just came in to admire the view."

It was quite impressive—half of Wall Street lay at my feet. And if I turned my head just right, I could see the top of WT1—also known as Freedom Tower—rising over the site of the World Trade Center.

I looked at Veep. "The amazing thing to me is how someone with this kind of view could encourage terrorists."

"What the hell are you talking about?" Veep's voice choked as he finished the sentence—evidently he did have a bit of a conscience somewhere.

But just a bit.

"I have nothing to do with terrorists," he added.

"Not Allah's Rule on Earth? Not al Qaeda?"

"Al Qaeda doesn't exist anymore," said Veep quickly. "It's like the boogeyman the government throws up to justify whatever it feels like doing. And your implication that I am somehow associated with terrorists is reprehensible."

"That's right." I turned from the window. "What I really should be doing is accusing you of associating with the CIA. A renegade member of the CIA who's even greedier and more ruthless than you. But you did know about Scorched Earth. Or what it would mean. Because you're the one that kicked it off when you realized how close we were to you."

"What the hell are you talking about?"

I turned to Danny. He opened the briefcase he'd brought in with him and took out an eight-by-ten glossy of the photo Junior had snapped in the New York restaurant of the meeting between Magoo and Veep.

Veep frowned at it.

"The transfers are what's really interesting, since they're the money trail. We don't have all of them," I admitted as Danny took a thick ream of paper from the briefcase and put them on Veep's desk, "but we have the important ones. Shunt managed to track down three of your accounts in the Austrian bank, but I'm sure you have a lot more. All of this would have hardly been worth it if you only cleared a few million dollars."

Veep's face had started to blanch. There was a slight commotion behind us. I turned and saw Barbara Freemason, one of the FBI's supervisory agents, entering the room. About a dozen people were lined up behind her, including a member of the CIA internal affairs unit, a few bank examiners, a deputy U.S. attorney, and a lawyer representing the bank.

The U.S. marshals and the local NYPD liaisons and uniformed cops were out in the hall. The office was big, but not that big.

"Before you say anything else, Mr. Veep," started Freemason, "I am going to read you your rights."

I would have loved to have stuck around, but Danny and I had a plane to catch.

Magoo's.

You know and I know that he planted that gun on the terrorist to make it look like he was justified in killing him. Junior knew that as well. But Junior wasn't around to press the case, and even if he had been, few people would have been inclined to believe him. After all, Habib was definitely part of a plot to blow up the Supreme Court Building, and but for Junior's pigheaded insubordination, he would have succeeded. So in a lot of minds, Magoo—a CIA officer on the fast track—had done the People a favor, sparing them the expense of a trial and, at least in his version of events, preventing the conspiracy from succeeding, since Magoo's information implied that Habib was the one who was going to detonate the bombs.

That of course was Magoo's interpretation of events. Mine was somewhat different.

Magoo's plane for Europe was about ten minutes to boarding when Danny and I strolled up to him. He was sitting near the wall, reading a book.

Not one of mine, alas.

"Marcinko," he said disgustedly as I approached. "Don't tell me you're on this flight."

"Not this one," I said. "Don't you think it's a little tacky for you to be going to France so soon after Scarface's death?"

"What?" He made a face. I will give Magoo this: he makes very good shows of disgust; he's practically a connoisseur of disdain. "Don't talk in your usual riddles."

"How long had you been grooming Scarface?" I asked. "Who was your cutout with the mosque? Is that who you're going to meet?"

"Who's Scarface?"

"Come on, Magoo. Tell me you didn't celebrate when you heard I blew him through the window at the stern of *Bon Voyage*. Did you know he was going to blow that up? You must have, right?"

"You're talking about Abdul Gharba, the terrorist? Okay, now I know who you're talking about. Sure, I'd celebrate his death—even if you killed him."

"Who are you going to get to run your drugs now?" I asked. "Is he already waiting, like Scarface was, for the bust on Allah's Rule? You had your network completely in place, moved in on Shire Jama and al-Yasur, and the network never lost a beat. Taking over the operation from al Qaeda was clever, and having Scarface think that he was getting instructions from al Qaeda was genius. I assume that's how you set it up."

"What's al Qaeda have to do with anything?"

"Nothing. You pushed them out so you could run the drug operation yourself. You set up the attack on the Supreme Court Building to divert attention from your operation as we closed in. I assume that was the deal with the *Bon Voyage* as well, though we haven't found the messages yet. Maybe Scarface double-crossed you."

Magoo gave me one of his nearsighted blinks. I assumed that he had primed Scarface for the operation through surrogates, then sent a message telling him to carry out the takeover of the ship, but Shunt hadn't found the evidence yet. Truthfully, it could have played as a straight double-cross, with Scarface acting on his own.

"You were playing a pretty dangerous game," I told Magoo. "But that's how you rose so quickly through the ranks to begin with. You were capable of real work, good work—penetrating one of the cells of Allah's Rule was really a coup. But why did you get so greedy?"

He pressed his lips together.

"You set up the bank explosions for Veep, didn't you? Did you tip him off? I should have caught the connection right away."

He didn't say anything. Just to clarify—the hit on the bank was done by people[51] Magoo had hired through another cutout after the board of direc-

---

[51] Chechen exiles in need of cash. Rumor has it they're turning state's evidence in exchange for leniency.

tors started asking questions and it looked like I might actually figure out what was going on. The attack was made to look like the terror groups. This gave Veep cover to change the computer records, losing the ones that would have revealed what was going on. It also gave Magoo another "case" he could solve at his leisure: bust some isolated tango, plant a modicum of evidence, and ship the bastard to Guantanamo for the rest of his natural-born days.

Not that I had a problem with the last part.

"In another year, you might have made deputy director," I told Magoo. "Or at least been close. Then, who knows? Get the admiral's job, maybe? Though I don't know why anyone would want to be head of the CIA."

"I earned my promotions."

The gate attendant called for the first-class passengers to board.

"The irony is, killing Habib is what's going to nail you, at least for now," I told him. "Because the whole thing is on video tape. And it's murder."

"Right." Magoo rose, retrieving his ticket from the papers in the back of his book. "I looked at the garage security cameras myself. Not one of them was pointed in the right place."

"Lucky for you, huh?"

Magoo started past. I grabbed the sleeve of his jacket to stop him.

"The camera over the runway approach was working, though," I said. "And it happens to have caught the entire transaction. There's no sound track, unfortunately. But Habib definitely seems relieved to see you, walks up freely to the car when you get out, then quickly backs away when you shoot him. You walk over, take the gun out, and drop it down."

"There's no evidence of that."

"We have a witness," said Danny, opening his briefcase and pulling out a photo. "And this." The image was extremely grainy, but you could just make out Magoo reaching for the pistol in his jacket.

"This could be anyone," said Magoo. "I have a plane to catch."

"Clayton Magoo?" said a plainclothes D.C. officer behind me. "I have a warrant for your arrest."

Two TSA cops and a pair of New York City detectives had fanned out behind him. Magoo looked from one to the other, his expression growing more solemn.

I was hoping he'd run. That would have justified my jumping on him and kicking the crap out of him. I would have relished giving him a physical demonstration of what I think of greedy, avaricious traitors. I would have loved to have paid him back for every American he put into harm's way, directly and indirectly. I don't guess we could blame the deaths of the people on the *Bon Voyage* solely on him, but I would not have minded giving him a bit of retribution on their behalf.

Unfortunately, he didn't run. So there was no way to justify my punching his lights out.

I did it anyway, with one punch, a solid smash to the side of the face as he looked away.

True, I'd cold-cocked him, but no worse than he'd done to the rest of us.

(II)

The charge of murder against Magoo wasn't going to stick, because no jury, even in Washington, D.C., would convict a CIA officer of killing a terrorist, even if the evidence showed that that officer not only lured the man to his death but had masterminded the entire ill-fated bomb attempt to begin with. Magoo wasn't in total control of Habib's operation; he had recruited him through an American imam, and funded him without ever meeting him. But he had given him enough aid, including information on how to set the bombs, to make the attack on the Court possible.

The information on bomb-making he passed along included two flaws that made the bombs harmless, but Habib hadn't known that. His operation existed solely to make Magoo look good.

"It was a brilliant setup in a lot of ways," I told Danny over a pair of Sapphires that evening in New York. We were up at the Rock, a fancy-schmancy bar in the RCA Building with a view to die for, and waitresses who convinced you not to end it too soon.

"Here's the thing I don't get," said Danny. "If you're Scarface, why abandon a profitable drug-running operation to blow yourself up?"

"You're thinking like a cop."

"No, I'm thinking like the thugs I used to lock up eons ago." He took another sip of his drink. "They all wanted to be rich. God knows what they would have done to get into Scarface's position. And to stay there."

"The drugs were not about making money for him. They were about funding jihad. Anything else would be a great sin—drug selling is one of those universal sins."

"So is suicide."

"It's not suicide if it's jihad. You don't die—you end up in Paradise, where you live forever. He gave me a big lecture on it."

Danny shook his head. He's been through a lot of ops, but he still has the head of a policeman. The motivations he thinks about are greed and lust, not religion.

Magoo and Veep's motivations, at least, were more in Danny's line. There were still some loose ends that night—in fact, there are still a couple as I write this. Neither Veep nor Magoo has come to trial. The prosecution sounds confident of convictions of both; I'm not so sure.

But only two loose ends really bothered me as I drained my glass and asked for a refill: the pain in my knees, which the doctors insisted had to be corrected surgically, and Junior.

I reluctantly went under the knife to get my knees refurbished a few weeks later. As for Junior . . . his story will have to wait for another day. I will say, though, that he is definitely a chip off the old block. And like all clichés, that's not necessarily a good thing.